W9-BUR-234

THOMAS CRANE PUBLIC LIBRARY
QUINCY MA

CITY APPROPRIATION

AUG

2011

OUT OF THE WATERS

TOR BOOKS BY DAVID DRAKE

Birds of Prey

Bridgehead

Cross the Stars

The Dragon Lord

The Forlorn Hope

Fortress

The Fortress of Glass

From the Heart of Darkness

Goddess of the Ice Realm

The Gods Return

The Jungle

Killer (with Karl Edward Wagner)

The Legions of Fire

Lord of the Isles

Master of the Cauldron

The Mirror of Worlds

Mistress of the Catacombs

Out of the Waters

Patriots

Queen of Demons

Servant of the Dragon

Skyripper

Tyrannosaur

The Voyage

OUT OF THE WATERS

DAVID DRAKE

A TOM DOHERTY ASSOCIATES BOOK
NEW YORK

This is a work of fiction. All of the characters, organizations, and events portrayed in this novel are either products of the author's imagination or are used fictitiously.

OUT OF THE WATERS

Copyright © 2011 by David Drake

All rights reserved.

A Tor Book
Published by Tom Doherty Associates, LLC
175 Fifth Avenue
New York, NY 10010

www.tor-forge.com

Tor® is a registered trademark of Tom Doherty Associates, LLC.

ISBN 978-0-7653-2079-7

First Edition: July 2011

Printed in the United States of America

0 9 8 7 6 5 4 3 2 1

To Sharon
Who read the galleys on Hammer's Slammers so long ago that
they really were galleys, not page proofs

ACKNOWLEDGMENTS

Dan Breen continues as my first reader. He catches typos and mental lapses—dropped plurals, subject and verb agreement, not infrequently missing words; that sort of thing. More important, he highlights some really clumsy constructions. I have tendencies to be both overprecise and elliptical, sometimes in the same sentence.

Dorothy Day and my webmaster, Karen Zimmerman, archive my texts in distant places and search them when I don't remember a name (for example, "What was the name of the night doorman?"). If an asteroid hits Pittsboro, Tor will still be able to retrieve my work in progress. (Unless it's a really big asteroid, of course.)

For the most part, I took my quotations of *The Book of the Dead* from the E. A. Wallis Budge version, which I've owned and used for many years. I needed one particular phrasing which did not appear in Budge. Karen found it for me in a Normandi Ellis paraphrase. I could cite many similar examples, from this book and from earlier ones, of how valuable it is to a writer to know a librarian.

While I was writing the very last sections of *Out of the Waters*, the screen of my first-line laptop got wonky because of a loose connection. A minor thing, I assumed. It isn't. My son, Jonathan, determined it was a job for factory repair and immediately ordered a replacement, which he then set up for me.

I have said that I'll continue writing even if I need to chip my words out on a block of stone—and I will. I am very fortunate that my family and close friends include professionals at all levels of the IT industry, making it unlikely that I *will* have to resort to chisels.

I don't care what anyone else thinks of the content of my fiction, but I run my nonfiction—including the author's note which immediately follows these acknowledgments—by Mark Van Name for a useful outside viewpoint. Mark is more circumspect in what he says than I am (almost everyone is more circumspect than I am), but he's very good at pointing out places where people who don't know me will misunderstand what I'm saying and also places where I might in a few days wish that I had chosen to be a little less brutally frank.

I do not always do what Mark suggests, but I listen to him. Only a fool would not.

My wife, Jo, continues to maintain the nest in which I live and work. The bills get paid, appointments are remembered, and I eat extremely well. When I'm working, which is most of the time, I focus very sharply on the work itself. That's good for the work, but it would be disastrous for life in the broader sense were it not for Jo's unflagging support.

My thanks to the people above and to all the other friends who make my life not only possible but worthwhile.

Out of the Waters is set in a fictional city named Carce (pronounced CAR-see). Things occur in this novel and in all The Books of the Elements which did not happen and could not have happened in the historical Rome of A.D. 30. This is a fantasy novel, *not* a historical novel with fantasy elements. I'm trying to keep that fact at the front of readers' minds by referring to Carce (in homage to *The Worm Ouroboros* by E. R. Eddison, by the way).

That said, I have hewed closely to Roman culture and to events from Roman history in creating the background of the series. The literary works which occur in the series (including the *Sibylline Books* and *The Book of the Dead*), and the quotes from them, are real.

The Native American myths which form the core of *Out of the Waters* are real also. I found the story of Uktena very powerful when I first read it. In reworking the story for my use here, I at last understood why it resonated so strongly with me.

While you should not assume that everything in the series is historical truth—it isn't—you *can* be sure that I research the details which go into my fiction. This brings me to another reason for setting The Books of the Elements in Carce, not Rome.

Most educated people have an idea of what ancient Rome was like. Much of what they think they know is false. I find it distressing to have folks write (and even phone!) me to complain about some "mistake" in my fiction when in fact my statement was correct.

For example, I've learned not to refer to Roman shields as being plywood, though in fact they *were* plywood and archeologists use "plywood" to describe the material from which they were molded. If I say the shields were "laminated wood," people don't complain (and I hope that I avoid breaking their suspension of disbelief).

Whereas I could say that the legions of Carce go to war wearing topcoats and tails without anybody claiming I was historically wrong. (They might think I was a complete twit—*I* would think I was a complete twit if I did something so silly—but that's a separate matter.)

My purpose in writing is to tell interesting, exciting stories that many people will take pleasure in reading; my role is not to educate readers. I hope, however, that those who read The Books of the Elements will get glimpses of a culture very different from our own—but which is nonetheless one of the major supports on which our culture has been built.

Still, I'll be satisfied if you tell me that you had a good time reading *Out of the Waters*. I certainly hope that you do.

DAVID DRAKE
www.david-drake.com

OUT OF THE WATERS

Varus sat upright at his father's side in the Tribunal—the patron's box—over the right edge of the stage in the Pompeian Theater, jotting notes in the waxed memorandum book on his lap. Staring at him from the vast bowl of the theater was an audience of thousands: perhaps twenty thousand all told, including the slaves standing—they weren't allowed to sit—in the aisles and the surrounding colonnades.

It was disquieting to look out at so many human faces, though he knew that only a handful of them were even vaguely aware of Gaius Alphenus Varus. Indeed, very few of the spectators would pay any attention to his father, Gaius Alphenus Saxa: senator of Carce, replacement consul, and destined governor of the province of Lusitania on the Atlantic coast of the Iberian Peninsula.

The spectators didn't worry Varus as much, though, as the vision forming in his mind: a very old woman, seated on a throne. He wasn't sure if she really existed or if she ever had existed; but he knew why he was seeing her.

Varus was too well schooled in philosophy to lie, even to himself, about his father's personality. Saxa was a cultured and well-read man, but not a particularly wise one. He had chosen to commemorate his consulate by putting on a mime written for the occasion: *The Conquest of Lusitania by Hercules.*

The replacement consul sat on his gilded, high-backed chair, beaming with pleasure. If the emperor had been present, the Golden Seat would have been his. The Tribunal wasn't the best place from which to view the three-hundred-foot-wide stage, but it *was* the best place in which to be seen by the audience.

The citizens of Carce would probably have preferred watching exotic animals being slaughtered by the hundreds and perhaps even convicted criminals being devoured by cats and bears, but Saxa was wealthy enough that the present spectacle was keeping the audience in its seats.

Varus had once imagined he could become a great poet, one whose readings would fill a hall and might even fill this theater. His first public performance had been a disaster, not so much in the eyes of those attending as in his own.

On that occasion, the audience had been of freedmen and hangers-on of his father's wealthy friends, sent as a courtesy. They had expected to be bored. Varus himself was too intelligent and too well taught . . .

He glanced over his shoulder toward his teacher, Pandareus of Athens; the scholar nodded crisply in reply. He sat in the Tribunal as a mark of Saxa's gratitude.

. . . not to understand how bad his epic was when he heard the words coming out of his mouth.

Under the careful direction of two handlers each, the Cattle of the Sun—big animals with bright bay hides—were marching across the stage. Though they had been gelded and their horns sparkled with gold paint for this show, they were of the same Iberian stock as the bulls which not infrequently gored to death the lions and tigers set to fight them in the arena.

While even more dangerous animals sometimes appeared on stage, these steers were nothing to have loose in the belly of the theater. That was especially true since the seats in the orchestra were reserved for senators and their families.

A steer bellowed peevishly and lashed its tail. The actor playing Hercules stood at the back of the scene on a "rock"; he twitched noticeably. It was unlikely that an angry animal would crash through the spiked iron fence protecting the orchestra, but one certainly might knock down the mountain of plaster on a wicker frame and then start in on the actor who had been standing on it.

The audience would love it, Varus thought, smiling faintly. He wasn't the sort of aristocrat who sneered at The Many, the common people; but even at seventeen he was enough of a philosopher to be wryly amused by the difference between his tastes and those of his fellow citizens of Carce—including the tastes of many who were just as wellborn as the Alphenus family.

Varus gestured Pandareus to slide his chair up a few inches. The Greek had been careful to take a subordinate place rather than imply his equality with citizens of Carce, but that had now been established. Varus wanted to talk with his teacher, the only person in the box who shared his own passion for truth.

Saxa had a capacious mind, but it was like a magpie's and his learning was slanted toward the marvelous. The more remarkable a report was, the more likely he was to believe it.

Varus preferred sober facts. His smile quirked again. It disturbed him that some of the events he'd recently seen—and participated in—were more amazing than the fantastic myths which charlatans retailed to his father.

Pandareus advanced his chair to the railing. He and the others in the Tribunal sat on backless folding chairs with fabric seats. They were identical to the chairs of the senators in the orchestra, except that the frames were of oak or fruitwood instead of ivory.

Apart from the senators, free persons in the audience sat on stone benches. The wealthier had brought cushions, while the poor made do with a cloak or an extra tunic. This mime was scheduled to last all afternoon, so even a toil-hardened farmer visiting the capital needed something between his buttocks and the stone.

Pandareus followed his pupil's eyes to the slaves in the gallery and murmured, "I wonder how many of them are Lusitanians themselves? It's supposed to be a rather wild province, of course. If there are any of them here, they may not have enough Latin to realize that they're supposed to be looking at their homeland."

The last of the cattle stamped and clattered off the stage below the Tribunal. An actor dressed as Mercury with a silver helmet and winged sandals cried, "Behold, the treasures of Lusitania, now yours by right of conquest!"

The first of what was obviously a long line of donkeys followed the steers. Instead of ordinary pack saddles, the animals were fitted with shelves which displayed silver and gold plate, bronze statuary, silks, and expensive pottery. Some of the dishes were decorated blue on a white background, products of the same Far Eastern peoples who produced the silk.

"Master?" Varus said as a question occurred to him. "There were twenty cattle. Is there some literary basis for that? Because frankly—"

He lowered his voice, though there was no likelihood that Saxa on his right side could have overheard.

"—I would have expected my father to provide more, just for the show."

Pandareus allowed himself a pleased smile. "As it happens," he said, trying to keep the pride out of his voice, "your father's impresario, Meoetes, asked me the same question while he planned the mime. I told him that annotations by Callimachus on Euripides' claim that the 'cattle' are actually a metaphor for the twenty letters of the Greek alphabet which Heracles—"

He used the god's Greek name.

"—brought to replace the alphabet of Cronus. Meoetes was doubtful, as you surmise, but the senator insisted on accuracy over spectacle." He coughed and continued, "Since I couldn't give any guidance on the loot of Iberia, I believe they decided to, ah, spread themselves."

Varus grinned again, feeling a rush of unexpected warmth toward his father. Saxa had not been harsh toward his son and daughter—he wasn't a man who could be harsh to anyone, even a slave; though of course he had foremen and stewards who could do what they thought was necessary. Neither had Saxa showed any interest in his children, however.

That had changed very recently. Saxa appreciated the real erudition which he was honest enough to know that he lacked himself. He had learned that Marcus Priscus, a member of the Commission for the Sacred Rites and reputedly the most learned man in the Senate, respected Varus' scholarship and regarded Pandareus as his equal in knowledge. That had raised son and teacher enormously in Saxa's estimation.

Alphena, Saxa's sixteen-year-old daughter, had gained status for an even better reason: Hedia, Saxa's third wife and the children's stepmother, had taken the girl under her wing. Hedia was lovely and could be charming, but she knew her own mind—and got her way in everything that mattered to her.

Varus wouldn't have believed that his tomboy sister would ever want to act like a lady, let alone that she would be capable of doing a creditable job of it. The fact that Alphena was here in the theater, wearing a long dress with a silk cape over her shoulders, was almost as remarkable as other things that had happened in the course of the past week.

Almost. Varus had seen the earth open and demons rise from the blazing rivers of the Underworld. He had seen that, or he thought he had seen that; and it had seemed that he himself was the magician whose chanted spell had dispersed those demons and sealed the world against them.

Varus prided himself on his intellect; intellectually he knew the things he recalled could not be true. Unfortunately for logic and reason, his teacher recalled the same things. When a scholar of the stature of Pandareus accepted the evidence of his eyes over common sense, a mere student like Varus was left with a dilemma.

The line of mules moved steadily except when one stopped, raised its tail, and deposited dung on the stage. Pandareus leaned forward, watching with more interest than he had shown for the splendid goods themselves.

"How will they clean the stage after the performance, Lord Varus?" he said. "That is, I understand there are to be eight hundred mules. If even a small portion of such a herd . . . ?"

Varus laughed. He wasn't a frequent spectator at Carce's mass entertainments, but he obviously got out more than his teacher did. He said, "They hold beast fights and hunts—"

So-called hunts, that is. Archers and javelin throwers behind metal fences shot corralled animals until they had no more living targets.

"—here also. Channels from the Virgin Aqueduct divert water over the stage and the cellars beneath to wash detritus into the sewers."

He met his teacher's eyes and added, "I don't believe that will be part of the performance though, as this mime doesn't include Hercules cleansing the stables of King Augeas."

They smiled together. Varus was proud to be able to make literary jokes with his teacher, and he suspected that Pandareus was pleased to have students who actually appreciated literature as something more than a source for florid allusions to be thrown out during a speech. Of the ten youths studying with Pandareus at present, only Varus and his friend Corylus could be described as scholars.

Varus let his eyes drift over the audience to where he had spotted Corylus while the jugglers and rope dancers were performing before the mime itself began. Publius Cispius was a Knight of Carce, entitling his son Publius Cispius Corylus to a seat in the first fourteen rows at any public entertainment. Corylus was in the fourteenth row, so that his servant, Marcus Pulto, could sit directly behind him.

The elder Cispius had capped a successful military career with command of a squadron of Batavian cavalry and had been knighted on retirement. He had purchased a perfume business on the Bay of Puteoli with the considerable money he had made while in service.

By ordinary standards, Cispius was wealthy—but Saxa was wealthy by the standards of the Senate. At Varus' request, Saxa had invited Corylus to watch the mime with them in the Tribunal. Corylus had refused, politely but without hesitation.

Part of Varus deplored the stiff-necked determination of a sturdy provincial not to look like a rich man's toady. There was no question of anything of the sort: Varus just wanted his friend to sit with him at this lengthy event.

On the other hand, if Carce's citizens hadn't been so stiff-necked and determined, the city would not rule all the land from Mesopotamia to the Atlantic, from the German Sea to Nubia. Logically, Varus would admit that being without his friend's presence was a cheap price to pay for an empire.

In his heart, though, he wasn't sure. Corylus was a soldier's son and destined for the army himself. He had grown up on the Rhine and the Danube, where mistakes meant not embarrassment and expense but death in whatever fashion barbarian ingenuity could contrive. Corylus projected calm.

Varus needed calm right now. He wasn't really watching the stately procession of treasures across the stage. That vision of the wizened old woman seated on a throne in the clouds was becoming sharper in his mind.

She was the Cumean Sibyl, and she prophesied the approach of Chaos.

HEDIA'S FACE WAS TURNED toward the stage, wearing a look of polite pleasure. That was the appropriate expression for the wife of the noble patron of the entertainment, so *of course* that was how she looked. She would have tried to appear just as politely pleased while torturers used a stick to roll her intestines out through a slit in her belly if that were what the duties of her station called for.

Moved by a sudden feeling of fondness, Hedia patted the back of her husband's hand. He looked at her in surprise, then blushed and faced the stage again.

Saxa was a thoroughly decent man, a *sweet* man. There were people—there were quite a lot of people, in fact—who felt that Hedia in her twenty-two years of existence had encompassed all the licentious decadence which had flowed into Carce along with the wealth of the conquered East. There was evidence for their belief, but even Hedia's worst enemies would never claim that she wasn't a perfect wife in public.

As for what happened after dinner parties at the houses of friends or in Baiae while the business of the Senate detained her husband in Carce, well—there were stories about any wealthy, beautiful woman, and not all of them were true. In Hedia's particular case, most of the stories *were* true, but she maintained a discreet silence about her private life. That was, after all, the appropriate response to impertinent questions.

The dreadfully long line of mules seemed to have passed. Another patron might have made a hundred mules do, leading them around behind the stage and exchanging their loads for fresh goods. Saxa's wealth made that unnecessary.

The actor draped in a gilded lion skin raised his hands, one of which held a glittering club. Hedia thought he was supposed to be Hercules, but she hadn't paid much attention. She had always found life to hold quite enough drama without inventing things to put on stage.

"As a sign of my prowess!" the actor boomed. He seemed a weedy little fellow, despite his armor and the lion skin, but his voice filled the hollow of the theater. "I raise these pillars to mark my conquest!"

On cue, a pair of gilded "hills" began to rise from the basement, through trap doors in the stage. Hedia frowned: bizarrely, monkeys were tethered in niches in the steep cones. The animals had been dusted with gold also, but in between bouts of angry chittering they were trying to chew their fur clean.

"In later years, another conqueror and god will come to this strait!" said the actor. "He too will bring the whole world beneath his beneficent rule before he returns to the heavens; but greater than I, he will found a line of succession. Each of his descendents will be more magnificent than his predecessor. Hail Caesar, and hail to your mighty house!"

A monkey shrieked and made a full-armed gesture. Something splattered the ornate shield displayed on a frame beside the actor.

Hedia blinked, uncertain of what she had just seen. *Oh by Venus! The little beast is throwing its own feces!* she realized. She started to whoop with laughter, not because what had happened was particularly funny but because its unexpectedness had broken the shell of fear that had enclosed Hedia since last night's dream.

She stifled the laughter into what she hoped would pass for a coughing fit. She was horrified at herself. The incident would embarrass Saxa if he noticed it, and to have had his own wife leading the seeming mockery would shrivel his soul.

Hedia reached over and this time gripped Saxa's hand firmly. The last thing she wanted to do was to hurt the gentle man who had, very likely, saved her life: he had married her when the relatives of her first husband, Gaius Calpurnius Latus, were claiming she had poisoned him.

Maybe some of the relatives had believed that. Latus had been an unpleasant man with unpleasant tastes; one of his partners—particularly the sort of boys he favored—might well have poisoned him. Hedia wasn't the sort, though if someone had brained Latus with a statuette . . .

She realized she was grinning at the thought; she softened her expression instantly.

Most likely Latus had died of a perfectly ordinary fever, as thousands did every year across the empire. He had been a wealthy man, however, and if his widow was executed for his murder, that wealth would be distributed among his surviving relatives—some of whom were well-connected politically.

Hedia knew that if matters had continued in the direction they were going, she would probably have been strangled by the public executioner—though in the entrance of the family home, in deference to her noble status. Instead, Saxa—a distant cousin of Latus—had asked her to marry him. Saxa's wealth and unblemished reputation immediately made the threat of prosecution vanish.

Hedia continued to caress her husband's hand. He glanced halfway toward her, then faced the stage again. He didn't pull away, though he seemed puzzled.

Hedia had never understood why Saxa had married her. Despite his relationship to Latus, they hadn't moved in the same circles. She was as attractive as any woman in Carce, and she was more—talented, one might say—than most highly paid professionals, but that couldn't have been an important factor in his decision.

Hedia made sure that her husband got full value whenever she enticed him into her bed, but she was invariably the instigator. Saxa appeared to enjoy himself, but he was past fifty and couldn't have been much of an athlete—in any fashion—even in the flush of youth.

As best Hedia could tell, Saxa was a sweet man who had chosen to protect a pretty girl who was being bullied. That she was one of the most notorious women in Carce may have had something to do with it as well. Saxa, for all his wealth, had been considered a foolish eccentric when anybody thought of him at all. The husband of the noble Hedia was a subject of interest to both men and women.

Storm clouds painted on flats descended over the stage. A troupe of attractive boys representing the Winds—a placard identified them—danced, while the actor playing Hercules' companion Ithys sang about his leader's battle with Geryon.

According to the song, this was merely a prefiguring of the greater battles which the divine Caesar and his heirs would fight in coming days. Silver foil on the scenery reflected torchlight to mimic lightning, and pairs of stage-hands rattled sheets of bronze thunderously between stanzas.

The fellow playing Ithys was well set up. In other circumstances, Hedia might have invited him to perform at—and after—a private dinner some night.

In her present mood, though, Hedia didn't want to think of darkness, even when it was being spent in pleasant recreation. The night before, Hedia had dreamed of Latus in the Underworld, screaming out the agonies of the damned.

If those who wrote about gods and men told the truth, her first husband was certainly worthy of eternal torture . . . but until recently, Hedia had never imagined that such stories—such *myths*—were true. A few days ago she had visited the Underworld herself. She had talked with Latus, who had been in the embrace of broad, gray-green leaves like those which wrapped him in her dream.

In last night's dream, three figures had coalesced through the shadowy fronds about Latus. They looked like men; or rather, they looked like human statues which had been found in a desert where the sands had worn their features smooth. These were of glass, however, not bronze or marble; and these moved as though they were human.

In the dream, Latus was screaming. Hedia had awakened to find her personal maid Syra leaning over her with a frightened expression and a lamp. Behind Syra were three footmen and a gaggle of female servants, all wearing expressions of excitement or concern.

Hedia had closed her mouth. Her throat had been raw; it still felt tender, though she had sucked comfits of grape sugar most of the day to soothe it. The screams had been her own. Something terrifying was going on, though she didn't know how she knew that.

On stage, the painted storm had lifted, and Hercules was back on his plaster hill. A large mixed company danced on, wearing silks and chains of tiny metal bells which tinkled to their movements. Hedia wasn't sure whether the troupe was meant to be the conqueror's companions, his captives, or more nymphs and sprites.

She didn't know, and she didn't care. Something was wrong, badly wrong; but there had generally been something wrong in Hedia's life, before her marriage to Latus and most certainly afterward. She would see her way through this trouble also.

Hedia gave her husband's hand a final squeeze, then crossed her fingers on her lap. Composed again, she glanced to her right at Alphena, Saxa's daughter by his first wife. The girl sensed her stepmother's interest and immediately blushed, though she didn't respond in any deliberate fashion.

Hedia nodded minusculely and turned her attention to the audience. She suppressed her knowing grin, just as she had swallowed her laughter at the monkey's antics.

As she expected, Alphena had been looking toward Publius Corylus, who sat at the edge of the knights' section. He was a striking young man, taller than most citizens of Carce. His hair was buttery blond. His father had been a soldier, so the boy probably had Celtic blood. Soldiers couldn't marry, but informal arrangements on the frontiers were regularized on retirement, for those who survived to retire. Acknowledged offspring became legitimate and, in Corylus' case, joined the ranks of the Knights of Carce to whom his father had been raised.

A very striking boy. Spending the afternoon with him would be a good way to climb out of this swamp of disquiet. . . .

Hedia's face hardened for an instant before she consciously smoothed it back to aristocratic calm. She could appreciate better than most why Alphena found the boy attractive, but she was by law the girl's mother and she took her duties seriously. Hedia would do whatever was necessary to keep Alphena a virgin until the girl was safely married; and marriage, for the daughter of Senator Gaius Alphenus Saxa, meant an alliance with another senatorial house.

After that, well. . . . After that, Alphena's behavior would be a matter for negotiation between husband and wife. Nothing to do with the girl's stepmother.

Hedia had never pretended to be a wife who embodied all the virtues of ancient Carce, but she had never failed to do her duty as she saw it. She would not fail in her duties now, neither to her husband nor to the girl to whom she was now mother. She would not fail for so long as she lived.

Trumpets and horns which curved around the player's body sounded harshly together. A military procession was entering from the other side of the stage.

As long as I live . . ., Hedia thought. She remembered Latus screaming and her own swollen throat; and she smiled with polite courtesy, because it was her duty now to smile.

THE ANTICS OF THE MONKEYS had amused Alphena, so she regretted it when they and their gilded perches slipped down into the sub-floors beneath the stage. Were there really monkeys on the Pillars of Hercules?

Varus will know. She glanced toward her brother, but Saxa and Hedia were seated in the way. It didn't really matter anyway.

Corylus would know if the monkeys were authentic too; or anyway, he might know. . . .

Alphena realized she was staring toward her brother's friend in the audience. She scowled, furious with herself and with Corylus also. He was so—

She drew her eyes away with a quick intake of breath. Corylus was enough of a scholar to impress Varus, who was a good judge of that sort of thing, and enough of an athlete to impress Lenatus, the ex-soldier whom Saxa had hired as family trainer and manager of the small gymnasium in Saxa's town house. His swordsmanship impressed Alphena too.

The actors marching across the long stage were supposed to be soldiers, or at least some of them were. Alphena eyed the hodgepodge of equipment with a critical eye.

Most of the helmets had been worn by the City Watch before becoming so battered they'd been replaced, but there were also gladiatorial helmets and various examples from the legions and the non-citizen cavalry squadrons. The remainder, a good quarter of the total, was odds and ends of foreign gear in leather, bronze, and iron. The impresario in charge of this mime seemed to have found it cheaper to buy real castoffs than it would have been to manufacture dummies.

The shields were wicker, though, covered in linen and painted with what for all Alphena knew really were Lusitanian tribal symbols. She sneered. The shields had to be fakes because actors wouldn't have been able to handle the real thing. The shield of a legionary of Carce was three thick layers of laminated wood and weighed forty pounds. The barbarians on the other side of the frontier generally used bull hide contraptions, less effective but even larger and equally heavy.

Alphena could use a real legionary shield and short sword: she had practiced daily for several years, determined to make herself just as good a swordsman as any man. She wasn't *that* good—she wasn't big enough, and she had
learned from experience that men had more muscle in their arms and legs
than a woman did. Alphena was better than most men, though.

She wasn't better than Publius Corylus. He had been training with
weapons all his life; and though Corylus didn't talk about it to her, Alphena
knew from her brother that he had crossed the river frontiers with army
scouts on nighttime raids.

Corylus didn't talk much at all to his friend's little sister. He shouldn't, of
course. He was merely a Knight of Carce, and Alphena was the daughter of
one of the greatest houses in the empire. For Corylus to have presumed on
his acquaintance with Varus would have been the grossest arrogance!

Alphena scowled fiercely again. She didn't have the interest in books
that her brother showed, but she had never doubted that she was as smart
as—smarter than—most of the people she dealt with in a normal day.

This wasn't always an advantage. Right now it prevented Alphena from
believing that she wasn't angry because Corylus showed absolutely no interest in her: he wasn't merely avoiding her for the sake of propriety.

But he *was* avoiding Hedia for the sake of propriety. *If he really does avoid
her—*

Alphena heard the thought in her head and shied away from it. Her skin
tingled as though she had rolled in hot sand.

Swallowing, she forced herself to focus on the stage again. Still more actors were marching on. Actually, they were marching and dancing: the ones
who weren't dressed as soldiers danced, men and women both. If she'd been
paying attention she might have known who the dancers represented, but
she doubted that she'd missed anything.

The only reason Alphena was here this afternoon was that Hedia insisted that the whole family be present to support Saxa in his consulate. In
her heart, Alphena knew that her stepmother was right: this was a great day
for Gaius Alphenus Saxa, and his family *should* be with him during his public honor.

She turned to look at Hedia, opening her mouth to protest, "Father
never went out of his way for me!" but that wasn't really true—and it wasn't
at all fair. Alphena faced the front and crossed her hands primly in her lap,
hoping her stepmother hadn't noticed the almost-outburst.

Hedia probably had noticed. Hedia *did* notice things.

Alphena had been amazed and appalled when she learned—from Agrippinus, majordomo of the Saxa household—that her father was marrying for a third time. Marcia was his first wife and the children's mother; she had been a coolly distant noblewoman from the little Alphena remembered of her. At Marcia's death, Saxa had married her sister Secunda. That relationship ended, but the children had seen almost nothing of their father's wife before the divorce, so that made very little difference to them.

But Saxa's third wife was to be the notorious Hedia: certainly a slut, probably a poisoner, and utterly *impossible*. Alphena thought she had misheard Agrippinus—or else that the majordomo was making a joke that would get him whipped within a hair's breadth of his life even though he was a freedman rather than a slave.

It hadn't been a joke. Alphena had known that as soon as she realized that Agrippinus was trembling with fear. He had obviously guessed how Alphena would take the news, and he knew also that Saxa would have allowed his furious daughter to punish the majordomo any way she pleased even though he had only been carrying out his master's orders.

Saxa had left for his estate in the Sabine Hills that morning. He too had been concerned about how Alphena was going to take the news.

When Hedia arrived, Alphena had found no difficulty in hating her. What she couldn't do—what nobody seemed able to do—was to ignore her stepmother. Instead of ignoring Saxa's children the way their birth mother had, she had become their mother in fact as well as law. That hadn't affected Varus much; he continued to take classes and, in his spare time, write poetry—an acceptable occupation for a nobleman if not a very heroic one.

Alphena, though, had found herself being forced into ladylike pursuits. She couldn't fool her stepmother, and she had found to her amazement that Hedia's voice was louder than her "daughter's" and that she had no compunction about causing a scene.

For that matter, the servants were more afraid of Saxa's wife than they were of his daughter. Alphena and her famously bad temper could no longer rule the household. For three months she had subsided into sullen anger, which Hedia had resolutely ignored as she ignored everything that didn't suit her.

Then Alphena had found herself trapped in a place she couldn't have freed herself from, and Hedia had rescued her. Alphena had already felt gratitude toward her stepmother even before she learned that Hedia had literally gone down into the Underworld for her.

A fragment of myth fluttered through Alphena's mind: Hercules had visited the Underworld too, but he had brought the monster Cerberus back to the surface with him. What would Hedia say if Saxa had commissioned a mime on that subject instead of the conquest of Lusitania?

Alphena giggled, then worried that she shouldn't do that now. Fortunately, what was happening on stage had absorbed everyone's attention.

Two tall Nubians had entered, bearing a platter with a domed silver cover. The actor playing Mercury cried, "Behold, great leader! The head of Geryon, conquered by your prowess!"

He whisked off the cover, pointing toward the platter with his free hand. On it was the head of a man whose tawny moustache flared back into sideburns of a paler color. His face had mottled during strangulation, and his eyes started in their sockets.

"The bandit Corocotta!" shouted a spectator who recognized the dead features.

"Corocotta!" shouted the crowd as a blurry whole. "The head of Corocotta!"

Alphena had heard—from gossiping servants—about the coup that Meoetes, the impresario, had arranged with a help of a great deal of Saxa's money. A noted Sardinian bandit, Corocotta had been captured after years of terrorizing the countryside. Instead of being crucified in Caralis, Corocotta had been brought to Carce and marched through the streets before being strangled in the prison on the edge of the Forum.

Corocotta's body had been dumped in a trench outside the religious boundary of Carce, but his head had been preserved for this performance. Saxa's triumph was greater than that of the governor of Sardinia, who had caught the fellow to begin with.

The audience stood and began stamping its feet in delight. Saxa sat straighter on his golden throne: beaming, flushing, and happier than Alphena had ever seen him before.

She grimaced. She hadn't given her father much reason to be happy in her presence. She had resented him, and she had resented the world that said that a daughter wasn't free to do the things that sons were encouraged to do. Varus could be a military officer, could rise to general even—but Alphena, who was easily able to have chopped her brother to sausage in battle, had to threaten a tantrum merely to be taught the manual of arms by the family trainer.

Being forced into close contact with Hedia had given Alphena a different perspective. Alphena's ability to use a sword had been helpful and occasionally very helpful. Hedia wouldn't have considered gripping a sword hilt and wouldn't have known what to do with the weapon if she'd been forced to handle one.

But for all her ladylike disdain for swordsmanship and combat, Hedia had shocked her stepdaughter with her ruthless determination. Hedia had brought Alphena back to the world she had fallen out of, alive and uninjured except for some scratches and blisters.

Alphena blushed, remembering the way she had sneered at the older woman as a pampered weakling. Hedia certainly pampered herself, and if threatened she would bend like a young willow in a storm. When the storm passed, the willow would stand straight again; and it wouldn't break, not ever, no more than Hedia would.

The Nubians pranced the length of the long stage, giving every section of the theater a good opportunity to view the head. *I wonder what my brother thinks of this?* Alphena wondered.

She bent forward slightly, then remembered that her father's plump bulk concealed Varus—and Pandareus—unless she leaned out over the Tribunal railing. There was no need of that.

From the time Alphena had begun to be aware of the world around her, she had been mildly contemptuous of Varus. He wasn't crippled, but he was completely disinterested in the physical sports that were open to boys. He spent his time with books and his writing, the sort of thing that an old man or a weakling would do.

Varus wasn't a weakling. When the blazing demons of the Underworld began to climb into Carce, he had sat as calmly as a Stoic philosopher, chanting a poem. At the time, Alphena would have preferred Varus help her fight the fiery onslaught; but—candidly—he wouldn't have been much use as a warrior.

She couldn't see that his poetry was much use either, but at the end of the night Carce and the world had survived. Alphena's sword had *not* defeated the threat, so perhaps her brother's verses had.

At any rate, Varus hadn't run. He was as true a citizen of Carce as any legionary who stood firm against charging barbarians; as true as the sort of man Corylus would be when he returned to the frontier as an officer.

Alphena's eyes slipped unbidden into the audience again. Corylus sat very close to the woman beside him. She wasn't young—she must be almost thirty!—but she wasn't bad looking in a coarse way.

A *lower-class Hedia*, Alphena thought, and for an instant embarrassment overcame her anger. *Hedia saved my life!*

Corylus' neighbor was from a knightly family like his own, shown by the two thin stripes on the hem of her tunic. She wore a linen cloak too, longer than the warm temperatures demanded but just the thing to conceal a man's groping hand.

Did Corylus and the hussy meet here by plan?

Alphena jerked her eyes away; but after a moment, she found herself looking at Corylus again.

"MY GOODNESS, the excitement just makes me *dizzy*," said Orpelia, the woman seated to the right of Corylus. "You'll keep me from falling over if I'm overcome, won't you, dear?"

She toppled—lunged would have been another way of describing it—against Corylus' shoulder, shifting her arm back so that her breast flopped against his forearm. As if that hadn't been a clear enough signal, she tried to wriggle closer.

Orpelia was the wife of a shipowner named Bassos, a Greek born on Euboea who had become extremely wealthy. Also, according to Orpelia, Bassos was very old and at present inspecting his estates in Sicily.

Corylus suspected "old" meant middle aged; and Bassos might well be here in Carce, though he probably didn't care a great deal about his wife's recreations. The claim of wealth was likely enough, though, given that Orpelia's jewelry included a ruby tiara along with other expensively flashy items.

Corylus didn't care how Orpelia conducted herself either, so long as her activities didn't include him. Which was much harder to arrange than he had expected it to be.

"Master Pulto," he said, looking over his shoulder. Pulto wore an amused expression which he quickly blotted from his face. "I wish to be a little higher for a better view. Trade places with me, if you will."

Pulto had served twenty-five years in the army with Corylus' father and had followed him into retirement. Pulto had been Cispius' servant, his bodyguard, and most importantly his friend. When it was time for Corylus to be trained in rhetoric by a professor in Carce, Cispius had sent Pulto along.

Pulto wasn't going to coddle Corylus any more than he would have coddled a new soldier in the company. On the other hand, if the boy showed signs of really going off in the woods, Pulto would bring him back to reality. A troop of Sarmatian lancers hadn't been able to move Pulto from where he stood over the unconscious form of his commander, and Hercules himself knew that no matter how drunkenly angry Corylus got, Pulto *would* be obeyed if he thought he needed to be.

"It's my honor to serve you, master," said Pulto in a sepulchral voice, "no matter how dangerous the duty may be. If I don't survive, I hope you'll see to it that my grieving widow is cared for in her final days."

Orpelia sat bolt upright, looking as furious as her rice-flour makeup allowed without cracking. "Well, really!" she said. "I'm astounded at the rural boors who claim to have been honored with knighthood!"

"Well, don't get too upset, honey," said Pulto as he and Corylus changed places. "His daddy and I were on the Rhine when your Greekling husband was being marched to Carce in chains, so it isn't us who made a slave of him."

Laughing, he chucked Orpelia under the chin. She squealed and made for the aisle, dragging her maid behind her.

Corylus allowed himself a smile. He'd grown up in the cantonments around military bases. He was a tall, good-looking youth and the son of an officer besides, so it hadn't been uncommon for older women to suggest they would like to know him better.

Even whores who were feeling the pinch toward the end of the army's pay cycle weren't quite as brazen as some of the women Corylus had encountered here in Carce, though. The metropolis had its own standards—and they weren't as high as those of the barbarian fringes of empire. Corylus wasn't a prude or a virgin, but neither was he desperate enough to be charmed by the attentions of a slut.

On stage, the head of "Geryon" had been placed on a stand beside Hercules. Its wax eyes stared out from beneath bushy brows as lines of actors paraded before it, wearing placards indicating what Lusitanian tribe they were supposed to belong to. *Nemetatoi, Tamarci, Cileni* . . .

Corylus frowned as a thought struck him: were they actors, or were they real Lusitanians, either purchased locally or shipped in from the province in order to make the production that much more lavish? If Saxa was paying his impresario a percentage over the expenses, Meoetes had every reason to run the costs up.

He glanced up at the Tribunal, looking for his friend Varus. Instead he saw the profile of Hedia, as crisply chiseled as the portrait on a coin. She started to turn toward the audience, and Corylus as quickly jerked his eyes away.

In the orchestra beneath him sat Marcus Sempronius Tardus, accompanied by three men of foreign aspect. Corylus knew little of the Senate, but he had met—better, had seen—Tardus seven days ago. He doubted whether Tardus would remember him; he certainly *hoped* the senator wouldn't remember him.

Tardus was a member of the Commission for the Sacred Rites, the ten senators who guarded the *Sibylline Books* and examined them if called on to do so when the Republic faced a crisis. Seven days ago, Tardus had been on duty in the Temple of Jupiter Best and Greatest on the Capitoline Hill; the *Books* were kept in a crypt beneath the temple floor.

The Underworld ripped open through the floor of the temple that night. Tardus had seemed to be asleep, the victim of a magician's spells. It might be awkward if he now remembered seeing Corylus when he awakened in the temple.

Tardus's three companions were thin-faced and, though they wore ordinary woolen tunics, were not natives of Carce or of Italy. Two had wizened cheeks and skin the color of polished walnut. They wore their hair over their left ears in tight rolls into which brightly colored snail shells had been worked. One had pinned a small stuffed bird with spread wings over his right temple, and the other had a tuft of small yellow feathers in a piercing in his right earlobe. Corylus had never met anyone with their particular combination of costume and features before.

The third man had short hair, a black goatee, and gold rings in both ears. If Corylus had seen him alone, he would have guessed the fellow was a seaman from somewhere in North Africa; in company with the other pair, his background was more doubtful.

Tardus sat upright on his ivory chair, as still as a painted statue. If he was following the action on stage it was only with his eyes, which Corylus couldn't tell from behind.

His three companions squatted instead of sitting on chairs of their own, and they were wholly focused on the Tribunal. The sailor-looking man curled the fingers of his left hand, then spread them one at a time as though he were counting. His lips moved; Corylus wondered if he was murmuring a prayer under his breath.

Why are they so interested in Saxa? Assuming that it's Saxa and not his wife or children that they're staring at.

While Zephyrs in flowing silks and mountain nymphs who wore revealing goatskins danced attendance, the Lusitanians continued to arrive from stage left and march past Hercules. They were carrying more treasures, this time in handbarrows instead of on mule back.

Corylus wasn't sure what the major products of Lusitania were, but he guessed hides and fish would cover the vast majority. This procession emphasized red-figured pottery of the highest quality.

A broad wine-mixing bowl, displayed on edge, showed the infant Hercules strangling the serpents which had attacked him in his cradle. *At least there's a connection with the mime,* Corylus thought. And in fairness, there were doubtless Greek colonies on the coast of Lusitania.

He looked at Tardus again, frowning slightly. The senator was completely still. He couldn't be sick or even asleep, not and remain upright on a backless chair. His lack of animation seemed unnatural, even granting that this display of Saxa's wealth would be of less interest to another senator than to the members of the urban proletariat who filled most of the seats in the theater.

For the first time, Corylus speculated on the relationship between Saxa and Tardus. The internal politics of the Senate weren't greatly of interest to the son of a provincial knight, but most of Pandareus' present students were themselves sons of senators; it was inevitable that Corylus would hear a great deal.

Much of it was gibes directed against Saxa, since Varus was clearly the best scholar in the class and held his well-born fellows in contempt. The fact that he associated with Corylus, a mere knight, made the implied insult to his peers even sharper. Nobody was going to physically attack the son of so rich a man, but there was free discussion of Saxa's reputation as a superstitious fool who lived in Aristophanes' Cloud-Cuckoo Land.

If that bothered Varus, he didn't show it. Corylus suspected it *did* bother him, simply from the fact that his friend never referred to the comments when the two of them were alone.

Tardus was the subject of similar comments, however. He was Saxa's elder by fifteen years and had become a Commissioner of the Sacred Rites through a combination of seniority and interest. Unlike Pandareus' friend Atilius Priscus, however, Tardus was known for credulity rather than scholarship.

Saxa had shouted at Tardus in the aftermath of the chaos at the Temple of Jupiter, blaming him for what had happened. At the time, Corylus had thought that was a clever ploy: it had prevented others, particularly Commissioner Tardus, from looking closely at the role Saxa's own family had played in those events.

Now Corylus found himself wondering what Tardus remembered of that night. He wondered also who the strangers accompanying Tardus were, and why they stared so intently at Saxa and his family in the Tribunal. There might, of course, be no connection.

On stage, the "suppliant tribesmen" were kneeling, and the various sprites and spirits had frozen in their dance. Mercury faced the audience, one arm pointing back toward the gleaming pomp of Hercules.

For an instant the only things moving in the scene were the twisting heads of the three metal snakes which protruded from the boss of Hercules' shield. According to Hesiod, Vulcan's genius gave the serpents the semblance of life. Here in Carce, a clever midget hidden in the belly of the shield moved them.

"All hail our ruler, the master of Lusitania under the majesty of the gods!" Mercury boomed, a neatly turned compliment for Saxa framed in a fashion that would not offend the emperor. The latter had by reputation been paranoid when he was young and in good health; the rigors of age had not mellowed him.

The actors on stage cheered; the audience echoed them, even most of the senators in the orchestra. Tardus remained as silent as a stone, and his three companions stared toward the Tribunal like greedy cats eyeing a fish tank.

CHAPTER II

Corylus stepped down into the fourteenth row again. He'd been punctilious about following the rules when he put his freeborn servant in the
row behind him, rather than getting Pulto a ticket for the knights' section
as Orpelia—and hundreds of others—had done for the slaves attending
them.

"No reason not to sit beside you now," he said.

"There was no reason not to before, except you're so stiff-necked,"
Pulto said with a broad grin. He glanced in the direction Orpelia had
disappeared and said, perfectly deadpan, "Too bad the lady had to go. We
could've had an improving conversation, I'm sure."

He nodded his head toward the stage and added, "Better than what's
going on up there, anyhow. What are they supposed to be doing now?"

The curtain had been drawn over stage left while the company, including Hercules on his rock, danced a complex measure. "They're moving,
marching," said Corylus after a moment's consideration. "I don't know
where to."

Mimes had their own visual language, as surely as birds and animals did.
Corylus hadn't spent enough time in Carce to be fluent in it yet.

Pulto snorted in disgust. "It's not what I remember route marches being
like," he said. "Which is good, mind you, because my knees aren't what they
once were."

The curtain drew back. The thirty feet of stage closest to that wing was
now water on which flats of sea creatures floated on shallow rafts: a ribbon-
fish, an octopus painted an unexpected green, and what was probably meant

for a whale. Corylus had never been to the mouth of the Rhine where it emptied into the German Sea, but he was pretty sure that the whales which were sometimes glimpsed there didn't arch their bellies, lifting their tail flukes and their long, grinning jaws into the air simultaneously.

"Here will I found a city," boomed Hercules. "In later years, great leaders will come here in the name of the Caesars, my equals in Olympus!"

Even granting that his mask contained a resonating chamber, the fellow's voice was impressive. Pulto must have been thinking the same thing, because he muttered, "That one's got the lungs of a first centurion on him. Wish he wasn't dressed like a clown, though."

Corylus chuckled. "I quite agree with you, old friend," he said, "but the impresario had literary justification for each of his choices. Well, a kind of justification. Probably because writers in the past were just as determined as Saxa is to give their audiences the most impressive show they could."

The Hercules of ancient legend carried a plain oak branch for a club and wore a lion-skin cloak. Later myth made the skin that of the gigantic Nemean lion, sprung from the blood of the monster Typhon. No writer before now had suggested that the lion's skin had been sprinkled with gold dust so that the spectators in the highest seats of the theater could see it sparkle, but Corylus supposed that might be an aspect which had simply gone unremarked in the past.

Euripides had given Heracles a brazen club, the gift of the god Hephaestus. Saxa had gone the Greek one better by gilding the club, but either metal was too sophisticated for the rustic hero.

Heracles' armor—here golden—and the shield banded with gold, silver, and ivory had even more ancient evidence: the poet Hesiod, second in time and—some said—second in literary importance to Homer himself.

Even a great writer could come up with a bad idea in search of an effect, though. When one did, he opened a passage through which a Replacement Consul of the future could drive whole herds of absurdity.

Saxa wouldn't have written the mime himself, of course. For a moment, Corylus wondered if Varus had. *No, he would've said something.* And besides, Varus had given up dramatic writing after his public reading last month.

Corylus glanced again at his friend and saw that he was jotting notes with a short bronze stylus on a tablet. Varus had decided to become a historian of the sacred rites of the Republic. That meant not only things like the auguries attending the appointment of a consul, but also theatrical performances like this one: they too were religious in character.

If something went wrong with a mime, a gladiatorial spectacle, or a beast hunt, it had to be repeated: restarted, in official terminology. That clause had been used to extend public events beyond the limits set for them by ritual.

In the past, a rich man could keep a spectacle going as long as he thought necessary to burn his name into the memory of the electorate. That wasn't required now that officials were elected only after being nominated by the emperor. Indeed, a thoughtful senator might conclude that it wasn't entirely wise to call the emperor's attention to one's wealth and popularity.

New "denizens of the deep" flowed along the channel: a cuttlefish lifting its arms, and a sea horse on which a painted triton rode. Floats in water so shallow wouldn't bear the weight of an actor, but overhead performed three rope dancers dressed as sea nymphs in diaphanous silk.

Hercules gestured with his left hand and said, "Blessed will the people of this land be . . . !"

Flats against the rear wall of the stage rotated on vertical axles to display city walls beyond which red roofs peeked. ". . . when my successor arrives to dispense the justice and mercy of godlike Caesar!"

"Say, how are they doing that?" Pulto said in a low voice. He nodded toward the stage. "The sea, I mean. That really looks . . ."

The right corner of the stage had gotten darker. Corylus frowned. He couldn't see the rope dancers anymore, and the water had become the dusty gray color of old lead.

Indeed, Corylus couldn't see the back of the stage: a sea covered with an angry chop seemed to stretch into the distance. The serpentine neck that lifted momentarily and disappeared again certainly didn't look like a bobbing flat.

"By Hercules!" Pulto said. "That looks *bloody* real!"

The oath had nothing to do with this mime. Hercules was the common man's god, a good-natured fellow who drank too much and got into fixes, and who therefore could understand the problems of an ordinary soldier or farmer.

Corylus looked at the Tribunal. Saxa was beaming. There may have been a touch of surprise in back of his pleased expression, but he didn't appear concerned.

Varus and Pandareus leaned forward transfixed. Varus continued to jot notes with a stolid determination which delighted Corylus but didn't surprise him.

Varus consistently displayed as much physical courage as anyone Corylus had witnessed on the frontiers. There were plenty of men in the legions who could stand before a charge of screaming Germans, but there were very few who could have done what Varus was doing now. Not if they knew what Varus—and Corylus—knew about what was really happening.

The "city" of painted canvas took on depth. The walls shone brighter than the armor of Hercules, who now cowered on his rock, and the tiled roofs had risen into high crystal towers.

"How are we seeing this?" Corylus said. Pulto might have been able to hear him, but he knew he was really speaking to himself, attempting to impose reason on something beyond all reason. "It's too clear!"

He wished he were with Pandareus and Varus now. They were talking in the Tribunal, two learned men discussing in the light of their philosophy the events they observed.

I am a citizen of Carce, a soldier and the son of soldiers. I will not flee.

The spectators began to applaud by shuffling their feet. *They think it's a stage effect!* Corylus realized. *They can't imagine anything else that it might be.*

The things Corylus had seen during the past ten days let him consider a broader range of possibilities than the general audience did, Gaius Saxa included. Ignorance would have been less uncomfortable.

Man-sized figures moved on the walls of the city, and the peaks of individual waves flicked foam into the breeze. A painter might manage the precision, but not the movement. No human eye could make out such detail from where Corylus sat. The spectators stamping delightedly from the base of the Temple of Venus at the back of the theater were hundreds of feet still farther away.

The sky continued to darken. Corylus could no longer see the stage, but the city and the sullen ocean spread to the limits of vision.

Tardus remained seated, unaffected by the scene or the clamor it provoked. His three companions had risen to their feet and were chattering with animation. Their words were lost in the applause and the howl of a wind that Corylus could hear but not feel.

The foreigners looked as frightened as Corylus felt. *I am a citizen of Carce. . . .*

The darkness spread, now engulfing the Tribunal. The last thing Corylus saw as he glanced upward was Hedia leaning forward for a closer look at what was before her. Her profile was cool and perfect.

I WONDER IF I'M GOING MAD? Hedia thought. The idea caused her to bleat a laugh. *Would that be a good thing or a bad one? Something that can be treated with a dose of hellebore would be better than what it means if I'm seeing what's really there.*

"Isn't it wonderful!" Saxa said, more excited than Hedia remembered him ever being during sex. "Why, Meoetes didn't suggest he was going to do this! Look at how clear the walls of Olisipo are! Marvelous!"

Hedia glanced at her husband, wondering if he were prattling nonsense to mask his fear. He wasn't. Saxa thought he would see a painting of the capital of Lusitania. He saw what he expected, stagecraft, and he was delighted that it was so good.

She patted the back of his hand with a wry smile; he gripped her fingers in excitement. *Obviously, he's seeing the same thing I am, so I'm not mad. Well, hellebore probably doesn't cure madness anyway.*

The city was becoming more distinct and spreading to fill . . . to fill her field of view, Hedia had thought at first, but it was more than that: she was becoming a part of the city. She could see and touch Saxa and—she reached to her left and squeezed Alphena's elbow just to be sure—her daughter, but the unfamiliar towers and gleaming walls were equally real, equally present.

Men looked out to sea from the battlements. Most wore fringed tunics of unfamiliar cut, but a few were in flaring armor of the same fiery metal as the walls themselves. They didn't disturb Hedia: Carce was full of foreigners, barbarians—people who, instead of speaking in Latin or Greek, chundered words that sounded like *bar-bar-bar* to civilized folk.

Among the humans were glittering figures, manlike but not men. They were the glass men which Hedia had seen in her nightmare, them or their close kin.

The audience here in the Pompeian Theater was as delighted with the spectacle as their patron was. They stamped their feet and waved scarves and capes to signify their approval.

The demonstrations had started at the highest levels of the theater. Hedia suspected the spectators there had been seeing detail beyond what they had thought was possible, causing them to react even more quickly than the folk in better seats.

Hedia's brief smile was as cold as the emperor's charity. The spectators had been correct: this detail *was* impossible to achieve—by human efforts.

If the vision on stage is real, Hedia thought, *then what I saw in my dream was real also.*

Varus would probably tell her that her logic was flawed. She wasn't a philosopher, but she *was* correct. *This is real, and the nightmare is real; and the nightmare isn't over.*

Hedia touched her dry lips with the tip of her tongue, then reformed them into her aristocratic smile. Any observer would think that she was as pleased as her husband by the drama being acted on stage.

The present audience had lost all sense of decorum in its delighted amazement, but even whispers would be loud when multiplied by tens of thousands. Nonetheless, Hedia heard screams of terror over the applause.

She couldn't see the actors and technicians on the other side of the stage where now another world was spreading. If they were alive, they knew that what was happening was more than theatrical trickery.

They must be terrified, Hedia thought. *They must be as frightened as I am.*

She smiled calmly as she watched and waited. She had no better choice than to behave like a lady; and perhaps that was always the best choice anyway.

The city before her was as clear as coral viewed through the waters of the Bay of Puteoli. Hedia—the whole audience, she supposed—saw more than mere eyesight would have allowed if the place had been as close as the stone stage front. It wasn't huge, certainly not as big as Carce. It seemed more the size of Herculaneum on the slopes of Vesuvius, where a sometime friend of Hedia's had a vacation villa.

I should make a point of seeing Maternus again when I next visit Baiae, she thought. The pleasant memory helped calm her, though no one looking on would have realized the patron's wife was in the least disturbed.

The buildings were shining towers, much higher than anything in Carce. The tallest of the lot was a smooth spire with no steps or stages, rising from the plaza which faced the seafront. Hedia had heard of the pyramids of Egypt, but those were described as being of stone and as broad as they were tall. This was a slender crystalline cone topped with a ball of the same blazing metal as had been used in the walls.

The city had been built on a bay, and the shore curved outward in both directions. In the corner of her eye Hedia thought she saw the glint of water inland as well, but that could have been another crystal building.

She couldn't look away from the moving statues on the walls. In dreams the most innocent flower or vista can terrify because it *is* terrifying, not from any property which the waking mind can recognize. The glass men frightened her only because they were frightening in her dream; and even there, they radiated doom only because of the nightmare ambiance.

Ships floated in the harbor at the foot of the city walls. They were larger than the barges which rowed pleasure seekers on the Bay of Puteoli to the Isle of Capri but no bigger than the fifty-oared liburnians of the naval detachment at Misenum, adjacent to Baiae. One ship moved, then a second.

Hedia gasped with surprise. Instead of moving out to sea on crawling oar strokes, what she had thought were sails were beating up and down. The ships lifted from the water like heavily laden gulls.

"Hurrah!" Saxa cried. "All honor to Meoetes!"

Hedia's smile became wry. She knew that her husband was cheering his impresario, but it must seem strange to the audience to hear the patron applauding his own spectacle. Except—

Her face became briefly expressionless before resuming its look of bland acceptance.

—that no one in the vast audience was paying attention to Saxa. Wonder at the performance had overwhelmed every other interest and speculation.

There were six ships in the air now, moving with increasing speed and agility as they rose. A few glass figures were on deck, generally standing at the tubular equipment in the bow. Each of these ships had a figure in gleaming armor in the stern where the helmsman of a normal vessel would grip the steering oar. A few ordinary human beings in tunics were scattered among the squadron, working at undecipherable tasks.

Though the sky was bright, the sun had begun to flatten and turn crimson on the western horizon. When the sea began to roil, Hedia thought at first that it was a trick of the light on the wave tops.

The flying ships curved toward the disturbance, continuing to climb. The water was suddenly as bright as blood. Something started to rise from it.

The thing was huge beyond all living measure.

As the ocean before them boiled, Alphena leaned forward. She felt an anticipation which she couldn't understand, let alone explain to anyone else.

A tentacled horror the size of an island rose on hundreds of twisting, serpentine legs. It paused for a moment, then surged toward the city. Two of the flying ships turned toward the creature and sprayed flame from the apparatus in their bows.

An arm hundreds of feet long curled out, coiled around the stern of one vessel, and clubbed it across the hull of the other. Both broke apart, spilling bodies and fragments. The bow of the free-flying ship splashed into the sea and sank. The monster hurled what was left of the ship it held toward the city.

This is wrong! Alphena thought.

As if she had blinked and cleared a distorting film from her eyes, Alphena saw a human giant where she had briefly imagined a monster. His iron gray hair had been caught in a pair of braids that hung down his back. His only garment was a leather breechclout on which colored splints picked out a border and a sunburst design.

The muscles wrapping the giant's broad, bare chest were as distinct as if a sculptor had chiseled them. Water cascaded from his body; he took another calm step forward.

The giant looked at Alphena. He smiled, the first expression she had seen on his face. He had an enormous dignity, the sort of feeling that the statues of gods should project, but never did in Alphena's experience.

He's not a giant! Alphena thought. She was certain of that, for all that he towered over the city walls and the tiny figures on them. *He's my brother's height!*

The four remaining ships flew toward the giant in line abreast. His face lost its smile; his right arm moved as swiftly as that of a gladiator casting his net. His fingers slapped the endmost ship, flinging it into its next neighbor. Both broke apart. The two surviving vessels curved off.

The man reached into the water as if groping for clams at the shore. The remaining ships slanted toward him. One pulled ahead and sprayed flame across the man's left shoulder.

Instead of reacting to the attack, the man straightened slowly; the muscles of his back and arms bunched with the effort. A plate of rock tilted up in his hands; a section of the city walls lifted with it. The thick metal walls bent like foil, then tore from bottom to top.

Spectators on the battlements, tiny by contrast, had begun to flee from the man's approach. Those who had not yet gotten clear fluttered away like chaff from a threshing floor.

The vessel which had sprayed fire now sheered away. The second, no longer blocked by its fellow, slid in. As part of the same smooth motion that had torn the slab from ground, the man threw it.

The rock sailed through the air like a hard-thrown dirt clod, but each of the pieces weighed tons. The nearer ship vanished like a cherry blossom caught in a hailstorm. The more distant might have escaped had not a sheet of gleaming wall tumbled through it lengthwise.

He knew what he was doing from the moment he bent over, Alphena realized. *He had decided how to destroy them before they even attacked.*

Varus studied history and literature, making connections between separate events in a fashion that astounded scholars far older than he was. Alphena was interested not in books but in gladiators. That might be unladylike, but she had come to suspect that her own mind was as good as her brother's, or nearly so.

A successful fighter swam through his battles the way a hawk did the air. Alphena had never seen anyone in the amphitheater who displayed more liquid grace than this half-naked barbarian.

He's magnificent. He's as old as my father, but he moves like a weasel. A huge, powerful weasel.

The man wriggled his shoulders, loosening his muscles after the effort of moments before. His left arm was angry red, and blisters were popping up on the skin. Alphena thought he might rub the injury, but instead he merely shrugged and grasped another shelf of rock.

This time he rose from his knees instead of lifting with his back muscles. A quarter of the city toppled inward, shattering tower against tower to fill the streets with fragments.

The great slab rolled back. The man caught it, braced himself, then lifted it overhead. *It must be as heavy as the cone of Vesuvius,* Alphena thought.

She was as thrilled as she had been the afternoon she watched the swordsman Draco defeat seven netmen consecutively, a feat never before accomplished in the amphitheaters of Carce. *He's magnificent!*

The giant smashed the slab down onto what remained of the city. The vision was soundless, but pulverized dust exploded outward to settle on the sea and the surrounding forest promiscuously, like a gray pall.

The man turned his head. Alphena thought he was looking straight into the Tribunal. He smiled minusculely—

At me!

—and reached down for another mass of rock. The sea behind him bubbled, surging up the passage he had torn into the land.

Magnificent.

VARUS TOOK NOTES as he observed the monster. He had filled the four leaves of his first notebook and was already well into the extra one he had brought as an afterthought.

He smiled slightly. Perhaps he could scribe additional notes on the Tribunal's stuccoed railing. If he had considered that possibility, he would have inked notes on shaved boards instead of scribing them on wax with a bronze stylus. Of course, he would probably have run out of ink by now also.

Pandareus had been making odd motions with his hands, curling and opening his fingers in a complex pattern. *Is he praying?* Varus wondered. *Or is that some foreign gesture to turn away evil?*

He was just opening his mouth to ask when Pandareus said, "I've counted three hundred and eighteen legs on the side we can see. And we don't know with a creature like this that the entire underside isn't covered with legs, instead of them being placed only around the outer rim of the body."

He's been counting, using the position of his fingers as an abacus! Varus realized in a gush of relief. He wasn't as willing to claim prayer and charms were superstitious twaddle as he might have been a month ago, but it still would have been disturbing to see his teacher descending to such practices.

Aloud Varus said, "You said, 'A creature like this,' master. You think there are more of them?"

Pandareus laughed. They were probably the only two people in the theater who found humor in the situation. That spoke well for philosophy as a foundation for life, or at least for a dignified death.

The creature was tearing a path into the island, hurling increasingly large pieces of soil and bedrock into the ocean behind it. Its hundreds of tentacles worked together, waving like a field of barley in a breeze. They groped down into the land, then wrenched loose great chunks of it.

"Master?" said Varus as he jotted down details of the creature's legs. They were all serpentine, but some had scales, some had nodules like a gecko's skin, and the rest included a score of different surfaces and patterns. "It . . . Does it look to you as though it's growing larger as it proceeds?"

"Very well observed, Lord Varus," Pandareus said approvingly. "Note that the channel behind the creature is narrower than the front which his body is cutting now. Perhaps it's devouring the rock, do you suppose? Though that doesn't appear to be the case."

Varus could see his companions in the Tribunal, but the audience in the belly of the theater was either hidden by the vision of destruction or had vanished into the blur that extended from the visible margins. Except—

Where the orchestra had been, the three strangers who accompanied Tardus were sharply visible. They glared at the creature as it tore through whatever stood in its way. The mixture of fear and fury in their expressions reminded Varus of caged rats, gnashing their chisel teeth in a desire to chop and gash in the face of certain death.

"Lord Varus?" Pandareus said without any hint of emotion in the words. He raised an eyebrow. "Is this your doing, I wonder?"

"No!" said Varus, angry for an instant. Then, when he had analyzed his response, he was embarrassed.

"I beg your pardon, teacher," he said. "I was afraid you might be correct. I *am* afraid you might be correct."

"You have mistaken a question for an accusation, my lord," Pandareus said dryly. "The teacher who failed to train you out of that defensive reflex is to be censured. Furthermore, my question was rather hopeful."

He gestured with his open left hand toward the vision. The monster was wreaking destruction at an accelerating pace.

"I'm quite certain of your goodwill toward mankind generally and toward me in particular, you see," Pandareus said. "I would have been glad to learn that you had brought this thing into being; because if you did not, I have to be concerned about the intentions of who or what *is* responsible."

The creature lifted a block of land greater than its own huge bulk, spun it end for end in its tentacles, and sent it crashing into the sea. The vision dissolved in spray.

Varus flinched instinctively, but the gout of water seemed not to reach the Tribunal. He had an impossibly good view of what was happening, but none of his other senses were involved.

"Master," Varus said, "if I knew what was happening, I would tell you; and if I could stop it, I . . ."

The words dried in his throat. Pandareus and, on Varus' other side, his family, were fading into a familiar gray mist which replaced the spray thrown up by the vision.

He was not moving, but reality shifted around him. He knew that he was walking through a foggy dreamworld in which other shapes and beings might pass nearby without him seeing them; but he knew also where he was going and who would be waiting when he arrived there.

Varus climbed up from the fog; it lay behind him in a rippling blanket, as though it filled a valley. The ancient woman sat under a small dome supported by pillars. Framing the top of her high-backed chair were two huge boar tusks.

No pig is that large! Varus thought. *It would have to weigh more than a ton.*

The ivory was yellow, and the tips had been worn by heavy use. He remembered that Apollonius claimed that Hercules sent the tusks of the Erymanthian Boar to Cumae.

"Why do you come to me, Lord Varus?" the old woman said. "The power is yours, not mine."

"Sibyl, I know only what is in books," Varus said, using her proper title. "Tell me what I saw in the theater."

Then, because he knew his body remained seated with his family in the Tribunal, he said, "Tell me what I am seeing."

The Sibyl turned her head, looking down the slope opposite to the direction from which Varus had approached her. He followed her eyes to the scene he had been viewing in the theater, but now he watched as if from a great distance above. The creature ravaged an island or rather a series of six rings, each inside the next larger and all touching or nearly touching at the same point of the circles.

Volcanoes, Varus realized. Or anyway, *a* volcano which had erupted six times on successively smaller scales. The craters were nested within one another, but cracks in their walls had let in sea to create a series of circular islands.

Even the most recent event must have been far in the past. Except where crystal palaces sparkled, heavy jungle covered the rims of the cones and their slopes above sea level.

The creature itself had grown to the size of an island as it demolished the linked cones. Varus remembered waves washing over the sand palaces he had built on the beach at Baiae when he was a child.

"You see Typhon destroying Atlantis," the Sibyl said. Her voice was as clear and unemotional as the trill of nightingale. "The Minoi, the Sea Kings of Atlantis, were not such fancies as Plato believed when he invented stories about them. But I know only what you know, Lord Varus."

I didn't know that! Varus thought. He grimaced. *She knows what I think, whether I speak or not.*

"Mistress?" he said. "Is it real, what we see? Is it happening?"

Spray and steam concealed whatever was left of the ring islands. *Will the creature break through to the fires remaining under the surface of the sea? And if so, what then?*

He doubted that Typhon would be harmed even by a fresh eruption. As for Atlantis, it could scarcely be more completely uprooted than it was now.

"It may have happened, Varus," said the Sibyl. "There are many paths, and on this path Typhon destroyed Atlantis."

"What happened next?" Varus said. He looked into the old woman's eyes. Her skin was as wrinkled as that of a raisin, but her features nonetheless had a quiet dignity. "After, after *Typhon* destroyed Atlantis, what did it do?"

The Sibyl turned her palms up, then down again. "If Typhon destroys Atlantis, will it not destroy this world, Lord Varus? Who but Zeus with his thunderbolts could halt him?"

The linked islands were a sludge of steam and drifting ash. Typhon, larger by far than the monster of his first appearance, crawled eastward. The setting sun threw his shadow across a red-tinged sea.

"Mistress?" said Varus. In this place he no longer had his notebook. He regretted that, because holding it would have given him something to do with his hands. "Is Zeus real?"

The Sibyl laughed. She said, "I know only what you know, Lord Varus. Are the Olympian gods real, philosopher?"

Of course not, Varus thought, though he didn't open his mouth. *I'm an educated man, not a superstitious bumpkin.*

The Sibyl laughed again. "Then let your philosophy console you!" she said.

The mist rose, lapping Varus' waist and stretching wisps toward the Sibyl's chair. He could feel words of closure trembling in his heart. Before they could burst from his mouth he cried, "Sibyl, was the Erymanthian Boar real? Did Heracles kill it?"

Without turning her head, the Sibyl lifted her right hand and caressed the great tusk beside her head. She said, "You are a clever, educated boy, Lord Varus. Something was real, and someone killed it. If you wish to say they were the Erymanthian Boar and Heracles, who is there to stop you? Not I, surely."

"Open the Earth and the World to me!" Varus' lips shouted. His soul plunged through ice and fire until it filled his body again. He rocked on his stool and would have fallen if Pandareus had not caught him by the shoulders.

The illusion had vanished. The actor playing Hercules sprawled sobbing against the stone backdrop. Others of the performers huddled together or had fled from the stage.

The entire audience was on its feet, stamping and shouting, "*Saxa! Saxa! Saxa!*"

Father must be very pleased, Varus thought. *I wish I knew as little about what happened as he does, so that I could be pleased also.*

CHAPTER III

The vision disappeared as suddenly as a lightning flash, leaving nothing behind but memories. Hedia was so cold inside that she continued to sit in numb silence, oblivious of the change.

The spectators, all the many thousands of them, were going wild. *That's dangerous!* she realized. Fear for her husband and family broke her out of the gray chill that had bound her.

Hedia got to her feet. She wasn't fully herself—she knocked the stool over behind her—but nobody would notice in this confusion. Alphena glanced up as Hedia walked toward the back of the Tribunal. The girl looked as though she wanted to say something, but Hedia had no time for chatter.

Servants waited in the rear of the box. Though excited, they didn't seem worried—or anyway, not more worried than could be explained by the fact that their mistress was approaching with a hard expression.

Hedia ignored her personal maid, Syra, and instead stepped close to Candidus, a deputy steward and the senior servant present. She gestured him to bend over so that she could speak into his ear and be heard.

I'll probably have to shout anyway. Shouting was undignified, but Hedia supposed that under the circumstances she couldn't complain about a minor indignity.

She smiled. She couldn't change how she felt, but she was too self-aware not to be able to view herself clearly.

"Candidus, find the impresario Meoetes and tell him in the senator's name to draw the curtain at once," she said, holding the lobe of the servant's left ear between her thumb and forefinger. "At once, do you understand?

And go yourself; don't pass this off to an underling who might be disregarded."

She wasn't pinching him, but her touch reminded the servant that he was dealing with Hedia, not her gentle, diffident husband. Candidus *would* obey, without question or hesitation.

The fellow made Hedia want to slap him. Well, cane him; she certainly didn't want her bare hand to touch his greasy skin. She had decided when she took charge of Saxa's household that so long as the servants obeyed *her* instantly, she would ignore any behavior that didn't directly touch the honor of her new family.

"At once, your ladyship!" Candidus said. He went down the stairs at the back of the Tribunal, taking each step individually but quickly.

Though a slave, Candidus affected a toga at public events like this one. The thick wool made him sweat like a broiling capon. In Hedia's present mood, the fellow's mere presence seemed an almost unbearable provocation.

She turned and almost cannoned into Alphena, who must have followed her. Hedia stifled a curse—*she's following me to help, but this isn't the time for it!*—and hugged her daughter by the shoulders and swung around her.

"Give me a moment, dear," Hedia said. "I must speak to your father."

Saxa sat with his hands on the arms of his chair, beaming and blinking. *He no more understands the situation than a bull being led to the altar does!* Hedia thought, then muttered a prayer that the metaphor might not be a prophecy.

Syra had righted the stool. Hedia leaned across it, graceful despite her hurry, and touched her husband's upper arm.

"Dearest," she said, hoping that concern wouldn't give her voice the whip-crack edge she knew it got at times. "Get up and thank the emperor. Raise your hands for silence. When things quiet a little, say that this was done by the emperor's gift. Make sure that at least the orchestra hears you. Do you understand?"

"What?" said Saxa. He looked at her, blinking. He seemed surprised to hear words in the midst of applause that had as little content as a crashing thunderstorm. "The emperor, my dear? No, Meoetes did all this, but he was doing it for me."

"My lord and master," Hedia said, chipping the words out and no longer trying to hide her frightened anger. "Tell Carce that it owes this entertainment to the emperor. Otherwise you and Meoetes and your family will be entertaining the city from the tops of crosses!"

Saxa looked blank for an instant. "Oh!" he said. "Yes, this was . . . this was . . ."

Apparently he couldn't decide how to describe the vision any better than Hedia could have, so he lurched to his feet instead of finishing the sentence. He raised his arms. For a moment the cheers increased, but Saxa turned his palms outward as though pushing the sound away.

Hedia sank onto her stool, feeling unexpected relief. She couldn't do anything about the glass figures of her dreams, but at least she had gotten Saxa—gotten her whole family—out of the immediate trouble. At any rate, she had done what was humanly possible to avoid immediate repercussions from this vision, this waking nightmare.

The curtain was canvas and split ceiling to floor down the middle. Ordinarily only half was used at a time, concealing set changes on a portion of the long stage. Now both right and left portions began to move toward the center, but they jerked and stuttered instead of sliding smoothly as they had before. By leaning over the railing, Hedia could see that three and four men were manhandling the heavy curtains rather than the dozen stagehands in each of the original crews.

Candidus must have carried the message successfully; that, or Meoetes had come to the same conclusion on his own. The actors still on stage looked like casualties of a gladiatorial show that the doctors and Charon—the costumed slave who drove the dead wagon—hadn't gotten to yet.

"My fellow citizens!" Saxa said. "Hail to the noble and generous emperor who has granted you this gift. Carce rules the world, and the emperor is the soul of Carce!"

His voice was pitched too high to command authority, but he was managing good volume; he would be heard. Hedia nodded approvingly.

"Long live the emperor!" Saxa said. "Long live the emperor, our father and god!"

Cheers and the banging of sandals on stone again overwhelmed the theater. Hedia noted wryly that her husband's fellow senators were the most enthusiastic, capering like monkeys in the orchestra. *Nobody wants word to get out that he was behind-hand when everyone around him applauded the emperor.*

Hedia started to relax, but now that the immediate danger was past, memory of the dreadful glass figures returned. The memory gripped her like a hawk sinking its talons into a vole. She felt dizzy for an instant; she felt Alphena take her arm to steady her on the chair.

She recovered, straightening like the noble lady that she was. She patted her daughter's hand affectionately.

There was something very wrong going on, but there had generally been things wrong in Hedia's life—before her first marriage to Calpurnius Latus and most certainly ever afterward. She had seen her way through those troubles, and she would see her way through this one also.

She had to, after all. What would poor dear Saxa and his children, her children now, do without her?

Tomorrow she would visit Anna, Corylus' housekeeper and his former nurse. Anna was the wife of the boy's servant Pulto—and she was a Marsian witch.

And if Anna couldn't send away those glass nightmares, Hedia would find another way. It was her duty as a wife and mother, and as a noblewoman of Carce.

But oh! She wished Corylus was holding her now in his strong young arms!

THE SPECTATORS WERE BEGINNING to drift toward the exits. Corylus led his burly servant through them against the flow. Pulto would have been more than willing to force a path, but Carce wasn't a frontier cantonment and Publius Corylus was no longer the son of a high military officer.

Still, though Corylus didn't push people out of his way, the senator's toady who thought to shove the youth aside got a knee in the crotch for his bad judgment. He heard Pulto chuckle behind him. *I am a freeborn citizen of Carce, and I learned on the Rhine how to handle lice.*

They got clear of the audience and found that the steps from the orchestra to the stage were concealed behind an offset panel. "Just like a Celtic hill fort," Pulto said as he followed his master up them.

Corylus' face blanked as he tried for an instant to fathom the deep inner meaning of what his servant had just said; then he smiled. *There isn't any deep inner meaning, here or ever with Pulto. He'd seen the entrances to Celtic hill forts designed the same way, so he said so.*

Corylus ducked behind the curtain. A few actors were still standing on stage. One had been dressed as a naiad in silk pantaloons painted to look like a fish's tail with flowing fins. She had stripped off her costume and stood nude, weeping desperately.

"What's all that about, do you think, lad?" Pulto asked in puzzlement.

Corylus glanced at him; they were side by side again. *Pulto still thinks it was all stagecraft!*

Picking his words carefully, Corylus said, "I think it must have surprised the actors even more than it did us in the audience. They were closer, you see."

The performers had been inside the vision. Perhaps the effect simply blinded them, which would be frightening enough. From the stunned looks and worse on the faces of the actors he saw, the experience had been worse than that.

Pulto would realize before long that there had been more than trickery behind the vision. Corylus didn't see any reason to hasten his servant's discomfort, however.

And Pulto would *be* uncomfortable, because magic frightened him in a way that German spears did not. He knew how to divert a spear with his shield—and how to deal with the blond pig who'd thrust it, too. Magic, though, was as unfathomable as a storm at sea.

Corylus felt the same way. His smile became wry. He had too good an education, however, to allow him to pretend something hadn't happened simply because he wished that he hadn't seen it happen.

A great number of people waited in the wing beneath the Tribunal. A senator never went out without an entourage of both servants and clients—freemen who accompanied him in expectation of gifts, dinners, and similar perquisites. They had nothing better to do with their lives than to be parasites on a rich man.

"I wonder how they'd look in armor?" Corylus whispered to his companion.

Pulto snorted. "I'd sooner train a cohort of fencing dummies to hold the frontier," he said. Unlike Corylus, he spoke in a normal voice. "At least they wouldn't talk back to me. And they'd stop spears just as well as this lot."

Besides the normal entourage and the similar band which attended Lady Hedia, Saxa had a consul's allotment of twelve lictors. They had been hired from the Brotherhood here in Carce, though there was no absolute requirement to do so. An official who wished to save money could outfit his household servants as lictors instead.

From weapons drill, Corylus knew that it wouldn't be as easy as a layman might think to handle the lictor's equipment. Each man carried an axe wrapped in a bundle of rods, symbols of the consul's right to flog and to execute.

The additional cost of professionals meant nothing to Saxa. The mental cost to him if a servant turned lictor dropped an axe on someone's foot or spilled his rods at a gathering of dignitaries was beyond calculation.

There was room for the mob of attendants backstage: the emperor sat in the Tribunal when he attended performances. Besides the retinue of a civilian magistrate, he was always accompanied by fifty or a hundred German bodyguards.

Corylus smiled grimly. This complex included, along with the Temple of Venus at the front and the portico and gardens behind the theater proper, a fine Senate Hall. It had not been used since the afternoon Julius Caesar was assassinated in it.

Caesar had dismissed his Spanish guards, saying that a magistrate of Carce did not need foreigners to protect him from his own people. None of his successors would be so naive.

The chief lictor watched Corylus approach, but here in the city the lictors generally took their cue from the consul's household whose members knew their master's friends. Manetho, a deputy steward, and Gigax, a doorman, stood to either side of the steps up to the Tribunal.

"Hullo, Master Corylus!" Gigax boomed. He would have to lose his thick Illyrian accent before he was promoted to daytime duties on the street door, but he was a good-natured fellow who sometimes fenced with Corylus in Saxa's private gym.

"I'm sure the family will be glad to see you, Master Corylus," Manetho said. He was Egyptian by birth, but his Latin was flawless and his Greek would have served an Athenian professor. "But if you please, room is a little tight in the box . . . ?"

"I'll stay down here, never fear," Pulto said. He grinned. "If you think you'll be safe, master?"

From being raped by Hedia, he means, Corylus thought. *She wouldn't do that! She's a lady!*

He blushed, and an instant later blessed Fortune that Pulto hadn't completed his thought aloud. That was the sort of joke that soldiers told one another. It would *not* be a good idea in the middle of the household of the husband, who was also consul of Carce.

"One moment!" said another voice sharply. Candidus, also a deputy steward, was crossing from the other wing of the stage at a mincing trot. "Manetho, you're exceeding your authority. Exceeding your authority *again*, I should say!"

Manetho turned toward his fellow servant, hunching his shoulders like a Molossian hound about to tackle a boar. Corylus made his face blank, but mentally he grimaced. If only he'd hopped up the stairs a few heartbeats quicker! An outsider had nothing to gain by becoming the token by which a rich man's powerful servants battled over status.

"Manetho," called Varus from the top of the stairs, "my friend Corylus— oh, there you are, Publius! I saw you coming this way. I was just telling Manetho to send you up as soon as you got here."

"I was just doing that, your lordship," said Manetho unctuously. "Despite some Bithynian buffoon trying to prevent you from meeting your friend."

Corylus had never known where Candidus came from originally: the fellow had no accent. Apparently he'd been born in Bithynia. . . .

Corylus took the steps in three long strides. He wasn't bothered by the number of people in the crowd beneath the Tribunal, but the fact they were divided into factions was disturbing. Saxa and his wife had rival establishments, and the lictors were a further element. Add that the individual servants got along badly with one another—as witness the scene of a moment before—and the emotional temperature was very high.

At least in a battle, there's only two sides, Corylus thought. He smiled.

Varus clasped hands with Corylus at the top of the steps. They'd become surprisingly close in the months since they'd met as students of Pandareus of Athens.

Corylus quirked a smile as he edited his own thoughts: it surprised him to be close to a senator's son, certainly; and he suspected it surprised Varus to be close to anybody at all. They were both outsiders in Pandareus' class, but Varus must have been an outsider all his life.

Saxa was still looking out over the hollow of the theater. He seemed dazed, but Corylus thought his vague smile was sincere.

Pandareus stood close to the senator but not with him. The Greek had moved back from the railing, but he hadn't chosen to join Varus until he was summoned.

A foreigner who moved in the highest levels of Carce's society had to be extremely careful not to give offense. Varus wasn't the sort to snarlingly order an uppity Greek to take himself off, but Pandareus was showing his present hosts the same punctilious courtesy that might have saved him from a beating if they had been, say, Calpurnius Piso—another of his present students.

Candidus reentered the Tribunal and murmured to Saxa, who suddenly came alert. He began giving the steward instructions, tapping his finger up and down in animation. Candidus bowed and disappeared down the stairs again.

Alphena and her stepmother talked intently at the back corner of the box while their maids hovered attentively. Alphena was an enthusiastic girl, but she had generally seemed to Corylus to be angry about something. Now she looked happily transfigured.

Hedia, on the other hand . . . Corylus had seen Varus' stepmother both icily calm, her public face, and letting her warmth and quick intelligence show when she relaxed in private. This was a different woman: frozen in the way a rabbit freezes when the weasel hops toward it.

"Did you see the three men with Sempronius Tardus?" Varus said without preamble. "Where did they go, did you notice? Because they weren't in the audience after I came back. Or Tardus either, but we know who he is."

Came back from where? Corylus thought, but the whole line of questioning had surprised him. Not for the first time, of course. Varus' rank as the son of Gaius Alphenus Saxa gave him access to every library in Carce; he read voraciously and apparently never forgot a word of the contents.

But Varus tended to forget that other people didn't have the same wide background as he did—and that they hadn't been listening to his thoughts to give them a context for whatever he said. Talking with him was often like having fragments of messages fall from the sky to your feet.

"I saw the attendants," Corylus said simply. He would get the context by listening carefully to his friend, and it seemed to him that answering the questions was as easy and far more useful than chattering a series of silly questions of his own. "I thought one of them might be a Moor, but I've never seen anybody like the other two. I didn't notice where they went after the performance. I was concerned with getting through the crowd to find you."

Varus made a moue. "It can't be helped," he said. "And anyway, questioning them might not bring us any closer to an answer."

"I don't even know what the question is," said Corylus, smiling but nonetheless bluntly truthful. "What did you notice about Tardus' servants that caused you to ask?"

Pandareus raised an eyebrow over Varus' shoulder. Corylus caught the gesture and beckoned him. Pandareus might know no more than his students did—which in Corylus' case at least was nothing at all—but his age and authority made everything nearby seem more stable.

"That I could see them at all," Varus said. "When I looked into the audience when the vision was at its height, I . . . it was as if I were on a mountain, looking over the tops of the clouds. Except for those three men, whom I'd noticed with Tardus. But I didn't see Tardus or any of the other senators."

He looked at their teacher. "Master Pandareus, did you see them?" he asked.

"I noticed them with Commissioner Tardus," Pandareus said, using the senator's title as a member of the Commission for the Sacred Rites. "I wondered what tribe they might be from."

He made a deprecating smile. "I was planning to ask my friend Priscus—"

Marcus Atilius Priscus, also a member of the Commission, and according to Pandareus, the most learned man in Carce. Priscus in turn assigned that honor to Pandareus.

"—to introduce me to Tardus so that I could learn more. Ethnicities are something of a hobby with me."

He turned his palms up, as if to show that they were empty. He went on, "I didn't see them during the, well, vision is as good a word as any. I might have missed them, however, because I was so engrossed in the vision itself."

"Master?" Varus said, licking his dry lips. "Could the city we were seeing be Atlantis?"

"I suppose it could . . . ," Pandareus said, pursing his lips. "If Atlantis existed, that is. Do you have reason to believe that it does exist, Lord Varus?"

"I was told it did in a dream," said Varus with a lopsided smile. "At any rate, I'm going to call it a dream for want of a better word. I was told that Typhon was destroying Atlantis."

"Ah!" said Pandareus. "What we saw fits the descriptions of Typhon in Hesiod and Apollodorus quite well. Rather better than the city matches the Poseidonis of Plato, in fact. Though I always believed that both were mythical."

Pandareus smiled like a cheerful parrot. "I would rather Atlantis would be real than Typhon, from what we are told," he said. "But I suppose our wishes in the matter aren't controlling."

Corylus coughed apologetically. "Master?" he said. "Speaking of dreams—you were visited by the sage Menre in the past. Have you dreamed of him again?"

"I'm not sure that I ever dreamed of Menre," Pandareus said, smiling faintly to take the sting out of his correction. "I believe I *saw* a man named Menre, yes; and he claimed to be an Alexandrian scholar who helped Demetrius of Phalerum create the Museum three hundred years ago . . . which certainly implies that I was dreaming."

He turned his palms up again, then closed them. "But this is a quibble, I know," he said. "The answer that matters is that I have not received further advice from Menre, in dreams or otherwise."

Varus hunched in on himself, looking as lost and miserable as a kitten caught in a thunderstorm. Corylus hesitated, then put his arm around his friend's shoulders. *Let people think what they bloody care to!*

"Master . . . ," Varus said. He started in a mumble with his face downcast. Remembering that he was speaking to his teacher, he caught hold of himself and straightened; Corylus stepped back.

Varus resumed in a firm voice, "Master, I believe Carce and the world are in danger. You can put that to my dream also, if you like."

"I share your belief in coming danger," Pandareus said in a dry tone. "I believe the vision of everyone in this theater will cause the Senate to call for examination of the *Sibylline Books*. At least it will if anyone beyond the three of us recognized what was happening."

"I'm pretty sure Meoetes and the stage company have figured that out," said Varus. He had recovered enough to smile wryly. "Though what actors and stagehands say won't carry much weight with the Senate."

"And I don't see much reason to convince anyone that it should," Corylus said. "Consulting the *Sibylline Books* in a crisis is a custom with the weight of six hundred years of tradition behind it, but I don't believe that it's a practical answer to the thing that threatens us. Whatever that thing is."

"Yes," said Varus. "That's what I thought too."

Taking a deep breath, he looked from Corylus to Pandareus and went on. "Which is why I hoped that your mentor—Menre that is—would have suggested a path for us to follow. Otherwise we have nothing."

Corylus exchanged glances with their teacher. Then he said, "In the past, Gaius, *you* provided the direction for us by quoting the *Sibylline Books*."

Varus had never seen the *Books*, nor would he be allowed to unless he were elected to the Commission for the Sacred Rites. He probably *would* be so elected; but not for perhaps forty years, when he had become a senior senator rather than merely a youth of learning. Nonetheless, responses from the *Books* had come from his mouth; though not from his conscious mind, he had said.

"I was told that if Atlantis was destroyed, then all the world was doomed unless Zeus again slew Typhon," Varus said, shaking his head slowly. "And it was strongly implied that Zeus didn't exist. I don't see that this is very helpful."

"Well, I'm pleased to have my skepticism about the Olympian gods to be confirmed by such a respectable source as the *Sibylline Books*," Pandareus said. His humor was so dry that even if Varus' superstitious father overheard, he wouldn't be shocked by the sacrilege. "Perhaps more will be offered to you later. As for me—"

Candidus brushed Pandareus as he bustled into the Tribunal, looking self-satisfied and important. He went immediately to Saxa.

Resuming with a faint smile, Pandareus said, "I will put my head together with my friend Priscus. We will peruse his remarkable library to see what we can find relating to Atlantis and to Typhon."

"Master Pandareus?" said Saxa, joining them to Corylus' amazement. From the expressions of Varus and Pandareus—the Greek lost all expression as he turned to face the senator—it was an equal surprise to his companions.

"I've just invited my colleague Marcus Priscus to dinner tomorrow night," Saxa said. "I'm hoping you will be able to join us. I cannot imagine a more worthy addition to a learned dinner than you, master."

Amazingly—given the difference in their ranks—Saxa bowed to Pandareus. The teacher bowed in return, careful to dip lower than the senator had. "I would be honored, my lord," he said.

Corylus felt a twinge of pity for Varus' father. For all his wealth and position, Saxa really wanted to be known as a wise man. It was his misfortune to be intelligent enough to realize that he *wasn't* wise.

Hedia left Alphena standing by herself and touched her husband's shoulder. When he turned, she whispered in his ear.

"Ah, yes!" said Saxa. "Varus, would you care to invite your friend Master Corylus to join us as well? He has a reputation for learning, and I believe he's already acquainted with Marcus Priscus."

Corylus' expression hardened. Before Varus could react, he said, "My lord, much as I would like to join you and your distinguished guests, I have a previous engagement. I regret that I must therefore refuse your generosity."

Corylus would be eating in his own apartment, as usual. That suited him; and it did *not* suit him to be a rich man's toady. Even less did he wish to dance attendance on the rich man's wife. . . .

"What?" said Saxa in obvious puzzlement. No one in his social circle expected lesser men to turn down a free meal prepared by his excellent chef. "What? Ah, of course, of course. Well, another time."

He started down the stairs, beaming again with the success of his entertainment. That applause, Corylus realized, was what had given him the courage to invite Atilius Priscus, whose real erudition was the standard to which Saxa vainly aspired.

Hedia glanced after her husband, then gave Corylus a knowing smile as she returned to Alphena's side. Corylus watched her, then realized Alphena was glaring at him.

The light in the Tribunal wasn't good. Corylus hoped that his blush wasn't as obvious as it felt when it painted his cheeks.

ALPHENA TURNED AWAY. She was suddenly angry with the whole world, starting with herself. She didn't know why she couldn't control these rushes of anger whenever she saw Corylus looking at her stepmother, and it made her *furious*.

Hedia's maid Syra babbled, "What a *hideous* monster! Meoetes should be *whipped* for building something so terrible! Why, if there were any expecting mothers in the audience, it'll be Juno's mercy if they don't miscarry, it was so awful!"

Alphena felt her face go white, then blaze red again. Her skin tingled as she turned to the servant.

Syra was talking to Florina, the maid who had been assigned to serve Alphena for the ten days which would end tomorrow. Alphena hadn't chosen a personal staff, so Agrippinus, the majordomo, rotated servants through her suite for various periods.

Alphena suspected that serving her was regarded as a punishment posting. In the past that would have pleased her. More recently she had been reconsidering her attitude, but right now there was room for nothing but fury in her mind.

"You little snip!" she said. "What do you mean by calling him a monster? He was a man, and a very distinguished man at that! Even if he was a foreigner."

Florina hadn't been speaking; even so she closed her eyes and began to tremble. Servants were not to talk in the presence of their owners unless they were directed to. Syra was on informal terms with her mistress, but there was no one to protect Florina from whatever torture the daughter of the house chose to inflict.

Syra, however, stood as though she'd been spitted on a javelin. Yes, she knew a great deal about Hedia's life away from her husband's house, but she didn't imagine that would save her if Alphena *really* wanted her flayed. Alphena was, after all, a fellow aristocrat; and Syra knew that she shouldn't have been chattering.

Though Syra would wonder—everyone in the Tribunal would be wondering—why Lady Alphena was so exercised at two maids discussing the recent stage presentation. That outside view of her behavior brought Alphena down from the heights of rage that she had climbed unaware.

Alphena relaxed, stepping back mentally from a battle she was losing. She took a deep breath, let it out, and gave a dismissive wave with her left hand.

"Never mind, girls," she said. Florina was a year older than Alphena; Syra was five or six years older than that. "I'm wasting my time discussing such a thing."

"I hadn't realized it was a man in costume myself," Hedia said from beside Alphena. "To tell the truth—"

She glanced at the maids. They hopped backward to the railing, getting as far as they could from their mistresses. Syra still looked white and tears were running down Florina's cheeks.

I'd like to slap the little chit! Alphena thought. Then, as sudden as the flash of anger, she felt a rush of revulsion at her behavior. *I wouldn't treat a kitten that way. Why do I do it to a woman? A girl!*

"As a matter of fact . . . ," Hedia said, now that the maids were making a point of being in a completely different world in which they could neither see nor hear their betters. She looked sidelong at Alphena. "I was afraid it wasn't stagecraft at all. I was afraid that it was a vision of things that might be real if our fates took a wrong turn."

"I don't know what it was," Alphena mumbled, wrapping her arms around herself.

"Daughter," Hedia said sharply. "Are you all right?"

Alphena came to herself. Her father was going down the stairs; preparing to return home, she supposed. She would like to go back now also, but Hedia obviously had things to say. She owed her life to her mother; and she certainly owed Hedia more courtesy than she had just showed her.

"I'm sorry, Mother," Alphena said, touching the back of Hedia's wrist contritely. "I didn't think it was a stage trick either. I don't think it could have been."

She cast her mind back to the vision. "Do you recall the walls of the city?" she said. "And the ball on the top of the tallest spire? You saw them?"

"Yes, of course," said Hedia, her eyes narrowing as she searched for meaning in what her daughter was saying. "They were gold, weren't they?"

"They were orichalc," Alphena said flatly. "Not brass like the edge trimming for shields that people call orichalc, but the real thing. I . . ."

She broke off and glanced toward the maids. Florina closed her eyes, her face scrunching in terror. She at least probably wouldn't be able to remember her name, let alone what she might hear today in the Tribunal; and neither she nor Syra was close enough to understand anything Alphena said in a normal voice.

"I saw orichalc where I was before you found me and brought me back, Mother," Alphena said, touching Hedia's wrist again, but this time not removing her fingers. That had been in a place of magic and terror, to which Hedia had come to rescue her. *She saved my life.* "You can't mistake orichalc if you've seen it once. Because of the fire in it."

"Ah," said Hedia, shrugging. "I thought that might be sunset on gold, but in all truth I wasn't paying much attention. I was . . ."

Hedia's eyes had been unfocused; or anyway, focused on something a great distance away. She turned her gaze on Alphena again. This time she wore a guarded, uncertain—perhaps uncertain; the light was bad— expression.

"You saw the walls, dear?" Hedia said. Her smile was false, but it had a trembling innocence instead of the brittle gloss Alphena had seen her show the world in normal times. "You mentioned that you did. I suppose you saw the people on the battlements, too? The figures, I mean?"

"Yes," said Alphena. "Some of them wore orichalc armor, yes. And each of the flying ships had a helmsman in orichalc armor, too. That's what you mean?"

She suddenly felt uncomfortable. There was something wrong with Hedia, but Alphena didn't know what. Framing the question in that fashion made her realize how much she had come to count on her stepmother's ruthless calm in the past ten days.

"No!" cried the older woman, her anger as unexpected as Alphena's own had been some moments earlier. Hedia's expression chilled; she tapped her left cheek with her fingertips, symbolically punishing herself for a lapse of control.

"I'm sorry, dear, I'm not myself," she said. "No, I meant the . . . that is, did you see glass statues on the battlements? And yes, in the ships as well. But they moved."

"Yes," Alphena said carefully. "I saw them and I don't understand. But I saw the ships flying, and I didn't understand that either."

She wondered how she could avoid provoking Hedia into another outburst, when she had no idea of what she had done before. She felt a rueful humor, but it didn't reach her lips: *Syra and Florina were probably wondering the same thing about me.* Then she thought, *I won't do that again to servants.*

"But you saw them and you saw them move," Hedia said. "As if they were men."

Alphena lifted her chin in agreement. "Yes," she said. "But I wasn't . . . I was looking at the . . ."

Varus was still talking earnestly with Corylus and their teacher. The two maids were trying to force their way into the stuccoed brick wall at the back of the box, and the male servants had gone down the steps with Saxa.

"I thought just for an instant I saw a, well, a monster that was all legs and arms," Alphena said. She didn't know why she was so embarrassed to admit that. "But then I saw he was a man, wading in the sea. I shouldn't wonder if he was a king himself, or a priest. He *wasn't* a monster, Mother."

Hedia looked at her and quirked a smile. Suddenly the familiar personality was back, the calm sophisticate who laughed merrily and, in season, killed as coldly as a Egyptian viper.

"If you say so, dear," she said. "I suppose whether it was a man or a monster doesn't matter a great deal, given that the rest of what we saw—I saw, at least—didn't make any more sense than a monster tearing a city apart did."

Hedia pursed her lips as she considered Alphena. "Once before you came with me on a visit to Pulto's wife," she said. "Now I have other questions that a Marsian witch might be able to answer. Would you care to join me tomorrow, dear?"

"To ask about the . . . ," Alphena said. "About what you say is a monster?"

"No," said Hedia, suddenly distant again. "To ask about the glass men."

"I'll come," Alphena said. "I'd come anyway, Mother. I want to help you. However I can."

Hedia patted Alphena's shoulder and said, "I'll inform Pulto of what we intend. Up here in front of Corylus, so that he won't object."

Hedia stepped over to Syra and gave crisp directions, leaving Alphena with her thoughts.

I don't know why I care. But he's not a monster.

"MASTER?" VARUS SAID. Hedia's maid had gone down to the stage floor a moment earlier; now she was returning. "Could I—and Publius, if he wishes, of course. Could we help you and Lord Priscus in his library. We—"

Pulto was coming up behind the maid with his head lowered. He showed all the enthusiasm of a barbarian being dragged along the Sacred Way behind the emperor's triumphal chariot.

Corylus' head whipped around; Varus stopped before the next syllable. Pandareus waited politely a moment for Varus to finish, then turned also.

"Thank you for attending me, Master Pulto," Hedia said, strolling across the Tribunal to where Varus and his companions stood. Pulto turned his head to follow her. At the top of the steps he was already within arm's length of Corylus; the Tribunal wasn't meant for large gatherings.

"My daughter and I . . . ," Hedia said, halting beside Corylus but keeping her eyes on his servant. "Intend to call upon your wife tomorrow morning, while Master Corylus—"

Only now did she glance at Corylus, giving him a neutral smile.

"—is in classes with Lord Varus."

Another nod, another pleasant smile. When Saxa first brought home his new wife, Varus had been amazed and more than a little disgusted. He wasn't a member of the fast set or interested in its gossip, but even a bookish youth who spent his time at lectures rather than at drinking parties heard things.

In the past six months Varus had observed his stepmother closely, seeing both her public and her private faces. She was—he was sure she was— everything which rumor had painted her, but she was also a great deal more.

Pandareus spoke. Varus heard the sound but not the words. At the moment laughter relaxed him, his grip on present reality loosened.

Varus was drifting into the mist in which he met the Sibyl. His companions continued talking, apparently unaware of what was happening to him.

He was climbing a trail through jagged mountains. The encircling cloud was too thick for him to see much beyond the length of his arm, but the sun scattered rainbows around the edges of outcrops.

Varus trudged on. He was never sure of time when he was in this place—or in this state, for a better word. Something large moved in the bright blur; coming toward him . . . and it was past, crossing the path ahead of him. It walked on two legs, but even bent over—as it was—it stood twice his height and taller than any man. Its long hair rustled, and it had the sharp, dry odor of fresh sawdust.

Can I die here? Varus thought. Then, smiling like the philosopher he wished to be, *Does it matter if I do?*

He came out into sunlight so bright that in the waking world, the contrast should have made him blink and sneeze. The Sibyl waited at the edge of a precipice which plunged off in the opposite direction. Every wrinkle of her face, every fold of her soft gray garment, was sharply visible. She had thrown back her hood so that she stood in a halo of her thick silver hair.

"Greetings, Sibyl!" Varus said. He bowed, then straightened. "Why did you call me here again?"

"Greetings, Lord Varus," the old woman said. "Who am I to summon you? You are real, Lord Magician, and I am only the thing your powers have created."

Varus looked out toward a great city far below. It was a moment before he recognized Carce, lying along the Tiber River and spreading in all directions from the villages which were its genesis.

Instead of the familiar Alban Hills to the southeast, the horizon lived and crawled forward on myriad legs. Tentacles flayed the ground to rock as bare as this on which the Sibyl stood. Typhon, growing with each innumerable step, advanced on Carce.

"Sibyl . . . ?" Varus said, sick at what he was seeing. *How long before that vision is the reality which my neighbors see loom above Carce's ancient walls?* "What am I to do? Where do we look for the answer, my friends and I?"

"I am a tool that your mind uses, Lord Varus," the old woman said. Her tone was that of a kindly mother to a child who demands to know the secrets of life. "I exist only through your powers. You know the answer to your questions."

"I know nothing!" Varus said. "I know—"

Immeasurable and inexorable, Typhon crashed across villas and the tombs on the roads leading out of the city. Varus' view shifted from the danger to a house on the slopes of the Palatine Hill, facing the Citadel and great temples on the Capitoline across the Forum. It was still luxurious, though it had been built to the standards of an older, less grandiose, time.

That's the house of the Sempronii Tardi, Varus thought. He had visited it a year past to read the manuscripts of three plays of Ennius which, as best he could determine, existed nowhere else in the city.

"You know all that I know, Lord Varus," said the Sibyl, smiling. Then she lifted her face and cackled to the heavens. *"There is a dear land, a nurturer to men, which lies in the plain. The Nile forms all its boundaries, flowing—"*

Varus was in the Tribunal with his startled friends. Corylus held his shoulders; Pandareus had taken his right hand in both of his own.

In a strained voice, Varus heard himself shout, "—by Libya and Ethiopia!"

"It's all right, Gaius," Corylus was saying. "Here, lean against the railing and we'll get a chair back up here for you."

Varus shook his head, partly to scatter the drifting tendrils of cloud.

"No," he said. He hacked to clear his throat, then resumed in a firm voice and standing straight, "I'm quite all right."

The humor of what he had just said struck him, so he asked, "Well, I'm all right now. But thank you for holding me, Publius, because mentally I was in a different place for a time."

"You were speaking of Egypt," Pandareus said. He considered for a moment with his head cocked sideways, then said, "A voice spoke which didn't sound at all like yours but came from your throat. Was speaking of Egypt. What bearing does Egypt have on our situation?"

"I don't know," Varus said. He shook his head ruefully, remembering the way he had said the same thing to the Sibyl in his . . . his dream? His waking reverie?

He considered the whole dream, frowned, and said, "I saw—I focused on, I mean; I saw all Carce. But I focused on the town house of Commissioner Tardus. I suppose I might have been thinking about him because of the strangers who accompanied him in the theater."

"It's equally probable," said Corylus, "that the thing that disturbed you in the theater is the same thing that you saw, saw or sensed or whatever, in the vision you just experienced. That's what you did, isn't it? Have a vision?"

Varus bobbed his chin up in agreement. "Yes," he said. "I saw Typhon starting to destroy Carce. It was much bigger than what we all saw here in the theater, but it was clearly the same creature. Then I was looking at Tardus' house."

"If we assume that the connection with Egypt is important . . . ," Pandareus said. He was in professorial mode again; he turned his right palm outward to forestall the objections to his logic.

"Then the crypt to the god Sarapis beneath the house of the Sempronii Tardi might explain the cause."

"But, master?" said Corylus. "Private temples to Serapis—"

Varus noted that his friend pronounced the god's name in Latin fashion while Pandareus had used Greek.

"—were closed by order of the Senate more than eighty years ago. Were they not?"

Pandareus chuckled. "Very good, my legalistic friend," he said. "But my understanding—purely as a scholar, of course—is that the Senator Sempronius Tardus of the day chose discretion rather than to strictly obey to the order closing private chapels. His successors have continued to exercise discretion, since closing the chapel now would call attention to the past."

He shrugged. "I'm told this, you understand—" probably by Atilius Priscus, but Pandareus would never betray his source "—but it's entirely a private matter. The aristocracy of Carce do not open their temples—or their family secrets—to curious Greeklings, however interested in philosophy and religion."

Varus sucked in his lips to wet them. "I think," he said, "that Commissioner Tardus would open his house to the authority of a consul."

Pandareus and Corylus both looked at him sharply. "Will your father help us in this?" the teacher said.

"I think he might do so at my request," said Varus.

He smiled. Looked at in the correct way, everything is political. He said, "And I'm quite sure he will obey his wife in the matter. Judging from Hedia's actions, she is just as concerned about this business as the three of us are."

CHAPTER IV

Pulto was part of the rear guard, chatting in German with a footman who had been born in the quadrilateral between the Upper Rhine and Upper Danube, but Corylus walked beside Varus in the middle of the procession. His expression must have caught his friend's eye in the torches which the linkmen carried.

Varus looked concerned and asked, "Is something wrong, Publius?"

"Nothing at all," Corylus said. He gestured to the twenty-odd servants ahead of them—as many followed—and explained, "In the cantonments, a procession like this at night would be the Camp Police, is all. So I guess part of me is expecting some drunk to fling a wine bottle at us—or a chamber pot, to tell the truth."

"We're far more civilized here in Carce," Varus said, relaxing into a smile. "A poor man might be set on and robbed, but we of the better classes travel in perfect ease and security. Unless we slip on the paving stones and fall on our backs, as I've been known to do."

Two linkmen and two servants with cudgels led the entourage, singing about a girlfriend who had run off with a trapeze artist and now performed with him. This version was rather tamer than what Corylus had heard sung on the Danube, where the lyrics dwelt on the endowments of the acrobat which had lured the errant girlfriend away.

The song was to warn away footpads, drunks, and any poor citizen who happened to be sharing Orbian Street with them tonight and didn't want a crack on the head. Corylus had learned quickly that in Carce, rich men's escorts had a rough-and-ready way with potential dangers to those they were protecting.

"Manetho?" Varus called to the steward walking a pace ahead of his master. "We'll go in through the back garden. I expect my father's clients will be clogging the front entrance for hours yet after the—"

He paused. Corylus knew why, but the servants probably thought nothing of it.

"—the success, that is, of his mime."

"As your lordship wishes," Manetho said. He trotted forward, though the men in front had probably heard the command without it needing to be relayed.

Pandareus had insisted on going home on his own to his tiny apartment off the Sacred Way. He'd insisted he would be in no danger because he had many years of dodging trouble at night in Carce.

No doubt that was true, but Corylus still wished that Varus had succeeded in getting their teacher to accept a couple husky servants to convey him. Marmots had a great deal of experience foraging on grassy alpine meadows, but eagles still caught their dinners.

One of the linkmen waited at the mouth of the alley as a marker, while his partner and the cudgel-bearers turned down it. From the near distance ahead a deep voice boomed, "Who's there?"

"Keep your tunic on, Maximus!" the linkman said.

"Both of you pipe down!" said Manetho. "Let's not embarrass the consul in his own home, shall we? He'll be meeting in his office with the leading men of the Republic right now."

"That isn't how I would have described my father's clients," Varus said, leaning close to Corylus. Even so his voice was barely audible. "But I suppose it sounds better than 'feckless parasites'."

"Well, I'm sure they're the leading feckless parasites," Corylus whispered back. That he dared make such a joke to a noble showed—showed Corylus himself—how much he trusted Varus and considered him to be a friend. *He's a man I'd take across the Rhine*, Corylus thought, putting it in army terms.

The alley was narrow; the procession slowed to a crawl while Maximus, the nighttime doorkeeper, pulled open the back gate. He had been waiting in the alley with his lantern instead of watching the portal from inside.

Pulto slipped—more likely, pushed—through the intervening servants to join his master. If Varus hadn't been present he would probably have asked Corylus what he intended to do now, but under the circumstances he merely grunted, "Sir," politely.

The line was moving again. The footmen who'd been in front were blocking the other end of the alley against rampaging housebreakers or other equally unlikely threats.

Most of what a rich man's servants did was either make-work or simply sit on their hands. There were too many of them for it to be any other way. Saxa had well over two hundred servants here in his town house: he could have rebuilt the whole structure with a smaller crew.

"Unless you want me with you, Varus . . . ?" Corylus said, raising an eyebrow.

"No, I think it's best if I see Father alone," Varus said. "I can take him away from his clients, but to bring my friend with me would be insulting. I'm perfectly willing to insult them if I need to, but I don't see the necessity in this case. Would you care to wait in the gymnasium until I have an answer?"

They'd reached the gate; Maximus raised his lantern. Varus' smile in the flickering light was engaging, but Corylus recognized an underlying hardness that he had noticed before in aristocratic tribunes posted to the frontiers for a year on a legion's staff. The nobles of Carce were pampered, certainly, but their enemies had rarely found them soft.

"If you don't mind . . . ," Corylus said as they passed through the gate. "I'll wait here in the garden."

He gestured. The central court had a pool and extensive plantings, but the walled back of the property was a garden also. Seven days ago there had been a peach tree and a pear tree as well as flower beds. The blooms were generally cut for decorations inside the house, but there was a little summer bedroom with wicker screens on either side of the enclosure.

"Certainly," said Varus. "Would you like something to eat or drink while you're waiting?"

"No," said Corylus. "I'll be fine. I just like flowers, you know."

"If it's all the same with you, master . . . ?" Pulto said. "I'd like to chat with my buddy Lenatus in the gym."

"Yes, of course," Corylus said. Pulto nodded gratefully as he strode through the gateway to the house proper on the heels of the servants.

There was nothing unusual about the request. Lenatus, whom Saxa had hired as the family trainer, was an old soldier whom Pulto had known when they were both stationed on the Rhine. The haste with which Pulto moved would have puzzled Corylus if he hadn't known the reason, however.

So long as Pulto thought the vision in the theater was stage trickery, it hadn't disturbed him. Now he had realized that it was real. That made him all the more uncomfortable about magic and the traces it left.

Corylus looked around. He was alone in the garden except for Maximus, who had pulled the gate closed and stood against it with the lantern, looking unhappy.

"Ah . . . ," said the doorkeeper. "I suppose you'll want me to keep you company back here, sir?"

Maximus had the shoulders of a bear and arms that hung almost to his knees. His strikingly ugly looks caused him to be stationed at the back gate, not at the front where the senator's distinguished visitors entered, but Corylus had found him intelligent and, surprisingly, literate in Greek with a smattering of Latin as well.

"I don't see why," Corylus said, smiling. "It seems to me that you can guard things just as well in the alley as here. I'll just think for a while."

"I guess you know what you're doing, sir," Maximus said. "Only me—it doesn't feel right back here since the pear tree died, you know? It used to be that other fellows would come sit with me, you know? But none of the servants like to come back here now. And, ah . . . I sometimes think I'm seeing somebody. In the corner of my eye, you know?"

"I'm sure I'll be all right," said Corylus; he gestured toward the back gate. "And you can take the lantern. There's plenty of moonlight for me."

"*Thank* you, sir!" the doorman said with an enthusiasm that a gold piece for a tip couldn't have bettered. He was out into the alley again, banging the gate closed, almost before he'd spoken the last syllable.

Corylus looked around again, his smile rueful. The garden wasn't a ruin, not yet, but even the crescent moon showed him that it was neglected.

Ten days since, Saxa and the Hyperborean sorcerer who had gained his confidence had held an incantation here. Their magic had resulted in a blast of intense cold which killed the pear tree, and it had also worked deeper changes to the setting.

Corylus had his own reasons for being here, but he wasn't surprised that the servants kept away. That included the gardeners: the dead pear had been removed, but no one had watered or weeded the flower beds since the incantation.

There was a covered walkway against the partition wall between the garden and the house. Corylus settled himself on the pavement, facing the alley. The peach tree on the left side of the garden was in full flower. Its branches, fluffy and white in the moonlight, overhung the wall at several points.

If all those flowers are allowed to set fruit, Corylus thought, *the weight will break the branches. If the gardeners won't do something, perhaps I should—*

A woman—a female figure—stepped into the moonlight, as he had expected she would. Corylus rose to his feet. "Good evening, Persica," he said.

The dryad flinched, but she didn't disappear. "Are you angry with me?" she said in a small voice. She turned her face away, but he could see that she was watching out of the corner of her eye.

"No, Persica," he said. "I think we've both learned things since we met before."

The nymph had tricked him into a past time. Her malice came from petty stupidity rather than from studied cruelty. She—"Peaches"—was small-minded and not over-bright, so how else could she have acted?

"I'd be angry if you tried to do it again, though," he added.

Persica sniffed. "No fear of that!" she said bitterly. "The woman here—she's a demon! She said she'd peel my bark off with a paring knife. She meant it!"

"If you mean Lady Hedia . . . ," Corylus said, hiding his smile because the dryad would have misinterpreted it. "Then I suspect you're right."

Persica gave a peevish flick of her hand. "I don't pay any attention to humans' names," she said. "Why should I?"

She kicked morosely at loose dirt where the pear tree had been. Though the gardeners had grubbed out the frost-shattered trunk, they had neither planted a replacement nor resodded the soil turned when they ripped up the roots.

"I never thought I'd miss Pirus," the dryad muttered. "So full of herself because she had nice hair. As if nobody else had nice hair!"

Persica tossed her head but swayed her body as well, so that her long red-blond hair swirled in one direction and her garment in the other. The fabric was sheer. It had scattered light in bright sun, as Corylus remembered, but now in the moon glow it was barely a shadow over her full breasts and the rippling muscles of her belly.

"I used to watch you humans, at least," she said. "You aren't much, but you're company. Now I don't even have that."

She looked squarely at Corylus and pleaded, "Is it because of me? I wouldn't hurt them! I didn't mean to hurt you, just, well, I was angry. Who wouldn't have been angry with that Hyperborean sorcerer killing Pirus right beside me?"

"I don't think it's you, Persica," Corylus said. He touched one of the flat marble spinners which hung from the roof over the walkway. They turned in the breezes, scattering light into the shadowed interior. The nymph had used their reflections to send him to another time and place. . . .

But if Persica hadn't indulged her whimsical malice, Corylus wouldn't have gained the tool and the knowledge that had helped save Carce from destruction. As a matter of fact—

"If you hadn't tricked me the way you did, Persica," he said, "I would have been burned to ash or less. And so would you."

Every land and perhaps the seas as well would have burned, would have been buried under fire. Except that a peach dryad had, in a pet, sent the youth who rejected her advances to the place where he needed to be and where the world needed him to be.

Perhaps the Stoic philosophers were right and gods did look after men. Chance, the whim of atoms clashing together, seemed a slim reed on which to support the series of events which had saved the world.

"Well, anyway, I didn't mean any harm," Persica muttered. She seemed to be walking aimlessly, her eyes on the ground, but she meandered closer to Corylus. Looking up, she said, "But I'm so lonely. I don't let humans see me, but I just wish they'd come here to the garden again."

She tossed her head and gave him a knowing smile. "You can see me," she said, "but you're one of us. Your mother was, and on her side you are."

"That may be true," Corylus said. "But it doesn't matter."

He was uncomfortable talking—thinking—about what Pulto had recently told him about the mother who had died giving birth to him. It didn't really matter whether she was a beech nymph or the Celtic girl his father would have married as soon as he could at the end of his military service. *I am a citizen of Carce!*

Aloud Corylus said, "The Hyperborean's magic clings here, that's all. It's like the smell of rotting blood in the arena, even though they change the sand after every performance. It makes the servants uncomfortable, that's all. That'll wear away."

He smiled encouragingly, knowing that what he said was only partially true. The powerful magic which had been worked here created a weak spot in the fabric of the cosmos. Ordinary humans in this garden—Maximus, for example; the doorkeeper who spoke of seeing things out of the corner of his eye—became more sensitive to matters that would ordinarily be hidden.

"It won't have time to," Persica said bitterly. "The Hyperborean is gone, but it's still going to end quickly."

She shivered and hugged herself. Looking up she said, "You can feel it too, can't you? The sea will do what fire did not."

Corylus rubbed his mouth with the back of his hand. His lips were dry. "You mean Typhon?" he said, remembering what Varus had said in the theater.

The nymph flicked her hand again. "What do names matter?" she said. "It will be the sea and the thing that *is* the sea."

She had sidled to within arm's length of Corylus. Now she leaned closer, not quite to the point of touching him.

"A little warmth would be so nice," she said. "It isn't much to ask, is it, when the end is coming so soon."

"Persica, please don't," Corylus whispered.

Varus would be back shortly, but even if he weren't . . . Corylus thought of the monster he had seen, then imagined that it was tearing apart Carce instead of some crystal echo of a philosopher's dream. He was frozen inside, and the only emotion he felt was fear.

Persica didn't edge closer as he thought she would do. She hugged herself again and said, "I don't really mind dying. I'm a peach, after all, not an oak or one of those ugly pine crones. But a little warmth, cousin . . . ? Just a little warmth?"

"I can't, mistress," he said. He heard a babble of voices in the central courtyard. *Varus must be coming back.* "Please, I can't."

Corylus expected a tantrum or worse, remembering the way the nymph had behaved the first time they met. Instead her face scrunched up in misery.

"Will you at least come back and talk with me?" she whimpered. "Before the end? Please, I get so lonely."

He swallowed. "I'll try, Persica," he said. "I'll . . . yes, I'll come back!"

The gate to the house opened. Varus strode through, beaming with success.

MANETHO REACHED THE SIDE DOORWAY from the central courtyard into the owner's office. A footman stood there, blocking it, and Candidus trotted over immediately.

"Make way for Lord Varus!" Manetho said. The footman turned sideways, squeezing back against the pillar. He was letting the deputy stewards snarl at one another while a lowly footman pretended to be back herding goats in the Pyrenees.

"The consul is receiving his clients in his office," Candidus said, carefully looking at Manetho and pretending not to be aware of Varus himself behind the servant. "No doubt he will attend to his household when he has finished his duties to the Republic."

I wonder if he would take that line if I were Alphena? Varus thought. *He certainly wouldn't do this to Hedia.*

The idea made him smile. If Candidus had been paying attention, the expression might have disconcerted him; but of course he wasn't. Why be concerned about Saxa's bookish, ineffectual son?

Varus tapped Manetho on the shoulder and gestured him aside. "Candidus?" he said pleasantly. "Get out of the way or I will ask my sister to have you tortured. I'm sure she can find something interesting to do to an uppity slave."

Candidus blinked, stepped back, and blinked again. He wasn't so much ignoring Varus' order as too stunned to obey it.

Agrippinus appeared. Varus hadn't raised his voice but the majordomo, overseeing the whole levee while his deputies handled specific areas, demonstrated his ability in a fashion that Varus wouldn't have recognized till recently.

Agrippinus touched Candidus' neck with his right hand; his fingers were pudgy and each had at least one ring, but the tips dimpled his deputy's flesh. Candidus staggered—half propelled, half jumping—into a corner of the office.

Agrippinus nodded minusculely to Varus, then turned and announced in a carrying voice, "Clear this room for the honorable Lord Varus, who wishes to address his noble father, Consul Gaius Alphenus Saxa!"

The client in the office with Saxa was one of the Marcii Philippi, a distant cousin of Saxa's first—and his second; they were sisters—wife; he was therefore a relative of Varus as well. Despite Philippus' rank, he lived in straitened circumstances; though that hadn't, Varus noted, kept him from eating himself into grotesque obesity.

"I say!" said Philippus in offended surprise.

Agrippinus walked toward him with his arms spread slightly and his hands raised, as though he were pushing the client's considerable weight. He didn't actually touch Philippus, but he moved the fellow back by force of personality. He said, "The consul will summon you when he is ready to receive you again, your lordship."

"But I—" said Philippus. Four junior members of Saxa's household moved toward him; one was the footman who had been in Varus' path to the office. He acted with particular zeal, apparently concerned to redeem himself in the eyes of the son of the house. Philippus returned to the entrance hall, backing so hastily that he almost fell into the pool fed by the opening in the roof.

The hall would normally have been crowded with clients. Now all but two clients at a time had been relegated to the street outside, because the consul's twelve lictors took precedence. Varus had considered the lictors a pointless complication, but he realized now that they might turn out to be useful.

Varus joined his father, feeling a mixture of amusement and disgust at the servant's reaction to his threat. Alphena had a vicious temper. She had been known to throw things at people who had made her angry, and it wasn't unimaginable that worse might happen if she flew hot when she happened to have a sword in her hand.

Alphena was not, however, cruel: torture would have been as unlikely for her as sexual congress with a donkey. If the servants had bothered to think, they would have known that as well as her brother did.

Varus had learned that generally people didn't think: they just reacted. He supposed that should have pleased him, because it gave him an advantage over most of the world. Instead, it tended to make him sad.

Saxa was seated on his ivory chair. He faced the hall, the anteroom, and the street beyond on a single axis. The entrance was designed to put the householder in a frame, focusing all eyes on him.

Varus stepped around in front so that his father didn't have to twist sideways; folding senatorial chairs weren't very stable and neither was Saxa. He said, "I'm very sorry to trouble you, sir."

"What's the matter, b-b . . . ," Saxa said in concern. He composed his expression and said, "What's the matter, my son?"

Rather than "boy." Varus had risen in his father's estimation—more accurately, had risen into Saxa's awareness—when Commissioner Priscus had made a point of praising the boy when he met Saxa ahead of a session of the Senate five days recently.

"Sir," said Varus. The office had a high ceiling and two mosaic scenes on the floor. The panel to the householder's right showed Pentheus being torn to pieces by women maddened by their worship of Bacchus. To the left was Acteon, human-headed but with the body of a stag, being devoured by his own hunting dogs; the goddess Diana, whom he had glimpsed bathing nude, gestured angrily from a pool.

The room had been decorated by Saxa's father. Varus didn't suppose he would ever know what his grandfather had been thinking of when he ordered the mosaics.

At least a dozen clerks and other servants watched expectantly from the service aisles on three sides of the room. There was no privacy in a noble household, any more than there was in a poor family's apartment where three generations were squeezed into two rooms and as much of the staircase they could claim against other tenants.

On the other hand, there was no reason why anything Varus was about to say to his father would seem worth repeating, even within the household. Not if he phrased it carefully.

"Father," he said with quiet earnestness. "My studies have reached an impasse of sorts, and I need to enter the house of Marcus Sempronius Tardus. I was hoping that you might help me in this."

"Tardus?" Saxa said, frowning in concentration. "Well, we're not close, you know, son. Indeed, I probably know as little of him as I do any other member of the Senate. The ones who live most of the year in Carce, that is."

He coughed into his hand. "Ah . . . ," he said. "And there was that business at the Temple of Jupiter a few days ago, when Tardus was there as Commissioner of the Sacred Rites. That was necessary, but it didn't, well, endear me to him."

Saxa was obviously hoping his son would say something to let him out of what threatened to be an embarrassment. When that didn't occur, he grimaced and resumed. "I suppose I can send a note to him. What in particular is it that you wish to see? His library, I suppose?"

"Not exactly, sir," Varus said. "My, ah, studies indicate that the Sempronii Tardi have a secret temple to Serapis in their town house. I would like to—that is, I think perhaps I *must* see that temple. In order to, ah, gather information of importance to the Republic."

Saxa blinked. For a moment he looked like a fish displayed for sale on a marble slab; then his cheeks and the lines of his mouth became curiously firmer.

"Marcus Priscus spoke very highly of you the other day," he said. "I believe it's the first time he has addressed a word to me except in answer to a question of my own. He's a very erudite man, you know."

Varus bowed slightly again. "Yes sir," he said. "The Republic is very fortunate to have men as learned as Marcus Priscus and yourself at its helm."

Saxa snorted; his expression went sour for an instant, or as sour as someone as pudgy and good-natured as he could look. That cleared and he said, "Not me, my son, much as I wish it were. But perhaps you in time; Priscus believes you will grow into his equal. I hope I may live to see that."

Varus didn't know whether or not he should speak. Since he was in doubt, he held his silence.

If more people followed that practice, he thought, *the world would be a quieter and less obviously foolish place.* His smile didn't reach his lips.

"I was going to ask if Marcus Priscus intended to make the inspection with you," Saxa said. He was trying to sound neutral, but there was evident hope in his voice. "I suppose you couldn't tell me, though?"

Father is so in awe of Priscus that if I said this was his idea, my request would be granted immediately. I won't lie, but if I tell the truth in the right form of words . . .

"I would not expect Commissioner Priscus to be present, sir," Varus replied carefully. "I believe his friend—and my professor—Pandareus of Athens may accompany us, however. If you are able to effect entrance to Senator Tardus' house, that is."

"I believe that Tardus will respect the authority of a consul," Saxa said. "And I rather think the emperor would have something to say about it if he did not. The emperor is notably traditional in his regard for the forms of government."

His smile widened as he considered the situation. His replacement consulate was an honor, of course, but he probably hadn't considered it to be a position of authority before this moment.

He sat straighter and looked firmly at his son. "We'll go tomorrow afternoon, then," he said. "Let's say in the eleventh—" counting from dawn to dusk in twelve equal segments, regardless of the season "—hour. Please inform Master Pandareus of the plan. And anyone else you believe should be present."

"Thank you, sir," Varus said. "I had considered asking Publius Corylus to accompany us, as his different viewpoint might be helpful."

Saxa smiled faintly. He said, "He's the boy with an army background, isn't he? Just as you like, son, though I hope *that* particular specialty won't prove necessary."

Before Varus could turn to leave, his father coughed and said, "Ah, son? As you doubtless heard, Senator Priscus and your Pandareus will be dining with me in two nights' time. I hope you will choose to join us? Priscus was very complimentary about you."

My father is willing to risk his life by using consular authority in a fashion he knows may be open to question, Varus thought. *If all he wants in return is for me to add a little extra luster to a dinner which already glitters with intellectual capacity—so be it!*

"I will be honored to join you and your guests, Father," he said formally. Bowing, he backed from the office and turned toward the garden.

I'm risking my life too, I suppose, he realized, *but I'm doing it to save the world from destruction by Typhon. My father is doing it merely on my word that it is necessary.*

May the gods grant that I be the worthy scion of so brave a man.

ALPHENA HAD RETURNED to the house with Hedia, in the double litter. She found it odd but nonetheless comforting to regard her stepmother as an ally—a friend even—instead of a demon sent to torment her.

Hedia was the perfect lady: beautiful, her hair and garments in the current style; familiar with all the trivia of Carce's highest social circle. Hedia had seemed all the things that her stepdaughter had been determined never to be.

Hedia *was* all the things she seemed, but Alphena had learned that her stepmother was also as hard as a blade of fine steel and every bit as deadly when the need arose. She had determined to bring Alphena safely through whatever troubles arose, no matter what her own risk was.

Alphena wasn't sure how she felt about that. She prided herself on being independent. She was certain, though, that it was much better to have Lady Hedia as a friend than as an enemy.

There had been no place in particular where Alphena had to be after they reached the house. There was *never* anywhere she had to be, a realization that brought a familiar flush of anger to her face.

Varus was being educated in literature and the arts of rhetoric. All aspects of public life were governed by oratory. The most brilliant general

would be laughed at—albeit behind his back—if he couldn't report his ac-
complishments using *chiasmus* and *litotes*, *praeteritio* and *asyndeton* and a
thousand other absurdities. Absurdities!

The empire had been won at the point of a sword, but Varus could no
better wield a sword than he could fly. Alphena had practiced weapons drill
as assiduously as any army recruit, but she would never be allowed to join the
legions.

She didn't want to spend her life reading poems that didn't make any
sense she could see, nor in learning scraps of history from eight centuries ago
because they might make useful embellishments for her summation speech
in a murder trial. She didn't want to do those things—but she wouldn't be
allowed to, whatever she wanted. She was a woman, so she had no share in
government or the army or in *anything* that mattered!

But while all that was completely true and completely unfair, Alphena
found herself thinking about her stepmother. If Hedia set out to accomplish
something, Alphena would *expect* it the way she would expect the sun to rise
in the east. She couldn't have given a logical explanation of why she was so
confident of her stepmother's abilities, but logic—

Alphena grinned. Logic was a matter for students, like her brother Varus.
Hedia's competence was *real*, which was a very different thing.

Alphena found she had walked the length of the house, to the private
gymnasium and bath located between the courtyard and the back garden.
She used the gym regularly, so it wasn't surprising that she would find herself
at the door if she wandered without paying attention.

She looked around. Her maid, Florina, was close behind but flinched
back when her mistress turned. Six other servants were following Alphena,
presumably people Agrippinus had assigned to her suite. They stopped dead
when she did, their eyes focused on various things but never on Alphena
herself.

I should slap their sniveling faces! Alphena thought, then felt a little
queasy. She took a deep breath.

*They're treating me like a viper. Except that they wouldn't be afraid to look at
a viper.*

Calmly, smiling slightly—she hoped it was a smile—Alphena said, "I
believe I will take a little exercise now to settle myself before I have a light
supper in my suite. Florina, you're dismissed to eat something now before
you'll need to attend me."

Alphena entered the small gymnasium, feeling virtuous. *Hedia would be proud of me*, she thought; but that wasn't really true. She would never match her stepmother's icy superiority to every one and every thing, any more than her chunky form would ever rival Hedia's willowy beauty. *It's not fair!*

"Your ladyship!" said Lenatus. He and his guest—Pulto, Corylus' man—lurched to their feet. A wine jar leaned against a corner, and each man held a broad cup. A water jug was part of the gym's furnishings, but Alphena didn't see a mixing bowl: the veterans were apparently drinking the senator's wine as it came from the jug.

Alphena looked at them. They weren't frightened like the bevy of servants back in the passageway, but they watched her warily. They were freeborn citizens who as soldiers had fought the most dangerous of the Republic's enemies . . . but from their expressions, they would rather be back on the frontier than in the center of Carce, facing a senator's daughter.

I wonder if Florina thinks that life has treated Lady Alphena harshly? Alphena wondered.

Aloud she said, "Master Pulto, I didn't expect to see you here. Is your master in the house as well? I suppose you came from the theater with my brother?"

"My understanding . . . ," Pulto said carefully. He wasn't a member of Saxa's household, but technicalities wouldn't matter if Alphena lost her temper, as she had a reputation for doing. "Is that Lord Varus wished to have a conversation with his father, the senator. Publius Corylus chose to wait in the back garden, but he gave me leave to visit my old friend here."

He gestured toward Lenatus with his free hand. His eyes never left Alphena's face.

"Oh!" said Alphena, feeling a tiny jump of excitement that she hoped she had kept out of her voice. "Well, I'll leave the two of you to your reminis—"

She broke off. She could see from the faces of both men that something was badly wrong.

"What is it?" Alphena said. She heard her voice start to tremble, which made her angry. She continued in an unintended snarl, "Is Corylus with someone, is that it?"

Lenatus looked at his friend, who in turn looked as though he had been stabbed in the belly. "Your ladyship," Pulto said, "I got the impression that my master might be talking with somebody, yes."

He's with Hedia.

He's having sex with Hedia in the garden!

Alphena blushed, then staggered as the *stupidity* of her thought struck her. Oh, Hedia's reputation was deserved: she'd as much as told Alphena so when they were fighting for their lives and very souls. As for Corylus, he was a man, which meant he was a pig; and there was no doubt that he found Hedia attractive. The way his eyes followed her whenever she was in sight proved it!

But Hedia didn't rub her husband's nose in things he would be expected to object to. She was a lady, and Alphena had good reason to know that she loved Saxa—in her way.

Just as Corylus was a gentleman, if not an aristocrat. He would turn up his nose at actions which the perfumed wastrels of Hedia's social set would have performed without thinking twice.

Alphena swallowed, then forced her lips into a smile. "Well, I won't disturb him, then," she said. "I will have some of that wine, though. But mix mine with two parts water, if you will."

"At once, your ladyship!" Lenatus said. He and Pulto spun toward the wine jar so swiftly that they almost collided. Without a signal Alphena could see, Pulto took the other cup as well as his own and Lenatus snatched an empty one from a cupboard intended for bath paraphernalia.

Alphena expected the trainer to lift wine from the jar with a narrow, deep-bellied dipper, a wine thief. Instead he hooked his thumb in the handle, then lifted the jar on his elbow and forearm to pour. Returning the wine to its corner, he lifted the water jar in the same fashion and brought the level up to a proper distance below the rim of the cup.

"Your ladyship," he said, offering it to her.

Alphena was trembling from all the emotions that she *hadn't* given in to over the past short while. "Sit down, both of you," she said. With that for an excuse, she quickly seated herself on the end of a bench intended for swordsmen tightening the straps of their sandals before they began their exercises.

When she had entered the gymnasium, the men had been beside one another on the raised stone slab into which posts were set when the grounds were used for fencing practice. They sat down as directed, but Alphena noticed that they had moved as far from her bench as they could get.

Pulto gave a little cough and swigged wine. Avoiding eye contact by looking into his cup, he said, "Master Corylus has spoken well of your judgment, your ladyship."

Alphena froze. *What does he mean by that?*

She smiled. At first she was forcing the corners of her lips upward, but the humor of the situation struck her.

"Thank you, Master Pulto," she said. "Though if you mean that I can recognize circumstances in which a proper young lady knows better than to walk in on a male acquaintance, I can only say that Mother hasn't yet made *that* proper a young lady of me."

Lenatus choked, blowing a spray of wine out his nose. Pulto simply froze.

"Fortunately . . . ," Alphena continued. She enjoyed the feeling of being in control of a situation without screaming at people. "Master Corylus *is* a proper gentleman. Despite my own failings, the worst would not have happened."

Mother really has taught me things. As soon as I was willing to learn them.

"But let's change the subject," Alphena continued calmly, looking at the old soldiers over the rim of her wine cup. "What do you—both of you—think about what happened in the theater this afternoon?"

If she had asked that question bluntly when she walked into the gymnasium, they would have mumbled and lied. They were off balance now, because she'd delicately hinted at a bawdy joke that they understood very well. They would *much* rather talk frankly with a senator's daughter about magic and sorcerers than to join her in a discussion of sexual shenanigans.

"Your ladyship . . . ," Lenatus said. He wasn't mumbling, but his voice was low. "I wasn't . . . I mean, I was here in the house when all that happened."

"Yes," said Alphena crisply; no one could mistake her tone for agreement. "But you were talking to your friend about it, were you not?"

Pulto croaked a laugh. He emptied his cup and said, "This is dry work, your ladyship. Do ye mind if I have some more of this good wine while we talk?"

"Not at all," said Alphena. Her nose was too snubby for her to look down at it with aristocratic hauteur, but just trying made her grin; which was perhaps an equally good way to get information out of these veterans. "Here, you can top off mine—"

She held the cup out.

"—too. Don't worry about more water."

"It's going to be hard times if his lordship needs me escorting him when he goes out to a show," Lenatus said wryly. He offered his cup when Pulto had filled Alphena's. "Mind you, I'd prefer that to what's going on now. Whatever it is."

"Right," said Pulto, sitting down again. "You always know where you're at in a fight."

"Of course," Lenatus offered, "where you're at may be so deep in the soup that you'll never see the surface again."

They were . . . not so much treating Alphena as one of them as talking as if she wasn't present. Which was good enough.

"I hate for my wife to be mixed up in it," Pulto said, taking half the cupful without lowering it from his lips. He looked at Alphena. "You know about that, right, your ladyship? That Lady Hedia is going to see my Anna tomorrow?"

"Yes," said Alphena. "I'll be accompanying my mother."

After a pause for thought, she went on, "I think in these times that we all should help to the degree we can. Help the Republic, I mean."

Lenatus looked at her without expression, then took a silent swallow of wine. Alphena had the uncomfortable suspicion that if she hadn't been his employer's noble daughter, he would have spat onto the dirt.

"I guess Lenatus and me know a bit about serving the Republic, your ladyship," Pulto said. He sipped wine and swizzled it around his mouth before letting it go down. "And Anna too. She was there on the frontier as sure as me and the Old Man and the boy. Who isn't such a boy now, is he?"

"I'm sorry, Pulto," Alphena said, feeling her cheeks burn. Ordinarily she would have reacted by shrieking angrily at the cause of her embarrassment, but she *wasn't* going to do that again. Or anyway, she wasn't going to do that this time. "I'm uncomfortable about it too, that's all."

She cleared her throat. "But what *was* it you saw?" she said. "What did you think it was?"

Looking at Lenatus, she said, "What did you just tell your friend Lenatus it was?"

The trainer barked out a laugh. "I can answer that, your ladyship," he said. "Pulto here told me he had no bloody idea of what he'd just seen except it scared the living crap out of him, and could I maybe find a jar of wine."

He lifted the cup in his left hand; he'd emptied it again. "Which I did, begging your pardon, but I'll pay it back to your father out of my salary."

Alphena waved the thought away brusquely. This was as proper a use for her father's wine as any in the Republic.

"Mistress?" said Pulto. He grimaced and corrected himself, saying "Your ladyship, I mean. You were there. What did *you* see? If a fellow can ask, I mean."

Alphena looked at them. At last she said, "I saw a man wearing a breech-clout, with his hair in two braids. He was as old as you are, but he looked very fit."

When she heard the words come out of her mouth, she paused in renewed embarrassment. "I didn't mean—" she blurted. She stopped because she didn't know what to say that wouldn't make the insult worse.

"Go on, your ladyship," said Pulto calmly. He clapped his belly with his cupped left hand. "I live in this flesh, so you don't need to tell me I'm not the hard young cockerel I was when first I enlisted."

"Well, anyway," said Alphena, "that's what I saw: a man. And he was destroying what looked like a city, only it was so tiny."

She closed her eyes and forced herself to add, "Just for an instant I thought I saw tentacles and snakes like Syra said. Like a lot of other people thought, I suppose. But *I* saw a man."

"I saw the tentacles and all," Pulto said, speaking to his empty cup. "Only then I didn't think it was real, so it didn't bother me."

He looked up with a lopsided grin. "It wasn't till I saw how your brother and the Greek professor were taking it that I started to get worried," he said. "And then Lady Hedia coming to see my Anna for charms—because that's what it is, I know from how she asked it—well, that pissed in the wine for sure."

"But do you know what it means?" Alphena asked. She suddenly felt very young. She wanted these two hard men to protect her, but she didn't know from what. "You've been in, well, battles! What's going to happen now?"

The men looked at one another. Lenatus unexpectedly chuckled. "You remember Stellio?" he said to his friend. Both of them laughed.

Alphena felt her anger rise despite trying very hard to choke it down. Pulto read her reaction correctly. "Your ladyship," he said, "what we mean is that nobody can tell you what's going to happen in a battle. Even if that's what this is, though I don't much see it."

"Stellio was a lazy scut, even for a Sicilian," Lenatus said. He sounded apologetic for being insultingly unclear when he first mentioned the fellow. "*And* I've seen rabbits with more stomach for a fight than he ever showed."

"We were going to assault a couple German hill forts the next day," Pulto said. "Only Stellio gets his foot under a cartwheel, by accident—he says—and he won't be able to hold his rank when we charge. So he got assigned to the artillery. He can turn the crank of one of the dart throwers, bad foot or no bad foot. But staying well back from German spear range, you see."

"So we're lined up and waiting the word," Lenatus said, speaking as he refilled all three cups. "The Germans are up on their mound, shouting and booming their spear shafts against their hide shields, and I got to say, I've been places I was happier being. Up rattles a mule cart and hauls around, and it's Stellio in the back with the dart thrower."

"He's grinning like anything," Pulto said, picking up when his friend took a swallow of wine, "and he starts cranking the arms back. And I hear *whack!*"

"I was looking right at him when it happened," Lenatus said, almost bursting with suppressed laughter. "The lever snapped right at the spring and come flying around on the cord. It caught Stellio on the back of the neck and broke it neat as a chicken for dinner!"

The men laughed together, more freely than before. Alphena wondered for a moment how much wine they had drunk, but she'd drunk more than her usual as well. She joined the laughter.

"And the beauty of it," Pulto said, his voice rising as if to be heard during a drinking party in barracks, "is that we didn't lose another bloody man that day. Not a one! The first salvo, one dart pinned the top of the chief's shield to his forehead and helmet. He tumbled down the hill, stiff as a board, and the rest all bloody ran off the other way."

"May my dick turn black and fall off if it didn't happen *just* that way!" Lenatus burbled.

The laughter died away. *They're probably hoping I didn't hear that,* Alphena thought. *Or at least that I'll pretend I didn't hear it, which I certainly will.*

"I understand that the future isn't really predictable," Alphena said carefully. "And I guess we can hope for a lucky dart shot, whatever that may mean now. I just wish I had something better to hope for."

"Your ladyship?" Pulto said. "We're not laughing at you. And we feel the same way. We wish we knew what was coming. Because we think something is, too."

"All I can tell you about a battle . . . ," Lenatus said, lowering his cup and looking at her with an expression something between calm and defiance. "Is that what happens is generally going to be worse than you figured it to be."

"But you deal with it," said Pulto earnestly. "You always deal with it, however piss-poor a deal it is you get handed."

That's what soldiers do, Alphena realized in a flash of understanding. She had thought being a soldier on the frontier meant fighting . . . but that was only part of it. They *dealt*; even though all they knew about the future was it would probably range from unpleasant to awful.

That was much the same as being a woman in a world which men thought they ruled. Hedia had shown her that. Hedia dealt, and thus far she had dealt successfully.

There was a bustle of voices in the passage from the house proper. Alphena set the cup down and rose.

"Thank you both," she said. "You've helped me to understand the situation. And now—"

She turned to the door.

"—I believe I'll join my brother for a moment before I dine."

And just possibly I'll chat with Corylus as well as Varus; but no matter what, I'll deal. Mother will be proud of me.

HEDIA ROSE FROM HER BED. A light burned in the alcove where her maid slept. Hedia didn't need the light because she was still asleep. She walked through the door of her suite, then drifted down the staircase.

Servants sprawled in the portico around the central courtyard. Five or six were dicing by lamplight, laughing and muttering curses. The familiar noise didn't disturb the nearby sleepers.

In a back corner was the miniature terra-cotta hill on which snails crawled till a cook's helper plucked them out for dinner. They continued to meander slowly along the molded curves.

Hedia walked past the doorman and through the thick wooden door. No one saw her. She wondered if she were dead. Part of her mind felt that the thought should make her smile, but her face did not change.

The sky was moonless, starless. Instead of starting across the square on which the house fronted, she had entered the mouth of a cave as great as all the night.

The opening was familiar: Hedia was walking down the long slope to the Underworld. In the lowest level she had seen her first husband: Calpurnius Latus, dead for three years.

She was going back to the place of the dead. She was going to death.

Hedia heard screams from a side passage. She would have turned to look, but her body could not move; it merely glided forward with no more effort or volition than a feather in a stream.

But she didn't have to look to see. The screams came from a score of women and girls, all of them familiar to her. Each was the age she had been when she died, of fever or accident or in childbirth; and one, Florentia Tertia, strangled by her husband's catamite while her husband watched, doubled up with drunken laughter.

Hedia's acquaintances—her friends, as she would have described them in public—were being devoured by a great lizard. Its jointed forearms stuffed the victims into its maw, where upper and lower jaws ground them like millstones. The women were scraped to chips and smears . . . only to reappear and to wail again, and be devoured again, endlessly. Endlessly. . . .

When Hedia had come this way before, she had walked on her own feet. Now she was . . .

No, I'm not, she realized. *I'm not really here. This is a dream, a nightmare if you will, but it isn't happening to Hedia, daughter of Marcus Hedius Fronto and Petronilla, his second wife.*

Again the smile didn't reach her lips. Her lips were with the rest of her body, asleep in a town house in the Carina District, rather than slipping with her mind toward Hades' realm. In a manner of speaking, it didn't matter: Hedia wouldn't have run if she could have. But knowing that this was unreal allowed her to feel smugly contemptuous of an experience which until that moment had been frightening.

Very frightening, in fact.

When Hedia walked this long corridor before, she had heard terrible sounds from side-branchings as she passed. Only the few paces of sloping track before her had been visible, however. Now she had a detailed awareness of what that was happening on either side of her route.

Flames that burned men but did not kill them. Insects that looked like locusts but which ate human flesh. Hair-fine quills that pierced to the victims' marrow by the thousands and drew out agonized cries but not lives.

Always the torture, always the cries, always the agony. And all of the victims were people whom Hedia had known while they were alive, but who had died.

The passage downward ended where Hedia expected it to, in a glade surrounded by trees with huge leaves. Her first husband, Gaius Calpurnius

Latus, stood in the embrace of a plant whose foliage was formed into vast green hands.

Latus did not see her. Around him, close enough to touch if she wished, were the three glass figures of Hedia's earlier nightmare. Their limbs did not seem to have joints, but the transparent material went milky when it bent and cleared when it straightened. Their eye sockets were indentations, their mouths were short notches.

One of the figures turned his empty visage slowly toward Hedia. Latus began to scream as though his guts were being wound out on a stick, screaming without hope and without relief. The figure reached toward Hedia's left wrist. She pulled away—

She sat upright in her bed. Her throat was raw. Syra stood beside her, her face terrified. Oil had spattered from the lamp in the maid's left hand as she jerked back; her right hand was outstretched. She must have touched her mistress; her mistress, who had been screaming in terror. . . .

Other servants had entered the bedroom or were peering through the doorway, drawn by the cries. They backed away or lowered their heads as Hedia straightened. They were afraid to be seen, afraid of what was happening, *afraid.*

I certainly can't blame them for that, Hedia thought. She smiled coldly at herself.

She stood up. "I—" she began. Her throat felt as though she had been downwind of a limekiln.

"Wine!" she croaked, but she reached the bedside table before Syra could. Silver ewers of wine and water stood to either side of a cup whose red figures showed Pasiphae welcoming the bull into herself. She ignored the cup, drinking straight from the ewer instead.

She lowered the container and looked around at the servants. "Go on about your business," she said brusquely. "Have you never had a bad dream yourselves?"

She lifted the ewer, then paused. "One of you bring more wine," she said. "A jar of it. The same Caecuban."

It was a strong vintage. The alcohol didn't so much soothe her throat as numb it after a moment of stinging.

Servants shuffled out, briefly crowding in the doorway. The ones who remained had probably been afraid to call attention to themselves by ducking away sooner.

Hedia poured the remaining contents of the ewer into the cup. She thought of adding water this time but decided not to. By now it wouldn't shock any of them that Lady Hedia sometimes drank her wine unmixed.

"Your ladyship . . . ?" Syra whispered. She didn't know what to do.

Hedia lowered the cup. She had been holding it in both hands as she drank, because her arms were trembling.

"As soon as the jar of wine arrives," Hedia said. "Which had better be soon. When it does, you can go back to bed. I may sit up for a little."

Until I've drunk enough to dull the memory of that dream.

"I'll stay up too, your ladyship," Syra said. "In case you need something."

The girl wouldn't be able to sleep either, Hedia supposed. Awake, she wouldn't have to worry that her mistress might strangle her in a fit of madness.

"Yes, all right," Hedia said.

She looked about her, suddenly aware of what had escaped her earlier in her fear. The walls of this room were frescoed with images of stage fronts: heavy facades above which stretched high, spindly towers. Hedia had had the suite redecorated when she married Saxa: her immediate predecessor had preferred paintings of plump children riding bunnies and long-tailed birds in a garden setting.

The room from which Hedia had dreamed her descent to the Underworld had been her bedroom also, but not *this* bedroom. The walls there were dark red, separated into panels by gold borders; in the center of each panel was a tiny image of a god or goddess identified by its attribute. Hercules carried his club, but adjacent to him Priapus gripped with both hands a phallus heavier than that club. . . .

That had been her bedroom when she was married to Latus, in the house facing the Campus Martius. She had sold the property when Latus died.

There was a bustle in the hall. Syra took a jar of wine from another servant, then brought it in and refilled the ewer.

Why did my nightmare show me Latus' house?

It wasn't an answer, but at least she was beginning to formulate the questions.

CHAPTER V

Alphena had allowed her stepmother to choose her garments for the outing: a tunic of fine wool, cut much longer—and so more ladylike—than Alphena preferred, with a shoulder-length cape which was quite unnecessary in this weather. She also wore earrings, bracelets, and a high comb, all of silver but decorated with granulated gold.

The one place that Alphena had refused to give in was her footgear. Instead of delicate silken slippers, she wore sensible sandals with thick soles and straps that weren't going to snap if she suddenly had to run. She didn't expect to run—she couldn't imagine any circumstances in which that would be necessary—but she would *not* wear flimsy shoes.

Instead of arguing, Hedia had nodded and said, "Very well," in a calm voice. She had sounded rather like a nurse telling her three-year-old charge that she could bring along all six of her dollies when they walked down to the river to watch barges from Ostia unloading their cargoes of grain.

In the entrance hall, Alphena turned to Florina and said, "I won't be needing you. Stay here and do whatever you like till we come back."

"I believe, your ladyship," said Agrippinus, "that it would be better if Florina accompanied you."

Alphena snapped her head around to face the majordomo. He froze; so did everyone else in the hall, which was still crowded even though Saxa had left for the Senate with his lictors and general entourage.

But Alphena froze also. "Thank you for your concern, my man," she said, choosing the words carefully. That wasn't the sort of thing she was used to saying, but she was determined to learn not to scream abuse whenever some-body tried to direct her. "I believe that Mother's staff will be able to care for me adequately, should the need arise."

She even smiled. It wasn't a very nice smile, she knew, but she wasn't feeling very nice.

"As your ladyship wishes," said Agrippinus, bowing low enough that he no longer met her eyes. He held the obsequious pose until she turned away.

Feeling both virtuous—because she hadn't raised her voice—and triumphant—because she had gotten her way nonetheless—Alphena stepped through the jaws of the entrance and into the street. Servants milled there. Saxa's still larger entourage of lictors, servants, and clients was turning into the Argiletum on their way to the Forum and the meeting of the Senate in the Temple of Venus.

The double litter had arrived from the warehouse on the Tiber where it was stored. Its frame was inlaid with burl and ivory; its curtains were layered Egyptian linen; and the upholstery inside was silk brocade.

The litter's weight required four trained men to carry it and four more to trade off with the original team at regular intervals to prevent fatigue—and therefore possible accidents to the wealthy passengers. Agrippinus had bought eight matched Cappadocian bearers along with the vehicle itself, all at Al-phena's order.

Though she had demanded the double litter as an angry whim, it had proven very useful now that she and her stepmother had become one an-other's confidante: they could speak while travelling in as much privacy as anyone in Carce was able to claim. Only the foreman of the Cappadocians spoke Latin, and even then the bearers' deep breathing and the rhythmic slap of their clogs effectively prevented them from listening to those within the vehicle.

Candidus was in charge of the entourage. He minced unctuously toward Alphena and bowed. "Everything is in order, your ladyship," he said. "I sent a courier to the warehouse myself to be sure that the vehicle would be here at the third hour, as Lady Hedia ordered. Manetho was supposed to have done it, but for your ladyships' comfort I thought it well to make sure."

Hedia swept through the doorway, turning the facade of Saxa's town house into a setting for her jewel-like beauty. She was so stunning and per-fect that Alphena's breath caught in her throat.

Not long ago she would have been furious at her stepmother for being, well, what Alphena herself was not. Now, she just accepted it as a reality of life, like the fact that she would never be emperor.

Reality wasn't a wholly one-sided thing, of course. She would never be teasing some other woman's hair, in constant fear of a slap or a slashing blow with the comb, the way Florina was daily. And there were women less fortunate than Florina.

"You're looking well, daughter," Hedia said, touching the pendant in Alphena's left ear. "You have flecks of gold in your eyes, and these bring it out. Your eyes are one of your best features, you know."

Alphena felt her jaw go slack if not exactly drop. "I didn't . . . ," she said. Then, "I do? I—thank you, Mother."

"Let's get started, shall we?" Hedia said in her breezy, pleasant voice. She gestured Alphena toward the litter.

She hadn't bothered to ask whether it was ready. Either she had seen that it was—though the bearers weren't gripping their poles yet—or she assumed that it *would* be, because the servants were terrified not to have accomplished whatever Lady Hedia expected them to have done.

"After you, Mother," Alphena said, mirroring Hedia's gesture.

Laughing, the older woman mounted the vehicle, placing herself on the front cushion. She moved as gracefully as a cat, or a snake.

Alphena got in on the other side, facing Hedia and the route ahead. As soon as Alphena settled on the cushion, the Cappadocians braced themselves and rose.

Candidus called an order, but that was an officious waste of time. The bearers didn't pass visible signals to one another, but they nonetheless moved as though one head controlled all four of them.

The litter swayed as the Cappadocians fell into step. The motion wasn't unpleasant—the passengers could have read if they wanted to—but it did serve to separate those inside from the rest of the world.

Hedia drew the curtains on her end. They were black netting, woven fine enough that they caught much of the dust as well as blurring the features of those inside the vehicle. Alphena quickly pushed forward her curtains also.

She eyed her stepmother carefully. She had heard—nobody had told her, but the servants had been murmuring about nothing else all morning—that Hedia had had a bad night with all sorts of shouting and threats. There was no sign of that on her face or in her calm, clear gaze.

Alphena mentally rehearsed her words before saying, "Have you been thinking about the vision in the theater yesterday, Mother?"

Hedia grinned with wry amusement. "Was that what gave me nightmares last night, dear?" she said. "Is that what you mean? No, monsters can destroy all the foreign cities they like without causing me to miss a wink of sleep."

Her eyes had drifted toward something outside the present. She focused again on Alphena and added, "Or distinguished older men can, if you like. I learned long ago, dear, that two women never see the same thing in any, well, man."

Alphena blushed, but the comment was kindly meant; and Hedia had been polite to her own clumsy prying. *I should have just come out and asked. With Hedia—not with most people.*

Before the younger woman could apologize, Hedia continued, "No, it was seeing the glass men again. Which I don't understand."

She turned her hands up in a gesture of amused disgust. "I could explain being frightened by dreadful monsters, couldn't I?" she said. "I'm sure people would be very understanding and say they feel sorry for me. Telling people I'm afraid of men would give a very different impression."

"Well, they're not really men," Alphena said.

Hedia's laughter caroled merrily. "Neither are eunuchs, dear," she said, "and I assure you that *they* don't frighten me. And they're not nearly as useless as you might think, the ones that were gelded after they reached manhood, at least."

The streets were noisy at this hour; they were noisy at most hours except in the heat of early afternoons in summer. The normal racket was doubled by the shouts and threats of the escort—and the curses of the pedestrians, peddlers, and loungers who felt they too had a right to the route that their ladyships wished to travel. Occasionally Alphena heard the smack of blows and answering yelps.

"Whatever they are," Alphena said, "the glass men, I mean, they must be terrible. I don't think I've ever seen you frightened before, Mother."

Hedia chuckled. "You've seen me frightened many times, my dear," she said. "You've never seen me unable to do whatever was necessary, though; and you're not seeing that now."

She indicated her calm, disdainful face with one careless hand. "Don't mistake acting ability for my being too dim-witted to recognize danger," she said. "And you should learn to act too, dear. Even though I'm sure you'll live a life with less to conceal than I have, it's a skill every woman needs to acquire."

They were passing through the leatherworkers' district. The reek of uncured hides warred with the stench of the tanning process. Alphena's eyes watered, and even Hedia's face contorted in a sneeze.

"I'll try, Mother," Alphena said, barely mouthing the words. She was afraid her voice would tremble if she spoke loudly enough for the older woman to hear.

She had faced demons, faced them and fought them. She had a sword that seemed to be able to cut anything and had certainly sent fire-demons to bubbling death.

She didn't know what they were facing now. That was the frightening thing. What use was the keenest, best-wielded sword if you had nothing to turn it on except the ghosts in your own mind?

"I suppose Pulto thinks that we're visiting his wife in order to buy charms," Hedia said. Her voice fell naturally into the rhythm of the Cappadocians' pace.

"Aren't we?" said Alphena. "That is, well, I thought we were too."

"If I believed that a sprig of parsley wrapped around a human finger bone would keep away those walking statues from my dreams," Hedia said tartly, "I'd be far less concerned than I am."

Her lips twisted into another smile. "I don't believe there's a charm to keep away distinguished older men with braided hair either," she said. "But as I told you, I'm not worried about them."

She's mocking me! Alphena thought. But that wasn't really true, and if it *was* true, it was good-natured. Hedia had risen from her bed screaming this morning. If she could smile and compliment and plan when she was under that much strain, then her stepdaughter could smile at a harmless joke and go on without snarling.

The litter continued pattering forward, but at a minutely quicker pace: the teams of bearers must have changed places. Alphena would not have noticed the difference had she not spent so much time studying swordsmen. Tiny patterns of movement indicated alertness and fatigue, victory and death.

"What do you want from Anna, then, Mother?" she said aloud.

Hedia looked momentarily weary, though her cheeks quickly sprang back to their normal buoyant liveliness. "Advice, I suppose, dear," she said. Her smile was real, but not as bright as usual. "Or at any rate, someone besides one another to commiserate with. I . . ."

She paused, then wriggled her shoulders as if to shake away a locust that had landed on them. "Dear," she said with renewed confidence, "I want to discuss the matter with Anna because she's the closest thing to an expert whom we have available, even though I don't really believe she can help. If she says she can't help, *when* she says that, I'm afraid, then we go on to the next possible pathway to enlightenment."

Alphena opened her mouth to ask the question. Before she could voice the first syllable, the older woman continued. "We'll determine what that next possibility is when we reach that point."

"Your ladyships, we are arriving!" Candidus cried. He sounded on the verge of collapse. Even though the Cappadocians had a heavy litter to carry, the pace they set through the streets had strained the deputy steward almost beyond his capacity.

The vehicle swayed gently to a halt. There was excited babble outside the curtains.

"Yes," said Alphena, trying to sound as assured as Hedia did by reflex. "We *will* determine that."

HEDIA SWEPT THE CURTAINS back but allowed the younger woman to get out of the litter before she herself did. She had been puzzled by the cheering, but it wasn't until she stood up that she could see past the wall of attendants surrounding the vehicle.

When she did, the slight smile that was her normal expression vanished. She wasn't angry, yet; but her mind had slipped into a familiar mode in which she decided how to deal with a problem—and absolutely any answer was acceptable if cold reason told her that it was the correct choice.

The apartment block in which Corylus and his household lived was the newest in the neighborhood and the tallest—at five stories—this far out the Argiletum. Anna—Corylus' nurse from the day he was born and his housekeeper here in Carce—was waving from a third-floor balcony. Arthritis made it difficult for her to navigate stairs; otherwise she doubtless would have greeted the litter on the street.

Scores of other people *were* waiting, however. At a guess, every tenant in the building who was home this morning stood outside, waving scarves or napkins and cheering, "Hail to their noble ladyships Hedia and Alphena! Hail!"

"I didn't expect this," Alphena said, edging close when Hedia walked around to her side of the litter.

"Nor did I," said Hedia. The background commotion probably concealed the flat chill of her voice; but if it didn't, that too was all right.

There were relatively few men in the crowd, but those present were neatly dressed. The women wore their finery and all the jewels they possessed. The children were clean and wore tunics, even the youngsters of three or four who would normally run around in breechclouts or nothing at all.

This litter would draw a crowd anywhere in Carce; it was exceptional even in the Carina District where Saxa and similarly wealthy nobles lived. This demonstration had been prepared, however, which was a very different thing.

Anna has bragged to her neighbors that she's so great a witch that noblewomen came to visit her. She's trafficking on my name—and perhaps my secrets—to raise her status in the neighborhood.

"Candidus," Hedia said, "you and the escort can remain here with the litter. All but one, I think."

The deputy steward didn't object as she had expected him to. He must have understood her expression.

Hedia looked over the entourage, then said, "Barbato?" to a footman whom she thought would set the right tone. "Precede Lady Alphena and myself to the third floor."

The name—Bearded, with a rural pronunciation—was a joke; his whiskers were so sparse that he could go several weeks between shaves by the household barber. He was a slender, muscular youth from the southern Pyrenees, with clear features and a good command of Latin.

He wasn't a bruiser, but he could take care of himself. Because this was daytime, the escorting servants didn't carry cudgels as they would at night, but Barbato wore a slender dagger in an upside-down sheath strapped to his right thigh where the skirt of his tunic covered it.

"Come along, my dear," Hedia said, stepping off with a pleasant smile. Barbato was swaggering pridefully; the crowd parted before him, still cheering.

"Anna must have said we were coming," Alphena said quietly.

An eight-year-old girl offered Hedia a bunch of violets, wilted because she'd had nothing to wrap the stems in to keep them wet. Hedia took them graciously and continued into the stairway entrance. To the right side was a shop selling terra-cotta dishes; on the left—the corner—was a lunch stall and wine shop.

"Yes," Hedia replied. "That's something I'll want to discuss with her."

To her amazement, the stairwell was not only empty but clean. When she had visited the building before, there was litter on the treads and a pervasive odor of vomit and human waste. There were benefits to Anna having turned the event into a local feast day.

The door at the third level opened. Barbato called pompously, "Make way for the noble Hedia and the noble Alphena!"

Anna waved him aside with one of her two sticks. "Bless you both, your ladyships!" she said. "Welcome to the house of my master, Gaius Corylus!"

She wore a long tunic which wavered between peach and brownish yellow, depending on how the light caught it, under a short dark-blue cape to which leather horse cutouts had been appliquéd; Celtic work, Hedia guessed, and probably a very good example of it. She herself couldn't imagine anybody finding it attractive; but then, she wasn't a Marsian peasant who had spent decades among barbarians on the frontiers.

"Thank you, Anna," Hedia said. She turned and added in a sharper tone, "You may wait on the landing, Barbato. We'll call you if we need you."

She shut the door firmly, then slid the bar across. The panel was sturdier than she would have expected on a third-floor apartment. Not that she spent much time entering or leaving third-floor apartments.

"I hope you didn't mind all the fuss below, your ladyship," Anna said. "It's for the boy, you see. How would you like your wine? Oh, and I had Chloe from the fourth landing, right above, you see, fetch some little cakes from Damascenus' shop in the next building. I do hope you'll try them, won't you?"

"I'll pour the wine, Anna," Alphena said, forestalling their hostess as she started toward the little kitchen of the suite. She and Hedia knew that the old woman had better days and worse ones. Even at her best now Anna had no business struggling with a tray of wine, water, and the paraphernalia necessary for drinking it.

"You said that the gathering was for Master Corylus?" Hedia said, letting her very real confusion show in her voice. "I had the impression they were expecting my daughter and myself."

"Oh, that, yes, of course they were," Anna said, obviously unaware of Hedia's suspicions. "Do sit down, won't you? I've gotten new cushions. The blue one is stuffed with goose down, so why don't you take it, your ladyship?"

Hedia settled carefully on one end of a clothes chest being used as a bench. She said, "I don't see, then . . ."

"Well, it's like this," said Anna, lowering herself onto a stool of polished maple. "The boy grew up in camp, you know. He's used to fetching for himself and he likes it that way, so it's just me and Pulto does for him—and I get the neighbor girls to fetch the shopping, since I'm such a clapped-out old nanny goat myself."

Hedia opened her mouth to protest; Anna waved her blithely to silence. "It suits me better that way too, to tell the truth," she said, "because, well, you know the stories that go around about Marsian witches. If we had servants, they'd be making up tales to cadge drinks and the like. That can get pretty nasty, as I know to my sorrow from when we lived in Baiae before the boy come here to school."

The small round table between the stool and the chest was cedar with a richly patterned grain, oiled and polished to a sheen like marble. Alphena set the tray on it and handed out the cups, already filled.

"I mixed the wine three to one," she said, a little too forcibly. That was the normal drinking mixture which she was used to, and she was making a point that she didn't intend to get tipsy by drinking to limits that her companions might be comfortable with.

"Thank you, my dear," Hedia said, taking her cup—part of a matched service which impressed her as both stylish and beautiful. Clear glass rods had been twisted, slumped together in molds, and polished.

She sipped; it was like drinking from jewels. She wondered if Corylus had chosen the set. Certainly Anna had not, given the taste shown by her garments.

"I'm not clear what the crowd down there . . . ," Hedia said, nodding toward the window onto the balcony, "has to do with Master Corylus, however."

She wasn't on the verge of anger anymore. Clearly she was missing something, but she now knew that Anna hadn't turned Lady Hedia into a carnival for plebeians as a way of bragging to her neighbors.

"Oh, well, you see . . ." Anna said. Her face was so wrinkled that Hedia couldn't be sure, but she seemed to be making a moue of embarrassment.

"Because we don't have servants and because we're up on the third floor—
the boy said he liked to be able to look out at the Gardens of Maurianus, and
you couldn't from any lower down—folks don't really believe he's quality."

Ah! The higher levels of apartment blocks were successively flimsier in
construction and—of course—that much farther to climb on narrow stairs
when coming and going. Lower rents reflected this. Corylus apparently wasn't
concerned about whether the neighbors thought he was an impecunious
phony who only pretended to be a Knight of Carce, but his old nurse cared
on his behalf.

"I've been having dreams, Anna," Hedia said. "Bad ones, of course, or I
wouldn't be seeing you. And I suppose you heard about what happened yesterday in the theater?"

Anna had been using "their ladyships" as a status tool, but Hedia couldn't
be angry about that now, however much she wished it hadn't happened. The
old servant was completely absorbed with her boy. No objection, no threat—
nothing but death itself—would change that focus.

And Hedia wouldn't have forced a change if she could. Oh, it was excessive, no doubt, but Master Corylus was certainly an impressive young man.

Hedia let a smile play at the corners of her mouth. Corylus even had the
good judgment to refuse to become entangled with his friend's beautiful
mother. Which was a pity, though Hedia was no longer concerned that a
physical relationship would be necessary to bind the boy to her. He would
support her for so long as he believed that she had the best interests of the
Republic at heart.

"I didn't hear much," Anna said with a sort of smile. "A sight of a monster, is all. The boy won't talk, which is as should be for an officer. My Pulto
was afraid to talk; afraid of what he doesn't know, pretty much, and I don't
blame him. But I could guess things, and—"

She shrugged.

"—I could feel them, too, when they're as strong as what happened yesterday."

"Mistress?" Alphena said. "Anna? Do you know what it is that we saw in
the theater?"

"No, dear," the old woman said, "no more than I knew what made the
ground shake so one winter in Upper Germany. It wasn't for two weeks that
we learned that the snow had come down the slopes in Helvetian territory
and buried a thousand people in a village."

She looked at Hedia. "You've been dreaming of this monster come up from the sea, then?" she said. "Is it the same as it was in the theater?"

"Nothing like that," said Hedia, more sharply than she had intended. "In the theater, though, there was a city and there were glass men on its walls. Does that mean anything to you?"

Alphena sat down, offering the older women a burl walnut tray of small sweet cakes. There wasn't room for it on the table with wine containers.

Hedia had emptied her cup. She hesitated—she never ate sweets; she loved them and knew she would bloat like a dead cat if she didn't exercise rigid control over what she ate—but finally took a cake and nibbled. It was delicious.

"I've never heard of glass men, Hedia," Anna said, reverting to previous familiarity now that they were completely alone. "Real men, moving you mean?"

"Moving, certainly," Hedia said, forcing herself to visualize the images that terrified her without reason. "Real, I don't know. Certainly not real *men*; but they acted like men."

She took a deep breath. Her eyes were open, but for the moment she wasn't seeing anything beyond her memory.

"I dreamed of them in the Underworld, Anna," she said. "I dreamed of them with Latus, where I visited him before. I couldn't hear them, but I think they were questioning him. He was screaming."

She sniffed with bitter amusement. "Screaming like the damned, in fact," she said, "which is likely enough with Latus."

Hedia forced her eyelids closed, then opened them and met Anna's calm gaze. "I think they're hunting for me," she said. "I don't know why or why I feel that. But I feel it, and I'm afraid."

"When we opened the passage to the Underworld," Anna said, "it couldn't be closed again. I'm sorry, but that was one of the risks."

Her face twisted into a smile. "It wasn't one of the risks that I worried most about," she said. "I didn't expect to see you ever again."

Her gaze flicked to Alphena. She added, "Either of you."

Hedia laughed, finding the humor of the thought. "Rather like virginity, you mean?" she said. "Well, that wasn't much good to me either. Perhaps keeping the passage to Hades' house open will turn out to be just as pleasurable in the long run."

Alphena's lips pressed together, but she tried to smile when she felt Hedia glance at her. *She's really everything one could wish in a daughter. Even her playing with swords turned out to be useful.*

"Is there anything you can suggest, dear?" Hedia said. Then, blurting, "Can you *do* anything? Please!"

Alphena had refilled her cup. She drank, to hide her embarrassment and to soothe her throat. She was dry, and her thoughts were dry and withered.

"A charm, you mean?" Anna said.

Hedia waved her hands, disgusted at her own weakness. "No, of course not," she said. "I know better, but I'm . . . frightened."

"Some of my charms do help," Anna said. She spoke softly, but there was rock not far below the surface. "Some help, and more help because people think they're being helped. But not for this, no. My usual work is for sick people; and sometimes for girls who want something or want to get rid of something."

She spread her hands. "I won't lie to you, your ladyship. Love charms and abortions. But what happened in the theater is beyond such neighborhood business."

Hedia opened her mouth to object, but Anna stopped her with a raised hand. "You may not be concerned with what happened in the theater, dear," she said, "but I am. It reeked on my men when they came home last night, and it's nothing I'll pass over lightly."

Her tone was polite but no longer obsequious. They were in Anna's realm now, and however much she might respect Lady Hedia, she wouldn't leave any doubt about what she knew.

Hedia's cup was empty again. She thought for an instant, then covered it with her hand as Alphena reached to refill it from the mixing bowl.

"I think that's enough for me," she said, rising smoothly. She might feel as though she should hang herself; but if she did, she would expect to writhe gracefully. "Thank you, Anna. You've helped me understand the situation better."

Anna struggled to rise from her stool. Alphena braced her while she got both her sticks planted.

"I told you I'm not passing over this, your ladyship," Anna said. "I . . . I won't promise you. But there's another thing that might be tried. It means danger for those I would die to keep from danger, but I fear—"

Her eyes locked with Hedia's.

"—that there's no safety anywhere if this thing isn't scotched. So I'll try."

"Mistress," said Hedia. "He's a soldier, in his heart at least. He'll understand."

Anna laughed. The sound would have been appropriate at a funeral. "Aye, we all understand," she said, "but it's still bloody hard to send them off. Well, we women know about that kind of hard, don't we?"

"Yes," said Alphena unexpectedly. "We do."

She reached out; for a moment, the three of them linked hands. It didn't make any sense, but Hedia found herself more hopeful than she had been since she awakened from her nightmare.

As CORYLUS AND PULTO approached the apartment block, one of the daughters of the cobbler on the fourth floor leaned out the window and called, "Hello, Master Corylus! I'm glad you're back!"

Corylus waved a halfhearted acknowledgement and tried to smile. He probably didn't succeed very well.

"I wonder if that's Tertia or her sister?" Pulto said, sounding mildly curious.

Corylus looked at the older man, uncertain whether the implication was a joke. He said, "Quartilla's pretty young, Pulto."

"Well growed, though," Pulto said. "And from the way everybody on the street's looking at us now, you could probably parlay one visit into a two-fer."

Then, with the break in his voice he'd been trying to avoid with the crude jokes, he said, "I wonder what it is my Anna said to everybody to get them so excited? Well, there's nothing to do about it now."

"Ah," said Corylus, who now understood a great deal more than he had a moment ago. Yes, a parade with elephants could scarcely have drawn more attention than he and his servant were getting right now.

Corylus had been thinking about the oration his fellow student Clementius had given today, urging Hannibal not to storm the walls of Carce. Pandareus had responded by "predicting" all the disasters which had beset the Carthaginian cause when Hannibal marched away without attacking.

Corylus would be speaking tomorrow. His set subject was to advise the imprisoned Socrates either to flee to Macedonia or to stay and drink the hemlock poison. He had planned to argue that Socrates should stay, honoring his principles—but that would give Pandareus the opportunity to blame Socrates for all the misfortunes "the gods" had heaped on Athens after his execution. Perhaps Corylus should argue that from exile in Macedonia, Socrates could foment a revolt of reason within the body politic. . . .

But Publius Corylus had duties and obligations in the real world also, as Pulto had just reminded him. Hedia and her daughter had visited Anna today, and the visit apparently had consequences here in his neighborhood on the Viminal Hill. Now that Tertia—or Quartilla—had addressed Corylus directly, a score of other people were calling to him also.

Hercules! Some are even cheering! He waved again as he ducked into the staircase behind Pulto.

"I'll just have something light to eat and go straight over to Saxa's," Corylus muttered to the servant's back. "Ah—Pulto? You don't need to come with me tonight. There'll be more than enough attendants, I'm sure."

"I guess I do have to come, don't I?" Pulto growled. "I would if you were heading for a dustup, wouldn't I? And this is a bloody sight worse, the way I look at it."

The way I look at it too, old friend, Corylus thought. But though Pulto wouldn't be of the least use in a situation where the danger was from magic, it *was* his duty. That was a way a soldier had to think, and it was the way Corylus thought as well.

The door opened before they reached it. "Anna, my heart!" Pulto said, his voice much harsher than was usual when speaking to his wife. "What in buggering Mercury did you say that's got them so worked up down in the street?"

"Never mind that now, Marcus Pulto," Anna said. "You'll give me a hand up to the roof where I'll talk to the master, and you'll stand at the bottom of the ladder making sure other folks understand that he wants his privacy. Do you understand that?"

I do not, Corylus thought. But it took his mind off a quick dinner and what they were going to find in the home of Sempronius Tardus.

"Yes, ma'am," Pulto said in a tone of supplication. That was even more unusual when he talked to Anna than the anger of a heartbeat earlier.

Corylus had wondered how long it would take her to reach the fifth-floor landing, let alone mount the ladder to the roof. Pulto must have had the same thought, because he took her arm as directed, but even that was probably unnecessary.

Anna clumped up the stairs in normal fashion, without pausing or slowing. The doors on the upper landings were all ajar, but nobody actually stuck her head out as they normally would when strangers passed.

"Anna?" Corylus said. "Let me go up ahead of you."

"I can still climb a ladder, master!" she said.

"So that I can help you out over the coaming," he replied, keeping his voice artificially calm. *She must be* very *upset.* "And there may be somebody on the roof already."

"There's not," Anna said, her tone contrite; she stepped aside on the narrow landing to let him pass. "But I shouldn't wonder if they'd lift the trapdoor and listen in once we were up there. I reckon my Marcus can take care of that, won't you, dearie?"

"I guess I could if I needed to," Pulto said. "Which I won't, since nobody in this building is going to show his ass to you. Me included."

He gave his wife a peck on the cheek. Things seemed to be back to normal between them.

The roof was empty, as Anna had claimed. It was tiled, but the pitch was so slight that it was easy to walk on. A poulterer on the second floor supplemented his merchandize by keeping a large dovecote here, and there were eight or ten terra-cotta pots with flowers and vegetables growing in them.

There was even a spindly orange tree. Corylus lifted Anna from the third rung down, then touched the tree trunk while she closed the trapdoor. He thought for an instant that flesh wriggled gratefully beneath his fingertips.

"I don't like what I'm going to ask you, master," Anna said. "But sometimes 'like' don't make no nevermind."

She was standing beside him, looking southeast toward the center of Carce instead of meeting his eyes. He put his arm around her shoulders and hugged her. He didn't speak.

"Aye, you know," Anna muttered. She gave him a half-hug also. "You're a soldier's son, and anyway, you're a good boy."

She turned her head to look at him. "It's her ladyship," she said. "She needs something I can't fetch her and I won't ask my Marcus to go for. He'd try, but I think it'd kill him, stop his heart. He'd be that fearful."

"Tell me what you need, Anna," Corylus said. He felt calm. Tell me what the Republic needs, or so I think."

He had been very young, certainly no older than three, when his father came into the room Corylus shared with Anna one night. Something had happened, though at the time he hadn't known what.

Later Corylus learned there had been a battle—not the kind that the historians wrote about, but the sort of little skirmish that happened regularly on the frontier. A party of young Germans had crossed the river for loot, but they got too drunk to return after they captured a handful of wagons loaded with wine.

They were too drunk to surrender also, but Germans never seemed to get too drunk to fight. It had been a nasty one, because the Germans had the wagons in a circle and horses wouldn't charge home. Cispius had dismounted his troop and stormed the laager.

Cispius had taken off his armor before he shook his son awake, but his tunic reeked of sweat and blood. In a voice as rough as stones sliding, he had said, "Don't ever let them know you're afraid, boy. And by Hercules, if you play the man, you'll find you really *aren't* afraid. Don't let your troops down, and you won't let yourself down either."

Corylus hadn't understood that at the time. He understood it now, with his arm around his old nurse.

Anna nodded and stepped away, visibly calmer. "Lady Hedia came to see me today," she said in the same normal voice in which she would have discussed taking her sandals to be mended. "It isn't her coming, though, because I already knew I'd have to do something."

She sniffed angrily. "I knew from the smell on you when you come back from the theater, boy," she said. "It was her ladyship visiting that showed me I couldn't put it off. I'd been telling myself it wasn't so, like I was a foolish girl."

"Tell me what I must do, Anna," Corylus said, firmly but calmly. He'd never seen his nurse in such a state. Shouting wouldn't help matters, but he did need to get her to the point at some time before Carce's thousand-year celebrations—in two or three centuries.

"There's a thing under the ground," she said, suddenly herself again. "An amulet I think, but maybe something else. I can't see it myself—I don't have that sort of power, boy, you know that. But . . ."

She swallowed and walked awkwardly over to the dovecote. She used her sticks. She had thrust them down the neck of her tunic so that she could climb the ladder, but they were a doubtful help on the tiles. Still, the surface wasn't any worse than wet cobblestones.

Corylus wasn't certain what to do, but after a brief hesitation he followed her. He tried to keep his weight over the beams, but a flash of humor lighted his face. *I wonder what Tertia—or perhaps Quartilla—would say if I entered through the ceiling instead of by the door?*

It was good to laugh at something when he felt like this. Especially something silly.

Anna rubbed a dove's neck feathers through the grille; it cooed, squirming closer to her. She looked again at Corylus and said, "I couldn't see things, but the birds, I thought, might; and the little animals. Which they did. Last night I went with a vole down his burrow into the place that the thing was; and this morning, after their ladyships were gone, I hired a chair to the Esquiline with Dromo, Cephinna's boy from the fifth floor. We marked the place, and he'll guide you back to it tonight."

Corylus licked his lips. "On the Esquiline. That will be to the old burial grounds there."

"Aye," said Anna. She looked as fierce as a rebel waiting to be crucified.

"All right," said Corylus, since there was nothing else to do. "We'll leave as soon as it's dark. Ah—will there be difficulties with Dromo? That is, how much does he know?"

Anna sniffed again. "He knows enough not to like it," she said, "but he'll do it for me. And for you, master. He trusts you."

"Ah . . . ," said Corylus. "I'll pay whatever you think . . . ?"

"A silver piece," Anna said. "A day's pay for a grown man, which is fair enough. Mind, there's few grown men who'd do what Dromo will tonight. He's a brave one, which is why I picked him. Though . . ."

Corylus hooked his hand, as though trying to draw the thought out of the old woman by brute force. It would be simpler if Anna simply spat out all the information in an organized fashion; but then, it would be simpler if everyone loved his neighbor, worked hard, and behaved courteously to others.

There wouldn't be much use for soldiers, then, or attorneys either. Corylus had seen enough of oxen to know that he didn't want to spend his life following a pair of them around a field while leaning into a plow to make it bite. Though a return to the Golden Age, where the fruits and grain just sprouted—that might not be such a hardship.

"I told Dromo all he had to do was show you where the place to dig was," Anna explained. "You and Pulto would do the rest. I've already bought mattocks and a pry bar; they're in the kitchen."

"That will save time," Corylus said, smiling faintly. Anna might have trouble saying things she wished weren't so, but she certainly didn't hesitate to *do* anything she thought was necessary.

He looked west over the city. Because this apartment was the tallest building for half a mile, he was largely looking down onto tile roofs much like the one he stood on. Potted plants and dovecotes and rabbit hutches;

and now and again there was a shed of cloth on a wicker frame that might have anything at all inside it.

People lived ordinary lives here in Carce, the greatest city in the world. None of them perfect, including Publius Cispius Corylus, a student of Pandareus of Athens . . . but generally decent folk.

He thought of Typhon, ripping its way through a vision of crystal towers and walls of sun-bright metal. No one had told Corylus that would result unless he—and Anna and Pandareus and Varus and all of them—managed to stop the creature, but it was a logical inference from what he had heard—and what he had seen ten days before, when the Underworld vomited forth its flaming demons.

"Pulto should stay here with you, Anna," he said. There was no reason to force a brave man and a friend into a night's work that would torture him worse than hot pincers.

"No," she said. "You'll be going into the ground, but you'll want a solid man up above to watch your back. My Marcus is that; and anyway, you couldn't keep him away unless you chained him."

She coughed. "I think it's a tomb, master," she said. "An old one, maybe; very old. Etruscan, I'd venture, from before Carce ever was. Though—"

She fluttered her little fingers, since her palms were braced on the smooth knobbed handles of her sticks.

"—that's a lot to draw from a vole's mind, you'll understand. Anyway, it's cut in rock, the place the thing is."

Corylus laughed and hugged Anna again. "We'll find you your bauble, dear one," he said. "How could any man fail someone they love as much as Pulto and I love you?"

He'd made the words a joke, but it was the truth just the same.

I'd best send a messenger to Varus, telling him I won't be able to join him this afternoon after all, Corylus thought.

On his way back from class, he'd been concerned about what they might find in Tardus' home. Now, entering the cellars of a senator's house seemed a harmless, even friendly alternative to the way he would really be spending the evening.

"OH!" SAID SAXA as his entourage formed around him with all manner of shouting and gestures. "My boy, I don't see your friend Corylus. You don't think he's gotten lost on the way here, do you? We really shouldn't wait much longer or we'll arrive at the dinner hour, which would be discourteous."

Tardus will probably regard our arrival to search his house under consular authority to be discourteous enough, Varus thought. Aloud he said, "Corylus was detained on other business, your lordship. We will proceed without him."

Saxa bustled off, surrounded by Agrippinus, who would stay at the house; Candidus, who would lead the escort; and the chief lictor.

It hadn't occurred to Varus that Saxa would remember that Corylus might accompany them. He'd underestimated his father, a disservice which he would try hard not to repeat.

Pandareus had dropped into the background when Saxa approached; now he joined Varus again. With his lips close to his teacher's ear, Varus said, "It seems a great deal of argument for what is really just a six-block walk, doesn't it?"

"It would be, I agree," Pandareus said, for a moment fully the professor. "But I take issue with your terms, Lord Varus. If we were simply to walk to the home of Sempronius Tardus, we would be wasting our efforts. If this is to be a rite of state—a religious act, in effect—then the litanies are to be accepted as being of spiritual significance even though their human meaning has been blurred."

Varus chuckled. In an undertone he muttered the refrain of the priests during the rites of Robigus—the deity of corn smut. It was a string of nonsense syllables to anyone alive today.

"Yes, my teacher," he said. "It does have a great deal of similarity to what we're hearing now. Or at any rate, to what my father is hearing, merging the three speeches."

"Plato believed in Ideal Republics," said Pandareus, watching the commotion with an attitude of bright interest. He was chatting now, no longer lecturing. "I am . . . willing, I suppose, to accept them also—for the purpose of argument. I don't find them any more useful in studying real conditions than the Chief Pirate's Beautiful Daughter would be in formulating the Republic's mercantile policy."

Varus chuckled at mention of one of the standards of school orations, like the Reformed Prostitute and the Undutiful Son. "I wouldn't say that the reign of Dion of Syracuse was a Golden Age, despite Plato's earnest coaching of his would-be philosopher king," he said. "I accept your point about real politics generally looking like—"

He gestured to the confusion of servants, lictors, and citizen-clients. It looked as though the procession was close to moving off.

"—that. What I don't understand is *why* it looks like that instead of being, well, smoother."

"It may be that you are asking the correct question," Pandareus said, reverting to his classroom manner. "You're asking it rhetorically, however, instead of using the moment as a real opportunity to learn. Why *is* it that human societies generally organize themselves in fashions that we philosophers deplore as inefficient? Surely it cannot be possible that human wisdom is limited while the cosmos is infinite?"

Varus laughed again. "I'll want to spend an hour or two considering the question before giving you a definitive answer, master," he said.

Pandareus had a remarkable ability to puncture displays of excessive ego—by using the Socratic Method, proving that his disciple already possessed the information. That was certainly true in the present instance. Varus wouldn't go so far as to claim that the fact something existed proved that it was good—but he did accept that everything happened for a reason.

Candidus spoke to a musician holding a double-pipe. Varus believed the piper was the same man—if that was the correct term for someone so slender and feminine—who had led the music during yesterday's mime. If so, he had come through the ordeal very well.

"We'd best take our places," Varus said. He moved into the place directly following Saxa. Behind them would come the most respectable of his clients, most of them impoverished relatives.

Varus and Pandareus had just reached the column when the pipe began to sing cadence from the front, among the lictors. The procession started off—not in unison, but a good deal closer than most arrays of this sort.

"In the army, Corylus says they sing to keep time," Varus said as they ambled through the city. "From the songs he describes, it's probably as well that we're not doing that. Otherwise Tardus would be in a panic to lock up his daughters."

"Or sons," Pandareus said, straight-faced. "Though I'm sure that the standards of the eastern legions that I'm familiar with are less manly and rigorous than those of the Rhine frontier."

I didn't expect to be laughing repeatedly on this expedition, Varus thought. The obvious answer—because everything was a question, looked at in the correct fashion—struck him. He looked at Pandareus and said, "Thank you, master. You have taught me more by example than even from the knowledge you have accumulated."

"I would not be a good model for most of the young men who become my students," Pandareus said, looking up with interest at the imperial palace on their right. Only servants were present, since the emperor was—as usual—on Capri. "Certainly not for Master Corylus, of course: he is far too forceful and decisive to gain from my style of self-management. But you, Lord Varus. . . . I believe you understand my own qualms and uncertainties all too well, so my practiced ways of dealing with them could be useful."

Changing the subject almost before the words were out, the teacher gestured up the steep slope to the ancient citadel. The great temples of Jupiter and Juno glowered down at the city. In a breezy, less contemplative tone, he said, "I'm seeing *this* Carce for the first time."

"But surely you've been here before, master?" Varus said. "Why, I'd think you regularly came this way to get from your room to the Forum when you hold class there."

"So speaks the son of the wealthy Alphenus Saxa," Pandareus said. "Yes, my feet tread this pavement—"

He half-skipped to rap the toe of his sandal on the flagstone.

"—regularly. But on an ordinary day I would be dodging a crowd of those who would trample a slender scholar who dawdled in front of them. Today, I'm in a capsule formed by the companions of a consul, like a hickory nut in its shell."

"Ah!" said Varus. "The armor of righteousness, no doubt."

"I would be the last to claim that the father of my student and—if I may— friend Gaius Varus is not a righteous man," Pandareus agreed solemnly.

Varus thought about being insulated from the world. Pandareus was talking about physical protection here, but that was really a minor aspect of the way Varus was walled off. His father's wealth wasn't really a factor.

Varus had come to realize that though he lived in the world, he was not and never would be part of it. If footpads knocked him down and slit his throat, a part of him—the part that was most Gaius Alphenus Varus— would be watching them through a sheet of clear glass, interested to see how far his blood spurted when the knife went in.

Corylus could probably tell me from having watched it happen to somebody else. That would be a better way to learn.

Pandareus was watching him intently. Varus let his smile fade. He said, "Master, what do you think we'll find in this chapel? What should we be looking for?"

"Your lordship . . . ," Pandareus said, being particularly careful in his address because they were in public. "We are intruding on Senator Tardus because of inferences which we deduced from your vision, coupled with additional knowledge which I brought to the discussion. All I can do is to say that I think we are acting in the most logical fashion that we could, given our limited information."

He grinned, becoming a different person. He said, "I will not lapse into superstition by saying that whoever or whatever sent you the vision was wise enough to give us as much information as we would need. I will particularly not say—"

The grin became even wider.

"—that he, or she, or it, is all-wise. But the less rational part of me believes those things."

"A textbook example of *praeteritio*," Varus said. "And I accept the principle underlying your statement, which I deduce to be that the wise man, when faced with an uncertain result which he cannot affect, should assume it will be beneficial. The price is the same as it would be for a gloomy prediction."

"I've taught you well, my boy," Pandareus said. They were no longer joking. It was one of the few times Varus had heard what he would describe as real warmth in the older man's voice.

At the head of the procession the lictors stopped in front of a house and faced outward. Its walls were of fine-grained limestone, rather than marble over a core of brick or volcanic tuff as was the more recent style.

The chief lictor banged the butt of his axe helve on the door and boomed, "Open to Senator Gaius Alphenus Saxa, consul of Carce!"

Varus drew a deep breath. He wondered what it would be like to wait for howling barbarians to charge, shaking their spears and their long, round-tipped swords.

At the moment, he would rather be out on the frontier, learning the answer to that question.

CHAPTER VI

Alphena would have been happier walking, but Hedia had insisted that they take the litter to the Field of Mars. This shopping expedition was part of the business—business or trouble or mystery, Alphena didn't know what to call it—so she'd agreed, but it still made her unhappy.

Her face must have been squeezed into a petulant frown. Hedia raised her slippered foot and wriggled the big toe at her. Because they were seated facing one another in the litter, it was like somebody pointing an accusatory, short, but nonetheless very shapely, finger at her.

"Cheer up, dear," Hedia said. "We really have to do it this way, you see. No one would imagine me going shopping on foot. And though they'd let us into the shops I want to visit even with your original footgear—you'd be with me, after all—the last thing we want is to appear eccentric. We'll learn much more if Abinnaeus is thinking only about the amount of money he'll get from their gracious ladyships of Saxa's household. Besides—"

She touched the tip of Alphena's slipper with her finger. The upper was silk brocade instead of a filigree of gilt leather cutwork, and the toe was closed. Sword exercises wearing army footgear had left Alphena's feet beyond transformation into ladylike appearance in the time available, despite the skill of Hedia's own pedicure specialists.

"—these shoes wouldn't be at all comfortable to walk across the city in, dear. And we really do have to dress for the occasion. Think of it the way men put their togas on to go into court, even though there's *never* been a more awkward, ugly garment than a toga."

Alphena giggled. Even a young, gracefully slender man like Publius Cor-ylus looked rather like a blanket hung to dry on a pole when he wore his toga. Father, who was plump and clumsy, was more like the same blanket tumbled into a wash basket.

The Cappadocian bearers paced along as smoothly as the Tiber floating a barge. They were singing, but either the words were nonsense or they were in a language of their own.

Only the thin outer curtains of the litter were drawn, so Alphena could see what was going on about them. They were making their way through the Forum built by Julius Caesar; the courtyard wasn't less congested than the streets to north and south, but there was more room for the crowd which was being pushed aside. The brick and stone walls bounding the street wouldn't give no matter how forcefully Hedia's escorts shoved people who were blocking the litter.

Alphena nodded in silent approval: someone had chosen the route with care and intelligence. This heavy vehicle required that sort of forethought.

The particular servants in attendance must have been chosen with equal care, because they were *not* Hedia's usual escort. "Ah, Mother?" Alphena said. "That's Lenatus walking beside Manetho, isn't it?"

"Yes, dear," Hedia said approvingly. "Manetho is in charge of things under normal circumstances, but Master Lenatus will take command if, well, if necessary."

Alphena didn't recognize every member of the entourage, though she didn't doubt that they were all part of Saxa's household. She'd seen at least one man working in the gardens. Several more had been litter bearers before Alphena bought the new, larger vehicle with the matched team of Cappadocians; simply by inertia the previous bearers remained members of the household, though they had no regular duties.

The escorts wore clean tunics, most of which appeared to have been bought as a job lot: they had identical blue embroidery at the throat, cuffs, and hem. Further, the men's hair was freshly cropped and they'd been shaven, though that had been done quickly enough that several were nicked or gashed.

The razor wounds stood out sharply against chins which since puberty must have been shaded by tangled beards. Alphena supposed that was better than being attended by a band of shaggy bravos. Though they *still* looked like bravos.

She leaned sideways, bulging the side curtain, to get a better look at the trainer toward the front of the entourage. She said, "I don't think that's a club that Lenatus is hiding under his tunic, is it, Mother?"

Hedia shrugged. "I didn't ask, dear," she said. "I leave that sort of thing to men."

She leaned forward slightly, bringing her face closer to Alphena's. "I told Lenatus to choose the men," she said. She was as calm and beautiful as a portrait on ivory. "I told him I didn't care how handsome they were or whether they could communicate any way except by grunting in Thracian. I just wanted people who would stand beside him if there was real trouble."

She laughed briefly. "Beside him and in front me, of course," she said, "but I didn't need to tell Lenatus that. I think he felt rather honored. I've never quite understood that, but men of the right sort generally do."

Of course men feel honored to be given a chance to die for you, Alphena thought, suddenly angry. *And* don't *tell me you don't understand why!*

But that wasn't fair to Hedia, who was risking her life too. Or seemed to think she was.

"Mother?" Alphena said, shifting her thoughts into the new channel with enthusiasm. "What's going to happen? Are we going to attack this Abinnaeus?"

Hedia's mouth opened for what was obviously intended for full-throated laughter, but she caught herself with a stricken look before a sound came out. Leaning forward, she caught Alphena's wrist between her thumb and two fingers.

"I'm sorry, dear one," she said. "No, Abinnaeus is a silk merchant with a very fine stock. His shop is in the portico of Agrippa. My husband Latus' house is just up Broad Street from the portico."

Alphena saw the older woman's expression cycle quickly through anger to disgust to stony blankness—and finally back to a semblance of amused neutrality. "My former husband's house, I should have said," she said. "And briefly my own, when the lawsuits against the will were allowed to lapse after your father took up my cause."

Hedia's lips squirmed in an expression too brief for Alphena to identify it with certainty. It might have been sadness or disgust, or very possibly a combination of those feelings.

"I got rid of the house as quickly as I could," Hedia said, falling back into a light, conversational tone. "There wasn't anything wrong with it. I didn't have bad memories of it, no more than of any other place, but I didn't want to keep it either. I told Saxa's agent to sell it and invest the money for me. I suppose I have quite a respectable competence now, dear one—by any standards but your father's."

"Father has never been close with money," Alphena said, thinking of her childhood. She had been angry for as far back as she could remember: angry about the things she couldn't do, either because she was a girl or because she was the particular girl she was.

She forced the start of a smile, but it then spread naturally and brightened her mood. She said, "I envied you so much, M-Mother. Because you're so beautiful."

The smile slipped, though she fought to retain it. "And I'm not."

"You're striking," Hedia said, touching Alphena's wrist again to emphasize the intensity she projected. "In a good way, a way that shows up much better in daylight than I can."

She leaned back, suddenly regally cool. "If you want that," she said. "Not if you're going to wear clodhoppers—"

She gestured dismissively toward Alphena's feet.

"—and scowl at everyone as though you'd like to slit their throats, though. *Do* you want that? *Do* you want people to say you're beautiful?"

Hedia grinned like a cat. "That is," she said, "do you want it enough that you're willing to spend as much effort on it as you do now on hacking at a stake, or as your brother does on reading Lucilius and similarly dull people who didn't even write Latin that ordinary people can understand?"

"I shouldn't have to—" Alphena blazed. Part of her mind was listening to the words coming out off her tongue, so she stopped in embarrassment. She closed her mouth.

Hedia's smile had chilled into silent mockery, but that didn't, for a wonder, make Alphena flare up again. *She's right. She's treating me like she'd treat an adult; and if I flame up like a four-year-old, then I'm the only one to blame for it.*

"I *have* spent a great deal of time on the training ground," Alphena said with careful restraint. "And of course my brother almost lives for books. For them and with them. But he could put just as much effort hacking at the post as I have and he'd still be a clown rather than a swordsman; and if I struggled with Lucilius and the rest for my whole life, they'd be as useless to me as my trying to read prophecies in the clouds."

Hedia gave a throaty giggle at the thought.

"I don't think I'd be much better at being a beauty than at being a scholar, Mother," Alphena said. "But I can stop resenting the things I won't take the effort to succeed at."

She felt her smile slipping again. "I don't know what that leaves me," she whispered. "I'm not really a good swordsman, even. Not good enough to be a gladiator, I mean, even if Father would let me."

"Your father wouldn't have anything to do with it, dear," Hedia said. She was smiling, but Alphena had seen a similar expression on her face before. A man had died then. "I would not permit you to embarrass that sweet man so badly. I hope you believe me, daughter."

"I wouldn't do it," Alphena said. The interior of the litter seemed suddenly colder, shiveringly cold. "I used to think I wanted to, but I really wouldn't have."

She swallowed and added, "And I do believe you, Mother."

Hedia held both her hands out, palms up, for Alphena to take. "I apologize for saying that just now," she said. "I—your father is very good and gentle. People of his sort deserve better than the world often sends them, and I want to protect him. I am neither good nor gentle."

Alphena squeezed the older woman's fingers, then leaned back. "Thank you for what you do for Father," she said. "And what you've done for me."

"Well, dear," Hedia said with a tinge of amusement, "I quite clearly recall you chopping away at demons with what seemed at the time to be a great deal of skill. That needed to be done, and I certainly wasn't going to do it. And I strongly suspect that none of those gladiators whom you admire would have faced demons either."

What does she mean by that? Alphena thought; then she blushed at the way her mind had tried to turn Hedia's words into a slur. Aloud but in a low voice, she said, "I should just learn to accept compliments, shouldn't I?"

Hedia laughed merrily. "Well, dear," she said, "I don't think I would suggest that as a regular course of conduct for a young lady. But with me . . . yes, I generally mean what I say."

The litter slowed. There was even more shouting than usual ahead of them. Alphena touched the curtain, intending to pull it aside and lean out for a better look.

Hedia stopped her with a lazy gesture. She said, "Ours isn't the only senatorial family going by litter to shop in the Field of Mars today. I'm confident that our present escort could fight their way through anything but a company of the Praetorian Guard, but I warned Manetho before we started that if he allowed any unnecessary trouble to occur, he'd spend the rest of his life hoeing turnips on a farm in Bruttium."

Alphena forced herself to relax. "I guess if there's going to be trouble," she said, "we'll get to it soon enough."

She pursed her lips and added, "I didn't bring my sword."

"I should think not!" Hedia said. She didn't sound angry, but she appeared to be genuinely shocked. She turned her head slightly—though she couldn't look forward from where she sat in the vehicle—and said, "I thought of suggesting that Lenatus go along with Saxa this afternoon. Just—"

She shrugged her shoulders. She looked like a cat stretching.

"—in case. But I understand that Master Corylus will be accompanying the consul, and I'm sure his man Pulto will be equipped to deal with unexpected problems."

"Father?" said Alphena, taken aback. "He shouldn't—"

She stopped, unwilling to belittle Saxa by saying he had no business in anything that might involve swords. It was true, of course, but it wasn't something that her stepmother needed to be told.

"That is," she said, "what's Father doing? I didn't know about it."

She didn't know—she didn't bother to learn—very much about what other people were doing. If Hedia hadn't taken family obligations more seriously than her stepdaughter had, Alphena would either be wandering in fairyland or be in the belly of something wandering in fairyland. Or be in a worse place yet.

"Your brother wants to visit a senator's house," Hedia said. "He thought the consul's authority might be necessary to gain entry. I don't know all the details. I don't expect Saxa to have difficulty, but—"

That shrug again.

"—I do worry about the poor man."

The litter slowed again, then stopped. Manetho came to the side of the vehicle and said, "Your ladyships, we have arrived at the shop of the silk merchant Abinnaeus."

Hedia grinned and said, "Come, dear. At the very least, we can outfit you with a set of silk syntheses to wear at formal dinners. Since we're coming here anyway."

She slid her curtain open and dismounted, allowing the deputy steward to offer his arm in support. Alphena grimaced and got out on her own side.

Maximus, normally the night guard at the gate of the back garden, held out his arm. Alphena lifted her hand to slap him away. She stopped, thinking of Hedia; and of Corylus, who had mentioned Maximus' intelligence.

"Thank you, my good man," Alphena said, touching the back of the fellow's wrist with her fingertips but pointedly not letting any weight rest there.

She turned, eyeing their surroundings. The Altar of Peace was to the left. Not far beyond it was the Sundial of Augustus—a granite obelisk brought from Egypt and set up to tell the hours. The metal ball on top of the obelisk blazed in the sunlight.

Alphena stared, transfixed. She felt but didn't really see her stepmother walk around the vehicle to join her.

"Is something wrong, my dear?" Hedia said.

"That ball," Alphena said. Her mouth was dry. She didn't point, because she didn't want to mark herself that way. "On top of the pillar."

"Yes, dear?" Hedia said. "It's gold, isn't it?"

"No," said Alphena. "It's orichalc. Mother, I'd swear that's the ball that was on top of the temple we saw in the vision. The temple that w-was being torn apart!"

HEDIA STARED AT THE SUNLIT GLOBE in the middle distance, trying to empathize with what Alphena was feeling. With whatever Alphena was feeling, because despite real mental effort Hedia couldn't understand what was so obviously frightening about a big metal ball.

Did it come from a ruined city as the girl said? Well and good, but so did the obelisk it stood on top of; and the huge granite spike must have been much more difficult to move and re-erect here in Carce.

"Is there something we should do, dear?" Hedia said. "Ah, do you want to go closer?"

She didn't understand why Alphena was concerned, but she understood all too well what it was to feel terrified by something that didn't seem frightening to others. She hadn't particularly noticed the temple Alphena talked about, because her mind had been frozen by the sight of glass men like those of her nightmare, walking on the walls of the city.

"No!" Alphena said; then, contritely, clasping Hedia's hands, "I'm sorry, Mother. No, there's no reason to . . . well, I don't know what to do. And—"

She grinned ruefully.

"—I certainly don't want to go closer. Though I'm not afraid to."

"We'll shop, then," Hedia said, linking her arm with her daughter's. "But when we return, we'll discuss the matter with Pandareus. I think he'll be with Saxa and the boys, but otherwise we'll send a messenger to bring him to the house. He's a . . ."

She paused, wondering how to phrase what she felt.

"Pandareus is of course learned, but he also has an unusually clear vision of reality," she said. "As best I can tell, all his choices are consciously made. I don't agree with many of them—"

She flicked the sleeve of her cloak. It was of silk lace, dyed lavender to contrast with the brilliantly white ankle-length tunic she wore beneath it. It was unlikely that Pandareus could have purchased its equivalent with a year of his teaching fees.

"—obviously. But I respect the way he lives by his principles."

As I live by mine; albeit my principles are very different.

Syra waited with Alphena's maid behind the litter. They had followed on foot from the town house. Ordinarily Hedia would have had nearly as many female as male servants in her entourage, but for this trip the two maids were the only women present.

They didn't appear to feel there was anything to be concerned about. Syra was talking with a good-looking Gallic footman, though she faced about sharply when Hedia glanced toward her.

Alphena noticed the interchange, but she probably misinterpreted it. She said, "I've asked Agrippinus to assign Florina to me permanently. I'm not going to get angry with her."

Hedia raised an eyebrow. "My goodness, dear," she said. "I doubt the most committed philosophers could go through more than a few days without getting angry at the servant who forgot to mention the dinner invitation from a patron or who used an important manuscript to light the fire."

"I don't mean that, exactly," the girl said, flushing. "But I'm not going to hit her. And I'm going to try not to scream at her either."

Alphena was upset, but Hedia wasn't sure who she was upset with. Perhaps she was upset—angry—at herself, though she might be directing it toward the stepmother who was forcing her to discuss something that she apparently hadn't fully thought out.

"I really can change, Mother!" she said. "I can be, well, nicer. To people."

"Let's go in, dear," Hedia said. As they started toward the shop between a double rank of servants, she added quietly, "In law, slaves are merely furniture with tongues, you know. But slapping your couch with a comb isn't going to lead to it informing the palace that you've been mocking the emperor. I applaud your new resolution."

Abinnaeus had chosen an outward-facing section of the portico. The majority of his trade arrived in litters which could more easily be maneuvered in the street than in the enclosed courtyard. There was a gated counter across the front of the shop, but clients were inside where bolts of fabric were stacked atop one another. There was a room behind and a loft above.

Within, a pair of no-longer-young women were fingering the silk and speaking Greek with thick Galatian accents. Their maids were outside, watching the new arrivals with interest verging on resentment.

That pair came to Carce with their feet chalked for sale, Hedia sneered mentally. They were the sort to have moved into the master's bedroom and made a good thing out of his will, but she doubted whether they were wealthy enough to do real business with Abinnaeus.

Only a single attendant, a doe-eyed youth, was visible when Hedia approached. A moment later the owner waddled out behind a second attendant—similar enough to the other to have been twins—who had gone to fetch him. Abinnaeus beamed at her, then directed his attention to the previous customers.

"Dear ladies," he said. "I do *so* regret that a previous engagement requires that I close my poor shop to the general public immediately."

"For them?" said one of the women, her voice rising shrilly. "I don't think so! Not till you've served me!"

She turned to the stack of silk and started to lift the top roll. It was colored something between peach and beige and would clash with every garment the woman was wearing now; but then, her hennaed hair, her orange tunic, and her vermillion leather shoes were a pretty ghastly combination already.

Abinnaeus put a hand on the roll, pinning it down, and reached for the woman's arm. She shrieked, "Don't you touch me, you capon!" but the threatened contact did cause her to jump aside—and toward the counter.

Hedia waited, her fingers on Alphena's wrist to keep the girl with her. The events of the past few days had put Hedia in a bad enough mood that she found the present business amusing. She didn't scorn people because they were former slaves—but she scorned former slaves who gave themselves the airs of noblewomen.

"I'm sure my colleague Cynthius in the courtyard will be delighted to serve you, ladies," Abinnaeus said. He spoke with an oily solicitude; nothing in his tone or manner indicated that he was sneering. "I think you'll find his selection suitable. Indeed, *very* suitable for ladies as fine as yourselves."

The youthful attendants were urging the women toward the opened gate. One went quickly, but the protesting woman tried to push the boy away.

Something happened that Hedia didn't quite see. Off-balance, the woman lurched toward the street and into it. The youth—who wasn't as young as he had first seemed; he was some sort of Oriental, childishly slight but not at all a child—walked alongside her without seeming to exert any force.

Hedia saw the woman's arm muscles bunch to pull away. She wasn't successful, though the youth's smile didn't slip.

"Well, you'll *never* see me again!" the woman cried. Her companion had been staring first at Hedia and Alphena, then—wide-eyed—at their escort. She tugged her louder friend toward the entrance into the courtyard; their maids followed, laughing openly.

"Ah," Abinnaeus said in a lightly musing voice that wasn't obviously directed toward anyone. "If only I could be sure of that."

He turned and bowed low to Hedia. "I'm *so* glad to see your ladyship again," he said, sounding as though he meant it. "And your lovely companion! Please, honor my shop by entering."

"Come dear," Hedia said, but she swept the younger woman through the gate ahead of her. "Abinnaeus, this is my daughter, Lady Alphena. We're looking for dinner dresses for her."

"You could not do better," Abinnaeus agreed. He was a eunuch; his fat made him look softly cylindrical instead of swelling his belly. "Please, be seated while I find something worthy of yourselves."

One of the attendants was closing the shutters: barred openings at the top continued to let in light and air, but street noise and the crowds were blocked by solid oak. The other attendant had carried out a couch with ivory legs and cushions of silk brocade; he was returning to the back room to find its couple.

Hedia gestured Alphena to the couch; she dipped her chin forcefully to refuse. Hedia sat instead of reclining and patted the cushion beside her. "Come, daughter," she said. "Join me."

Alphena hesitated only an instant, then sat where Hedia had indicated.

The youth appeared with the second couch. He eyed them, then vanished back into storage with his burden.

Abinnaeus returned with six bolts of cloth over his left arm. "Sirimavo," he said to the youth who had bolted the shutters, "bring wine and goblets, then go fetch some cakes from Codrius. Quickly now!"

"No cakes for me," Hedia said. "Though if my daughter . . . ?"

Alphena gestured a curt refusal, then consciously forced her lips into a smile. "Not at all, thank you," she said.

The girl really is trying. Soon perhaps I can introduce her to some suitable men without worrying that she's going to tell them she'll cut their balls off if they dare to touch her again.

"It would be remiss of me not to offer your ladyship every courtesy," the eunuch said. "What you choose to accept is your own affair, but I will say that my friend Codrius just down the portico has even better pastries than my beloved father at home in Gaza."

"No one has ever been able to fault your hospitality to a customer, Abinnaeus," Hedia said. The tramps he had just turfed out of his shop might have quarreled with her statement, but they weren't proper customers. "It's been too long since I've been here."

"We have missed you, your ladyship," Abinnaeus said, setting down five bolts. "Your custom is always welcome, of course, but even more I've missed your exquisite taste. So like mine, but more masculine."

He and Hedia laughed. Alphena looked shocked, then went still-faced because she wasn't sure how she should react.

Abinnaeus stretched a swatch from the last bolt and held it close to Alphena's ear. "There, your ladyship. What do you think about this with your daughter's coloring?"

Hedia gave the fabric sharp attention. It was faintly tan—the natural color of the silk, she was sure, not a dye—but it seemed to have golden highlights.

"Is that woven with gold wire?" she said in puzzlement. *Surely no wire could be drawn that fine.*

Abinnaeus chuckled. "To you and you alone, your ladyship," he said, "I will tell my secret. No, not wire—but the blond hair from women of farthest Thule. They let it grow till they marry, then cut it for the first time. The strands are finer than spider silk, purer than the gold of the Tagus River."

"And you, dear?" Hedia said to her daughter. Abinnaeus stepped back with the cloth spread in a shaft of sunlight through the clerestory windows. "It complements you perfectly, but do you find it attractive?"

Alphena had swollen visibly while Hedia and the proprietor discussed the matter as though she was a dog being fitted with a jeweled collar, but she had managed to control herself. "It's all right, I guess," she muttered. "It's— well, it's all right, if that's what you want."

When we're back in the litter, I'll remind her that we came for information; and that I had to put Abinnaeus at his ease. He wouldn't be able to imagine Lady Hedia caring about anybody *else's opinion on matters of taste and fashion.*

The attendants returned, each carrying a small table already set with a refreshment tray. There was a passage to the courtyard shops from the back room, but the wine was probably from Abinnaeus' own stock. He kept better vintages on hand for his customers than could be purchased nearby.

He eyed Hedia and gestured minusculely toward the wine. "Three to one," she said, answering the unspoken question. That was the only possible choice with her daughter present, and it was what she probably would have said regardless.

Turning to Alphena, she said, "I used to visit Abinnaeus more frequently before I married your father, dear. I lived close by; just across Broad Street, in fact."

To Abinnaeus she went on, "I sold the house to a Gaul from Patavium; Julius Brennus, as I recall. Do you see any of him, Abinnaeus?"

"Well, not Master Brennus himself, your ladyship," he said, kneeling to offer each of the women a silver cup. "But his wife, Lady Claudia, visits me frequently, I'm pleased to say."

So the wealthy—extremely wealthy—trader from the Po Valley married a patrician after moving to Carce, Hedia thought. *Good luck to both of them.*

She sipped her wine, which was just as good as she expected it to be. Alphena had leaned forward slightly to lift the silk for closer examination. An attendant moved the bolt slightly closer. He didn't speak or otherwise intervene for fear of causing the young customer to rear back. *It must be like bridling a skittish horse.*

Aloud Hedia said, "I recall Brennus having some very odd-looking servants. Is that still the case?"

"Odd?" said Abinnaeus, pursing his lips. Discretion warred with a desire not to lose the chance of a present sale. "Well, I don't know that I'd put it quite that way, your ladyship. But it is true that many of Master Brennus' servants did come with him from the north . . . and one could say that they brought their culture with them. One could scarcely claim that boorishness and bad Latin are unusual in Carce, though, I'm afraid."

Hedia laughed. "No, not at all," she agreed, holding out her cup for a refill. "I thought he had a number of fellows in shiny costumes, though. You've never seen anything like that?"

"Nothing like that, no," the proprietor said, clearly puzzled. "Ah—it is possible that Master Brennus added moving automatons to his courtyard, though. Alexandrine work, I mean, worked by water. I've never been inside the house."

"That could be the story I'd heard," Hedia said as if idly. "Well, I think this first pattern will be a fine choice. What else have you for us, Master Abinnaeus?"

The afternoon wore on. The familiar routine was pleasurable during those moments when Hedia forgot the danger which had really brought her here, and such moments were more frequent as she became absorbed in fabric and fashion. Alphena was showing real interest also, which was a success beyond expectation.

The maids waited silently, their backs against the counter. There was nothing for them to do, but they too were entranced by the lovely cloth.

It was time to be getting back. Hedia rose and stretched.

"Have these eight patterns made up," she said, "and send them to the house. I'll tell our majordomo to expect them. I daresay we'll be back for more, though."

"You are always welcome, your ladyships," Abinnaeus said. The attendants were rattling the shutters open as he bowed. "Your intelligence and taste brighten an existence which sometimes threatens to be about money alone."

He made a quick, upward gesture with a plump hand. "Taking nothing away from money, of course," he added. "But there can be more."

The sun was well into the western sky when Hedia followed her daughter into the street. "You did very well, dear," she said; truthfully, but mostly to encourage the girl.

Hedia looked idly toward the great sundial. In the wavering sunlight she saw three glass figures glitter like sun dogs in the winter sky.

"Ah!" she cried, grasping Alphena's arm.

"Mother?" the girl said. The alerted escorts were pulling weapons from beneath their capes and tunics.

None of them saw anything. Hedia didn't see anything—now.

She forced a clumsy laugh. "I tripped on these foolish shoes," she said, "but I don't seem to have turned my ankle."

She wiggled her shapely leg in the air.

"Let's be getting back to the house, shall we?" Hedia said. The others were staring, though they had started to relax. "There's nothing more for us here."

She hoped that was the truth; but she was sure in her heart that it was not.

VARUS REALIZED he was holding his breath as he waited for someone inside the house of Sempronius Tardus to open the door. No one did. He breathed out, then snorted fresh lungsful of air.

The chief lictor banged again and growled, "Open it for me or by Jupiter you'll open it for a cohort of the Guard!"

Apparently Varus had been unable to hide his smile. Pandareus looked at him and raised an eyebrow in question.

"I was wondering how it would affect our mission if I were to faint from holding my breath," Varus said. "I think it better not to make the experiment."

He opened his tablet and resumed his notes. This was, after all, an official activity of the consul and therefore part of his self-imposed duty of recording the ritual business of the Republic. There was at least the possibility that his records would be of service to later historians, whereas there was no chance at all that anyone in the future would have wanted to read the *Collected Verse of Gaius Alphenus Varus.*

The door jerked open. A tall man with the beard of a Stoic philosopher and a cloth-of-gold sash that suggested he was the majordomo stood in the opening, looking flustered.

"Your Excellency," the tall servant said, "my master, Senator Marcus Tardus, will be with you in a moment. If I may ask your indulgence to wait here until the senator is ready to receive you—"

"You may *not*," said the chief lictor, prodding his axe head toward the servant's stomach. "This is the consul, you Theban twit!"

He shoved forward with the remainder of his squad following. The majordomo hopped backward.

"My goodness, what an unexpected slur from a public functionary!" Pandareus said. "Though he caught the Boeotian accent correctly, so I can hardly describe the fellow as uncultured."

They started into the house. Saxa seemed oblivious of the interchange between servant and lictor. Varus looked sharply at his father, wondering if he could really be as lost in his own world as he generally seemed to be.

Perhaps so. Saxa was insulated by his wealth, which would one day become the wealth of his son Varus. If Varus survived him. If Carce and the world survived.

Sempronius Tardus trotted into the entrance hall from a side passage. He was tightening the wrap of the toga which he must have put on only when the lictor banged for admittance. A dozen servants fluttered around him, all of them frightened.

"Saxa?" Tardus said. "That is, Your Excellency. You're welcome, of course, but I don't see . . . ?"

Tardus looked dazed. Well, this business would be startling to anybody, but it seemed to Varus that more was going on than surprise at a consul's unannounced formal arrival. Though the emperor was known to be erratic, and even the most loyal and honest of men probably had something in his life that could be turned into a capital offense.

"I am here with my learned advisors . . . ," Saxa said. "To inspect the Serapeum on this property."

He turned slightly and indicated Varus and Pandareus with a sweeping gesture. *This is probably the first time Father has used the rhetorical training that I'm sure he got when he was my age.*

"If you will lead us to the chapel," Saxa continued, "we will finish our business and leave you to your privacy, Lord Tardus."

"What?" squeaked Tardus. "I—this is a mistake! Saxa, I must ask you to leave my house immediately. You have been misinformed!"

Pandareus looked up quizzically, as though he expected Varus to do something. Varus felt the crowed hall blur about him. There was barely room to move, but he found himself walking forward in the familiar fog.

A bull snorted nearby. Varus turned his head sharply, but he could see nothing in the fog though the sound had come from very close. He walked on, picking his way past outcrops. Some of the rocks looked like statues, or anyway had human features.

He wondered where the Sibyl was. Usually in these reveries, he would have come upon her by now.

Varus heard the bull again, this time behind him, and glanced over his shoulder. The fog had cleared enough for him to see a figure that would have been a giant if its human body had not supported the horned head of a bull. It snorted angrily.

A voluptuous woman reclined on the stony ground behind the creature. She caught Varus' startled expression and smiled lazily.

He stepped into sunlight. The Sibyl held a small glass bottle in her left hand, the sort of container in which perfume was sold. Something moved inside it, but the glass was iridescent and Varus couldn't be sure he was seeing a tiny figure rather than the sloshing of liquid.

He bowed formally to the old woman. "Sibyl," he said. "My father has entered the house of Sempronius Tardus, but the senator denies there is a chapel of Serapis in the property. Will you help me find the chapel, please?"

The old woman's laughter was like the rasping of cicadas. She pointed with her right hand, down the craggy reverse slope of the ridge.

"Why do you ask me to tell you things you already know, Lord Magician?" she said. "You stand beside the entrance now."

Varus followed her gesture. He saw himself in the garden behind Tardus' house. The plantings were unusually extensive, covering a greater area than the building itself. Palms grew on either side, and water flowed down and back along a pair of lotus-filled channels in the center. The gazebo where Varus stood was between them, reached by small bridges to either side.

Pandareus was on his right; his father was to the left. Tardus was with them, but all the other people visible in the garden were members of the consul's entourage. The household servants had vanished into corners of the house where they hoped to escape attention.

"How . . . ?" Varus said. Then he said, "Thank you, Sib—"

As the final word came out of his mouth, he was again with his companions, beneath a dome supported by thick wooden columns shaped like papyrus stalks. Tardus stared at him numbly.

"—yl."

Varus blinked. His father and Pandareus were staring at him also: Saxa in concern, the teacher with keen interest.

"I'm sorry," Varus said. He coughed, because his throat was raw. "I've been daydreaming, I'm afraid."

"You have been repeating, 'There is a certain dear land, a nurturer for men,' Lord Varus," Pandareus said. "Repeating it quite loudly, in fact."

"Shouting, my son," Saxa said. "I was rather worried about you."

"And you led us here to this pavilion," said Pandareus, who beamed with cheerful satisfaction. Turning, he added to the waxen looking householder, "The motif is interesting, Lord Tardus."

Varus looked at the gazebo into which he had walked unknowing. The domed ceiling had an opening in the center, but around that was a frieze of men in boats in a landscape of tall reeds. Some were hunting ducks with throwing sticks; others were trying to net the variety of fish shown swimming on a bottom register which was painted sea-green.

"If that's meant to be the Nile," Pandareus said, musing aloud, "and I suppose it is, I would suggest that brown would have been a more suitable color. I recall thinking that it seemed thick enough to walk on."

Varus grinned; neither of the other men reacted.

The floor was a pavement of jasper chips in concrete, but in the center was a round frame about a mosaic of a priest with a bronze rattle. Varus looked at it, then raised his eyes to Tardus.

"There's a catch here," Tardus said, sounding as though he had received a death sentence. He opened a concealed panel in one of the columns, disclosing a lever. "You'll need to step off the mosaic."

Varus, Pandareus, and a moment later Saxa as well stepped back between pairs of pillars.

Tardus threw the lever. The circular mosaic sank into the darkness with a faint squeal. It must have been counterweighted, because it had not required more effort on the lever than to draw a bolt. Broad steps led downward; Varus couldn't see the bottom in the shadows.

"I had forgotten this old grotto existed, Consul," Tardus said, looking distinctly ill. "I suppose it's been here for many years. Since my father's time, no doubt, or even longer."

Tardus is an old man, thought Varus. That was true, of course, but in simple years he was younger than Pandareus. Official discovery of a banned chapel on his property seemed to have ripped all the sinews out of his limbs.

"The worship of Sarapis is legal nowadays, of course," said Saxa, apparently trying to calm his fellow senator.

"There are now official temples of Sarapis in Carce, Lord Saxa," Pandareus said. "Note, however, that they have not been permitted within the religious boundary of the city. This chapel—"

He gestured rhetorically. He was in his professorial mode again and probably didn't, Varus realized, notice the effect that his words were having on Tardus.

"—could not be erected today or at any time after the Senatorial edict when Aemillius and Claudius were consuls."

One of Saxa's footmen trotted out of the house, carrying a lighted lantern. Candidus waddled quickly behind him.

Varus nodded approval. The deputy steward wouldn't demean himself by actually lifting an object, but he had thought far enough ahead to get lights as soon as he saw his master would be entering a crypt.

The footman crossed the short bridge but stopped at the gazebo and held out the lantern. Saxa started to reach for it but paused and looked at his son.

"I think I had best go down," Varus said, taking the lantern. "Ah, your lordship. I will return with a report."

At any rate, I hope to return.

"With your permission, Lord Varus," Pandareus said, "I'll accompany you."

"Yes," Varus said. "That might be helpful, teacher."

They started down into the crypt side by side. Varus held the lantern out in front of them.

If it hadn't been for the Sibyl's roundabout direction, Varus would have been pleased and excited to enter a Serapeum. It was a link to Carce's past; not so ancient as the crypt in which the *Sibylline Books* were stored, but old and part of a mystery cult besides.

The Sibyl *had* sent him here, however. Therefore, more was involved than viewing the decoration and appointments of a secret chapel.

"I doubt," said Pandareus in a mild, musing tone, "that we will encounter Apis in the form of an angry bull. Though I'll admit that I'm less confident than I once was at my ability to predict events."

"I was thinking more along the lines of the goddess Isis loosing cobras on us," Varus said. "Unlikely, but less unlikely than other things that have occurred recently. Or that I imagined happened."

They reached the bottom of the stairs: only twelve steps down. It had looked deeper. There was no door at the base of the staircase, but the archway there was too narrow for more than one person to pass at a time.

Varus, holding the lantern high, stepped into what was clearly an anteroom. There was a doorway in the opposite wall with a niche on either side. To the left was a statuette of a male figure with a bull's head; on the right stood a female figure with a cow's head and a crescent moon rocking between her horns.

"If this were an Egyptian temple," Pandareus said, looking past Varus' shoulder, "I would describe them as Apis and Isis. The Ptolemies were eclectic when they created the cult, however, and they may have made other choices."

He sighed. "My friend Priscus—" Senator Marcus Atilius Priscus "—would know that sort of thing without having to look it up, but I didn't think it would be right to involve him in this matter."

"If the question becomes important," Varus said, "we can answer it at leisure when we return. Unless we're arrested for some political crime, as you suggest."

Varus would have said he was the least political of men, unless that honor was due his father. Yet here they both were, invading the house of another senator under consular authority, an action that could easily be described as rebellion or insult to the emperor as head of state.

"I don't think Tardus will be reporting this intrusion to the authorities," Varus said.

"Probably true," Pandareus said. "In that case, we have only a monster capable of wrecking a city to worry about."

Varus chuckled.

They entered the second chamber, twice the size of the first. Stone benches were built into three walls, intended for diners who were sitting upright instead of reclining as was the custom for men in Carce. Servants would set tables of food and wine in the hollow within the three benches.

In place of a fourth wall, passages to either side flanked an alabaster slab carved in relief. Varus raised the lantern again to view the carving, a man with a full beard seated in a high-backed chair and glaring outward.

"Sarapis joining his worshippers for the sacred meal," Pandareus said. Then, looking upward, "The frieze is interesting."

Varus moved the lantern. The reliefs were of very high quality: a bearded man flanked by a youth and a young woman in flowing robes; in the next panel, the youth thrusting back the woman who, bare-breasted, was trying to pull him onto a couch; in the last—

"This is Hippolytus and Phaedra," Varus said aloud. "Hippolytus cursed by his father Theseus, who believed his wife's false claim that her stepson had raped her."

"Yes," said Pandareus. "Those three, and the monster which executed Theseus' curse."

On the third panel, a tentacled, many-legged monster climbed out of the sea in the background. Hippolytus' chariot raced through brush, dragging behind it the youth whose reins remained wrapped around his wrists when he was thrown out.

"Do you suppose this is what we were meant to see?" Varus said.

Pandareus shrugged. "There must be another room," he said.

They walked to right and left of the carving of Serapis. On the other side, Varus found a tunnel stretching farther into the distance than his lantern could even hint. "This seems to slope downward," he said, turning toward Pandareus.

The teacher was not there. Varus was alone in a tunnel. Behind him was a faint rectangular glow, the sort of light that he might have seen creeping past the edges of the slab from the trap door in the distant gazebo.

Varus took a deep breath, then walked forward at the measured pace of a philosopher and a citizen of Carce. He wondered what he would find at the other end of the tunnel, but it was pointless to speculate. If Typhon waited for him, so be it.

The floor of the chapel had been of simple mosaic design, black frames each crossed by an internal X, on a white ground. Now Varus was walking on seamless sandstone: the tunnel had been drilled through living rock.

There was something ahead: at first just a texture on the sidewalls. Then, as Varus proceeded with the lantern, he saw that the walls had been cut back at knee height to make shelves. On them were terra-cotta urns, similar to ordinary wine jars. Instead of ordinary stoppers, these jars were closed with the stylized heads of birds with long curved beaks.

One of the jars had fallen and shattered some distance down the long corridor. Varus paused and knelt to bring the lantern closer: there would be nothing at the other end of this passage that wouldn't wait for him to arrive. Given that his goal might be death, he wasn't going to have the regret that he'd hastened past his last opportunity for learning.

He smiled, but he meant it. Pandareus would understand; and perhaps Corylus would as well.

The jar had enclosed the corpse of a bird. It had been mummified—the smell of natron and cedar resin was noticeable even after what might have been ages—but the skull was bare beneath rotted linen wrappings.

It had been an ibis. There were thousands or tens of thousands of ibises in this necropolis.

Varus rose to his feet and walked on. He had to restrain himself from counting paces under his breath. He wasn't sure that he was really moving physically anyway. It would be unworthy of a philosopher to carry out a meaningless ritual to trick his mind into the belief that he was imposing control over his immediate surroundings.

I think I see light. But Varus knew that he could see flashes even when his eyes were closed; and he had to admit that his present state of mind wasn't wholly that of a dispassionate philosopher.

He wondered if Socrates had really been that calm when he prepared to drink the poison. Plato had *not* been a disinterested witness, now that Varus thought about it; given that Plato's stature as a teacher was directly dependent on the stature of the master whom he portrayed as showing godlike wisdom and fortitude.

Varus chuckled. He would have described himself as an Epicurean; but perhaps the teachings of Diogenes the Cynic better suited his present mental state.

"Greetings, Lord Varus," called the man standing at the end of the corridor. The pool of light surrounding him did not come from any source Varus could see. "I am Menre."

Varus stepped to within arm's length of the stranger who wore a woolen tunic, a semicircular cloak that hung to his waist, and a low-crowned, flat-brimmed leather hat. He would have passed for an ordinary traveller anywhere in Greece or the southern portions of Italy.

"Sir, you're Menre the Egyptian?" Varus said in puzzlement. The stranger—Menre—held a bulky papyrus scroll in his left hand.

Menre laughed. "Sarapis is more Greek than Egyptian," he said, "and perhaps the same is true of me. Regardless, the chapel was a useful connection between you and the place I am."

Varus found his lips dry; he licked them. He said, "Sir, I would have expected you to visit my teacher Pandareus, as you have in the past. Rather than me."

Menre looked him up and down as though he were a slave—or a couch—he was considering buying. Smiling faintly, he said, "Pandareus is a great scholar, worthy of a place in any learned academy. But he is not a magician, so this—"

He offered the scroll in his left hand.

"—would be of no use to him or to the world."

Varus took the scroll. He started to fumble with it, then set the lantern on the floor so that he had both hands free. There was as much light as there would be outside at midday in Carce, even if he couldn't tell where it was coming from.

He unrolled a few pages of the book; Menre watched him, continuing to smile. The text was in pictographs; chapters were headed—he unrolled more of the scroll to be sure—by paintings in the Egyptian style, full frontal or full profile; gods of terrible aspect confronted humans.

Still holding the book open, Varus met the other man's eyes. "Sir," he said, "this is written in Egyptian holy symbols. I can't read it."

"Can you not, Magician?" Menre said. To Varus, his words were an eerie echo of those the Sybil sometimes directed at him. "Try."

Scowling, Varus looked down at the page, as meaningless to him as bird tracks in the dust. He said, "All hail to Ra, the Sun, as he rises in the eastern quadrant of heaven!" He stopped, amazed.

"You will need the book," Menre said, smiling more broadly. "Give my regards to your teacher, whose scholarship I respect."

The light began to fade; Menre faded with it, as though he had been only a mirage. Just before he vanished completely, his faint voice added, "You will need more than the book, Lord Varus. Perhaps more than your world holds. Good luck to you, but I am not hopeful."

Varus swallowed. For a moment, his surroundings seemed as dark as the tomb; then his eyes adjusted to the oil flame wavering in the lantern which sat on the ground beside him. He picked it up again. The large scroll had vanished, as though it never was.

He and Pandareus were in the service area of the chapel. Food couldn't be prepared here, but prepared dishes would be brought in ahead of time and then served in sequence to the diners.

"Lord Varus?" Pandareus said. "Are you all right?"

"I—" Varus said. He rubbed his eyes with the back of his free hand. "Did I disappear, master?"

"No," said Pandareus, "but you stopped where you were and put the lantern down. You didn't appear to hear me when I spoke to you."

"Ah," said Varus. "Was I, that is, was this for long?"

"Not long," said Pandareus. "Not much longer than it took you to pick up the lantern again. Did something happen to you?"

"We may as well go back," Varus said, turning. He felt queasy, as though he had grasped for a handhold while falling and felt his fingers slip off it. All that remained now was to hit the ground. "I thought I met Menre and that he gave me a book that he said I would need. That we would need. But I don't have it now."

"Can you remember any of it?" Pandareus said, leading through the central room of the chapel. The light from above was enough for him to avoid the benches now that they had been underground for long enough.

"I didn't read it," Varus said, feeling an edge of irritation. "I just glanced at the opening columns. And even if I had—"

Suddenly, unbidden, the phrase, "Let not the Destroyer be allowed to prevail over him!" leaped into his mind. He shouted the words aloud.

Pandareus glanced back at him and nodded in satisfaction. "It appears to me, Lord Varus," he said, "that you have what we need. What all the world needs."

They walked up the stairs together, as they had gone down.

"Do you think it should have kept the boy with us?" Corylus said. Pulto stared at a sunken place on the hillside, but he hadn't said anything for the long moments while his master waited politely for him to speak.

"It's where Anna showed me this morning," Pulto said in a dull voice. He turned to face Corylus. They carried a lighted lantern, but there was moon enough to show their features clearly.

"Master," Pulto said, "we shouldn't be doing this. I'm not a god-botherer, you know that, but it'd be better to lose than to win by the kind of magic that you find in graveyards. Though it was my own Anna as sent us here."

Corylus thought about the vision of Typhon, wrecking the world it crawled across. "No, old friend," he said. "Losing would be worse, for the Earth, at any rate. For me personally—"

He shrugged. "I don't know what it means for me personally. It doesn't matter. But Pulto? You can wait for me back where we crossed the old wall. I won't think the less of you if you're unwilling to be involved in this sort of thing."

That wasn't really true, but Corylus knew that it should be true. He'd known a man, a centurion with scars marking every hand's-breadth of his body—he couldn't remember the tale of half of them—who had frozen in mumbling fear when a wolf spider ran up the inside of a leather tent and stopped directly over him. If magic disturbed Pulto in the same way, well, there was more reason for it.

Pulto snorted. "I'm afraid," he said, "but I'm a soldier, so what's being afraid got to do with anything? And I've done plenty of things this stupid before, begging your pardon, master. Only—"

His smile was forced, but the fact he *could* force a smile spoke well of his courage and his spirits both.

"—this time I'm sober. Which is maybe the trouble, but it's one I plan to solve right quick when we're done with this nonsense."

Corylus grinned. "I'll split at least the first jar with you," he said. "Now let's get to work."

The tombs of Carce's wealthy ranged along all the roads out of the city. The great families had huge columbaria, dovecotes; so called because the interiors were covered with lattices to hold urns of cremated ashes.

Lesser, more recently wealthy, households had correspondingly smaller monuments. Often there was just a slab with reliefs of the man or couple and a small altar in front to receive the offerings brought by descendents.

But the poor died also, and even a slave might have friends and family. The slope of the Aventine outside the sacred boundary of the city received their remains. Small markers, generally wooden but occasionally scratched stones, dotted the rocky soil. Badly spelled prayers or simple names which were themselves prayers for survival, lasted briefly and were replaced by later burials and later markers, just as other wretched souls had moved into the tenements that the dead had vacated earlier.

By day this end of the Aventine was a waste of brush which feral dogs prowled and where crows and vultures croaked and grunted. Fuel for pyres was an expense which the poor skimped on, as they skimped on food and clothing during life. At night occasional humans joined the beasts, witches who searched for herbs which had gained power through the presence of death; and who sometimes gathered bones as well, to be ground and used in darker medicine.

No one would disturb Corylus and his servant, but Pulto had brought swords for both of them among the other tools: the mattock and pry bar, ropes and basket. By concentrating on the thought of human enemies, Pulto could push the other dangers from his mind.

"It's a well, I think," Pulto said, loosening up now that Corylus had broken the glum silence. "Under a lot of crap and full of crap, of course, but that's what I thought by daylight."

"Right," said Corylus, thrusting the blade of his mattock between two stones gripped by vines and levering upward. "People throw things down the well when they're in a hurry to leave. We should be able to find what we're looking for and get out before the wine shops close!"

Among the things people threw into wells were bodies, depending on who the people were. Well, they'd deal with that if they had to.

Corylus put on his thick cowhide mittens. He didn't need them for the tools—he spent enough time wielding a sword in Saxa's exercise ground that his calluses protected him—but the loosened rocks were often jagged or wrapped in brambles. He didn't mind a few cuts and scratches, but it was easy to wear protection when throwing rubble down slope.

He and Pulto worked together briefly, but when they had excavated the fill a few feet down, Corylus got into the shaft and filled baskets for his servant to lift and empty from the top. It *was* a well shaft as Pulto had guessed. The coping of volcanic tuff had mostly collapsed inward, but the remainder was cut through the hillside's soft limestone. There was no way to tell how old it was, but it was certainly old.

Corylus lost track of everything except the task. This was monotonous but not mindless work, much like ditching or cutting turf to wall a marching camp. He had to decide each next stroke, sometimes scooping loose dirt with the blade of the mattock, sometimes using the pry bar to separate rocks that were wedged together.

Once he found a human jaw. There wasn't room in the shaft to leave it, but he made sure it was on the bottom of the next basketful he sent up to Pulto.

Corylus wasn't sure how long he had been working—it didn't help to think about that, since he would work until the task was finished—but his feet were by now some ten feet below the level of the coping. He bent to work more of the light fill—gravel and silt—loose with the mattock while Pulto hauled up the basket with the latest load.

He stopped and put the mattock down. The light at this depth wouldn't have been good even without Pulto leaning over the top, so Corylus tried the seam between stones with his fingers and found what he thought his eyes had told him: a slot wide enough for passage had been cut in the living rock, then closed with a fitted stone with a stone wedge above it.

"Pulto?" Corylus called. "Send the lantern down to me on a cord."

Pulto only grunted in reply, but he jerked the basket up more abruptly than usual—a long task was better handled at a steady pace than by fits and starts. Moments later the lantern wobbled down, tied to the end of Pulto's sash. They could have passed it directly from hand to hand, but not without searing somebody's fingertips on the hot bronze casing.

Corylus set the lantern at an angle on the ground so that the light through its mica windows fell on the stones inset in the smooth shaft. He set the point of his pry bar, then used it to work the wedge sideways. When it bound, he blocked the widened crack with a pebble, then shifted the pry bar to the other side and levered the wedge the other way.

An inch of the wedge was clear of the wall. Corylus thumped it with the heel of his bare palm so that the pebble fell out, then gripped the stone with the fingertips of both hands and wriggled it back and forth while he drew it out. He hopped when it fell, but it landed between where his feet were anyway.

"What are you doing down there, boy?" Pulto asked with a rasp in his voice. He was worried, and that made him harsh.

"I think I've found what we're looking for," Corylus said. He didn't say that he'd found an Etruscan tomb, because he knew that the information wouldn't please Pulto.

As Corylus hoped, the larger slab tipped forward when the wedge was removed. He walked it awkwardly to the side, trying not to crush the lantern or trip over the wedge. Holding the lantern before him, he knelt to peer into the opening.

The chamber beyond was cut from the rock like the well shaft. It was about ten feet long but not quite that wide. Benches were built into the side-walls. At the back, facing the entrance, was a chair that seemed to also have been carved from the limestone.

On the chair sat a bearded man with a fierce expression. He wore a white tunic with fringes of either black or dark blue and a heavier garment of deep red over his left shoulder, leaving the right side of his chest covered only by the tunic. On a gold neck-chain was an elongated jewel clasped by gold fili-gree at top and bottom.

"Master, what are you doing?" Pulto said. His voice echoed dully in the well. "Hold on! I'm coming down!"

"Stay where you are!" Corylus said, twisting his head backward as much as the tomb door allowed him. "I'm coming right back!"

He stepped forward, hunching; the floor was cut down so that the ceiling might have been high enough for him to stand, but he didn't want to chance a bad knock in his hurry. He set the lantern on the floor, then took the jewel in his hands and started to lift the chain over the head of the bearded man.

The figure and his clothing vanished into a swirl of dust. A bracelet of braided gold wire clinked to the stone chair, then to the floor.

Corylus sneezed, then squeezed his lips together. He backed quickly out of the tomb, then dropped the chain over his own head as the easiest way to carry it. *I'm not going back for the lantern,* he thought.

"Pulto!" he said. "Drop me an end of the rope and snub it off. I'm coming up and we're getting out of here!"

The rope sailed down; the basket was still attached to the handle.

"That's the first thing you've said tonight that I agree with!" Pulto said. "By Hercules! it is."

CHAPTER VII

Daylight through cracks in the shutters awakened Corylus. He sat up quickly, angry with himself. Ordinarily he awakened before dawn and—

Pain split his head straight back from the center of his forehead. He wobbled, sick and briefly unable to see colors. He whispered, "Hercules!"

"Swear by Charon, better," said Anna as she hobbled over to him, carrying a bronze mug that she had been heating in a bath of water. "I've never seen anyone closer to dead but still walking than the two of you when you came in last night."

She offered the mug. "Here," she said. "Swallow it down."

Corylus lifted the warm bronze cautiously. The odor made his nostrils quiver; he started to lower the mug.

"Drink it, I tell you!" Anna said. "D'ye think you're the first drunk I've had to bring back to life in the morning? It's been your father often enough; but I don't think he'd be pleased to learn that my man, who he trusted, let you get into this state—and himself no better!"

"Yes, ma'am," Corylus said obediently. He held his breath and drank the whole mugful at a measured pace, then set it on the side table, empty. Anna gave him a napkin. He looked at it puzzled, then sneezed violently into it.

"There," said Anna with a satisfied smirk. "You'll feel better now, or so I believe."

Corylus lowered the napkin with which he had covered his mouth and nose. He *did* feel better, for a wonder. He would have thought that the sneeze would have shattered his head into more bits than the shell of a dropped egg.

"I meant to stop at the first jar," he said contritely. "I must have had more than that to drink."

"Aye, you must have," Anna said, her tone still grim but her face showing a trace of humor—if you knew what you were looking for. "Well, it's done and you're back safely, no thanks to that fool husband of mine. Are you going to your class today, then?"

"If I . . . ," Corylus said. He got slowly to his feet as he spoke. Somewhat to his surprise, he found that he was all right except for a slight wobbliness when he straightened. "Yes, I will. I want to talk with Varus afterward anyway, and Master Pandareus too."

A thought struck him. "Oh!" he said. "And we did find what you sent us for, or I think it was."

He reached under his tunic. The chain wasn't around his neck.

Anna gestured with her free hand toward the storage chest on the other side of the bed. The chain and the jewel wrapped in the net of gold wire were there. In a shaft of sunlight, the stone was a cloudy gray-green with very little sparkle.

"I took it off you," she said. "When I got you out of that filthy tunic and sponged you before I put you to bed."

Her grin suddenly widened. "As I've done your father half a hundred times. It takes me back, lad."

Corylus reached for the jewelry, then paused and raised an eyebrow in question.

"Aye, take it," Anna said. "Take it and wear it. I don't know what it means or what it does, but I know it's meant for a man."

Corylus didn't move. "I don't know what you mean," he said. "Meant for a man?"

Anna grimaced. "I don't have the words!" she said. Her voice was as harsh as he ever remembered her talking to him. "If a civilian asked me how you knew the shields on the far hill were Suebi and not Batavians, what would you tell him? You'd just know, that's all. Well, I tell you, that jewel's meant for a man; and whatever else I am, I'm not that."

Corylus picked it up by the chain and carried it over to the window for better light. He threw open the shutters.

"It's glass," he said, looking at the scalloped fracture lines at one end of the stone. "Slag from a glass furnace, anyway."

He held it up against the sky and squinted through it. "There's something inside, but I can't tell what it is," he said.

Then, lowering the pendant with a triumphant grin, "No! It's volcanic glass! But I still think there's something inside it."

"I tried to look," Anna said. Corylus tried to hand it to her; she waved it away and said, "No, I don't mean like that, so better light would show me more than the lamp did. Another way, boy. All I learned is that there's something inside, all right, and that it *doesn't* like women. I set it down then—"

She nodded to the chest.

"—and I stepped back, and I burned a little frankincense to Mother Lucina—"

A Greek would have called the goddess Hecate, but Anna was a Marsian born in the mountains a hundred miles south of Carce.

"—that I wasn't any deeper in when I roused it."

"Should I—" Corylus said. He stopped, lifting the pendant by its chain. He was seeing the complete object this time, not trying to peer into the depths of the cloudy glass.

He looked at Anna. "You said I should wear it, dear one," he said. "If it's dangerous . . . ?"

She cackled without humor. "A sword's dangerous, boy," she said. "But not to you when you're wearing it, I think. Nor is this, for you're a man if ever a man was born. The dream that guided me . . ."

She shrugged.

"I can only trust my guides, master," she said with a catch in her throat. Corylus realized that she was close to tears. "I would tear my own heart out if I thought it would help you, but it wouldn't. I can only tell you what I am told, or what I anyway believe. And I pray that I'm right, because I would so rather die than you be harmed!"

Corylus dropped the chain over his neck and tucked the pendant, the amulet, under his tunic. Then he folded his old nurse in his arms. She felt as light as a plucked chicken. He felt a rush of love.

"I love you, little mother," Corylus said. "You kept me safe as a boy, and you protect me still."

He squeezed Anna again and stepped back, smiling. "Now, I'm already late," he said. "I'll pick up a roll on my way to class. We'll deal with this business, whatever it is."

Corylus quickly laced on his sandals. He was still smiling, but that was for show. He wished he could be more confident of what he had just told Anna; and he wished he didn't feel that he had a vicious dog on the end of the chain around his neck.

Because despite Anna's words, he wasn't sure it was *his* dog.

HEDIA'S EXPRESSION REMAINED pleasant as the new doorman announced the arrival of Senator Marcus Atilius Priscus. In truth the fellow's South German accent was so broad that if she hadn't known who was invited for dinner, she wouldn't be any wiser now.

Keeping her professional smile, she murmured to Saxa at her side, "Dear heart, we *cannot* keep Flavus on the front door until his Latin has improved. Not if we're going to entertain senators as learned as Lord Priscus, at least."

Flavus was a striking physical specimen, tall and blond and ripplingly muscular. Hedia could certainly appreciate the fellow's merit, but she had never allowed appearances to interfere with her duty.

Hedia had never let *anything* interfere with her duty.

She was standing beside her husband as a matter of respect while he greeted his dinner guests, though she would not be dining with the men tonight. She didn't have a party of her own to attend: she planned to dine in her own suite, either alone or possibly with Alphena. She hadn't decided whether to issue the invitation, and she thought it likely that the girl would decline it if she did.

Varus wasn't present, though he would be dining with Saxa and his guests. That wasn't a protest, as it might have been with his sister in similar circumstances. The boy said he would work until dinner.

"Work" in his case meant that he would be reading something and taking notes. Hedia had recently looked through one of the notebooks Varus was filling, thinking that she should display interest in her son's activities. She had found them either nonsensical or unintelligible, though no more so than the passage from Horace to which they apparently referred.

Hedia's smile became momentarily warmer. Her son—stepson by blood but, in law and in my mind, her son—would never be the sort of man she socialized with; but he was a clever boy, and brave. Hedia had seen that the night in the Temple of Jupiter when Varus saved the world from fiery destruction.

Marcus Priscus waddled into the entrance hall, accompanied by a score of servants. There were no freeborn clients in his entourage. Sometimes a host would give his guests the option of bringing the number of diners up to nine with their own friends and hangers-on, but Priscus had not asked for this right and Saxa hadn't volunteered it. Hedia knew her husband viewed the dinner as a chance to frame his magpie's hoard of erudition with the solid scholarship of his guests and son.

"Welcome, my honored colleague!" Saxa called. "Your wisdom lights my poor house."

"Welcome, Lord Priscus," Hedia said, her voice a smooth vibrancy following her husband's nervous squeak. "Our household gods smile at your presence."

"Lady Hedia," Priscus said, beaming at her. "I recall your father fondly. He would be delighted, I'm sure, to see how his daughter has blossomed."

Priscus was badly overweight and nearly seventy, but his undeniable scholarship had not kept him from getting quite a reputation for gallantry in his younger days. *A pity Varus isn't more like him,* Hedia thought. *We might get along better if we had something in common.*

Hedia murmured something appreciative to the guest, then turned to a deputy steward—it happened to be Manetho—and whispered, "Go to Lord Varus—he's probably in the library—and tell him that the guests are arriving for dinner." Manetho nodded and vanished toward the back stairs.

Candidus was marshaling the members of Priscus' escort and leading them toward the kitchen where they would be fed with the household staff. There were probably as many more out in front, including litter bearers. Hedia was sure that Priscus hadn't walked here himself from his home on the west slope of the Palatine Hill.

Her husband and Priscus were chatting, waiting for Pandareus and perhaps Varus as well before they went up to the outside dining area, overlooking the central courtyard. Instead of permanent masonry benches built into the walls, wicker furniture was brought up from storage and covered with goose down pillows covered with silk brocade whose ridged designs made the guests less likely to slip off than slick surfaces would.

"The learned Master Pandareus of Athens!" Flavus said, butchering the words even worse, if that was possible, than he had the senator's.

The servant who whispered the names of those arriving was a wizened Greek from Massillia in Gaul. He was extremely sharp—Hedia had never known him to misidentify a visitor—and would have been a perfect doorman if he hadn't had the face and posture of an arthritic rat. *By Venus!, the trouble the gods caused for a woman who simply wanted to present her noble husband with the proper dignity.*

Hedia smiled more broadly by just a hair. She wasn't fooling herself, of course; but the experience of behaving normally for a woman in her position had thrown a little more cover over the figures of her nightmare.

The scholar entered, looking faintly bemused. He didn't have an attendant, and Hedia could only assume that the tunic he wore was his best. One heard of rhetoric teachers becoming very wealthy, but Pandareus had clearly avoided that experience.

I must remember to check with Agrippinus to make sure that Varus' school fees are paid.

Priscus greeted the teacher with obvious warmth. Varus had said that the men were friends despite the difference in their social position; this confirmed the statement.

Saxa glanced at Hedia and whispered nervously, "My dear? Do you suppose V-V . . . , my son, that is, will be joining us?"

"Yes, he'll be—" Hedia said. She stopped gratefully as Varus entered from the office with an apologetic expression. Two servants were trying to adjust his toga on the move.

"The noble Senator Marcus Sempronius Tardus, Commissioner of the Sacred Rites!" Flavus boomed.

There was silence in the hall, at least from the principals. Servants continued to chatter like a flock of sparrows, of course.

"What's this, Saxa?" Priscus said. "I wouldn't have thought you'd be inviting Tardus, not after that consular visit yesterday."

He didn't sound angry, though he probably felt that he should have been informed of who the other guests were when he was invited. There were senators who certainly preferred never to set eyes on one another.

"I didn't . . . ," Saxa said, looking stunned. He turned to Hedia. "Dear one, did you invite Tardus? That is, I'm not misremembering something, am I?"

"No, little heart," Hedia said coolly. "I'm sure Lord Tardus will inform us of why he is gracing us with his presence."

Tardus entered the hall with attendants, crowding it again. No toga-clad citizens accompanied him, but the three men closest to the senator were the foreigners whom Hedia had seen with him in the theater. Close-up they seemed even more unusual, especially the man with the stuffed bird pinned opposite to the roll of his long black hair.

"Greetings, Lord Tardus," Saxa said. "You are welcome, of course, but I confess that I was not expecting to see you today."

"I was equally surprised yesterday, Lord Saxa," Tardus said. "But your visit reminded me that we were colleagues with similar interests which we might be able to cultivate together."

Hedia didn't recall ever meeting Tardus before, and if she had seen him casually in the Forum, he hadn't lingered in her memory. He would have merited the term "nondescript" were it not that his toga was hemmed with the broad purple stripe of a senator. He had the reputation of being not only superstitious but involved in kinds of magic that were discussed in secret if at all.

Hedia's smile was cold. She wasn't the one to talk, of course; not after the task she had given Anna.

"Well, I . . . ," Saxa said, his words stumbling as he tried to understand the situation. "I'm pleased that you're, ah, reacting in that fashion, Marcus Tardus, but in truth this isn't a very good time . . . that is—"

"I see that you're gathering for dinner," Tardus said, nodding to the guests. The two senators and Varus wore their togas, showing that this was a formal occasion. "No doubt you'll have private matters to discuss, so I'll take myself away. Perhaps another time."

"Why, yes," Saxa said gratefully. "I appreciate your understanding."

Priscus jumped as though he'd been cut with an overseer's whip . . . which, if the stories about him in his younger days were true, had indeed happened on occasion.

My dear sweet husband doesn't have a clue! thought Hedia with a mixture of affection, exasperation, and fear. There was definitely reason for fear if this weren't handled properly—and at once.

"We would be delighted to have you join us for dinner, Lord Tardus!" Hedia said brightly. Smiling as though she had just received the gift of eternal youth, she went on to the majordomo, "Agrippinus, have three more places set; Lady Alphena and I will sit upright in place of the third couch."

Lowering her voice, she continued, "And Agrippinus? Ask Lady Alphena to prepare for dinner. I'll be up in a moment to discuss jewelry with her. Please press upon her the urgency of the situation."

The majordomo strode from the entrance hall, calling sharply to underlings. Hedia hoped Agrippinus intended to speak to Alphena himself rather than leaving the unpleasant task to a junior who might not understand its importance.

The men were all looking at her. Well, that wasn't the sort of thing that made her nervous. Saxa and Varus were puzzled, but Priscus was obviously relieved.

Hedia expected Tardus to smirk at his successful throw of the dice, but instead he seemed numbly accepting. The trio of foreign servants were sharply interested in everything around them but particularly, it seemed to Hedia, in Varus and herself. She couldn't tell how old they were. In their fifties, she had guessed from a distance; but close up, what she saw in their eyes suggested they were older than that, and perhaps impossibly old.

"Dear, is that correct?" Saxa said, completely at sea now. "I'd understood that you wouldn't be joining us. And Alphena, well, Alphena never dines with the family."

"Indeed, it's time that our daughter becomes more comfortable in polite society," Hedia said. "And what better place than a meal with erudite friends, discussing fine points of literature?"

She continued to smile. On the walls of the hall were death masks of ancestors going back almost two hundred years, and by Venus!, some of those wax masks would be less obtuse than her husband was showing himself at the moment.

"Well, just as you say, dear," Saxa said. "Ah—"

"Take your guests to the dining room, my lord and husband," Hedia said gently. She wondered if her smile looked as brittle as it felt. "Lady Alphena and I will join you very shortly."

Leaving Manetho to take charge of chivvying the men to the outside dining area, Hedia herself strode briskly to the back stairs. These were intended for the servants, but Hedia needed to get to her daughter as quickly as possible. It wouldn't have done to rush up the main stairs ahead of three senators, and she certainly wasn't going to wait until they had shuffled in chatty, leisurely fashion to the couches set on the roof above the black-and-gold hall, with a good view of the central courtyard.

A quick-witted footman saw Hedia coming and sprinted ahead of her, bellowing up the back staircase in a Thracian accent, "Hop to, you wankers! Her ladyship's on her way!"

Hedia grinned wryly. She'd been announced in more gracious and mellifluous terms, but this had the merits of being short and extremely clear. When she got a moment to catch her breath, she would learn who the footman was and tell Agrippinus to promote him for initiative.

The stairs weren't clear when Hedia reached them, but servants who had been lounging there only moments before were scattering like a covey of quail. She lifted the skirts of her long tunic in both hands and trotted up.

Part of her was appalled to think of how embarrassing it would be if she tripped on her hem and broke her neck. Another part—the part that made her giggle as her slippers pattered on the plain brick steps—realized smugly that if she *did* break her neck, her own problems were over.

Alphena was leaning over the mezzanine railing, watching Tardus' entourage being escorted toward the kitchen. Hedia approached her from behind, swallowing her initial flash of irritation. Florina and a bevy of other maids fluttered around the girl, afraid to warn her that Hedia had arrived but obviously afraid of what would happen if they didn't say something. Agrippinus stood by the public stairs, bowing as Saxa and his guests passed in their stately fashion.

"Come, daughter," Hedia said in calm, cultured tones. "Let's get you ready for dinner so that their lordships don't feel that you're insulting them. Syra—"

She turned her head slightly. Her maid, as expected, stood at her elbow; she panted, probably more from nervousness than the exertion.

"—go to my suite and fetch my jewelry box. I'll pick out pieces for Lady Alphena while she's getting into her synthesis."

"I've set out the violet one, your ladyship," Florina said. "It would be *ever* so nice with a set of amethyst ear drops."

Hedia looked at the maid. She whined like a stray cat, but that was a good suggestion.

"Yes," she said. "I believe I have a pair that will work." Then, to Alphena, "Come dear. This is really quite important."

Alphena allowed herself to be guided back into her room by a gentle touch, though she looked back over her shoulder once. Hedia wasn't approaching the limits of her patience because she *couldn't* allow herself to lash out in these circumstances, but she was certainly finding the business trying.

The girl doesn't understand. I must remember that the girl doesn't understand.

"Mother, did you notice the servants with the senator who just came?" Alphena said.

Hedia had untied the simple sash as they entered the suite. Now she lifted the tunic over Alphena's head, ignoring the girl's squeak.

"Yes, dear," Hedia said. "Now, be quiet for a moment while I explain why the family needs you at dinner as soon as possible."

"I don't see why—" Alphena said, her voice muffled until Hedia flung the tunic toward a corner of the room.

"Be quiet!" Hedia repeated. "The senator who arrived uninvited is Marcus Tardus. He is not your father's friend. He—"

"But—"

"Be quiet!"

Florina and five other maids—unexpectedly junior to Florina, whom Alphena had suddenly chosen to make her permanent attendant—were holding the violet dinner dress and a variety of possible undergarments. They had no idea of how Lady Hedia would choose to display her daughter, and they were rightly worried at what would happen to them if they guessed wrong.

Alphena had flashed angry, but she had quickly controlled that. Now she radiated a mixture of concern and defiance.

She's learned to trust me, Hedia thought. *Thank Venus for* that *mercy.*

"Tardus announced that he would leave because he saw that your father and his senatorial friend wanted to have a private meeting," Hedia said. "Do you understand what that means?"

Alphena's mouth dropped open. "But that's crazy!" she said, showing— rather to her mother's surprise—that she did understand the threat. "Saxa wouldn't plot against the emperor. He'd *never* do that!"

"No, he wouldn't," Hedia agreed grimly, "but it's very hard to prove that you haven't done something. I prefer not to take that chance, so I invited Tardus to join us."

The notion of wealthy senators plotting to overthrow the emperor might not seem crazy to someone who didn't know Saxa personally; and the emperor most certainly *was* crazy on the subject of possible threats to his life and government. A whisper in the wrong ear—which could be any ear in Carce nowadays—could mean a visit from the German Bodyguard and a quick execution in the basement of their barracks.

"But me?" Alphena said. She wasn't protesting now, and her curiosity was reasonable.

"One moment," Hedia said. To the maid holding the black bandeau and briefs she said, "Do you have gray?"

The maid—all the maids—looked stricken.

"Never mind," Hedia snapped. "Syra, bring a set of mine, they'll do in a pinch. And bring Lucilla too. There isn't time to do the hair properly, but Lucilla can manage something."

"Your ladyship, they're here," Syra said. "The clothes too."

Hedia looked around in surprise. At least a dozen of her personal servants—the line extended out onto the walkway—waited with undergarments ranging from pale gray-blue to dark gray, plus two caskets of jewelry and apparently—this was beyond the doorway—wraps and stoles.

She chirped a laugh despite the tension. Her staff had instantly realized what Hedia had forgotten: Alphena's wardrobe contained *nothing* suitable for formal occasions except the silk dinner tunics that Abinnaeus had delivered the day before. Why, up until a moment ago the girl had been wearing a single knee-length tunic as though she were a field hand!

"Yes," Hedia said aloud. She pointed to the palest gray combination and said, "Those."

Maids began to dress the girl. Her staff had taken over from Alphena's. Florina seemed briefly to have considered arguing. That wouldn't have been a good idea, because Hedia would have welcomed a way to reduce tension.

"As for why you and I will be present," Hedia said, feeling herself relax as her staff transformed Alphena from hoyden to young lady, "well, perhaps we needn't be, but this isn't a situation that I want to be blasé about. Nobody has ever imagined that I give a hoot about any government official—"

She paused, considered, and went on with a wicked grin, "Except in some cases for what they have between their legs. And you, my dear, have the reputation of being even less political than I am."

"Oh," said Alphena as the synthesis drifted over her like a violet cloud. "I guess I see."

Maids cinched the thin silk under her bosom. She looked at Hedia with a perfectly straight face and said, "I'll be sure to talk to Tardus about the fine points of swordsmanship, then."

Hedia's expression froze. Then she realized the girl was joking and burst into laughter.

"Here," she said, extending her arms to Alphena. "Hold me and raise your feet one at a time so that they can put your slippers on."

The girl's feet were too wide for Hedia's shoes, but she had a pair of black cutwork sandals which would do. *I really must get her properly outfitted, to-morrow if possible!*

"Then as soon as Florina—"

The maid had done a creditable job in caring for her mistress, given her limited resources. Hedia was making a point of not denigrating her in front of the other servants.

"—puts in the amethyst ear drops, we'll be ready to go."

Though Hedia hadn't expected to eat with her husband tonight, she had dressed to greet the guests. That was a blessing, though she had enough experience with throwing on—or throwing back on—formal clothing in a hurry that she could have managed.

Alphena raised her other foot. "But Mother?" she said. "Those men with Tardus? I've seen them before."

"Yes," Hedia said, frowning slightly at the return of a matter of no impor-tance. "They were with him in the theater. I noticed them at the time."

She stepped back and looked at her daughter, then beamed. "You look *lovely*, dear. Just lovely! Now, let's join the men."

Alphena followed without protest, but as they reached the main staircase she said, "Mother, I've seen them somewhere else than the theater. And I don't think I like them."

Alphena was excited to be dressed up like this—like a fine lady. She wouldn't have admitted that to a soul, certainly not to her stepmother and only in the very depths of her heart to herself, but she knew it was true.

"I don't see why I have to wear such a *long* tunic, though," she muttered to Hedia as they walked arm-in-arm down the mezzanine corridor toward the main stairs.

"Tush, dear," Hedia said easily. "Be thankful that you're not a man and having to wear a toga. And besides—"

She glanced to the side, assessing Alphena with the dispassionate preci-sion of a trainer judging a coffle of gladiators.

"—you look quite nice in a long tunic. You move gracefully, and the sway of the fabric sets that off."

Alphena glowed with pleasure, though that embarrassed her. "Ah . . . ," she said. "Ah, thank you, Mother."

They reached the staircase. There was a flurry of motion within the cloud of servants surrounding them. Two maids snatched the front hem of

Hedia's synthesis—it was a white as pure as sunlight on marble—and lifted it slightly as they skipped up the steps ahead of her; two more raised the back.

Oh! thought Alphena. She hadn't considered the difficulties of going up or down stairs in a garment that broke at her ankles. *I could have tripped and fallen! Oh, gods, that would have been awful!*

Then she wondered if Corylus would be dining with them. That thought made her so angry that she glared. She wasn't really looking at anything, but one of the maids lifting the front of her skirt began to whimper. The girl didn't stumble or let the fabric slip, but the sound brought Alphena back to an awareness of her surroundings.

Servants had set poles supporting vertical wicker lattices on the west side of the dining alcove. Lamps would be necessary before the meal was over, but for the moment the shades were keeping the sun out of the eyes of the diners on the central, west-facing couch. Priscus, the chief guest, reclined there, and a place for Tardus had been added below him.

Saxa was at the head of the left-hand couch, adjacent to Priscus. Below him were Varus and the teacher, Pandareus.

Corylus wasn't present. There was no reason he should have been. It was just a possibility, an obvious thing to wonder about, that was all.

There was no bench on the right end. Instead, two chairs had been placed there with little side tables to hold the dishes or cup that the diner wasn't using at the moment.

Alphena looked at the arrangement. *Because I'm a girl!*

"I prefer to recline at dinner," she said to the dining room steward. She didn't know his name; he was plump and had a touch of red in his thinning hair. "Set me a place on the couch beside Lord Tardus."

"My dear?" said her father, looking up with a startled-rabbit expression. "I think you'd, that is—"

"Nonsense, dear heart," Hedia said cheerfully to her husband. "There's nothing improper about a lady reclining at dinner. I just prefer to sit up-right."

Turning to the steward she said, "Borysthenes, remove one of the chairs and set a place for my daughter on the couch."

Servants were already bustling; when Lady Hedia gave directions, you obeyed or you wished you had. To the table generally she said, "I'm sure their lordships will be pleased to be joined by youth and beauty."

Priscus, twisting his body to better look toward the two women, chuckled. "If I were a great deal younger, your ladyship," he said, "I'd be tempted to show you just how much I would appreciate that opportunity. Younger or drunker."

Hedia laughed like a string of little silver chimes. "Perhaps a trifle younger, Marcus dear," she said.

Alphena settled onto the end of the couch, what would have been the middle couch if there had been the normal three. She took most of her meals in her suite, sitting upright. She'd only complained because her father had directed her to sit instead of reclining, and now she realized—as an instant's thought should have told her—that it was her stepmother, not Saxa, who had decided that.

She'd seen an insult where there hadn't been one. She *had* to stop doing that and not pick unnecessary fights.

Alphena grinned. She wasn't sure what the vision in the theater meant, but it seemed likely that it involved enough fighting for even the most pugnacious of young ladies.

The servants had finished washing the guests' feet, and the first round of wine was being served from the mixing table. "We're having it three to one, Hedia," said Priscus with heavy gallantry. "I fear that if it were stronger, I'd find myself too ensorcelled by your beauty to remember the proprieties."

Hedia and—a moment later—Saxa laughed. Tardus sipped his wine and said, "You mention sorcery, Marcus Priscus. Were you in the Pompeian Theater for our host's gift, *The Conquest of Lusitania by Hercules*? For it certainly seemed to me that the impresario was a magician to have achieved those effects. Quite marvelous, didn't you all think?"

Priscus turned to look at his neighbor on the couch. "I wasn't present, no," he said, "but I've certainly heard enthusiastic descriptions. I suppose—"

He gestured toward the teacher with a broad grin.

"—that the impresario was one of you clever Greeks, eh Pandareus, my friend?"

"So I've been told," Pandareus said blandly.

"He was indeed, Lord Priscus," Varus said, sounding calmly interested. "Sometimes I wish I were more of an engineer so that I could understand such wonders, but my talents seem to be limited to literature. And even in literature I'm only a spectator, I have learned."

He smiled, but Alphena saw momentary wistfulness in her brother's expression.

Alphena didn't know anything about rhetoric, but she understood duel-ing better than anyone else present. As servants placed a tray with deviled eggs and olives on the little table in the U of the diners, she said, "I noticed the attendants with you during the performance, Lord Tardus. If I noticed cor-rectly, they're with you tonight as well. I wonder where you found them?"

Tardus turned his head in surprise. "How interesting that you should ask, Lady Alphena," he said. He coughed onto the back of his hand, gathering time to respond.

Alphena didn't smile, but she felt fiercely triumphant. *I pinked you that time, didn't I, you old weasel!*

Tardus had been pushing her father to talk about something that he didn't want to. Indeed, Alphena wasn't sure that Saxa had any more knowl-edge of what had happened in the theater than Agrippinus, who'd been here in the house at the time. Perhaps Tardus was reacting to the embarrassing visit her father and brother had made to him the day before, but perhaps there was more to his curiosity.

Regardless, Saxa was her father. She wasn't going to let this old man badger him when simply asking a blunt question would change the dynamic of the bout. Nobody expected perfect deportment and courtesy from Saxa's boyish daughter, after all.

"Well, strictly speaking, I met them when they arrived here in Carce eight days ago," Tardus said, looking over his shoulder at Alphena. His gaze had a hard fixity that she hadn't expected from so old a man. "But as to where they're from, they say 'the Western Isles.'"

"The Hesperides?" Saxa asked, cocking his head with interest. "What language do they speak, if I may ask?"

"They speak Greek to me," Tardus said. He spoke with studied care, quite different from the aggressiveness with which he had begun the discussion. "I suppose they have some language of their own, but I haven't heard them speaking it. And as for the Hesperides—that isn't their name for their home. Perhaps their 'Western Isles' are what Hesiod meant when he spoke of the Hesperides, but apart from summoning him from the dead, I don't see how we could be sure."

"And even then," said Pandareus, "we couldn't be sure without teaching him modern geography first. In any event, I don't think—"

He smiled faintly. Alphena decided that her brother's teacher was joking, which she hadn't been sure of at the start.

"—that I would choose to start my discussion there if I had the opportunity. I would be much more interested in details of how he created his masterpieces. The style of the *Theogony* is quite different, it seems to me, from that of *The Works and Days*; more different than I would have expected to come from the pen—the throat, rather—of a single man."

Priscus and Varus both laughed; Saxa blinked, then grinned weakly. Tardus was frowning, which was understandable, but there still seemed to be something odd about his demeanor.

The discussion turned to how much Hesiod and Homer knew about geography. Tardus listened glumly.

Alphena grinned. She supposed the situation should please her: her mother's plan to convince Tardus that this was simply a literary evening was a resounding success. She was utterly, bone-deep, bored, however.

She took an olive from the dish, then paused and looked at it more closely. A man's face had been carved into it. She popped the olive into her mouth—it was stuffed with anchovy paste, a startling but tasty combination—and picked another one, green this time. The features were female.

"I wonder, Marcus Tardus?" Hedia said in a break as the fish course came in. "Are your Hesperians nobles from their own country who should be dining here instead of down with the servants?"

"I don't . . . ," Tardus said, clearly taken aback. "That is, I believe they are priests or wise men rather than, ah, nobles. From what they say. But they didn't wish to call attention to themselves."

Are you still pleased that you blackmailed your way into this dinner, Lord Tardus? Alphena wondered. She took what looked like a small crab, complete to the stalked eyes; it proved to be a thin pastry shell stuffed with a spicy fish paste.

"If I may ask, Lord Tardus?" Pandareus said. "You suggest that your guests are the western equivalent of the Magi. The Magi ruled Persia until Darius broke their power in a coup, and even now under the Arsacids they have a great deal of authority. They are certainly as worthy of a place at Gaius Saxa's table as—"

He curled his hand inward.

"—a professor of rhetoric."

Pandareus had done full justice to the eggs and olives, and he was now attacking a seeming mullet molded from minced crabmeat. Alphena decided that his lanky frame was a result of privation rather than ascetic philosophy.

"I don't know what political arrangements exist in the Western Isles!" Tardus said. "The, the . . . my guests, that is, they said that they would prefer to eat with the servants. They didn't expect to arouse comment, as I understand it. They've come to Carce to observe our customs, and they hoped to do that without their presence affecting those observations."

The conversation drifted back to literature when Saxa mentioned Plato's conceit of a Scythian visitor to comment on Athenian society. Tardus ate morosely without adding much to the discussion of fictitious Brahmins, Magi, and Egyptians.

Alphena didn't speak either. She neither knew nor cared anything about the books the men were talking about; and besides, she was puzzling over the westerners themselves.

Alphena knew them from somewhere; she'd felt that when she saw them in the theater. That didn't seem possible if they had arrived so recently in Carce, though; and if Tardus was lying—why should he be on a question like that?—then it still didn't explain why she had *no* recollection of where she had seen the trio.

The talk droned on. The men might as well have been chattering in Persian for how much Alphena could understand of it.

She thought of the theater and her vision of a man tearing his way through the sparkling city. She thought of the way he had looked at her, and the recognition she had felt in his gaze as well.

Alphena ate mechanically, and thought. She *almost* could remember.

"I SEE YOU APPROVE of Father's cook, master," Varus said in a low voice to Pandareus, who had just taken another fig-pecker stuffed with a paste of figs and walnuts before being grilled.

"My dear student," Pandareus said, pausing with the skewer just short of his mouth. "For a man who can't always afford sausage with his porridge, this meal is the very ambrosia of the gods."

He paused, pursing his lips in thought. "I misspoke," he said. "This meal would be the true ambrosia to anyone, whatever his background."

Varus smiled. The meal had been both pleasant and stimulating, which was a surprise after Tardus had invited himself to join them. Not that Tardus would have been an improper guest under normal circumstances, given his background and interests, but these circumstances were scarcely normal.

He glanced at his stepmother, sitting primly across from him as she nibbled a quail drumstick in which the bone had been replaced by a breadstick and the meat chopped with spices. Thank Jupiter for Hedia! Varus himself hadn't understood the threat until Priscus whispered an explanation while they mounted the stairs together.

"I am a collector of objects which are supposed to have, ah, *spiritual* properties, Gaius Saxa," Tardus said. "I suppose you are aware of that?"

He means "magical properties," Varus translated. But magic could be seen as a means of threatening an emperor who was reputed to be something of a magician and astrologer himself, whereas "spiritual" had no dangerous connotations.

"I believe many of Carce's older families have objects from the time when the city was rising to greatness," Saxa said. His tone was more cautious than Varus would have expected. His father probably didn't know what was going on, but at least he was beginning to realize that there was cause for concern. "I'm not surprised that the Sempronii Tardi do. We of the Family Alphenus do also."

"Yes, I had heard that," Tardus said. "I believe that you have in your collection a murrhine tube, do you not? About as big around as my thumb?"

Pandareus had reached for another fig-pecker. Now he withdrew his hand and looked sharply from Tardus to Saxa.

"I do, yes," said Saxa. "It was sent to me recently by Gnaeus Rusticus, whom I have been appointed to succeed as governor of Lusitania. He, ah, said he knew that I was interested in such things, so he was giving it to me in a gesture of goodwill and thankfulness that I was allowing him to come home."

"Might I see the object, if you please?" Tardus said. "I have a fondness for murrhine myself and I would like to observe the structure of the grain."

"I suppose . . . ," Saxa began. Then, as forcefully as he ever got, "Yes, of course. Simplex—"

One of the footmen standing near his couch nodded.

"—go to the library and tell Alexandros to bring me the murrhine tube from Rusticus. Hurry now!"

"Have you decided to go to Lusitania in person, Gaius?" Priscus said. Varus wondered if he was trying to change the subject. "I ask because it has the reputation of being a challenging post, all mountains and mule tracks; and you're no more of the active, outdoor type than I am myself."

He laughed and patted his belly. He had been eating just as enthusiastically as Pandareus had, and he'd been drinking quite a lot of the wine that the teacher had been avoiding.

Saxa smiled weakly. "In truth," he said, "I've been considering governing through a vicar, Quinctius Rufus. A very solid man, you know; a Knight of Carce who has served as legate of a legion in Upper Germany. But I suppose Rusticus wouldn't have known that."

"I do hope you'll stay in Carce, dear lord and master," Hedia said. "My heart would waste away if you were to go into exile off on the shore of Ocean."

She sounded sincere. Varus, though by no means a man of the world, was at least knowledgeable enough to know to doubt anything his stepmother might say to a man.

"I've requested an appointment with the emperor to discuss the matter," Saxa said. "Of course his will—that is, the will of the people, expressed through the emperor—is paramount, but I'm hoping that, well . . ."

He fluttered his hands with a wan grin.

"As Marcus Priscus says, I'm not well suited for clambering across the spines of mountains on muleback, which I gather would be required for any official in Lusitania."

Alexandros, the chief librarian, appeared, leading two attendants who carried a narrow wooden casket about the length of a woman's forearm. The container's weight didn't require two men to carry it, but the librarian's rank did.

Corylus would like the box. He would know the kind of wood it was, too, with that lovely swirling grain.

Alexandros was a corpulent man, and rushing up the stairs from the library had set him to wheezing. As he approached, Borysthenes signaled to a pair of his juniors who snatched the table holding the tray of fowls out of the space in front of the diners.

The librarian was an impeccable servant, with a good grounding in literature and a flawless memory regarding where things were filed. The only way to locate a scroll was to remember where in which basket it had been stored. This was a matter of some difficulty for Saxa's library of over three hundred books, but Priscus was reputed to own nearly a thousand; his librarian must be *very* good.

"Your lordship," said Alexandros, bowing, "we have brought the curio which you requested."

The two attendants knelt before Saxa. The librarian lifted the lid of the casket—it was separate rather than hinged—to display the blue-and-yellow crystals of a murrhine tube as long as a large man's thumb and as thick as two thumbs together; the hollow center was only half that diameter.

Saxa touched the tube, then gestured toward Tardus on the central couch. The attendants shifted to face the guest.

"Where does your librarian come from?" Pandareus whispered, his lips close to Varus' ear.

Varus turned and whispered, "He's a Greek from Gaza, I believe. From somewhere in Syria, at any rate."

"Ah," said Pandareus. "He's Jewish, unless I'm badly mistaken. His trying to pass for Greek explains that odd accent."

Varus hadn't noticed anything unusual about the librarian's accent, either the Latin he spoke to members of the family or the Greek he rattled off to other servants from the East. He didn't doubt Pandareus' assessment, though. The subtleties of speech were as much a rhetorician's stock in trade as was the literature of which rhetoric was a branch.

Tardus used his thumb and forefinger to lift the tube from its velvet-lined container. The murrhine had a soapy sheen in the lamplight. The material came from Britannia, generally worked into the form of whimsies like this tube.

Occasionally traders penetrated the interior of the island and convinced the savages to turn murrhine into cups or tabletops for which the aristocrats of Carce would pay astronomical amounts, but that was a difficult and dangerous business. The Britons were headhunters, as their Gallic kinsmen had been two generations before. Caesar's raid into the island hadn't been enough to civilize them out of the practice.

A warrior who took the head of a foreign trader didn't have to worry about the victim's family returning the favor before long. The difficulties that caused for commerce weren't a pressing concern to the island's tattooed savages.

"That's odd, Gaius," Priscus said, staring at the object which the man beside him held. "Bring a lamp closer. The ends—"

He pointed, though he didn't attempt to take the tube from Tardus.

"The one end is cut and polished, you can see the way they radiused it. But the other seems to have been melted, doesn't it? Cut with a hot knife, but how hot to melt stone?"

"Whose tomb did this come from, Gaius Saxa?" Tardus said, looking from the murrhine to his host.

"I don't know that it *did* come from a tomb," Saxa said. He drew his lips in, then let them out again.

"Rusticus said some of his soldiers dug into a cairn on a headland overlooking the Ocean," he continued with an uncomfortable expression. "They were looking for gold, but all they found was splinters of bone and this. It may be that it was a tomb, but a very ancient one. They brought it to Rusticus, and he gave it to me."

"I see," said Tardus. He weighed the tube in his hands before him, but he didn't seem to be looking at it.

As best Varus could tell in the lamplight, the old senator was lost in another world. His mouth seemed to go slack momentarily. *Is he having a fit?*

Tardus roused himself abruptly. He blinked twice and his body trembled.

"Well!" he said. He didn't return the murrhine tube to its box. "Gaius Saxa, thank you for returning in so lavish a fashion the hospitality I showed when you and Lord Varus visited me. I'm not a young man any longer and I wasn't given to late hours even when I was, so I think I'll take my leave now."

"A colleague of your learning is always welcome, Marcus Tardus," Saxa said in obvious relief. "Perhaps soon we can exchange visits in a more, well, regular fashion."

Tardus rose to a sitting position on the back of the couch, then stood. He still held the tube. Varus saw his teacher's expression harden as he watched what was happening.

"If I may, Saxa," Tardus said, "I'll borrow this tube for a day or two. I'd like to compare it with—"

"Lord Saxa!" Pandareus said. Varus was as startled as if a squeak of protest had come from the carved olive he was lifting to his mouth. "I know it isn't my place to speak, but I would appreciate it—"

"It most certainly *isn't* the place of a snivelling Greek to inject himself into a discussion between senators of Carce!" Tardus said. He bent his hands to his breast, still clutching the murrhine.

"Father, you *mustn't* let go of that thing," Alphena said in a carrying tone. "I have an idea for the most darling little ornament for my hair. I'm becoming—"

She rose gracefully to her feet. Standing, she blocked Tardus' natural path from the dining alcove.

"—very much the fine lady, don't you think?"

She fluffed her hair with the fingertips of her left hand. *She really is quite attractive*, Varus realized in surprise.

Alphena reached for the murrhine tube; Tardus hunched back, scowling fiercely. Priscus was leaning forward to whisper to Saxa on the adjacent couch.

Varus wondered if he should stand. *Is Alphena going to kick him in the crotch? No, that's more the sort of thing that Mother—*

Hedia rose and stepped forward from her chair, her right hand outstretched. Alexandros and his attendants slid out of her way like cork dolls bobbing in the wake of a trireme.

"I'm so sorry, Marcus Tardus," she said in a cheery voice. "I know you've heard that our daughter is a shameless tomboy and terribly spoiled, but my lord and I love her very much. I'm afraid I'll have to take the bauble now. Perhaps when fashions change, dear Alphena will allow you to borrow it."

Tardus stiffened, then sagged and opened his hands. Varus knew from experience that his stepmother had a stare like a dagger point when she chose to use it.

Hedia took the tube, then replaced it on its velvet bed and closed the box. Alphena stepped aside. Tardus scuttled past her, then walked briskly toward the stairs with his waiting attendants falling in ahead and behind him. The remaining diners watched him go in silence.

Hedia embraced Alphena. "We *do* love you, daughter," she said. "You are *such* a clever young lady!"

CORYLUS PICKED UP the cornelwood staff that leaned beside the door during daytime. When he went out at night, he carried it.

Carce at night was similar to the forests on the German side of the Rhine. A healthy young man who kept his eyes and ears open probably wouldn't have any trouble; but if trouble *did* crop up, you'd best have something besides your bare hands available to deal with it.

"Sure you wouldn't like me to come along, lad?" Pulto said. "I wouldn't mind stretching my legs."

That was a lie. Corylus knew that the old servant's knees had been giving him trouble, and the last thing he needed was to lace his hobnailed sandals back on and tramp over the stone-paved streets with a youth who wasn't ready to settle in for the night.

"Keep your wife company, old friend," he said. "I'm just going to sit in Demetrius' yard and relax for a bit. I've got a declamation to work on, you know."

"Wouldn't you—" Anna said.

Corylus raised his left hand palm out to stop her. "Little mother," he said, "I'm not hungry. If I get hungry, I'll have a sausage roll at the Cockerel on the corner. Don't worry, you two."

He slipped out the door quickly. Back in the suite, his servants were arguing about the cook shop's sausages. Pulto held that regardless of what Spica, the owner, put in them, they tasted better than a lot of what he or the boy either one had eaten on the Danube.

A pair of beggars were huddled on the second-floor landing. They were regulars; they scrunched to the side when they saw who was coming down and one of them, an old soldier, croaked, "Bless you, Master Corylus."

Corylus passed with a nod. Anna had probably seen to it that the fellow had eaten today. He was a former Batavian auxiliary whose Latin was still slurred with the marshes at the mouth of the Rhine; but he'd been places that Pulto and the Old Master had been, and he wouldn't go hungry while scraps remained in the suite.

Corylus stepped into the street and took his bearings. Someone moved in the shadows opposite; a quick waggle of the staff let the moonlight shimmer on the pale hardwood. The movement ceased.

Smiling, Corylus strode westward, toward the center of Carce. Half a block down, a large jobbing nursery filled a site large enough for an apartment block. A crew was unloading root-balled rosebushes from an ox-drawn wagon.

It would have been an easy enough task if the roses had been pruned back severely, but wealthy customers didn't want to wait till next year for their plantings to bloom. By definition, anybody who owned a house with a garden in Carce was wealthy. The workmen were cursing as canes whipped and caught them unexpectedly as they moved the bushes.

"Where's Demetrius?" Corylus said as he approached.

The man on his side of the tailgate turned his head and snarled, "We're closed! Come back in the bloody morning!"

He was a new purchase. The thorn slash across his forehead was still oozing despite his attempt to blot it with the sleeve of his tunic.

"You stupid sod, that's Master Corylus!" his partner said. "Do you want the back flayed off you too? Go on back, sir. The master's working on the accounts back in the shed, like usual."

Corylus walked through the crowded lot, feeling the tension recede. Not disappear; it was still waiting out in the night. But the presence of bushes and saplings hedged him away from the unseen dangers, the way they had insulated him from the pressures of Carce when he first came here to take classes under Pandareus of Athens.

He wasn't a peasant who grew up in a rural hamlet: the military bases of his youth were crowded, boisterous, and brutal. Legionaries lived as tightly together as the poor on the top floors of tenements in Carce.

But the total number of people gathered into this one city had stunned Corylus. The entire army which guarded the frontiers of the Empire was about three hundred thousand men, including the auxiliaries who were not citizens. There were far more residents in Carce than that.

A single lamp burned in the office, one end of the shed along the back of the lot where tools and shade plants were stored. Demetrius, a Syrian Greek, was usually there; Corylus suspected he slept in the office occasionally. He had married his wife while they both were slaves, but with freedom and wealth she had become increasingly concerned about status and appearances. Demetrius simply loved plants and having his hands in dirt, which made time spent in his luxurious apartment a strain.

"Granus?" Demetrius called. "Have you got those bushes—"

"It's just me visiting," Corylus said as he stepped through the doorway.

Demetrius grinned over the writing desk at which he worked standing. Two clerks were reading aloud invoices written in ink on potsherds; he was jotting the totals down on papyrus.

"Oh, you're always welcome, Publius," Demetrius said. "Say, I've got some apple grafts I'd like you to cast an eye over. I didn't have a chance to see them when they were delivered, and I'm not sure about the technique. They're end-butted on the twigs. You've got the best eye for how a tree's doing that I've ever seen."

I should, Corylus thought. *My mother was a hazel sprite.*

Aloud he said, "I'll take a look, sure. I just wanted to sit with something green for a while and work on a declamation. Is that all right?"

"Any time, boy, any time," Demetrius said cheerfully. "Say, you wouldn't like a pomegranate tree at a good price, would you? I had an order for six, but there was only room for five in the garden when I delivered them and they sent one back. You could have it for my cost."

Corylus laughed. "I don't think it'd fit on a third-floor balcony, my friend," he said. "It's a bit crowded with potted herbs as it is."

"Now, don't turn it down till you see it," Demetrius said. "Pomegranates need to be root bound to bear best, so it doesn't take up as much room as you'd think. And the pots are nice glazed work, blue with birds and flowers. One of them'd dress your apartment up a treat!"

"Sorry, Demetrius," Corylus said. "Where's the apples?"

"On the west side of the lot," Demetrius said, gesturing. Ever hopeful, he added, "And the pomegranate's there too. I'll bet she'd fit fine, boy."

Corylus made his way along the paths winding through the nursery stock. Demetrius brought only what he had under immediate contract into the city. Even so, his lot was stuffed to capacity.

He imagined Anna hauling enough water for a tree up to the third floor. Well, she would organize it as she did the household water already; other residents of the building, generally young women having problems with romance or with the results of romance, did the work that Anna's arthritis didn't permit her to accomplish herself. Corylus didn't care what sort of charms and potions Anna provided in return, and Pulto didn't want to know.

There were four grafted trees. The trunks were probably crabapples and appeared healthy, and the grafts appeared to have been done well also. Demetrius mitered twigs onto branches, but these mortise cuts were clean, tight, and tied with strips of inner bark in a thoroughly satisfactory fashion.

"I wonder how the gardener would like it if they cut his hands off and tied somebody else's onto the stumps?" said the woman suddenly standing beside him.

Corylus didn't jump, but his head snapped around quickly. She was short, no more than five feet tall, and remarkably buxom. She wore a shift that was probably red or blue—moonlight didn't bring out the color—but was so thin that her breasts might as well have been bare.

"Ah, mistress?" he said. *How did she creep up on me?*

Then he realized. "Oh," he said. "You're a dryad. Of one of these trees?"

He gestured to the apples, looking furtively at her plump wrists. They seemed unblemished.

Always before when Corylus had seen tree spirits, it was in the wake of great magic. Demetrius' nursery was a simple business concern, unlike the back garden at Saxa's house where the wizard Nemastes had worked spells that might have drowned the world in fire.

"Them?" the sprite sneered. "Well, I like *that*! I'm not one of those drabs. I'm sure they'll be giving themselves airs whenever they come out of that butchery, but they'll still only be apples. *I* am a pomegranate."

She threw her head back. The movement didn't exactly lift her breasts—that would have required a derrick—but it made them wobble enthusiastically.

"Of course, Punica, I beg your pardon," Corylus said. There at the end of the line of apples in terra-cotta transfer urns was a pomegranate tree in a fine glazed bowl, decorated with a garden scene. The pot was indeed very nice, but it was much smaller than Corylus had expected. The tree looked positively top-heavy.

Oh. He blushed.

"I was glad you came to see me," Punica said. "I've been lonely."

She put her arm around his waist; he shifted sideways, recovering their previous separation. He cleared his throat and said, "I'm surprised to see you. That is, I don't usually see, well . . ."

He made a circular gesture with his left hand, the one that didn't hold his staff.

"It's what you're wearing," the sprite said. "What's in the glass."

She leaned forward and twitched the thong around Corylus' neck, bringing the amulet out from under his tunic.

"Not the hazelnut," she said. "The other thing. And *I* wouldn't care to be wearing it, I promise you; though since you're half-hazel too, I suppose you're all right."

"What?" said Corylus. He lifted the bead—it was the size of the last joint of his thumb—up to the quarter moon. He knew he was being silly as soon as he did that: the glass had barely shown internal shadows against the full sun, and now it was as black as a river pebble.

He lowered the amulet. "What is it inside, Punica?" he asked.

She shrugged impressively. "I told you I didn't like it," she said, moving closer again. "That's all I want to know about it. I like you, though, Corylus. Why don't you just take off—"

She reached for the thong again. Corylus caught her hand and lowered it firmly to her side.

"I don't think so, Punica," he said. "I—maybe I'll come back. But right now, I have to get home."

"Oh, must you go?" she called as he squirmed between potted oleanders on one side and a planter of fragrant parsley on the other.

"Another time," he murmured over his shoulder. He was old enough to have learned that nothing a man said on these occasions was going to be sufficient, so you might as well stop with bare politeness. He didn't strictly *owe* Punica even that, except as to another living being; which Corylus believed should be enough to demand courtesy.

The crew which had unloaded the wagon was in the office when Corylus returned there. Demetrius had sponged the injured slave's forehead clean and was looking at it. The jagged tear didn't seem serious without the wash of blood, though the fellow would probably have a scar. He hadn't been much of a beauty to begin with.

"The apples are going to be fine, Demetrius," Corylus said. "Did you buy them from a new grower?"

"No, I got a Gallic arborist myself, a freeman, and I hadn't seen his grafts before," the nurseryman said. "Ah—you slipped a girl in, sir?"

Corylus understood the question, though it gave him a shock to hear it. "That's all right, Demetrius," he answered with forced calm. The workman must have heard him—and heard Punica as well, which meant the glass bead on his breast really did have power. "There's no hole in your fence. But just put it out of your mind, all right?"

"Sure, lad," Demetrius said, relaxing a little. "It's no problem, only I'd like to know if, you know, it comes up again."

Corylus cleared his throat. "I looked at the pomegranate too," he said, "and I think I will take it. But not for me. Senator Gaius Alphenus Saxa has a house in the Carina. Do you know where it is?"

"I can learn," Demetrius said. "I don't believe he's bought from me in the past."

"He's been letting me use his gym," Corylus explained, though in fact he wasn't sure that Saxa even knew his son was letting a friend use the training facility; certainly he didn't care. "A pear tree in his back garden died. I thought I'd give him the pomegranate as a little thank you."

"I can get in a nice pear tree in forty-eight hours," Demetrius said. "And if you're worried about the price—"

Corylus stopped him with a smile and a gesture. "I'm not," he said truthfully, "but I've taken a liking to that pomegranate. Only—plant it in the ground, will you? I think it'll be more comfortable if its roots have a chance to spread out."

Demetrius shrugged. "It won't bear as well," he said, "but I don't suppose I'm going to change *your* mind about how to plant trees. Sure, I'll send it over in the morning. Just one tree, Bello and Granus can carry it on a hand-barrow so we don't have to wait for nightfall to use a wagon."

"Send the bill to me," Corylus said as he started toward the front gate. "I'll clear it on the first of the month."

He wondered how Punica and Persica would get along. They'd squabble— the spirits of fruit trees tended to be self-centered and quarrelsome, in his experience—but he thought they'd both be happier than they would be alone.

Corylus began to whistle as he crossed the street. He was ready to sleep now.

Two men were running toward him; from the way one clutched his cloak to his side, he was using it to hide a sword—illegal to carry in the city and a bad sign anywhere except on the frontier. Corylus paused and put his back to the wall.

"Lad, is that you?" Pulto called hoarsely.

"Right!" Corylus said, relaxing again. He recognized the other man as a courier from Saxa's household. "I'm glad it's you."

"Well, turn right around," Pulto said. "There's trouble at the senator's house and Lord Varus said to bring you!"

CHAPTER VIII

Pandareus wanted to leave by the alley after dinner, saying it would be shorter by two blocks for him to get home, so Varus walked his teacher into the back garden. To his surprise, Alphena came with them.

By now he wasn't surprised that none of the servants followed them into the garden, though Varus hadn't felt the sense of unease that the staff claimed to. He wondered whether the problem had been a single nervous footman worrying himself twitchy and infecting his hundreds of fellows with fear of nothing.

Alphena stood arms akimbo as they entered the garden and glared at the surviving fruit tree. Varus looked at her with lips pursed, but whatever had brought that on seemed to be satisfied when nothing had happened after a moment or two.

"I'll stand outside, your lordships," said the doorman on duty. "I'll leave the lantern—or would you rather I take it into the alley, your lordships?"

"Take it with you," Varus said before it struck him that his sister might not find the moonlight as adequate as he did. *Well, if that's the case, Alphena has never had trouble making her opinion known. . . .*

Instead she hugged her arms around herself, then smiled wanly. "I don't know what was going on at dinner," she said. "I was hoping one of you could tell me."

"For somebody who didn't understand," Varus said, "you certainly re-acted quickly enough. Quicker than I did, anyway."

He shook his head, feeling disgusted with himself. "Actually, I don't think I would have thought to demand the, well, artifact myself if I'd had all night. My brain doesn't work that way, I guess."

"All I knew," Alphena said, "is that Tardus wanted to take the tube and you—"

She was looking at Pandareus.

"—didn't want him to. Is there something you want to do with it, ah, master?"

As soon as Tardus and his attendants had gone down the staircase, Hedia gave the chest with the murrhine tube to Alexandros to return to its place in the library. Saxa had a collection of similar curios among the baskets of scrolls, as well as busts of those he considered the wisest men of past ages.

Along with Solon, who gave laws to Athens; Lycurgus, who gave laws to Sparta; and Socrates, who chose to die to uphold his philosophy, there was a bust of Periander, the famously ruthless Tyrant of Corinth. Varus had always considered that an odd choice for his gentle father.

"I'm sorry, no," Pandareus said. "I'm not a magician—"

He quirked a smile toward Varus, who felt his cheeks start to warm. Fortunately the moonlight wouldn't show his blushing. *I'm not a magician either!*

"—and scholarship doesn't take me beyond the obvious, that the object is very old and probably came from a tomb. I was reacting to the fact that Lord Tardus wanted it very badly; and though I don't have any idea why, I had—I have—the feeling that his purposes would not be to the benefit of anyone I could consider a friend."

Varus nodded in understanding. He said, "And Father wouldn't have refused a fellow senator simply because a foreigner—no offense meant, master."

"None taken, my pupil," Pandareus said with a nod of deference.

"A foreigner, even a very learned foreigner as Father knows you to be," Varus said, "didn't approve. But the wishes of his own daughter certainly did matter."

He shook his head again. "Or his son," he said. "Except that his son wasn't quick enough off the mark to intervene."

Alphena looked at him with an expression he couldn't read, then hugged him. Varus stood stiffly. He didn't believe there was anything his sister could have done that would have surprised him more.

"Dear Gaius," she said, stepping away again. "I don't think you could have accomplished anything no matter how hard you tried. You've just been so *nice* to everybody all your life. But I've been a screaming bitch often enough that Father would listen to me."

She smiled wryly. She wasn't boasting, which was also a surprise. Alphena had always seemed proud of the way she made people cringe when she was in a bad temper.

"Well . . . ," he said. "Thank you, sister."

Varus smiled. He'd never really approved of Alphena's behavior—not that he would ever have said anything—but her past behavior was paying dividends. Her unladylike practice with a sword had saved his life when she stood between him and an army of fire demons.

"Did either of you notice the men who came with Tardus?" Alphena said. "They were the same ones who'd been with him in the theater when the city appeared. I mean, three of them were."

Pandareus was answering. Varus heard the teacher's voice, but the words didn't seem to have meaning. He felt himself drifting into the fog that separated him from the Sibyl's dreamworld. He tried to speak, to warn his companions, but grayness closed in before he could force words out through his throat.

There was laughter in the fog, silvery and cheerful. Varus felt his heart jump as if he had heard a scream of fury, though there had been nothing frightening in the sound itself.

His smile was bitter for a moment, then warmed into humor. Quite a number of frightening things had happened recently. He couldn't help being afraid, but he could simply walk on regardless.

He had no choice, after all. Not if he were to help save the world. He thought of the monster he had seen engulfing Carce.

The fog brightened; in another step, he burst out into sunlight. The old woman stood on the edge of an escarpment, holding a hank of yarn and a pair of bronze shears. She turned toward Varus.

"Greetings, Sibyl," he said. He cleared his throat and went on, "Why have you called me here, your ladyship?"

"I call *you*, Lord Magician?" she said. Her smile was almost lost in the wrinkles of her face. She seemed tired, now that he was close to her; but perhaps she was just weary of life. "Not so. It may be that you wanted to view Poseidonis again—"

She gestured with the shears; Varus followed their points to look over the escarpment. The city he had seen in the theater spread below them.

Flying ships flapped toward the harborfront and landed like giant dragonflies, each guided by a figure in fiery armor. The streets were of the same glassy, glittering substance as the towers; catwalks as seemingly fine as spider silk tied the structures to their neighbors at three or four levels above the ground as well.

People hastened about their business. They wore sandals, broad-brimmed hats that seemed to be made of stiffened fabric, and tunics that left their left shoulders bare; Varus did not see any of the loiterers or street vendors that he would have expected in Carce. Among the humans were scores, perhaps hundreds, of the glass figures which walked at a measured pace like so many living statues.

"Why do I need to see this?" Varus said. "Help me to understand, mistress!"

"The Minoi of Atlantis threaten your world, Lord Wizard," said the old woman. "They are one threat of three, and any one will be sufficient to doom you."

The armored men from the airships and similar figures from distant towers were walking toward the tall spire. Ordinary humans thronged the broad plaza that separated it from the sea, but they made way for the converging shapes in armor.

"But why?" Varus said.

But as he spoke, the Sibyl's mouth twisted and she cried, *"How many evils does the sea devise against you?"*

Varus plunged through darkness. He awakened in moonlight, standing with Alphena and Pandareus. He was shouting.

ALPHENA JUMPED BACK AS HER BROTHER, who had been slouching as if asleep on his feet, suddenly stiffened. He shouted in a squeaky voice, *"How many evils does the sea devise against you? She will suddenly encroach on the grieving land, causing it to flood as the Earth tears asunder!"*

"Brother?" Alphena said sharply.

"What?" Varus snapped, looking about wildly as though he expected to see something that wasn't there. "Alphena? Oh. I'm sorry. What happened?"

"You shouted a warning that the sea will flood," Pandareus said, his head cocked to the side in interest. "Using a proleptic gerundive, I might note. Were you quoting?"

"I think I was . . . ," Varus said. He licked his lips. "That is, I heard the Sibyl calling a prophecy. About the sea."

"You said it yourself, brother," Alphena said. She felt sick with uncertainty; she didn't know what was real or if *anything* was real.

Varus gave her a wan smile. "I suppose I did," he said. Then he added, "Master Pandareus means that the land won't really grieve until the sea encroaches, but the poet describes it as grieving already."

"My comment was out of place, Lady Alphena," the teacher said, dipping his head contritely. "When human beings feel threatened, they revert to habitual behavior; and I fear my habit is pedantry."

Alphena was only half listening. She had caught movement out of the corner of her eye. She turned toward what should have been the gate to the alley. A vortex of pale light spun there. As she watched, the light deepened.

"Look!" she said. She wasn't sure whether her companions could hear her. She couldn't see them, and when she tried to point at the coalescing vision, she couldn't see her own hand and arm. "It's the city from the theater!"

No, it's more than what we saw in the theater. This isn't just the city, it's an island too.

The vision changed with her thoughts: first the city sparkling like a polished diamond, then the backdrop of jungle-covered hills behind and beside the crystal towers. A heartbeat later she saw a panorama of seven ring islands, each inside the next larger.

"*A volcano like Aetna,*" said a voice at the edge of her hearing. Was Pandareus speaking? "*Seven eruptions, each slighter than the one before.*"

The rings almost touched close to the point where the city spread and sparkled. Spotted at intervals among the forested curves of each island were glittering specks, single towers similar to the much larger buildings of the city.

The vision shrank inward, reversing the way it had appeared. For a moment a dull glow remained, like the wick of a lamp that had run out of oil; then that too was gone.

Alphena let out a shuddering breath. "Brother?" she said.

Varus looked as drawn as she felt. With a touch of anger he said, "I didn't do that!"

Pandareus raised an eyebrow. Varus looked at his teacher in sudden dismay, then turned to Alphena. He bowed formally and said, "Your pardon, sister; I misspoke. I am not consciously aware of having caused that vision—"

He made a rhetorical gesture toward what was again only the back gate. Light from the doorman's lamp in the alley glowed through the slight gap between the panel and doorpost.

"—but as Master Pandareus rightly pointed out, I may be having an effect of which I'm not aware. Indeed, given that I was seeing a similar vision when I was dreaming."

He paused. His expression was suddenly that of a frightened little boy.

The young philosopher reasserted himself with a wry smile. "When I was in a reverie, I'll call it," he said. "I think I probably did cause what we all just saw, though I don't know how."

Her brother's smile returned, broader. "Nor do I know how to stop it," he said.

"We have much to consider," said Pandareus with a smile that made him look like another person. "Which is always true of the philosopher, as I'm sure we three strive to be. I believe I will do my further consideration to-night in my bed, and I hope in my sleep."

He bowed. "Repeat my thanks to your father," he added. "The food was wonderful, and the evening has been even more remarkable than the menu would have made it."

Pandareus pulled the gate open. The doorman standing in the alley turned, lifting his lantern on the short hooked pole it hung from.

"Are you sure you won't accept an escort, master?" Varus asked.

"I prefer to retain my own habits, Lord Varus," the teacher said, "though I thank you. I have gone out virtually every night since I arrived in Carce. If I get used to linkmen and guards, where will I be when they're no longer available? Like a once-wild rabbit who has been fattened in a cage before be-ing returned to the forest, I fear—an easy meal for any predator."

Alphena looked at the teacher in a new way. She had never wondered how ordinary people—that is, people who didn't travel with scores of attendants—went anywhere at night. The answer seemed to be, "Carefully."

She knew that Carce's streets were prowled not only by robbers, but by violent drunks and by beggars who would willingly turn thief if they met someone sufficiently weaker than themselves in the darkness. Publius Cory-lus was young and strong and carried a hardwood staff that made him more than a match for a footpad with a knife. Pandareus had none of those ad-vantages, but he seemed to have gotten along quite well.

The gate closed behind him. It reopened a crack, then shut again. The doorman was making sure that the young lord and lady were still in the garden—so that their privacy gave him an excuse for staying in the alley where he was more comfortable.

Varus stared after his teacher for a moment, then looked at Alphena and said, "Master Pandareus shows himself as wise in his present assessment as I have found him in every other matter where I've heard him give an opinion."

His smile was affectionate, but it seemed to Alphena to be sad as well. "I'll take his advice and go to bed, sister. Shall we go back into the house together?"

"Help!" Pandareus called from the near distance. At any rate, it sounded like Pandareus and sounded like the word *help*, but the cry was muffled.

"What's going on there!" the doorman bellowed.

Alphena was through the gate before her brother, but he was only a half-step behind. That was a surprisingly good performance for a youth with no pretensions to being a man of action.

The doorman was just outside the gate, standing in the middle of the alley and looking to the left; he was brandishing his cudgel. Alphena couldn't see anyone else.

"Come on, you!" she shouted, wishing that she knew the fellow's name. "Master Pandareus has been attacked!"

She started down the alley, hiking the long tunic up with her left hand. Behind her the doorman called, "Your ladyship, come back! I can't leave the gate! It may be a trick!"

Alphena ignored him and ran toward the intersecting street. She looked both ways. The moon was close to setting, so all she could see was rapid movement to the south.

She started to follow, then stopped after two strides. From the slap of sandals on the pavement, there were a dozen men or even more in the gang which must have abducted Pandareus.

If I had my sword . . . But she didn't have a sword, and she couldn't even run in this accursed dinner dress.

Varus came up behind her; several servants were with him, holding hoes and shovels. He'd apparently grabbed the nearest men and opened the gardeners' tool shed to equip them. "Are they gone?" he said.

"Yes," Alphena said, pointing. "But don't follow them. There's too many, and I think I saw swords."

She was gasping for breath, though she hadn't really run very far. It must be the sudden shock that was making her tremble. Looking at her brother, she said, "We need to tell Father."

"Ah . . . ," said Varus. "I don't think that would be a good idea just now. I don't think Father would be able to do anything, and, ah, I think he's busy. With Mother."

I don't understand—Alphena thought. Then she gasped, "Oh!"

"I sent a messenger to Publius Corylus, though," Varus said. "When he arrives, the three of us can discuss the best way to proceed."

He looked away; he was obviously embarrassed about having shocked his sister. *Though of course I know that it happens. Or it can happen. I know it does!*

"Yes," Alphena said aloud. "That's a good idea. Corylus will know what to do."

She really did believe that, she realized. Though she didn't have the faintest notion of *why* she believed it.

Corylus reached the alley to the back of Saxa's house, loping at well below the best speed he could have managed. He wasn't in quite the shape he had been on the Danube frontier, but he used running—and sports more generally—to cushion himself against the stresses of Carce as well as to stay physically fit. He could keep up with even a professional courier over the distance from his apartment block to here.

The footing over Carce's streets, even on a familiar route, wasn't safe for a dead run after moonset. Even at a measured pace Corylus had slipped several times, saving himself by tapping one end of his staff or the other down on the pavement.

Men with lanterns and clubs blocked the middle of the alley outside Saxa's back gate. Corylus slowed to a walk as he started toward them. A voice with a harsh German accent called, "Hold it right there, you, or I'll split your head!"

A number of replies bounced toward Corylus' lips. The same reflex readied his staff for a straight thrust that would show that barbarian what it meant to threaten a soldier of Carce. But—Corylus' grin, though wry, was nonetheless real—that wasn't what he'd come here for.

"I'm Publius Corylus, here at the summons of Lord Varus!" he said. He didn't halt, but he slowed further with half-paces. "Who's in command here?"

"Ajax, *get* your bloody ass back here!" shouted Lenatus from the gateway. "Otherwise you'll be lucky if there's enough left of you to strap to the flogging horse. He's his lordship's friend!"

"Here I am, Publius," Varus said as he broke through the clot of servants. "And, ah, my sister."

Corylus clasped his friend. Varus wore slippers and a knee-length linen tunic, probably what he had worn under his toga at dinner. Alphena was in a short wool tunic of military cut and heavy sandals. She wasn't wearing a helmet or body armor, but she had belted on a long sword.

Corylus had seen Alphena use the weapon. The edge of the gray blade was sharp enough to shave sunlight, and the point had ripped open fire demons; whatever it was made of wasn't ordinary steel.

Lenatus had followed the siblings, but he stayed politely in the background. He too carried a sword, but his was the ordinary weapon of a legionary. With him was one of the night doormen; and Agrippinus, the majordomo, stood a pace behind the two lesser servants.

Varus looked around. "I sent Culex with the message," he said. "Didn't he return with you?"

"The runner?" Corylus said. "He'd told me what he knew—that Pandareus walked onto Fullers Street and somebody, a gang, apparently grabbed him. I asked your man to follow along with Pulto. I could get here quickly, but I didn't want to chance Pulto stumbling and, well, being alone at night on the streets. He wasn't pleased at being babysat, as he put it, but—"

His mouth twisted into a smile of sorts.

"—he wasn't able to catch up with me to clout me into proper respect for the man my father depended on to keep me safe."

"I don't think any of us are safe," Varus said with a tired grin. "But I suppose that's always true. Demons are no more deadly than the ordinary summer fevers; they're just different."

"Fevers weren't going to burn the whole world to a cinder," Alphena said. "Anyway, I don't think it was demons that took Pandareus, though I don't know why anyone, demon or human, would."

She frowned and said, "They may have killed him and carried off the body. I couldn't see that well."

"Master Corylus?" Lenatus said, choosing to address himself to the soldier—or semi-soldier—rather than to the children of his noble employer. "I checked the alley mouth, and there wasn't a splash of blood on the pavement. From what Ferox here says—"

The doorman nodded vigorously but didn't speak. He held an oak cudgel with an iron ring shrunk over the business end.

"—they were waiting for Master Pandareus. It wasn't a chance robbery."

"Aye," said Ferox. "They come from both sides, slick as garroting a rabbit.

I figure they threw a bag over him. They was waiting for him, no doubt about that."

Corylus looked to where the alley met the next street over. The sky was pale enough that he could see the top of the peach tree which leaned over the wall of Saxa's garden.

He thought for a moment, then shrugged—after all, there could be no harm in asking—and said, "Gaius, can you arrange for me to be alone in the garden for a little while? Without any servants or, well, anybody?"

"Yes, of course," Varus said. He looked at his sister with a worried expression. "Ah—that is . . . ?"

Alphena wrinkled her face in irritation. "We asked Master Corylus to come because we thought he might have a suggestion," she said. "Of *course* we'll do any reasonable thing that he asks!"

She turned to Agrippinus and said, "Get everyone out of the garden. Then you stand in front of the inside gate and make sure nobody comes back. You personally!"

"Your ladyship!" the majordomo said as he went back through the gate with little mincing steps. As soon as he was inside he cried, "Get out of here at once, all of you! Back into the house unless you want to spend the rest of your lives chained to plows in Sardinia!"

"I'll see to it that nobody comes in from the alley," Alphena said, drawing her sword and placing herself in the gateway. The gray blade gleamed like a stream of ice water.

"Thank you," Corylus said as he stepped past her into the garden. He shut the outer gate. Agrippinus had already closed the interior one behind him.

Alphena's gesture seemed unduly melodramatic, but it had certainly worked. Soldiers learned to appreciate tactics that worked, because you didn't have to be on the frontier very long before you had plenty of experience with things that *didn't* work.

The garden had three stone benches. Corylus sat on the end of the one nearest the peach tree. When nothing had happened immediately, he said in a quiet voice, "Persica, I'd like to speak with you, if you don't mind."

There was a further long pause. Well, it seemed long. Then the peach nymph appeared, seemingly from behind the trunk.

She hesitated. Corylus patted the bench beside him; she settled onto it sinuously.

"I didn't have anything to do with the men who took the old fellow,"

Persica said; her tone was a defensive whine. "I know what I did before, to you and the little trollop who fancies you, but I didn't do this."

"I didn't imagine you did, mistress," Corylus said. "But because of where you're standing, I thought you might have seen something."

He paused, but the nymph didn't volunteer a reply. "In fact I'm sure you saw something," he said. "Who took my friend Pandareus?"

The nymph looked at him sidelong. "Will you be nice to me if I tell you?" she said in a tiny voice.

"Tell me out of the goodness of your heart, Persica," Corylus said calmly, as though he were speaking to a child. That was true, in a way: dryads were as quick and light as children in their enthusiasms and their malice.

The nymph sniffed and made a face. "You humans," she said. "I *have* no heart."

She met Corylus' eyes. "But I get very lonely. You're hard, though, so you don't care."

"Pandareus is my friend, Persica," Corylus said.

"What would I know about friends?" the nymph said. "But it doesn't matter, *I* don't matter. Anyway, it was the attendants of the old man who came with the three sorcerers. The sorcerers were in charge; I think they're telling the old man what to do, too."

"Sorcerers?" Corylus said. "And what old man? Do you mean Senator Priscus? He was coming to dinner, but not with sorcerers."

"Not Priscus," Persica said petulantly. "The other senator, the one named Tardus."

She slid closer on the bench. "Can't you at least hold me?" she said. "I'd like to be held. I don't think it's going to be very long now before the end."

Corylus put his arm around her waist. She snuggled against him as though she were warm liquid.

Why would Tardus have dined with Saxa? But perhaps Saxa had invited his colleague to make amends for searching his house. And the sorcerers—

"Persica?" he said. "The sorcerers you mentioned? Were they the dark men with Senator Tardus? One of them had a stuffed bird in his hair when I saw them in the theater."

"Hold me," the nymph said. "That's right. Your arm is so strong."

Corylus didn't speak, but his muscles stiffened with frustration. Persica said, "I suppose. A Carthaginian and the other two from the Western Isles. They're all very old."

"But why should they have taken Pandareus?" Corylus said. He didn't doubt what the nymph had told him, but it came as a complete surprise. The pieces of information were piled on top of one another, none of them fitting with the others or with anything that Corylus and his friends had known before.

"How would I know why humans should do anything?" Persica said, treating the question as though he had meant her to answer it. She took his right hand in her left and moved it to her breast. "I'm so *lonely*."

"No, dear," Corylus said, firmly removing his hand. He kissed the nymph on the forehead, then stood. "You'll have company coming soon, but I'm not at all comfortable with this."

The nymph rose supplely, looking as though she was about to plead. She saw his face and instead made a moue.

"Company?" she said. "Are they going to plant another pear?"

"A pomegranate," said Corylus. "She should arrive in the morning."

"Oh, well," Persica said. She sounded contemptuous, but her expression seemed speculative if not unreservedly positive. "Even a pomegranate is better than no one, I suppose."

Corylus reached for the gate latch. He grinned: he hadn't bothered to slide the bar through its staples, not with Alphena outside with a bare sword.

As he started to pull the gate open, there was a hoarse shout from the house. Over it, cutting through the night like a jagged razor, came a woman's scream.

He thought it was Hedia screaming.

Ordinarily Hedia allowed—directed—Syra, her chief maid, to deal with her hair. Tonight it had been made up for her husband's formal dinner, however, which had required the services of three specialists. Removing the pad onto which the hair was teased, and the combs and pins which anchored and embellished the waves, was just as complicated as the creation had been.

A librarian read aloud notes which friends had sent to Hedia; they were mostly froth discussing gossip and parties, past or planned. A clerk stood at a writing desk of Celtic bronzework, a tracery of serpents which twined in curves too complex to follow with the eye. His brush was poised over a sheet of thin birchwood, smoothed into a glossy writing surface to take down Hedia's replies.

There were low voices in the hall outside her suite. The reader stumbled over two more words and stopped without Hedia directing him to. She raised her eyes to him without moving her head: he stood transfixed, his glance trembling from his mistress to whoever had come to the doorway behind her.

It might be a ravening beast, Hedia thought, letting a dry smile quirk her lips. *But a beast would probably be noisier. Therefore it's more likely that—*

"Your ladyship," Syra announced, "Lord Saxa requests an interview with you."

Hedia thought that most of the hardware was out of her hair. Regardless, if she continued to sit with her back toward her husband, she would appear to be sending a message which was quite the opposite of how she really felt about the dear man.

"Step back, girls," she said calmly, gesturing to her sides. If she got up abruptly, she was likely to be jabbed with a pin. Flaying the back of the hairdresser responsible wouldn't make the jab any less uncomfortable.

When she was sure that her staff was out of the way, Hedia rose smoothly, turned, and bowed to Saxa. He looked flustered, the poor thing.

"Ah," he said. "Your ladyship, I'm, ah. . . . I came to apologize, and to thank you from the marrow of my bones."

"You bless me with your presence, my dear heart," Hedia said, walking to him with her arm out. She hooked her hand gently around his neck. He still wore his dinner tunic. "Come and sit with me, dear one."

Hedia's clerical staff trickled out of the suite, mixing with Saxa's considerable entourage which milled in the hallway. None of the servants had attempted to enter with Saxa: the four footmen on Hedia's staff stared at potential interlopers, but the real threat that kept them out was her own temper.

Her reputation had preceded her when Saxa brought his new wife home. His household hadn't forced Hedia to prove the truth of the stories about how she dealt with disrespectful servants; but they were true, or anyway enough of them were.

The hairdressers didn't leave the room because their job wasn't quite finished, but they clustered with their equipment at a small side-table on an outside corner. The sun had set, and stars gleamed through the clerestory windows.

Syra stood with her arms akimbo, glancing alternately toward the door, the hairdressers, and her mistress. Hedia, catching the sequence from the corner of her eye, noticed that the glare directed at Syra's fellow servants became a meekly downcast expression when it fell on her ladyship.

As it bloody well had better.

"Marcus Priscus explained that Tardus was threatening me," Saxa said. He allowed Hedia to sit him on the couch beside her, but he sat looking at his hands in his lap. "Threatening all of us, I suppose. I suppose you think I'm an awful fool not to have seen that. I, well, you saved us all, your ladyship."

"I think you are a very sweet, decent man, my husband," Hedia said, kissing his cheek. "The world we live in isn't nearly as nice as you are, but that's not a reason to reproach yourself."

She paused, then kissed him on the lips. "Don't *ever* be sorry that you're so decent!" she said fiercely.

She thought of sending out the servants, but she didn't want to frighten Saxa away. It was much like coaxing a sparrow to take a breadcrumb from her fingers; though he seemed to enjoy the exercise as much as any other man once he got properly started.

"I would be lost without you, my wife," Saxa muttered. "I don't know how I got along before I married you."

Instead of answering—even in the depths of her heart, Hedia wasn't sure whether the value she brought into Saxa's life was worth the stress which she undeniably also brought with it—Hedia kissed him again and leaned closer. She heard Syra chivying the other servants out with harsh whispers. Hedia would reward the maid for her initiative . . . but if Syra hadn't responded without direction, she would have been demoted to the scullery, or worse.

"Dear heart?" Saxa said. "Do you think . . . ?"

"Hush, my dear lord," Hedia said as she lifted the skirt of his tunic and fondled his genitals. She would have preferred the bed because it was wider, but she knew from experience that it took very little to break her husband's mood. She knelt before him and took his penis into her mouth.

Saxa mumbled something, though Hedia wasn't sure that the sounds were words. Matters were proceeding as she had planned; well, as she had hoped.

She reached up with one hand to unclasp the brooch pinning the right shoulder of her tunic, a gold lion's head with polished garnet eyes. She heard the whisper of slippers; Syra expertly unlatched the brooch, then untied the bandeau holding Hedia's breasts as the tunic spilled to her knees on the floor.

Hedia rose, kicking off her slippers as she loosed her G-string. "Now lean back, my lord," she said, guiding Saxa around on the couch so that his whole torso would be supported. "Let me do the work tonight."

She lowered herself onto Saxa, pleased to find that he was rigid enough to enter her without additional coaxing. For a moment she gave herself up to the pleasure of the moment, wriggling her hips gently.

Syra gasped. The sound was little more than an intake of breath, but it would still get her a whipping shortly.

Saxa shouted and tried to sit up. His eyes were wild and he was looking at something in the room.

Hedia turned her head. The three glassy figures from her nightmare stood around her, closing in. She screamed.

The figures gripped her by the arms and waist. Hedia continued to scream as she and her captors fell out of the world.

CHAPTER IX

Alphena stood in the courtyard as Saxa's frightened household scurried and chattered around her. With her forearms crossed before her, she scowled. She didn't know what to do. While she was too intelligent to do something pointless just to be acting, it made her *furious* to stand here in the midst of chaos.

People running to and fro would have stumbled into Alphena in the bad light and confusion, were it not for the squad of footmen which Florina had gathered about her mistress. They weren't Alphena's own servants—at least she didn't think they were; she didn't even recognize the faces of most—but they seemed pleased to stand and glare at anybody who came too near.

A few of them were even armed, more or less. Two had iron rods that were probably turnspits from the kitchen, and one fellow with drooping moustaches and a shaved scalp was holding a decorative marble post which he'd pulled from the bed of peonies beside them. The head of Hermes that topped the post made it an effective mace.

Alphena found herself smiling. The men around her were happy because she had given them purpose in the midst of confusion: they were guarding the young mistress. Well, Florina had given them purpose. It was time and past time that the young mistress found a purpose for herself.

"Florina," she said crisply, "who was with my mother when she disappeared? Really there, I mean. Ah, besides my father."

"Syra, your ladyship," the maid said. "She was the only one inside the bedroom, though there were plenty in the hall."

Florina added with a sneer, "To hear some of them talk, they were all

standing around the bed, but everybody knows that isn't the way her ladyship behaved. Your mother, I mean."

"Very good," Alphena said, trying to keep her tone firm but detached.
"Florina, bring Syra to me at once."

"Yes, your ladyship!" Florina said. She patted two footmen on the shoulder to move them out of the way, then scampered toward the stairs.

Alphena had thought she might need to coax or threaten the girl to make
her obey; Hedia's chief maid might, after all, be with Saxa or Agrippinus,
which would make the task of dragging her away potentially dangerous.
Apparently the opportunity to give her recent superior orders in Lady Alphena's name was worth the risk of trouble with the master or his majordomo.

Varus had gone upstairs. Alphena didn't know whether he was just looking over Mother's room or if he was speaking to Father. She didn't think either
of those things would do any good; certainly she wouldn't help by tagging
along in her brother's footsteps.

Corylus, Lenatus, and Pulto—who had arrived just before Hedia began
to scream—were talking to the doorman and the servants who had been
in the entranceway and office at the time. No one had broken into the house
through the back gate, so they were checking to see what had happened in
front.

Nothing, obviously; this hadn't been an attack by ordinary human enemies like the ones who had earlier spirited away the teacher. The former
soldiers hadn't been able to accept that, but Alphena didn't see why Corylus
was wasting his time with them.

Not that Alphena was doing anything useful, or anything at all for that
matter.

Mother would know what to do! Which meant that she had to find Hedia.

Florina reappeared, tugging Syra along by the wrist. Hedia's maid wore a
stunned look. She wasn't fighting Florina's guidance; she didn't even appear
to be aware of it.

"Here she is, your ladyship!" Florina said triumphantly. "She was just
standing in Lady Hedia's room as if she didn't have a thing to do!"

She didn't, Alphena thought. Aloud she said, "Syra, describe the men who
took my mother away."

The maid's numb expression suddenly melted into misery and tears. Syra
threw her hands to her face and began to blubber, "I didn't I didn't I d-didn't—"

"I'll make her talk!" said Florina. She jerked Syra's left hand down with her own and cocked her right arm back to slap the cheek she had just uncovered.

"No!" said Alphena, thrusting Florina aside to underscore the command. *Though if the girl hadn't been so enthusiastic, I might have slapped Syra myself.*

"Syra," Alphena said, "nobody thinks you did anything wrong. Tell me about the men who took my mother."

Syra swallowed. She turned slightly toward Alphena but didn't raise her eyes. "They weren't men," she mumbled. "They were all shiny like glass. They just . . ."

She stopped and swallowed. "I was standing by the alcove where I sleep like I, well, like usual when the mistress is, well, you know. I'd put out all the lamps but the one beside me on the wall because the master is kinda skittish sometimes. Anyway."

Syra took a deep breath. She was talking more easily now that she'd gotten started.

"They were just *there*, these three statues, I thought they were," she said. "But they moved. They couldn't come through the door, and the windows have grates besides being just under the roof. I dropped the towel I was holding for afterward and I guess I said something. The master shouted and her ladyship turned. I don't know if she started to get up but they, the statues, grabbed her."

Syra forced both fists against her mouth. Past her knuckles she whispered, "They fell, it was like. They just fell into the air, her ladyship and the statues holding her, spinning and getting smaller but they weren't going *down*. They were going away. And they were gone and the master was shouting and everybody came in from the hall and they were *gone!*"

The maid began to blubber again. Alphena made a moue: Syra's behavior infuriated her. She couldn't really blame the woman, but if she had to listen to more of this whining, Alphena was going to slap her just to shut her up.

"Syra," she said. "Go back to your cubby and stay there until morning. Go on, now!"

Florina took the other maid by the shoulders and turned her around, then shoved her out of Alphena's protective circle. The push wasn't brutal, but it was more forceful than necessary.

"Next," Alphena said, "where's Agrippinus? Oh, never mind, there's Callistus. Callistus, come here!"

Her mind had direction now. She was proceeding logically, with a feeling of relief because she *was* proceeding.

The deputy steward had just come from the office. He heard his name and looked around with an angry expression to see who was calling him.

Alphena waved imperiously. That might not have been sufficient, but a Po-Valley Gaul from her escort bellowed, "Callistus! Get your fat Syrian ass over here! Lady Alphena wants to talk to you!"

The deputy steward's expression went from being furious to being terrified in an eyeblink—the length of time it took him to get past the insulting nature of the summons to what the words actually meant. He came over to Alphena as quickly as his feet could mince.

"Your ladyship?" he said. "Is there something wrong? I assure you—"

"Hush," said Alphena. "Find one of the clerks and a runner for me. I want to send a letter to—oh!"

Anna couldn't read and write. Her husband could, but Pulto was here already with Corylus. And besides, Anna wouldn't be able to—

"Your l-ladyship?" said the frightened deputy steward.

"The double litter is still here at the house, isn't it?" Alphena said, making her decision as the words came out of her mouth. "Get it around to the front with the crew immediately. I'm going to see Master Corylus' nurse at his home."

She gestured to the servants standing around her. "These men will be my escort," she said. "And find Iberus for a guide, he's been to the apartment block before."

"You should be talking to Nestor," Callistus said. "The litters are—"

He closed his mouth and swallowed when he saw Alphena's face contort.

"Want me to pop him one, your ladyship?" the big Gaul asked cheerfully. "Let him see how those pretty teeth feel going down his throat?"

"I'll see to it at once, your ladyship!" Callistus said. He turned, shouting, "Nestor! Spartax! I need you!"

"Your ladyship?" Florina said. "The regular litter hasn't been taken back to the warehouse either, from when your father was using it. The little one would be handier if you're going alone."

Alphena looked at the girl. "I'm *going* alone," she said. "But I'm bringing Anna back with me."

She took a deep breath and added what she hadn't intended to say to anybody but Anna herself. "When Anna gets here, I'm going to have her help me to find Hedia. Because Hedia came to save me."

CORYLUS FOUND VARUS STANDING in his stepmother's bedroom, staring moodily at the wall. The painting of Neptune and Amphitrite in a conch-shell chariot being drawn by sea horses was attractive—under other circumstances, Corylus might have spent some time examining it himself—but he doubted that his friend was really thinking about art at the moment.

Dozens of servants were in the suite, chattering, shuffling, and peering closely at the furniture. As Corylus entered, a maid opened a wardrobe cabinet, stared at the contents, and closed the wicker door just in time for a footman to open it and repeat the process.

"Gaius?" he said quietly. Then, when Varus didn't react, he said in a louder voice, "Gaius Varus?"

Varus turned; his look of fierce intensity became welcoming. He said, "Publius, I'm glad to see you. Have you had any luck, ah . . . ?"

He apparently didn't know how to end the question. Corylus smiled faintly; that was understandable, since framing the questions was the really difficult problem.

"Perhaps," Corylus said. "Is there a place we can talk privately?"

"Right here, I think," Varus said, "if Lenatus and your man—"

He gestured past Corylus to the pair of veterans who had followed him into the suite.

"—can clear the room and then stand in the hallway."

Corylus looked over his shoulder. Lenatus grinned like a drillmaster—a position he had held with the Alaudae Legion—and bellowed, "All right, you pansies! On the orders of Lord Varus, out! Every bleeding one of you. And if my buddy Pulto and me don't think you're moving fast enough, you're out the bleeding window!"

"And we *won't* take the grating off first!" Pulto said.

Servants either looked up in shock or hunched and stared at the floor, but they moved with surprising unanimity toward the door. Corylus heard a few whines of complaint, but no one tried to argue.

Varus leaned close to Corylus and said, "Could they really do that? The windows are too high, aren't they?"

Corylus grinned, remembering a fight he'd seen in a tavern in

188 ✦ DAVID DRAKE

Moguntiacum. There were no windows, but openings under the peak of the high thatched roof allowed smoke to trickle out.

"I think they could," he said. "But I don't think it'll come to that."

Lenatus and Pulto were the last out of the suite. Before he banged the door behind him, the trainer looked back and grinned again.

Corylus grinned also. "You've impressed Lenatus," he said.

"What?" said Varus, looking puzzled. "I just stood here. Goodness, I couldn't have emptied the room like that."

"You *did* empty the room," Corylus said. "You identified the correct subordinate for the job, gave him clear instructions, and stayed out of his way while he executed them. Any time you want a career that involves freezing your butt on the Rhine, the army is ready to give you a home."

He visualized his friend creeping through the Hercynian Forest in loose woolen leggings with a cape over his shoulders. His laugh was real and spontaneous, a release after a very tense day. *Hercules! A lot of very tense days!*

"You learned something about Hedia from talking to the doorman?" Varus said, smiling mildly at his friend's pleasure. He didn't ask what had caused the laughter, for which Corylus was thankful. Varus would think he was being mocked.

"No," Corylus explained, "and I didn't expect to. I was able to talk to Pulto and Lenatus about how we might find Pandareus, or at least find out more about him, though. Which is why I was prowling around with them."

He grinned and added, "Your other servants were scared to death of being blamed for intruders getting in, so they kept as far away as they could while the three of us were muttering to one another in the door alcove."

"Very good," Varus said, nodding. "Yes, at least we know who abducted Pandareus."

He pursed his lips with a frown and said, "It seems very unlikely that Tardus and his associates were involved with whatever happened to Hedia, however."

Corylus shrugged. "I can't imagine that there's *no* connection, however," he said. "Anyway, we have an entry point on Pandareus and none at all on her ladyship."

Until now he'd kept his friend in the dark about his plans, which would have irritated many people. He hadn't really been worried about how Varus would react—he was too smart not to realize that this discussion had to wait for complete privacy—but it was good to get past the concern.

"Right," said Varus. "Explain your plan. And—"

A real smile lit his face.

"—if you're going to tell me that it's dangerous, as your expression suggests you are, then save your breath. I watched Typhon, if that's what it was, destroying Carce. Nothing can be more dangerous than letting that happen."

Corylus started to speak and found his throat was dry. He coughed to clear it, then said, "A tribune with a squad of the Praetorian Guard and an imperial writ would be able to enter Saxa's dwelling, I believe. Ah—"

Spit it out!

"You were able to find the concealed entrance to the Serapeum," he said, his tone level and his eyes on his friend's. "I think, I hope, that you would be able to find Master Pandareus if he's hidden in the house also. But because you've entered the house recently and by daylight, you would certainly be identifiable after the event. The others involved might possibly be able to conceal themselves from an investigation."

Varus shrugged. "As I say, I don't believe any risk is as great as the risk of doing nothing," he said. He seemed truly nonchalant instead of putting on a brave face before his friend. "But how under heaven are you going to get a squad of Praetorians to escort me?"

"Ah!" said Corylus. "Pulto has connections with the equipment manager in the Praetorian barracks. For a sufficient payment, ten sets of accoutrements can be declared unserviceable and sent out to a scrap dealer. That won't include swords, of course, but swords are available from the gladiatorial schools. They're no problem."

"I see," said Varus. "But the men? I know we could hire idlers easily enough, but I wouldn't want to trust them not to be drunk—or to run off when they really understand what they're expected to do."

"Nor would I," Corylus said, pleased to see how quick his friend was, even on a matter that had probably never crossed his mind before. "Lenatus has sounded out seven of your male household servants; he's had time to get to know your staff pretty well, of course. All of them agreed to join us. Ah, I'll be the tribune, of course."

"Yes, of course," Varus said absently. He glanced toward the wall painting of Hercules spinning yarn for Queen Omphale. As before, Corylus doubted that the—excellent—painting figured in his friend's thoughts.

Varus turned back. "You're talking about slaves," he said. "If this goes wrong, they will certainly be tortured and then crucified. Unless they die sooner under torture."

He pursed his lips for a moment as he thought. "Well, I suppose we all will," he said, "but we're freemen—you and me and the two at the door. Why would any slave take such a risk?"

"Gaius," Corylus said, his grin spreading into a slow smile, "I don't have the faintest idea, but it doesn't surprise me. Men do lots of crazy things they don't have to do. The scout detachments on the borders, they're all volunteers, and believe me, there's nothing the emperor's torturers can do that the Germans and Sarmatians haven't done. I've seen the recovered bodies."

He took a deep breath, silent for a moment with the memory. "I've helped recover the bodies, though I was a civilian kid who shouldn't have been across the river," he said, so softly that he wasn't sure his friend could make out the words. *It doesn't matter.*

He cleared his throat again and said, "Anyway, Lenatus trusts them so I trust them. They'll mostly have to keep their mouths shut, because some of them speak bad Latin and the rest speak worse. Keeping their mouths shut is right for soldiers on a raid like this, though."

"Well, that's in your hands," Varus said. "You're the officer, after all. What is my role, besides acting as your rabbit hound?"

"Well, there's money," Corylus said reluctantly. "I mean, I could swing it with a little time, but Father's banker would send to Puteoli before he'd clear the amount we'd need. There isn't time. We need to move tomorrow, as early as we can get it together."

"That's not a problem," Varus said, gesturing with his open left hand. "I'll talk to Father as soon as you've told me everything you think I need to know. What else?"

"Nothing else, I think," Corylus said, again relieved of more stress than he had realized he was feeling. "I'll be in front with Pulto; you'll be right behind us, and then the rest of the squad with Lenatus at the rear. Wear a toga. Tardus' servants can think what they want, and I'll make sure Tardus himself has plenty to think about if he tries to argue. Beyond that—"

He tried to grin. It came out lopsided, but Varus seemed to appreciate the effort.

"—we'll place our counters according to the throw of the dice."

"Yes," said Varus, nodding. He threw his shoulders back and shook himself. "Wait here, if you would. I'm going to go talk to my father."

Corylus watched his friend leave the room, standing straight. Building Carce from huts on a hilltop to the metropolis of today had taken more kinds of men than just those who were willing to charge the enemy's shield wall.

It had taken men like Gaius Alphenus Varus.

THE ENTRANCE TO SAXA'S suite was open. Varus didn't know which of the ten or a dozen servants clustered there was technically the doorman on duty, so he said, "Ask my father if I may speak with him," in a firm voice and trusted that the right party would hear him.

Servants oozed away, some turning their backs on Varus and bending away. They left a worried looking footman standing alone. He swallowed and piped, "Your lordship! His lordship has gone downstairs. I don't . . . I don't . . . your lordship, his lordship didn't say where he was going!"

It's quite amazing how useless our hundreds of servants are in a crisis, Varus thought. *They're all frightened to death.*

So was he, of course, but that didn't keep him from trying to find a solution.

Manetho had reattached himself when Varus left his mother's rooms. "I'll find him, Lord Varus!" he cried as he rushed down the stairs.

Varus managed to keep his expression blank as he followed in the midst of his considerable entourage. Normally he had very little to do with the household staff unless he brought himself to their attention, and even that sometimes took an effort. Lord Saxa's bookish son didn't shout and decree beatings as his sister did, so he could be—and often was—safely ignored.

Hedia's abduction and the rumors about it—though it was hard to imagine rumors that would be more frightening than the reality—had so unsettled the servants that many were clustering about Varus simply because he appeared calm. He wasn't calm, of course, but his Stoic appearance was sufficient to calm others.

Master Pandareus will be pleased to learn of this proof of the value of philosophy, Varus thought. *And I will be even more pleased to be able to tell him of it.*

Before Varus reached the bottom of the staircase, Manetho came from the side entrance to the office with a wild expression. "The master isn't here!" he said. "They say he's gone to the back garden, your lordship!"

"Well, then, we'll go to the garden," said Varus. Did everything have to be treated as a crisis? "Or at any rate, I will. I don't believe I need help in accomplishing that, Manetho."

"Of course, your lordship!" said the deputy steward, striding toward the back of the house with his head high and his chest thrown out. "You two! Take those lamps from their sconces and precede Lord Varus!"

Varus smiled, though the expression didn't really reach his lips. *Apparently I'm still being ignored,* he thought. *But I'm being smothered rather than shunned by the servants who ignore what I say.*

There were so many people crowded into the rear of the house—the training ground, private bath, storage rooms, and the corridor to the back garden—that it took some moments for Manetho's threats and bluster to clear passage. There wasn't deliberate resistance, just a lack of room for frightened servants to displace into.

I wonder if Archimedes would have had a better answer? Varus thought. As many times before in the recent past, philosophy brought him a smile in a disturbing situation.

"I'll announce you, your lordship," Manetho said. Before Varus could decide how to proceed, the deputy steward turned the wooden gate latch and bellowed, "Lord Varus to see his father, the noble Lord Saxa!"

That probably wasn't the form of address I would have chosen, Varus thought wryly. *My fault for not reacting more quickly.*

He stepped into the open gateway and stood, waiting to be recognized from the garden. To his surprise, Saxa was sitting on a bench along the sidewall—he looked up at the announcement—and was accompanied only by his chief secretary, Philon. A single lamp burned on a stake which had been driven into a planter of poppies close to the bench.

"Oh, I'm glad to see you, son," Saxa said. He sounded more as though he were announcing that the emperor had ordered him to commit suicide. "It's kind of you to join me."

"Would your lordships like me to give you your privacy?" Philon said. He moved quickly toward the gateway, ready to slip through as soon as Varus took a step. "I'll be waiting in the passage, your lordship!"

There was no question that Philon would prefer to be somewhere other than on this haunted site. In all that had happened Varus had forgotten the garden's bad reputation; it was obviously still at the top of the servants' minds.

He was surprised to find his father here. There were people who liked trees and flowers, but Saxa had never displayed any interest in such things. Varus had expected to find his father in bed, perhaps curled with his knees lifted to his chest.

"Lord," Varus said, standing formally in front of his father. "I need funds to carry out a project that may put you in a great deal of danger."

"Sit down, my son," Saxa said. He patted the bench but didn't raise his eyes to meet those of Varus. "And yes, of course you can have whatever you need; just tell Agrippinus. I haven't been a very good father, I know, but I hope—"

He finally looked up.

"—that at least you never thought I pinched you for money."

Varus seated himself gingerly. He hadn't expected to be alone with Saxa, so most of his mental preparation had involved choosing words that he could use in front of the servants without flatly saying what he planned. The plan, after all, would be treated as armed rebellion if it came to the emperor's notice.

"L-l . . . ," he said. He caught himself and took a deep breath, then said, "Father, it isn't that. I need you to know that the money will be used for. . . ."

He swallowed and resumed, "We will be committing treason in the eyes of the emperor. That isn't our intent, but the means we're using are, well, treasonous, I suppose."

"Will you be able to bring my wife back?" Saxa said, suddenly speaking with animation.

"I—" Varus said. *This is so hard.* "No, I will not. Not tomorrow, or at least I don't think so. I hope that it will help us—"

He shouldn't have been involving Corylus and the others, even by implication. Well, too late to worry about that.

"—rescue Mother at some later point. If we succeed. If we survive."

"Well, do what you can," Saxa said sadly. He looked around the garden. "It's my fault, you know. I brought Nemastes here, and that's what started it all. Right here in this garden, we worked a spell that—"

He gestured toward the gap where magic had blasted the pear tree with unnatural cold.

"—did this. Caused demons to take my Hedia. *I* did it."

Varus took Saxa's right hand in his left. He didn't remember ever doing that before. "Father?" he said. "Look at me, please."

Saxa turned with a look of mild surprise. "Yes?" he said.

"I don't understand what's happening," Varus said. "Not even Pandareus does. But I've seen enough to know that you weren't the cause any more than I was or Mother was or Alphena. What you did do was to help save Carce; and by providing funds, you'll be doing that again."

He smiled. "A philosopher should be truthful and precise," he said. "What I should have said is that you will be helping us *try* to save Carce. I hope we'll succeed, but I'm not a soothsayer to speak with divine certainty."

In talking to Varus, Saxa had risen enough from the depths to chuckle. "I've known many soothsayers, my son," he said. "I've never known one whose opinion I would take in opposition to yours."

He pursed his lips and added, "My first wife had a pet sparrow. I would take its opinions ahead of those of most soothsayers, too."

Varus realized he must have looked shocked. Saxa smiled faintly. He said, "I probably seem rather an old fool to you, son, because I believe in things which cannot be logically proven. Unlike my colleague Marcus Tardus, however, I don't believe in things which have been logically *dis*proven. I place portents of the future found in the shape of an ox liver in the disproven category."

"I . . . see," Varus said. He hesitated because he *did* see, perhaps for the first time, a portion of his father as a man. "I, *we* will try not to disappoint you, your lordship."

He rose to his feet. Saxa got up also and unexpectedly gripped his hand. "You haven't disappointed me, my son. You couldn't disappoint me."

Varus felt a surge of warmth toward his father. He said, "Sir? Why don't you visit Marcus Priscus tomorrow, since the Senate won't be in session? Get to sleep tonight, then send him a note in the morning saying that you intend to come over."

"Do you suppose he'd be willing to see me?" Saxa said, noticeably brighter than he had been a moment before. "I don't, I mean we haven't been intimate friends, you know."

"Priscus will be very interested in what happened tonight," Varus said. Part of his mind wondered just how detailed a description of the event his father would provide. "And he's as able as any man in Carce to explain what it means."

He and Saxa shared a smile. It was the older man who voiced the thought of both: "Which means the chances are he'll be completely at sea. Well, regardless, I welcome the chance to become better acquainted with so learned a man."

Varus turned, thinking about the next step. He would offer Corylus a bed, though he wasn't sure that his friend didn't have more preparations to make yet tonight. After Varus confirmed that any necessary sum of money was available for the enterprise, all *he* had before him was sleep . . . which he was looking forward to.

Varus reached for the gate latch. Without warning, he was in the midst of a vision as sharply defined as the one that had filled the stage of the theater. He could no longer see the side of the house, and he turned to find the garden and his father had also been replaced by a crystal fortress squatting on a crag in the midst of jungle.

Huts not greatly different from those of a village in Greece or Lucania had been built around the fortress and spread halfway down the slope. They were burning now. The jungle smoldered in places, but the thick foliage was too green to sustain fire on its own. With the thought, Varus saw humans, some of them injured, crawling among the vines at the buttress roots of huge trees: refugees from the dwellings.

The fortress was shaped like an eight-pointed star. It was small and squat, no more than ten feet high from the ground to the flat roof and only fifty feet from point to the opposite point, but it remained untouched by flames from the score of flying ships which encircled it a quarter mile distant.

Some had penetrated closer: the wreckage of three vessels lay on the outskirts of the burning village. Each was charred around a hole the size of a bushel basket which had been burned through its hull.

A single flying ship moved slowly, bow-on, toward the fortress. The other vessels had hulls and masts of wood, but this one was of the same fiery metal as the armor of the figure in its stern. There were no other crewmen.

A bolt ripped from the fortress: not fire like what the ships had squirted on Typhon as it rent Poseidonis but rather a jet of white channeled lightning; the air glowed in its wake. The ship gleamed as if every surface was covered with ghostly corposants; it staggered, then resumed its slow progress.

A second bolt hit the vessel, then a third. The figure in the stern raised its hands to the flaring helmet, then lifted it off. Instead of a human head beneath the armor, Varus saw a grinning diamond skull.

Purple light flashed from the skull and licked across the face of the fortress. The wall crumbled like a stream bank during a freshet.

The light cut off; the ship wallowed closer. Overhead, what had been a clear sky now roiled with lightning and stormclouds.

Again the purple glare ate into the heart of the fortress, revealing an armored figure in a bubble of clear light against which the purple raved. In one metal gauntlet he held a murrhine bar crossways toward the attacking vessel.

The murrhine split; the halves flew out of sight in either direction. It had been a hollow tube.

Instead of blasting the figure as it had the fortress which sheltered him, a third spurt of purple light plucked the armor off like a diner shelling a crayfish. The mouth of the diamond skull opened: the victor was laughing.

The vision blinked away. Varus fell forward, but his father caught him.

Saxa's expression was as blank and frightened as Varus himself felt.

HEDIA GASPED, trying to get her breath. She thrashed for a moment, but that was pointless. The creature grasping her waist from behind had let go, but the two beside her each held a wrist. Their glassy hands were not uncomfortably tight, but they had no more give in them than if they had been carved out of stone.

She twisted to look at them. The creatures had opposable thumbs, but their fingers were fused into flat paddles. They were translucent, as though made from a dozen sheets of mica stacked together; she could see her wrists faintly through them.

She straightened again. The creatures seemed to pay her no attention. In silhouette they would have seemed human, but all the detail had been smoothed off. Hedia thought of statues worn by windblown sand.

She felt a smile twist the corners of her mouth. *At least they don't terrify me now, the way they did in my nightmares.*

She forced her body to relax. "Do you have names?" she demanded.

The figure on her left turned its head toward her, then turned back. It didn't speak, if it was even able to. The curves of its lips met in a shallow V and were seemingly carved from a single block.

"Where are you taking me?"

That brought no response at all. Well, she hadn't expected it to. She looked about her for the first time.

Hedia and her captors stood as though in clear air. At first she had thought she was falling, but now she wasn't sure. Things half-glimpsed swirled about them the way bubbles dance below a mill flume.

A man covered only by his gray beard and long hair suddenly *was* close: she didn't see movement. From the way his face contorted as he shook his fist, he was shouting curses; Hedia couldn't hear them; she heard only the *shush* of her own pulse in her ears. The figure shrank to a point and spun away, vanishing as suddenly as he had appeared.

Could he have touched me? Would the glass men have protected me if he tried?

A snake squirmed into view. Her captors faced it as stiffly as gladiators preparing to salute the Patron of the Games.

Why are they afraid? Hedia wondered. It seemed an ordinary blacksnake like the one in every temple of Apollo, fed by the priests on bread and milk when worshippers paid to receive the god's attention.

The snake looked toward Hedia; its forked tongue quivered from between its closed lips. As suddenly, it loomed like an avalanche before them; its jaws opened wide enough to swallow a cart and oxen. Releasing Hedia, the glass figures raised their arms at angles like the Egyptian dancers painted on the walls of a temple of Isis.

Hedia felt a wrenching. The snake was no longer visible. She sank to her knees, raising her hands to her face but not—quite—covering her eyes. She began to sob loudly.

Her misery was perfectly believable; it always was. Hedia was young and fit, but she wasn't large, and she tended to favor men of an athletic turn. Knowing when and how to weep had saved her from a beating or worse a number of times in the past, generally when a man entered unexpectedly and found her occupied in a fashion to which he took exception.

Once in fact she had been with the messenger who had brought a mistaken message saying his master, a military tribune, would be detained. The tribune had unfortunately hastened when his schedule had cleared again almost immediately. Hedia suspected things had gone very badly with the servant later that night, but she herself had come out of it with nothing worse than a bruised cheek and a table to replace.

It worked this time too. Her captors hedged her closely on three sides, but they didn't take her wrists again as she knelt weeping.

A blue sphere took form below them, growing denser the way fog rises from a pond on a cool evening. It swelled as it came into better focus, becoming a mass of forested islands. The surrounding sea was ultramarine in the distance, but the water was pale and greener where it fringed the curving shores of an island.

The figure behind Hedia began to gesture with its hands while the other two remained still. Her head was at the level of his knees; she wondered what would happen if she lunged against him.

Very likely I would cut myself as badly as if I'd slammed into the Temple of

Jupiter. Certainly their hands are like stone. Hedia smiled in her mind, though she was careful not to let the humor reach her lips. She began to sob as though her pet kitten had died.

The island now looked as solid as if she were viewing it from a high tower. She and her captors slid over the tops of giant trees, still descending at a flat angle. The air was humid and thick with the smell of rotting leaves.

When Hedia first had glimpsed the forest, it had seemed a solid green mass. Close-up she could see not only different shades of green but also masses of yellow blooms among the leaves or even purple and bluish white. Birds shrieked at them; once a lizard as long as a canoe barked an angry challenge from the top of a tree limb. Her captors didn't react.

Ahead was a hilltop which had recently been burned clear. It was enough higher than the ridge to either side that even bare it rose above the surrounding trees. The line on which they were moving passed very close above the crag.

Sunlight reflected in a dazzle. A building had stood here, but it had been shattered to stub walls and glittering debris over which the fronds of great fern were already curling.

A red-furred ape clambered through the wreckage; it turned and looked up at them. Its head was human with a pentacle tattooed in blue on its forehead. It screamed in fury.

The line of travel flattened still further; now Hedia and her captors were coursing parallel to the treetops ahead. *There won't be a better time.*

Without hesitation, she threw herself forward. The figures to either side grabbed for her, but they were too slow. Hedia somersaulted in the air and hit the slope feetfirst. She couldn't stay upright, but she somersaulted again. Bouncing up, she threw herself into the shadows among the giant trees.

"OH, LADY ALPHENA!" Anna said as two members of the escort started to hand Anna into the double litter. A third servant carried the old woman's walking sticks. "This is much too fine for me! I'll just hire a common chair, let me."

"I'm sure Mother would say that nothing is too good for the guest of our noble family," Alphena said, trying to speak in a properly arch tone. She thought she had come fairly close, which made her giggle. That didn't spoil the effect, since after she spoke she realized that Anna might not otherwise have realized she was joking. "Anyway, we'll talk on the way back to the house."

The servants who had carried Anna down from the third-floor apartment shifted their grips and now lifted her onto the couch. They weren't perfectly gentle, but Anna wasn't a hothouse flower who needed coddling.

The men were Illyrians, enough alike to be brothers, and very possibly former pirates: both were heavily scarred, and one was missing his right ear. Regardless of how they looked, tonight Alphena had found them cheerful, helpful, and—frankly—quite reassuring. Your viewpoint changed when you suddenly had to consider the possibility of glass demons appearing out of thin air.

Alphena sat on the opposite side of the vehicle, then swung her legs in. She performed the maneuver easily—it was child's play compared to the lunges and leaps she practiced on the training ground—but she found herself suddenly blushing.

She'd seen Anna's look of shock and the way she raised her hand to her lips to cover a gasp. Alphena's short tunic was the right garment for violent exercise, but it did very little to cover a woman who was being carried on a litter with her legs stretched out in front of her.

I'm not used to riding in litters! And anyway, Anna wouldn't be shocked if she didn't think I was a fine lady.

Scowling at herself, Alphena drew the side curtains. "Take us home, Manetho!" she called through them to the steward who had attached himself to her escorting servants.

The Cappadocian bearers lifted the heavy vehicle and started forward as part of the same smooth motion. "Oh, my . . . ," said Anna, though Alphena wasn't sure whether she was commenting on the quality of the team or more generally on the situation.

As a courtesy, Alphena had entered the building to announce herself to the older woman instead of sending the servants up alone. She had left the sword lying along the axis of the litter, like a divider between the two passengers. Anna tapped the metal scabbard with a fingertip, making it ring softly. She said, "Think this is going to be needed tonight, your ladyship?"

"I know how to use it!" Alphena said, her voice sharp with a second cause of embarrassment.

"Aye, I know you do," Anna said. "My boy has told me you do, and my Pulto has too. But that's not what I asked your ladyship."

"I'm sorry, Anna," Alphena muttered. "And—"

She leaned forward to squeeze the older woman's hand.

"—please, call me Alphena. I don't mean to be . . . Anna, I'm afraid."

"There's good reason to be afraid," Anna said, nodding. The lanterns on the vehicle's front corners cast enough light through the gauze curtains that Alphena could read Anna's expression; she herself was in shadow. "My boy told me that you're brave, too; but I didn't need him to tell me what I saw myself when we first met."

"It's not monsters or glass men or, or those sorts of things that I'm afraid of," Alphena said, realizing that she had to explain. She smiled wanly. "Anna, I have to save Mother. And I'm afraid I won't be able to. I know what she did for me."

The older woman's face grew unexpectedly hard. In a rasping voice she said, "You're a good girl and you mean well, but don't say you know *that*. Even if her ladyship told you what she'd done, you wouldn't *know* what it meant until you'd done it yourself."

Anna had straightened as she spoke. With a grimace she settled back— she didn't look relaxed, but at least she no longer looked as though she was going to lunge at Alphena in fury—and added, "Which you may have to, child. I'll help as I can, but I'd no more be able to go in your place than I could have in your mother's."

"I'm sorry," Alphena said. In a matter of heartbeats she had gone from embarrassed to furious—*What does this servant mean to be lecturing me?*—to calm and apologetic before she even opened her mouth. "I used the wrong words. I know that Mother risked a great deal to rescue me. I'll help her now in any way I can."

Anna remained sunk in thought for some moments. The litter bearers changed on the move. The only reason Alphena was aware of what was happening was that briefly there were eight voices rather than four calling cadence at the corners of the vehicle. Their chantey was in what might either be Cappadocian or nonsense.

"I'm sorry, your ladyship," Anna muttered. Her eyes remained downcast. "I know you'll help as it takes, that you won't funk it. You come to fetch me, after all. And if you don't know all of it, then—"

She smiled, weakly but honestly.

"—I guess you know that it won't be easy or good either one."

She reached out and squeezed Alphena's hand; Alphena returned the clasp with a feeling of relief.

"The truth is . . . ," Anna said. She was barely whispering, though no one could have overheard them through the singsong drone of the litter bearers. "That I'm afraid myself, for what my part is. But I'll help your mother and I'll help you. I'll do it for my duty."

She chuckled, deep in her throat, and raised her eyes to Alphena's. "Anyway," she said, "I don't guess anything that happens to the three of us is going to be worse than what'll happen to all the world if somebody doesn't stop it. And getting Lady Hedia back is at least a step that way."

"We're coming to the house, your ladyship!" Manetho called from ahead of the vehicle.

Alphena squeezed the older woman's hand again. "We'll bring her back, Anna!" she said, wishing that she really believed her own words.

CHAPTER X

Hedia awoke. She supposed that it was near morning, but she knew that she might be deceiving herself because she so desperately wanted this night to be over. Surely it was at least after midnight?

Sunrise wouldn't leave her much better off, but perhaps she could find something to eat. That was becoming one of her more serious concerns. She hadn't eaten since dinner with the two senators. Though she couldn't be certain how long ago that had been, it was certainly longer than she would usually have gone between meals.

Hedia heard a quick clicking from the branches above her. She didn't know what was making it. It wasn't threatening, just peevish; which was unfortunately how Hedia herself felt. She was bruised, scratched, and hungry, and she certainly couldn't threaten anybody.

The canopy had been as dark as a vault when she raced into the forest, though at the time the sun had still been above the horizon. The edge was a tangle of brambles, saplings, and vines. Hedia wriggled through and staggered on, bleeding on her thighs, the insides of her arms—she threw them up to cover her eyes—and most painfully her bare breasts.

Why didn't I leave my bandeau on? But that hadn't really been a choice: Saxa loved her breasts, and she had no intention of shorting him of anything that he really desired. *He's just a big baby, the poor dear.*

She grinned to realize that she in her present condition was feeling sorry for her husband. He generally seemed to be at sea, though, whereas Hedia always saw a course and followed it with no more hesitation than a rock has in falling when dropped.

The forest within the sunlit edge had been relatively open, but "relatively" was damning with faint praise. Trees as large as those still standing lay scattered on the ground, though they had fallen long enough ago that Hedia had not been able to find gaps in the canopy when she looked up. The downed giants were covered with mushrooms and even saplings, but their wood remained firm.

The trunks channelled her course, though she wasn't going anywhere in particular—just *away*—so she didn't suppose it mattered. It still made her uncomfortable.

She had kept going as long as she could; she couldn't ignore the pain, but she struggled on despite it. The cuts on her limbs and body were unpleasant, but the real problem was the soles of her feet. Thorns, broken twigs, and stones buried in the leaf litter had gouged them several times, but she had no choice except to go on.

They would *have to grab me when I was stark naked!* Hedia thought, then giggled. The garments she ordinarily wore even when she was going out—thin shifts and delicate silk slippers—wouldn't have been much more useful. *If I'd had a little warning, I could have borrowed a pair of heavy boots from Alphena.*

There hadn't been any sign of pursuit, but Hedia wasn't sure she would have noticed. Occasionally she looked over her shoulder, but sweat and the stinging tips of her hair—since her coiffure was down—would have made it difficult for her to see on a promenade ground. This jumble of vines, saplings, and fallen branches could have concealed an army, let alone three glass figures who had been perfectly silent during the time Hedia had been aware of them.

She had finally collapsed beside a fallen tree which was thicker than she was tall. Fine loam, sticky and damp, filled the angle between the trunk and the ground. Hedia didn't know whether it had blown there and been trapped or if it was the product of the tree itself, rotted bark and the excrement of wood-boring beetles.

Regardless, it was soft and cool. It had pillowed her head and had even, to her amazement, allowed her to fall asleep. It had been a busy day, and the stress of capture by demons and escape had drained her utterly.

Hedia got to her feet, pressing her hand against the tree bole more for mental than physical support. Something crawled over her toes. She froze where she stood. That was probably the right decision, because whatever it was—mouse? snake? insect?—vanished into the night, having left no more than a slight tickle on her skin.

Hedia stumbled on. The alternative was to huddle where she was. She wasn't going to do that. Many men—she smiled—could testify to the fact that she was not of a passive temperament.

The sun must have risen, because she was beginning to be able to make out shapes though not yet colors. She itched all over, and whenever a drop of sweat oozed into a scratch, it stung like a hot wire.

Birds called to one another in the canopy. They didn't for the most part sound very musical, and the cries of one in particular sounded like sheets of bronze rubbing.

Of course they might not be birds. Hedia was beginning to regret that she knew so little about plants and animals. She'd never really liked the outdoors, even in circumstances as controlled as the garden of a close friend. Afterward she generally found nicks and bruises that she had ignored in the throes of passion.

She saw a human figure and stopped where she stood. It was little more than an arm's length ahead of her, but because it was completely motionless she had almost walked into it before she noticed its presence: a bearded man, looking back over his shoulder in terror. It was stone, but it wasn't a statue.

Ahead of the male figure were a woman and a child. They had fallen over: their limbs stuck up from the ferns and leaf litter. None of them wore clothing, but the man had a bandolier woven from withies which had survived weathering better than cloth had.

Hedia turned in sudden reflex. She glimpsed a face watching her through a screen of the spindly saplings which grew until, light-starved, they died. The face vanished so quickly that she might have thought she imagined it, save for the blue pentacle tattooed on the forehead.

She was being watched—followed—by the man-faced ape which she'd seen clambering through the ruins just before she dived away from her captors.

Hedia began to run, which was pointless; and looked for a branch that she could use for a club, which was even more foolish. Any branch she could break off would be useless against the muscles beneath the ape's russet fur.

She didn't hear the creature following. Well, she hadn't heard it before, either, but it obviously *had* followed her from the ruins. *If it wanted to harm me, it could have done anything it pleased while I was asleep. Or now, for that matter.*

She had been aware of the slow thumping in the sky for some while, but as the sound became louder, she realized that it wasn't a bird's call. Understanding struck her; she stopped dead, wishing that she were closer to the petrified family so that she might be confused with them.

She craned her neck upward. *Can they see through the trees? What they're doing is a waste of time if they can't, though . . . even if they can see me, that doesn't mean they can land in this forest.*

The beating sails passed overhead. The thumping faded, then swelled again as a second vessel followed, slightly farther out than the first. Hedia couldn't see anything, not even a deeper shadow on the canopy.

She heard people on the ships speaking. Though she was sure the voices were human, she couldn't make out the words clearly enough to know whether the language was familiar to her.

Hedia set her hands on the trunk of a great tree and leaned against it; she closed her eyes. The men in the flying ships were hunting her: it can't have been a coincidence that they flew directly overhead. The glass men who captured her might be following her track; at any rate, she didn't dare go back the way she had come for fear that she would find them waiting.

And then there was the ape; she didn't know what its plans were, but she was certainly part of them. What *his* plans were: the creature's human face was masculine. Rather ruggedly handsome, as a matter of fact.

There was no point at all in her going on but she did regardless, pushing her way through more of these *accursed* saplings. Several were dead; their dried twigs scratched her no matter how careful she tried to be. She came to another fallen tree; she couldn't see over the trunk. *I'll turn left when I get past it so that I'm going the way I was before. Otherwise I'll be walking in circles, which—*

An eight-foot-long lizard hopped to the top of the great tree bole; it cocked its head to stare down at her. Half the lizard's length was tail, so it probably didn't weigh much more than a large hunting dog.

Hedia stopped in midstep. The creature stood on two legs; its thighs were disproportionately muscular, like those of the fighting cocks bred by the manager of Saxa's farm in the Sabine Hills.

Balancing as delicately as a sparrow on its right foot, the lizard raised its left leg and cocked it back. It hissed at Hedia. The middle of the three toes was armed with a hooked claw the size and shape of a sickle.

Something *thrummed* by close overhead. The lizard launched itself toward her, but a serpent—

A rope! A bark rope weighted with fist-sized pieces of crystal on either end!

—wrapped around the creature. Hedia ducked and the lizard crashed past, twisting its long neck to snap at her as it went by. It pulled a lock of hair, but she was already stumbling forward.

Over Hedia's shoulder, the lizard and the great red-haired ape were rolling in combat. The reptile shrieked like steam shrilling from a covered pot, but the ape was as silent as death itself.

Hedia ducked to shove her way through a shrub whose stems arched from a common center and touched the ground again with their tops. A day ago she couldn't have imagined plunging into such a mass; now it was only an obstacle to be surmounted as she fled.

She burst out into a broad glade covered with flowers and rank grass that grew no higher than her knees. Two of the flying ships lay before her, canted on their sides when at rest. Several score of men carrying ropes and hand nets were starting toward the forest under the command of one of the figures in blazing armor. This time the armored man had taken off his helmet, so that Hedia could see that he had a tattoo on his forehead like that of the ape.

Hedia turned to dodge back but stumbled to her knees from exhaustion. Three nets curled over her and tightened. The hunters would have caught her regardless before she pushed herself back into the brush.

"WHO ARE YOU HERE TO SEE?" Alphena demanded. She was tired and was feeling the strain besides, but she doubted she would have been able to sleep even if she hadn't needed to remain in the back garden with Anna.

The doorman and a carpenter's assistant held a wretched man who was clad in an uncertain number of layers. If they had been clean, he would have looked parti-colored; as it was, they were the uniform shade of filth.

He mumbled something. Alphena couldn't make out the words. "Speak up!" she said in frustration.

"Da noble Alpheno Saxo," the fellow said. He had a strong Gallic accent.

Alphena grimaced. She glanced over her shoulder toward Anna, but there was no need to bother the older woman with this one.

To the servants she said, "Beat him and throw him back into the street."

The carpenter pulled the maul from beneath his sash. Alphena snapped, "Don't kill him! Well, try not to kill him."

The beggar squalled as Alphena slouched back onto the garden bench. He was the third one who had tried to slip into Saxa's house with the steady trickle of delivery people, some of whom looked just as disreputable as he did.

Anna was busy with a growing array of paraphernalia. She had brought three small wooden chests from Corylus' apartment—members of Alphena's escort had carried them behind the litter—but she had sent a score of messengers out in the hours since they arrived here, to order more materials. Supplies, mostly in baskets or jars, arrived in response—sometimes with the messenger, but more often brought by unfamiliar men or women.

Some of the beggars living in the cul-de-sac had thought that gave them an opportunity. They had been wrong.

Alphena grinned at the recollection. At least the intruders had provided occupation for the considerable company of servants in the alley—footmen, messengers, watchmen. The deputy steward Callistus acted as paymaster, but he was under the observation of two clerks from the accounts division.

Alphena had directed a pair of servants to carry a bench just inside the open back gate. Though wicker, it would have been an awkward load for one person. Alphena had decided not to move it herself, especially while wearing the long sword. The servants could have lifted marble furniture as easily: it just would have required more of them.

There were scores lounging around nervously, after all. Nobody in the household seemed to have slept since Hedia was abducted.

Alphena stayed by the gate not so much because Anna needed help—she didn't—but so that anybody who arrived got a hearing instead of a blow. Several of the people bringing the old woman's orders would have been lucky to escape with their lives if they came to Saxa's door under normal circumstances.

Anna hummed quietly as she worked. Alphena didn't know whether the tune had magical significance or if Anna simply hummed while she was working. She seemed focused and content, if not exactly cheerful. Apparently her forebodings had been submerged as she lost herself in the activity.

Someone opened the interior door, peeked in, and quickly closed the door again. Alphena looked around, but she didn't see who it had been. Probably some servants, wondering what was happening. When they saw the Marsian witch at work in the middle of the garden, they fled as though demons were pursuing.

No demons as yet, Alphena thought, rolling the idea in her mind until it brought a grin. *Perhaps soon, though.*

Two deliverymen arrived at the head of the alley and were passed through after muttered questioning. The doorman escorted them to where Alphena waited. They carried a potted fruit tree between them on a handbarrow.

Why has Anna ordered a tree?

Before Alphena could speak, the man in front said, "A first-quality pomegranate in planting vase, a gift for Lord Saxa from his friend Publius Corylus!"

"But he says stick it in the ground, don't leave it in the pot," the other servant piped up unexpectedly. "Lord Corylus does, you know?"

"Shut up, Bello!" the leading man said over his shoulder. "And he's not *Lord* Corylus anyhow, he's a knight!"

Then, apologetically to Alphena, "But he did say that, yeah. He wants you to plant it where the dead pear was. Though it won't bear as well out of the pot."

"Bring it in, then," Alphena said. Then, thinking of the way the servants disliked the back garden—and what was going to happen tonight wouldn't change that feeling for the better—she added, "Say. Could you two plant the tree yourselves?"

The servants exchanged puzzled looks. The man in front said, "I guess we could, mistress, but, well . . . don't you have your own gardeners?"

"Never mind that," Alphena said. "There'll be an extra silver piece for each of you. And you'll find tools in the shed in the corner."

Why has Corylus sent us a pomegranate tree? Alphena thought. Well, she could ask him when they next met. For now, it was a simple enough problem to deal with.

The men set the pot close to the peach tree to keep it out of the way when they were digging, then sauntered to the toolshed. The younger one—he had a nasty gash in his scalp but it didn't seem to have harmed his cheerful nature—eyed Anna as he passed her, but there was no particular concern in his glance. He was just curious.

Anna ignored them both. Their presence wasn't even an interruption.

Another load arrived, this time a foreman leading two men who carried a large wicker basket. The sun was still below the eastern houses, but the sky was bright enough for Alphena to watch the servants questioning them. She thought of snarling to the officious fools to let the men through—they were obviously not beggars—but she held her tongue.

Maybe I'm mellowing. More likely, I'm just tired. She was certainly very tired.

"We're from Agrimandi the Potter," the foreman said officiously. His eyes had flicked down to the sword Alphena wore; disdain made his tone sharper than it might normally have been when greeting the person at a senator's door. "We've brought the basin that Lord Saxa ordered."

"Bring it in!" Anna called, no longer lost in arrangement of the powders and other articles that she was preparing. She grabbed both walking sticks and lurched upright. "That's what I've been waiting for. Bring it in, dearies."

The foreman hesitated. "Yes, do it!" Alphena said with a curt flick of her hand.

The potter's servants tramped through the gate. The goods would be made outside the city and brought in by wagon or more likely barge. Agrimandi might even be a jobber rather than a manufacturer; given the haste, the object had to be from the stock he had on hand rather than a special order.

"Set it there, by the well curb," Anna said, pointing with a stick. "Unpack it and set it on the ground."

The porters untied the top of the basket and withdrew a shallow basin from its packing of straw. It was four feet in diameter and glazed a bright blue; it was probably meant for a birdbath.

On the rim were four crouching figures. Alphena stepped closer and identified them: a gryphon, a chimaera, a basilisk, and a mantichore. She glanced at Anna but didn't speak.

"Ma'am?" said the older of the men who'd brought the pomegranate. His partner was at the ancient well, filling a bucket made from willow splits and tarred to make it waterproof. "We'll wet it down good and head back now, all right?"

The pomegranate was settled in the ground. The men had even trailed the extra soil neatly along the edges of the summer bedrooms in the inner corners of the garden.

"Yes, very good," Alphena said. "And take the pot back with you."

"Ah—ma'am?" the workman said, frowning in concern. "That's a valuable piece, you know?"

Alphena opened her mouth to snarl, then paused. *He was trying to do me a favor. He cannot imagine how wealthy father is.*

"Even so," she said with a negligent wave of her hand. *Publius Corylus would be pleased with me.* Looking toward the alley, she said, "Callistus? A silver piece for each of the men whom Master Corylus sent."

One of the clerks stared at her in surprise: a silver piece was a day's wage. If he had been about to say something, he was prevented by his partner who tugged him around to face the other way. Callistus merely bowed and said, "Of course, your ladyship."

The men who had brought the basin were leaving also. The foreman had caught the exchange with the nurserymen and watched her hopefully as he passed, but Alphena merely gave him a disdainful glance.

Anna turned to face her. The two of them were alone in the garden once more.

"I guess that's done it," Anna said with satisfaction. "There's nothing more to do but wait for moonrise."

"All right," Alphena said. She swallowed. "What should I do now, mistress?"

Anna stretched, raising her right arm and then her left separately so that she could keep one cane firmly planted on the ground at all times. "Get some rest, your ladyship," she said. "I'm going to try to do that myself, and I don't have near so far to go tonight as you do."

She pursed her lips. "And get something to eat," she added. "There's no telling when you'll be able to eat next. Ah—you might make it a good meal."

Because it may be your last, Alphena thought, completing the sentence.

"Yes," she said. "We'll both do that."

VARUS WALKED BESIDE PULTO at the rear of the squad of "Praetorian Guards." He had listened to the servant muttering curses all the way from Saxa's house where they started before dawn.

It wasn't until they clashed to a halt in front of the home of Sempronius Tardus that Varus realized the old soldier wasn't worried about what would happen if they were caught pretending to be soldiers on a mission for the emperor. Rather, he was furious that the troupe of servants was hopeless at marching in step.

Because of the circumstances Pulto couldn't even scream and slap them into better order with the vinewood swagger stick he carried in the guise of a centurion. Lenatus, at the head of the column with Corylus, was probably having the same mental problem.

Varus grinned. The situation was pretty funny when he thought about it. The risk of being tortured to death was an accepted hazard for any veteran of skirmishing on the frontier. The embarrassment of marching bumbling incompetents through the middle of Carce was a new experience and apparently a more harrowing one.

"Open in the name of the emperor!" Corylus said. The door was closed, but Varus could see movement behind the eye slot. "I have a petition with a rescript from the emperor, requiring the release of Master Pandareus of Athens!"

The acting guardsmen looked quite impressive when they halted, which was all that really mattered. Pulto seemed to have begun to relax. In truth, the reaction of most residents of Carce—citizens as well as slaves—to a squad of soldiers was to get out of their way, not to quibble about the quality of their close-order drill.

No one spoke from the other side of the door. Varus moved so that he—or anyway, his broad-striped toga—was visible behind Corylus.

Corylus nodded. Lenatus stepped forward and rapped a sharp tattoo on the door panel with his stick.

"I'll count to five!" Corylus said, standing arms-akimbo. His molded body armor, silvered and then parcel-gilt, was dazzling in the rising sun. "Then we're coming in whether you open the door or not!"

Bolts rattled inside. Pulto muttered what sounded like a curse. *He must have been looking forward to a chance to break the door down,* Varus realized. For an instant he was appalled; then he grinned. He thought, *I hope that looks like a sinister smile.*

The door creaked outward, pushed by the doorman. Lenatus and a "soldier" slammed it the rest of the way into the outside wall as soon as a crack wide enough for their fingers had opened. The doorman jumped inside and flattened himself against the back of his alcove.

Inside stood the majordomo Varus had seen the previous day. He looked, if anything, more frightened than he had been when Saxa arrived.

"Here, read this!" Corylus ordered, holding out the petition—supposedly from the urban praetor, countersigned in vermillion by the emperor and sealed with the imperial signet.

"Master, that won't be necessary," the majordomo said, bowing low. He was an Oriental of some sort, Mesopotamian or from even farther east than that. For a moment Varus thought he was going to genuflect. "Please, master, allow me to take you and your friends to Lord Tardus. Lord Tardus will explain."

Varus tried not to react, but he supposed the way his face suddenly became blank was a reaction in itself. He had expected protests or blank denials, but what was there to explain? All the servants looked terrified, which was understandable in the face of armed men entering with the threat of the emperor's displeasure; but there was something more going on here.

A pity that the majordomo hadn't bothered to read the petition, though. The calligraphy was the work of two of the finest scribes in Saxa's household—one acting as the praetor, the other for the emperor's secretary. The librarian, Alexandros, had not only provided a document with the imperial seal but had also made a mold of it in mastic, then duplicated the markings in wax on the false petition. Artistry like that forgery deserved an audience.

Corylus motioned Varus forward. Varus stepped through the doorway directly behind his friend and Lenatus, realizing that he hadn't gotten this far the other day. *I was talking with the Sibyl while my body apparently walked through Tardus' house and found the Serapeum below his garden.*

And as Varus thought that, he felt the mist close in on him again.

CORYLUS JUMPED AS VARUS SQUEALED, "Oh, grant thou to me a path!" in the voice of an old woman. He'd heard his friend do that often enough now that he supposed he should be used to it. Having someone shout it from behind when he was already as tense as if Germans might burst out of the thickets, though. . . . He decided to allow himself to have been startled.

"What, your lordship?" the majordomo said, his eyes opening wider. "Ah, Lord Tardus is in the office, where he'll, ah, he'll be glad to explain the situation to you."

Corylus glanced back at Varus, whose face was as stern as that of a father sitting in judgment. That could have been acting—Corylus himself was trying to look like a military officer on a grim errand when in fact he felt like a schoolboy in the midst of a dangerous practical joke—but his friend's eyes were focused on something in the far distance. It gave him an uncanny expression, more disturbing than fury would have been.

When Varus didn't speak or press ahead, Corylus nodded curtly. "Take us to Lord Tardus," he said, shaking the forged judicial order toward the majordomo's chest.

The man stepped back, bowed again, and turned, pattering into the office where Tardus sat on his senatorial chair. He bowed again and while still bent over said, "Your lordship, the, ah . . . this officer wishes to speak with you about Pandareus of Athens."

The servant sidled from the room as quickly as a startled crab. Tardus raised his eyes. There was a direct line from his ivory seat and through the anteroom to the front door. The master of the house should have been as aware of the soldiers as Corylus was of him, but instead he looked as puzzled as if he found himself addressing the Senate in the nude.

"I am Marcus Sempronius Tardus, Senator and Commissioner for the Sacred Rites," he said. His voice was reedy but seemed calm. "Why are you here, Tribune?"

Have we made a mistake? Corylus thought. He held out the document and said, "We're here to release one Pandareus of Athens. This is our authority."

"The teacher?" Tardus said. "Why ever do you think he's here? I've heard him lecture in the Forum, but we have never spoken."

You were at dinner with Pandareus two nights ago! Corylus thought. At least Varus had said that Tardus forced his way into the dinner.

He glanced at his friend. Varus, in the same ancient voice as before, said, *"Oh grant thou to me a path!"* and started toward the alcove at the back of the room where stairs led upward.

"I don't understand," Tardus said. He sounded confused and irritated, but Corylus didn't hear any hint that he was afraid. "Why did he say that?"

Lenatus strode forward and went up the stairs ahead of his master. He didn't draw his sword, but he cocked back the swagger stick in his right hand to use for a cudgel if the need arose.

Corylus followed Varus, wishing that he had something to fill his hand also. Only the "common soldiers" had shields. That had been the correct decision, but it increased Corylus' sense of disquiet. It *really* felt as though he was going into action.

They reached the second floor landing. Lenatus paused. Varus started to push by without speaking. The trainer hopped sideways up the next two steps to take the lead again, then turned and stepped quickly to the top of the staircase. He moved on his toes, skipping up the last six steps two at a time.

If he takes a spear through the belly when he turns into the third-floor corridor, Corylus thought, *I'll have time to get Varus out of the way, even if it means tripping him and jerking him backward.*

Which was probably what Lenatus was thinking also. That was a soldier's job, after all: putting himself between possible violence and the civilians who were paying him. This just happened to be a direct example of something that was performed by hundreds of thousands of men on the frontiers.

Only the central section of Tardus' house had a third floor; the wings, reaching back on either side, had two. Corylus expected this top level would be servant's quarters, but the decoration all the way along the stairwell was of the same high quality: a continuous rural landscape in which winged cupids plowed, sowed, and reaped on the left side and on the right tended vines and olive trees. At the top was a harvest feast which extended around the wall behind the head of the stairs.

Corylus heard Tardus protesting from some distance back. He had apparently started up the stairs but the armed servants directly on "the tribune's" heels prevented him from joining the leaders by. Doing that to the householder—and a senator besides—would have been insanely foolhardy under most circumstances, but every soul of them would be crucified if this went wrong anyway.

No one was in the upper corridor. Given the number of servants in Tardus' household, that was in itself remarkable enough to arouse suspicion. As with the stairwell, the decoration was expensively complete. The corridor floor had a simple white pebble background broken into squares by lines of black pebbles, but there were mosaic cartouches in front of the stairs—in which pigmies rode cranes and battled with winged serpents—and at the far end under a skylight.

"Sir, what do we do now?" Lenatus said, speaking to Corylus. He gave his master a sidelong glance that showed a degree of concern.

"*Grant thou me a path!*" Varus said and started down the corridor.

"I'll lead," Corylus said. He drew his sword without being conscious of what he was doing; it seemed the natural thing, like taking a deep breath after surfacing from a plunge into the sea. Varus walked at a measured pace, so it was easy to get ahead of him.

The door on the left side at the end of the corridor was open. That room held a profusion of books: baskets of scrolls, each tagged, and codices lying flat with their cut pages turned outward so that the titles written on the fore-edges could be read.

The doorway to the room across the hall was closed with a light panel that didn't quite reach either the lintel or the floor. Herbal smoke drifted over and under it, tickling Corylus' nose. Several people were speaking—droning a chant—on the other side, but he couldn't make out the words.

He poised, starting to try the latch but deciding instead to kick the panel. Varus tried to walk past, seemingly oblivious of the naked sword. Lenatus caught his shoulder and dragged him back by main force.

Corylus smiled, though mostly in his mind. *If Lenatus hadn't had to grab his master, he'd have tried to nudge me out of the way and go through first himself—just like he'd do across the Rhine if a young tribune decided to be a hero.*

When Corylus looked down at the gap at the bottom of the door, he noticed for the first time the mosaic cartouche he was standing on. It showed the priest Laocoon and his two sons wrapped in the coils of sea monsters, punishing him for trying to prevent his fellow Trojans from dragging the wooden horse within the walls of their city.

Memory of the vision of Typhon almost made him jump to the side, but there was a better way to get off the image. He lifted his hobnailed boot and kicked the latch and the panel around it into splinters. What was left of the door slapped the wall as Corylus strode into the room.

It was the mirror image of the library across the hall but fitted out with a couch and a writing desk instead of shelves and book baskets. Originally it must have been intended as a reading room to which Tardus would bring the chosen volume.

The lower two-thirds of the walls were dark red divided into panels by slender golden pillars. In the center of each panel was one of the Olympian gods, also painted in gold.

The upper register was a frieze of the wanderings of Odysseus. The Cyclops Polyphemus stood on a crag facing the door, holding a huge rock over his head to fling at the ship sailing toward the horizon with the hero in the stern. On the shore below the monster were wrecked vessels and the scattered bodies of men.

Corylus sneezed violently; there was much more smoke inside, welling from a murrhine tube like the one in Saxa's collection. *If they haven't somehow stolen Saxa's,* Corylus thought, *they already had the other one of a pair.*

"They" were the three servants that Persica said were controlling Tardus. They were squatting on the floor, facing inward, but they looked up when Corylus burst through the door. The North African had his mouth to one end of a reed; the murrhine tube was cemented to the other end.

Pandareus sat opposite to the North African, his back to Corylus. He didn't move when the door banged open.

One of the servants reached for the dagger in his sash; the hilt was fashioned from deer antler. Corylus kicked the fellow's arm.

The North African blew a ring of smoke toward Corylus and grunted a word.

The amulet from the Etruscan tomb burned like a hot coal. Corylus plunged through darkness into bright sunlight.

He stood on top of a crag, facing a Cyclops. The creature was easily twice his height and weighed as much as an elephant.

CHAPTER XI

Corylus staggered. His feet were still planted firmly, but now they were on gritty soil with a slight downward slope instead of a flat mosaic floor. That had thrown him off balance.

The Cyclops was thirty feet away. It turned its head toward him with a bellow; the sound was like a huge wave smashing into the shore. At the same time it shuffled awkwardly to bring its body around, like a duck trying to rotate in tight quarters. Over its head, the boulder quivered.

Corylus knew from experience that stone weighed three or four times as much as flesh did, and he could see that the boulder was the size of the Cyclops' torso. No man he knew could have lifted an equivalent mass. Even for the monster, it was a strain to be balanced rather than a whim to be toyed with. Still, the sea three hundred feet offshore—half the length of a foot race—bubbled and slapped where a similar missile must have landed.

The surface on which Corylus stood was a few hand-breadths higher than where the Cyclops' feet were planted. It wasn't much of a slope, but rather than turn and run uphill—

"Ears for Nerthus!" Corylus screamed as he charged the monster. It was the war cry of the Batavian Scouts; well, of the Scouts when they weren't slitting throats silently in the darkness. It wouldn't mean anything to the Cyclops, even if he wasn't a beast without language, but it put Corylus in the right frame of mind.

The Scouts had their own temple grove separate from the altars of the rest of the cohort which Publius Cispius had commanded on the Danube. An oak, a broad spreading wolf tree, stood in the center. They nailed to it the right ear—salted to preserve it—of every Sarmatian they killed.

The Cyclops grunted and hesitated, repositioning the huge boulder. The creature probably hadn't expected its victim to attack, which would have been justification for Corylus' tactics if he'd needed one.

He hadn't. The Batavians were a crack unit, as good as any non-citizen auxiliary cohort in the army—and better than the legions which were deployed in luxury in the eastern provinces, anybody on the Rhine or the Danube would have said. He could either have fled the monster or charged it. Neither seemed survivable, but *of course* you tried to cut the other guy's throat before he finished you.

I can't even reach his throat, Corylus realized. The thought made him grin.

The Cyclops strode forward, preparing to throw. Corylus stepped on a human arm bone. His foot flew out from under him and the bone—it was just the upper joint; the shaft had been cracked for marrow—sailed skyward.

The Cyclops gave the stone a savage push with both hands, not so much hurling it as snapping it forward in a straight line as though the springs of a catapult were driving it. Corylus landed on his back with a clang, skidding feetfirst toward the monster. He had lost his helmet and there were certainly dents in his thin bronze back plate.

The boulder hit the edge of the crag a dozen feet beyond where Corylus fell and bounced away in a cloud of dust and shattered gravel. He had thought—had imagined, though at the back of his mind—that he could dodge the missile.

He couldn't have. The monster's strength was beyond anything of which flesh should be capable. Only luck and the Cyclops' messy eating habits had gotten Corylus out of the way. The boulder would otherwise have struck him in the middle of the chest and splashed him into the ground like a fly clubbed against a brick wall.

The Cyclops bent, reaching for Corylus' outstretched legs. Corylus kicked, trying to roll himself away. The Cyclops closed a fist the size of a boar's ham over Corylus' left ankle. Corylus bent forward at the waist and thrust. The point of his short sword crunched through the gristle and small bones of the monster's wrist.

The Cyclops bellowed again—the sound felt like an avalanche of sand—and hurled Corylus inland. He wasn't sure whether the motion was deliberate or simply a twitch in reaction to the pain of the wound.

Corylus hit hard and bounced. He was twenty feet from where the Cyclops had grabbed him. He'd lost his sword. He rolled and looked back. The monster plucked the blade from the wound with his left hand and spun it far out to sea. Blood poured from the injured wrist and ran down the creature's dangling right hand.

The Cyclops turned toward Corylus, who drew the sturdy dagger from the scabbard on the right side of his equipment belt. The Cyclops strode forward, shaking the ground. Its eye was bloodshot and unwinking.

Corylus tried to curl his feet under in order to stand up. He wasn't sure that would be an advantage in this fight, but it would make him feel better. White pain exploded in his groin; he screamed and fell back. He may have lost consciousness for an instant. When the monster used his left leg as a handle, it had strained or torn the ligaments joining thighbone to pelvis.

The Cyclops seized Corylus by the shoulder and jerked him off the ground. Its body stank like a tanner's yard from the rotting blood and flesh tangled in its shaggy pelt. It crushed him to its chest and wrapped both arms around him.

Corylus stabbed. He couldn't see to place the point. It was like thrusting into a stack of bull hides.

The Cyclops continued to squeeze. Corylus couldn't see anything, but in the deepening shadows of his mind flickered a nude woman and a creature which stood on two legs but was utterly inhuman. It reminded him of a serpent, despite its fine golden fur and a triangular face like a fox.

The Cyclops was roaring. Corylus couldn't hear sound—any sound—but he felt the vibration of the chest against which he was being flattened like an olive in the press. He thought he still held the dagger, but he didn't know. All he could feel was the fiery pain which spread from his ribs and out through the skin.

Then the blackness was complete, until the woman and the slender, terrifying beast stepped from it and joined him.

VARUS FROZE in the flood of light. He had come down from the mountain on which he had been standing with the Sibyl. Below them in the infinite distance, his body led his companions through the dwelling of Sempronius Tardus and up to the room where three magicians held Pandareus.

But even as his soul reentered his body, a flash had numbed and blinded him. He fell backward, blinking and stunned. When he shook himself alert, he found that Pulto gripped the back of his toga and was holding him upright. The sword in Pulto's other hand searched for something to stab.

"You may loose me, Master Pulto!" Varus said, speaking sharply. He was embarrassed to have stumbled, and he knew that he had been wandering and no doubt speaking without conscious awareness.

What did I say this time? They must all think I'm crazy!

And in the back of his mind: *Maybe I am crazy.*

"Where's the boy?" Pulto said on a rising note. He let go of Varus; tossed him aside, very nearly. "Lenatus, where's Corylus? Where's the bloody boy?"

"He couldn't have gotten past!" Lenatus said, but as he spoke, he rushed to the doorway. "You lot! Did you see Corylus? Did the tribune go out this way?"

Varus looked over the trainer's shoulder. The hallway was choked with servants in Praetorian armor, their swords out. No one could have pushed through them quickly, even if the squad had been willing to grant passage.

The three servants whom Corylus said were at the bottom of the trouble had vanished also. Varus had seen them clearly from the Sibyl's eyrie, squatting on the floor of this room where Pandareus sat facing them. Pandareus had vanished with them.

Tardus stood behind the counterfeit troops with an expression of frightened amazement. Varus snapped to a decision.

"Lord Tardus!" he said. "Come join me, please. You men there! Make way for Senator Tardus, our host!"

I'm giving orders to a man whose home I've invaded with a forged document and a band of armed slaves, Varus thought. He'd always had an analytical mind, but recently he'd become aware of the limits of analysis. Sometimes you simply had to act, whether or not reason told you that the act was courteous, legal, or even survivable. This was one of those times.

Not that Tardus was objecting. Quite the contrary: he paused nervously until he was sure that the "Praetorians" were really making way, then bustled through to the doorway of the room where Pandareus had been held

"Varus?" Tardus said. "You're Gaius Varus, aren't you, Saxa's son?"

"Yes," said Varus, puzzled at the nervous doubt in the older man's voice. Austerely he went on, "You dined with us the night before last. And after dinner, you abducted Master Pandareus."

"That wasn't me!" Tardus said, but the denial was a prayer rather than angry disbelief. "Please, you have to believe me. I—"

He paused and looked around him. "Please, Lord Varus," he said. "Can we speak in private without these soldiers around?"

"No," said Pulto. He didn't sound angry, but there was only flat certainty in his voice. "Not when my boy's gone somewhere and I figure this fellow had something to do with sending him there."

Lenatus lifted his chin in silent agreement. Neither of the old soldiers had sheathed their swords, though at this point that was probably a matter of theater rather than real concern that they would have immediate use for the weapons.

"Sending who?" Tardus said. "I've only been allowed out myself when the sages sent *me* somewhere."

Varus gestured the thought away with his left hand. "Come," he said to Tardus. "This incense makes me want to sneeze. You and I will go into the library, but we'll leave the door open so that the centurions—"

He nodded to Lenatus. He and Pulto probably wouldn't have minded him using their names, but Varus felt that the less detail he gave about the others involved in this criminal enterprise, the better. *He* was doomed if things went wrong, but it was at least possible that the false Praetorians might escape.

"—can watch us, but you can speak privately."

Pulto snorted; Lenatus gave Varus a wry smile and said, "As your lordship wishes."

Varus remembered what Corylus had said about his behavior in the crisis after Hedia was abducted. Soldiers approved of clear, forceful orders, even if the orders themselves weren't what they wanted to hear. Confusion and hesitancy got people killed faster even than bullheaded courage.

He led Tardus across the hall and gestured him to the only couch in the library. That was partly out of respect for a man far his senior, but still more because that resulted in Varus looking down at—scarcely at his host; say rather, looking down at his potential enemy—as they spoke.

"Witnesses watched your servants abduct Master Pandareus outside my father's house," Varus said. He let the anger he felt as he spoke the words peek through in his tone. "There would be no point in you denying it, even if we hadn't seen them and Pandareus across the hall—"

He gestured.

"—a moment ago."

"They're not my servants!" Tardus insisted with a hint of fear. "They're sages from the Western Isles. They're magicians, and they were—"

He gestured with both hands as if trying to pull words out of the air. His expression was anguished.

"They were working me like a puppet. You must believe me!"

Varus didn't speak for a moment while he considered what Tardus had said. *Is that true? And whether it's true or not, what does it mean?*

"I could see and hear what was happening," Tardus said. He sat rather than reclining on the couch and he rubbed his temples with the tips of his fingers. "Mostly I could at least, but it was as though it was all behind a wall of glass. And what I remember seemed to be happening to someone else."

"Where did they go, the sages?" Varus said. "And where did they take Pandareus and Corylus?"

"I don't know," Tardus said, speaking with apparent satisfaction. "So long as they were controlling me, I saw what they were doing and heard what they said, even among themselves when I wasn't present. But when you broke in on them, I was freed. Thank Venus and Mercury, I'm free again!"

The goddess from whom Carce's founder Aeneas was descended, Varus thought, *and the god of luck. Good choices.*

Then, smiling slightly, he thought, *A pedant even now. Well, a scholar.*

Tardus frowned and lowered his hands. Apparently realization that he was his own man again had freed the senator from some of his terror . . . which might make him less cooperative.

"Who is this Corylus?" Tardus said. "I saw Master Pandareus, of course, but I don't remember a Corylus."

"Never mind," Varus said with another dismissive flick of the hand. He had no intention of letting the older man take charge of the discussion. "How did you meet these sages? Or how did they meet you?"

"I didn't—" Tardus said, alarmed again. He stopped and licked his lips. He was obviously willing to lie to Varus, but he seemed to be afraid to do so. "Well, perhaps I did. . . . That is, I carried out some, ah, researches to gain knowledge about Atlantis. I didn't learn anything and thought I'd failed, but it may be that by asking in certain fashions, I lit a beacon of sorts for the sages. They sailed here from the Western Isles and left their ship at Ostia."

He frowned and added, "Their ship flies through the air, like the ones I saw during your father's entertainment. I, ah . . ."

He lowered his face again and wrung his hands. In a barely audible voice, he continued, "They asked me questions. I couldn't deny them. *Couldn't*, no more than I could walk on air. They wanted to know who the magician was who caused the vision in the theater. I told them Pandareus did. I didn't realize it was you, Lord Varus."

Tardus gestured for words again, then locked his fingers together and stared at them. He said, "I had seen Pandareus in the Temple of Jupiter the night I was in charge of the *Sibylline Books*. I was asleep so I didn't see what happened, but I thought Pandareus must have been the cause. He's a great scholar, you know. Your father arrived, but he wasn't, well, wasn't a magician, and I never thought of a youth like you. So the sages took Pandareus."

This is actually funny, Varus thought. Though he wasn't sure his father would have thought so.

He wondered what would have happened if these sages had tried to abduct him. Varus had a considerable escort at any time he went out of the house, but these were magicians. He remembered how the Hyperborean wizard had put everyone in the Temple of Jupiter to sleep; including Tardus himself, now that Varus thought about it.

Instead of speculating about what had drawn the sages to Tardus in the first place, Varus asked, "*Why* did they want Pandareus? Or me, or *anyone*? If they're magicians themselves."

As they clearly were, given the way they had vanished—and taken Pandareus with them.

"They're afraid of a monster named Uktena," Tardus said. "He has a connection with Carce, but I don't know what it is. I don't mean they hid it from me—I couldn't understand what I saw in their minds. Your father has the other half of the talisman that they use in their own magic, the murrhine tube. Perhaps that's what drew them."

He appeared to be getting his mental bearings again, but Varus no longer feared that the senator would be uncooperative. It seemed that imagining Saxa's son was a magician of untold power had frightened him as much as his earlier concern for the emperor's torturers.

Tardus half-raised his arm, an orator making a gesture of emphasis. "When you showed a vision of the monster," he said, "they thought they could force you to help them. They thought Pandareus could, I mean. So they took me—forced me to take them—to Saxa's house when the teacher was present."

"Uktena?" Varus said, frowning. *He* knew what the monster of the vision was. *The Sibyl told me* . . . "You mean Typhon?"

Tardus shrugged with a look of irritation. "They called it Uktena," he said. "Called *him* Uktena; they said he used to be a man. But he's a monster, now, and they think he's about to break out of the prison they put him in."

Varus wished that Pandareus were here to discuss this with, for his wisdom. *And I wish Corylus were here, because he's sensible and he makes the world around him seem solid.* Even when the world clearly wasn't solid.

"What did your sages have to do with my mother's abduction?" Varus said, attacking the problem from another angle.

"Your mother?" said Tardus in surprise. "You mean Lady Hedia? Has she disappeared also?" He grimaced and made a gesture with both hands. "I don't know where she's gone," he said. "I don't know where the sages went, or Pandareus or this Corylus. The others don't matter, but the sages do."

Tardus looked up at Varus. The terror in his expression was unmistakable. This time it had nothing to do with the youth whom he thought was a magician.

"If the sages can't control Uktena, they'll try to release him somewhere far away from their Western Isles," Tardus said. "You know what the monster will do—you showed us all the vision of what would happen if he got free."

He swallowed and said, "The sages will release Uktena here in Carce."

HEDIA TURNED. She was draped in three nets which were being dragged in slightly different directions, but she drew herself up as straight as she could. The hunters chattered excitedly to one another in—bad—Greek, so it was in that language which she said, "I am Lady Hedia, wife of Lord Gaius Alphenus Saxa, Consul of Carce. Take these cords off me at once and bring me proper clothing!"

It was a challenge to be regally disdainful while naked, limping, and covered with cuts and scratches, but Hedia had generations of noble ancestors to fall back on. She didn't expect her captors to pay attention, but at least she wasn't disgracing her family.

Somewhat to her surprise, the hunters—servants, obviously—fell silent and slacked the net ropes enough that Hedia could straighten fully. Along with tunics that left the right shoulder bare, they wore ankle-length boots of some supple material. Some of them glanced back to the taller man in fiery armor who was walking toward them.

"Are you in charge of this rabble?" Hedia said. "What do you mean by behaving in this fashion?"

The man smirked at her in a comfortable, arrogant fashion. That wasn't an unfamiliar expression on the faces of men who were seeing Hedia nude; though usually her appearance was less bedraggled.

"I am the Minos Serdain," he said. "Kalpos and I—"

He nodded toward the similarly armored man who remained in the more distant of the two ships.

"—were sent by the Council of the Minoi to bring you back when the Servitors botched the job."

Serdain made a sour face. "Using the Servitors was a bad choice but a necessary one," he said. "Even the most powerful of us couldn't have gone to the Underworld and returned . . . but you did, Minos Hedia. Which is why we need you."

He wasn't speaking *bad* Greek, she realized, but rather a very foreign Greek. Among Saxa's recent visitors had been a delegation from the ancient Greek colony of Vipasca in Lusitania. Their speech had some of the same rhythms as this Serdain's did; perhaps it was the Phoenician influence.

"Release me, then," Hedia said, sounding as haughty as she could while naked and looking—literally—like a sparrow which cats had been playing with. "When you've done that, we can discuss my terms for helping you."

She was no more a magician than she was emperor, but if these Minoi wanted to think otherwise, then perhaps that would give her some bargaining power.

Serdain chuckled. "No, I don't think I'll do that, my dear," he said, "since I'm not a mindless automaton like the Servitors. We might not be lucky enough to get you back the next time. And you—"

His grin became suddenly cruel.

"—might not be so lucky either. The jungle can be dangerous, particularly where you were, in the ruins of Lann's keep after Procron destroyed it. Procron played with Lann's dependants, you see. Some of the results may still be alive, in which case they're worse than the creatures that nature herself created."

The ape with a human head, Hedia realized. *But that—*

Aloud she said, "Your forehead."

She tried to point, but she couldn't raise her arm high enough to make the gesture more than a hint of her intention. "The tattoo there. What does it mean?"

"Mean?" said Serdain. He raised his free hand—the other held the flaring helmet that covered even his face behind a mesh of the same metal as the remainder of his armor. His gauntleted finger stopped just short of touching the pentagram. "It means that I'm a Minos, of course. It's a sign of the favor of Zeus. But I see—"

His eyes narrowed.

"—that you do not have the mark. Has the Council made a mistake, I wonder?"

"You'll learn what a mistake you've made if you continue to treat me with disrespect!" Hedia said.

Serdain chuckled. "No doubt, no doubt," he said in a mocking voice.

A pair of glass men—Servitors—had come from the nearer ship. They reached under the tangled nets and locked hobbles around her ankles.

The restraints appeared to be made of the same translucent substance as the Servitors themselves. To Hedia's amazement they weighed as little as silk leggings, but when she tried to kick, they were as constraining as steel. They would allow her to take only shuffling, eighteen-inch steps.

When the hobbles were in place, the servants began to remove their nets. Their task was more difficult because they seemed afraid to touch Hedia. Some of the cords were looped on her elbows and even her chin.

She glared at Serdain, refusing to help or even recognize the servants. He continued to smirk. That appeared to be his normal expression.

The nets came free, one after the other in quick succession. The servants retreated in pairs and began to roll the nets without letting them touch the coarse grass. Serdain said, "Come to the ship and we'll be off, Minos Hedia. If you really are a Minos."

"Carry me," Hedia said, her arms crossed. It was a petty response, but she had noticed that the servants were afraid of her. "Since you've made it impossible for me to walk."

She *could* walk, of course, but she couldn't walk in a dignified manner. There was almost nothing she could do with dignity in her present condition, but she didn't intend to stagger along like a hunched beldame in addition to the other degradations.

Instead of responding, Serdain turned his back and stalked back toward the nearer vessel. The servants followed, murmuring among themselves again.

Are they going to leave me? Hedia thought. The two Servitors gripped her by the upper arms and lifted her off the ground. They walked toward the ship in perfect unison; they could have been one another's mirror images.

Hedia drew her legs up under her to kick but restrained the reflex in time to save herself a broken toe—or worse. *It'd be like kicking marble statues.* She held herself silent and upright as the creatures paced on.

The ship lay on its port side, canted at about a thirty-degree angle. That put the railing low enough for the servants to clamber aboard easily; despite his armor, Serdain mounted without apparent difficulty. He walked to the stern and used both hands to settle the helmet back onto his head.

With the helmet in place, Serdain took an object—it looked to Hedia like a simple pebble—out of a pouch of silvery cloth hanging from a stud on his breastplate. She had noticed it but had assumed it was simply a bangle.

The Servitors stepped aboard with Hedia between them and stood her against the single mast. One held her in place while the other bent at her feet. She heard a click and found her hobble was firmly attached to the mast step.

The ship trembled, then rocked upright on its keel. The crew didn't have anything to do with it, so far as Hedia could see. The humans, the hunters who had caught her, squatted along the rails. Other than shifting slightly, presumably for balance, and talking among themselves in low voices, they didn't seem concerned or even interested.

The Servitors—two on this ship with Hedia, but four on the deck of the other vessel—stepped into the bow and didn't move after that. She might have taken them for glass decorations if she hadn't seen them previously.

Serdain was motionless also, but the stone in his hands spat light which occasionally seemed to coat the stern. It faded from Hedia's sight as it wicked forward along the deck. She felt the hair on the backs of her arms rise for just an instant.

She grimaced. Alphena would understand—or at least experience—whatever was going on to make the ship move. The girl had a natural talent for magic, according to Anna.

To Hedia it was all a blank, like the literature Varus got excited about or the mathematics that the engineer planning an irrigation tunnel at her first husband's estate in Calabria tried to interest her in. She smiled, remembering the engineer; she hadn't thought of him in years.

Hedia had talents of her own. She wouldn't trade them for magic or literature or mathematics or anything in the world . . . nor, she was sure, would any of the men she'd gotten to know want her to trade.

The sails were carried on a pair of booms butted to opposite sides of the mast. Hedia hadn't paid much attention to ships, but that was unusual enough to have caught her eye when she first saw the ships flying above the city of the vision. There was a double *thump* above her and a gust of wind.

She twisted—her body was free—and looked upward. The sails were beating like a bird's wings, just as she had seen them in the vision.

The ship hopped once and a second time on the ground, then lifted from the glade. The "wings" weren't big enough relative to the hull to do that, at least not as slowly as they were flapping.

But the ship is flying, she realized, looking over the side. *There's no question about that.*

Hedia itched. She was extremely hungry, and she would have liked something to drink. Thirst during the night had caused her to slurp water from the upturned leaves of a plant rooted in the trunk of a great tree, but there hadn't been much even of that.

She wasn't going to beg, though; not yet. And if Serdain's apparent concentration was real—as it may well have been, if he was responsible for the ship flying—he might not have been able to respond to any request she made anyway.

She rubbed the deck with her big toe. It appeared to be ordinary wood, though with an oily slickness. Its broad grain showed sharp contrast between the white softer wood and the almost black divisions.

Does the kind of wood help the ship fly?

Hedia quirked a bitter smile. That question didn't matter in the least; except that it saved her from thinking about the questions that did matter.

How can I escape? How can I get back to Carce even if I do escape? Am I going to spend eternity being tortured in the Underworld alongside Calpurnius Latus . . . ?

She had no answers to those questions either, of course. Still, her worst enemies—and there was a long list of them, for one reason or another—had never claimed Hedia was a coward. She would focus on escaping, and after that on return to Carce.

What happened after she died could take care of itself. As no doubt it would.

When she had been stumbling among the lightless tree trunks, Hedia had thought of the forest as degrees of blackness and greens so dark as to be black themselves. Looking down on the same expanse, she was delighted by the amount of color.

Several of the giants emerging from the canopy were sending up spikes covered with bright yellow flowers. Butterflies with blue, transparent wings flitted among them like chips of brilliant glass.

The second ship was paralleling theirs about fifty feet to the side. A tiny monkey looked up at them and flung itself to cover deeper in the foliage. The ships were so quiet that Hedia could clearly hear its *cheep!* of alarm.

They were flying at about the speed of a trotting horse—faster than Hedia had ever been carried on a ship, though within the capacity—for a brief dash—of the triremes she had seen exercising in the sea off Misenum. Under other circumstances, this could be a pleasant, mildly exciting interlude.

She giggled, causing the nearer servants to look at her with concern. *It would be interesting to see what Serdain looked like stripped to the buff. He can't be more than forty, and he moves well despite that clumsy armor.*

They passed within a long bowshot of crystal buildings surrounded by ordinary huts which spilled down the hill from them. People, dressed and looking like Serdain's human servants, were at their occupations in the terraced yards between the ordinary dwellings. Most of them didn't bother to look up at the ships.

One of the crystal structures was a squat dome. The other, attached to it, was a tall cylinder whose thin walls fully displayed the contents. A sloping ramp wound from the bottom to the top of the interior. In layered beds grew grains, vegetables, and fruit, often of types which Hedia had never seen before.

She sniffed. Of course, to her food was something that appeared on serving tables, frequently in forms so modified that a farm manager wouldn't be able to determine the original.

Hedia turned to look off the right side of the ship; to starboard, seamen called it, though she had never understood why. She saw glints on top of a hill in the distance. *Those must be the ruins where I escaped.*

"What are those?" she said to Serdain in a crisp voice, pointing as much to emphasize her question as to indicate the shattered crystal.

The Minos seemed oblivious of all except the pebble in his hands. That continued to spit sparks like amber rubbed with silk.

As I expected, Hedia thought. She gestured to the servants along the railing. The ship was so narrow that if she had bent over and stretched out a hand, she could have touched several of them on the shoulder.

"You!" she said. "Why are those buildings broken that way? What happened there?"

The servants didn't move away—perhaps they couldn't without making the ship wobble in a dangerous fashion—but they lowered their eyes. One began singing a counting song as if to block out Hedia's voice.

"Do you want me to turn you all into toads?" Hedia said on a rising note. She was afraid, and she let that come out as anger in her voice. "Is that what you want? *Is it?*"

She straightened and pointed her right arm toward a hunter slightly astern of where she was fastened; her index and middle fingers were extended. He turned his head, but he couldn't help seeing the threat in the corner of his eyes.

I'm going to look like a complete fool if he calls my bluff.

"It's Procron's keep!" the servant blurted. Fear made his wretched dialect almost unintelligible, but at least he was trying. "Don't turn me into a toad. Don't turn me into a toad."

The rest of what he was trying to say was lost when he began to blubber. Hedia thought she could guess the words easily enough, though. She lowered her arm.

"It's not Procron's keep," said the hunter just ahead of Hedia's target. "It's Lann's, that Procron destroyed before the Council drove Procron out. Procron was a mile farther west."

He cleared his throat and risked looking directly at Hedia; from the scars on his chest and right shoulder, he must have tangled with a lizard like the one that she saw just before she was recaptured. The hunter added, "I was in the Council fleet."

I wonder what happened to the ape that saved me? Hedia thought. Aloud she said to the hunter, "Thank you, my good man."

That tiny bit of information raised her spirits enormously. The Minoi fought one another . . . and she already knew that at least some of the Minoi were male. She smiled kittenishly at Serdain, though he was too lost in his magic to notice her; for the moment.

There would be other times and other male Minoi. Hedia was no longer without resources.

They slanted out over water—one of the bands of water which separated the ring islands she had seen as she approached with the Servitors who had snatched her from her bed. *That certainly provided Saxa with an unexpected surprise,* she thought. She snorted a laugh which she throttled with her hand. *I do hope Saxa is all right.*

Mats of vegetation floated in the broad lagoon. At first she took them for islands, but they drifted in the sluggish current. Flowers rose on long stalks, following the sun; there were animals, too, popping up and vanishing to leave only green undulations behind.

And there were fish as well. Anyway, something was swimming so deeply under the water that Hedia saw only a huge shadow.

Ahead was the city of the vision in the theater, a jewel glittering against the dark green hills surrounding it. A dozen ships circled lazily over the crystal towers, their sails beating slowly; many similar ships bobbed in the lagoon, tied up at the seawall below the city.

The ships weren't in the wide plaza facing the temple, because that was full of spectators: many thousands of people, including as many as a hundred of the armored Minoi. Most of them had their helmets off. With each Minos was a band of retainers in distinct livery. The dyes were vivid enough to bring a fortune in Carce to anyone who was able to duplicate them.

Serdain's ship sank toward the seafront; the ship that had been escorting it joined those circling above the city. The hunters murmured in animation to one another, though Hedia couldn't catch words.

She drew herself up with as much dignity as circumstances allowed. *More than when they caught me in the forest*, she thought. *I will get out of this and return home. I will!*

Hedia had half-expected cheers from the crowd as the ship they waited for approached. Instead, she heard frightened whispers magnified many thousands of times.

She felt a touch of disquiet. *They didn't bring me here for a human sacrifice, did they?* The Gauls and Scythians did that, and Varus had told her that as recently as the war with Hannibal, the Senate of Carce had made human sacrifices.

I'll deal with the situation as it develops. And if some priest comes toward me with a golden sickle, I'll hope that my hands are still free.

The ship dropped below the seawall to settle into the lagoon. Hedia looked up. All she could see of the city was the top of the high temple. The ball gleaming there was the one she had last seen while shopping in Carce, on top of the obelisk of Psammeticus.

RATHER THAN USING A BRAZIER on a tripod, Anna had built a small fire on the ancient well curb at the side of the back garden. She fed it with splinters of maple wood and regularly dropped pinches of different powders onto the flames. Occasionally it spat sparks, and once Alphena had seen a bright glow in the shape of a cat form around the fire.

Alphena wore heavy sandals, a short tunic, and a belt from which hung the sword she had battled demons with. She was nervous and tired and occasionally dizzy, though she thought the dizziness was just from standing upright and not moving from the spot for so long.

Anna chanted in Oscan. The rhythms were more or less the same as those of Latin, but Alphena could only catch the occasional word. She smiled slightly: she was guessing about even those words. Maybe it wasn't Oscan, maybe it was all gibberish and Anna was playing a joke on her.

Alphena pressed her lower lip between her teeth. Part of her hoped that nothing was going to happen, except that afterward she would feel like a fool.

Heavy wagons rumbled along the Argiletum all night, their iron-shod wheels smothering other sounds. Even Anna's cracked voice only flecked that dull background, like bubbles on the sea after a storm. Somewhere a man shouted curses, repeating himself and slipping into a singsong pattern before finally falling silent again.

Alphena dried her right palm on her tunic, then gripped the sword again. She had thought of wearing armor and carrying a shield, but the weight would be a useless burden under most circumstances. She was going to find her mother, not to stand in ranks and battle Germans! Though it might be worse than Germans who were holding Hedia.

At least if demons started rising from the ground, she wouldn't feel so useless. *I don't want to just wait!*

Anna broke off her chant and rocked back on her seat, sighing. Instead of using a bench or having a stool brought out, she sat on a large upended mixing bowl from the kitchen. It wouldn't have been Alphena's choice, but—she grinned—it *hadn't* been her choosing.

"Is it time, mistress?" Alphena said, trying very hard to keep the quaver out of her voice. *I'll be fine when I have something to do.*

"It is not," the older woman said. Her tone made Alphena's breath draw in.

Anna must have shocked herself to hear also. She grimaced, pausing with a miniature billet of maple wood in her hand, and looked up at Alphena; she would probably have risen if her knees had been up to it.

"I misspoke myself, your ladyship," she said. "I'm tired to the marrow and the job isn't over yet. I'm tired and I'm frightened, may Venus protect me."

"You have nothing to apologize for, Anna," Alphena said. That was a lie, but it should have been the truth. Anna was a freewoman doing a favor at great personal risk. Lady Alphena should have been ready to accept a certain lack of deference as a result of strain. "And I'm still your friend, not some 'ladyship', I hope."

Anna sighed again and brought a skin of wine out from under her tunic. "I'm still sorry, dear," she said as she undid the lace clamping the wooden plug into the throat. "I'm old enough that I ought to be able to do better. And it's not like I've never done this before, though not often since I met Pulto."

She took a deep draft of wine. Lowering the skin, she added, "And maybe not quite this far into the shadows as this time. Except for, you know, for your mother."

Sending Mother into the Underworld in order to save me. Alphena took a deep breath, feeling better. She wasn't taking any risk as great as what Hedia had taken for her.

"Oh, Venus forsake me, where's my manners?" Anna said. She leaned toward Alphena, holding out the wineskin. "Here, girl, I wasn't thinking. Truly, I been that dry with saying the invocation over till I felt it start to take."

Alphena took the wine. She knew her face stiffened momentarily, but thank Mercury!, it seemed that Anna had missed the reaction. Raising the skin quickly to hide her expression, she took a reasonable drink and sluiced it around her mouth.

The wine was as warm as she expected. Goodness knew where the grapes had been grown, but the vintage had been mixed with not only resin but also seawater—the salty tang was noticeable even through the tar flavor—to stabilize it for travel.

Resin and the dash of seawater were the only things it had been cut with. It seemed much stronger than the unmixed vintages which Alphena had occasionally drunk with her mother.

She lowered the wineskin, then returned it to Anna. The drink certainly had cured her dry mouth. Numbed it, she shouldn't wonder.

"We're waiting for the moon now, child," Anna mused. She stroked the trussed rooster; it was part of the paraphernalia that messengers had brought when she started her preparations. "We can't hasten the moon."

The rooster tried to peck her. Its legs, wings, and beak were bound with rye straw, but it had been squirming like a hooked fish ever since Anna began chanting.

Six birds had arrived in response to Anna's summons—all cocks, and all white or mostly white. Alphena wasn't sure how Anna had picked the one she did, but it wasn't pleased by the honor.

The other five had gone to the cooks, so it didn't matter. It probably didn't matter. For an instant, Alphena was uncomfortably aware that being cooked and eaten wasn't necessarily the worst thing that could result from this night's business.

Anna took another drink—a very long one—from the skin, then looked about the garden. The moon was well up, but it was still short of mid-sky; Anna hadn't said, but Alphena supposed that was what she was waiting for now.

The witch laughed. "No gawkers, tonight. I thought somebody might be up on the roof—"

She gestured toward the house proper. Somebody standing on the parapet of the second floor could look down onto the back of this garden, though he wouldn't be able to see more than possibly the top of Alphena's head. Anna was more visible, even though she was sitting down.

"—watching."

She spat into a rose bed. "They're welcome to, if they like. Anybody who wants to try this theirself has my blessing."

Anna turned her head quickly. Alphena followed her eyes and caught a glimpse of a female figure. It faded like fog into the peach tree.

"Would ye like a closer look at this, girlie?" Anna snarled at the tree. "If not, then ye'd better keep your pointy little nose out of my way!"

The garden was as still as street noise allowed it to be; the peach nymph didn't reappear. Anna grasped the rooster by its legs. She hunched, holding the bird out at arm's length, and rocked to her feet.

"It's time if we're going to do it," she said with a lopsided smile. A small knife had appeared in her right hand.

"Yes, of course," Alphena said. She was no longer gripping the sword hilt. Patting her hands together, she was pleased to notice that her palms were dry. "What would you like me to do?"

"You just stand there, dearie," Anna said with a grim chuckle. "If this goes well, I'll summon something to take you to wherever her ladyship is. But girl?"

She paused until Alphena looked up and met her eyes.

"I can't do anything about it after you leave here," Anna said. "There's dangers, maybe worse ones than I know. And what I know is bad enough. That's for you alone to deal with, and I'm sorry to say that."

"Yes, of course," Alphena said brusquely. "I don't expect others to fight my battles, mistress."

Anna unexpectedly chuckled. "Spoken like a true officer," she said. "Line troopers have better sense."

Before Alphena could respond—she had no idea of how *to* respond to that—Anna resumed chanting. Without changing the rhythm of the incantation, she brought her hands together and slit the rooster's throat. The bird continued to thrash as its blood gurgled into the glazed bowl.

Drops splashed the animals molded onto the bowl's rim. It seemed to Alphena that a mist was starting to form.

CHAPTER XII

Anna wiped her knife on the cock's feathers, then flung its drained body to the ground. Her voice had become more resonant. Alphena couldn't be sure, but she thought the words of the incantation were the same as those she had heard earlier in the night.

The blood settled at the bottom of the bowl. Anna was looking into it, so Alphena glanced down as well. The moon was reflected in the black fluid.

The garden became dark. Alphena heard shouts and in the distance a wail of despair. Anna's voice had slowed and deepened into thunder through which other sounds sank.

Alphena looked at the sky in surprise. The stars still sparkled, but the full moon had vanished—except for its reflection in blood. Anna continued to chant.

The bowl was a window into another sky. A mist separated Alphena and the witch from the city outside. Anna's lips moved. Instead of hearing sound, Alphena felt the world tremble.

The reflected moon swelled and blurred and suddenly coalesced into the figure of a coldly beautiful woman glaring at her with a furious expression. The garden was still, but a wind whipped the woman's garments.

The woman held in either hand the leashes attached to a pair of three-headed vultures. When the birds opened their long beaks, their tongues quivered. Alphena heard no sound except the surrounding thunder.

The woman and the vultures faded into pale light. The gryphon on the rim of the bowl shrieked and flapped its wings tentatively. It twisted its eagle head around to stare at Alphena.

Light filled the bowl; Alphena could no longer see blood or the glazed pottery, just the four animals hanging in the air. Three—the chimaera, basilisk, and mantichore—groomed themselves, but the gryphon seemed to be struggling to break free of unseen bonds.

Alphena thought she could make out Anna's form on the other side of the window, but she wasn't sure; the light was swelling. An image formed within it: a series of ring islands nested within one another like ripples in a pond spreading from a dropped stone.

The islands sharpened into focus. They were forested, but crystal buildings glittered on crags. The city of the vision in the theater spread along the shore of a deep bay.

Mother's been taken to Atlantis. But how will I get there myself?

The gryphon called in high-pitched triumph. Either it was growing or Alphena was shrinking. Atlantis hung in the unimaginable distance, though she still saw it clearly.

Anna and the garden vanished, but Alphena and the gryphon stood on solid air. The creature's body was much larger than that of the lion it resembled; it was more the size of an ox.

It lifted a birdlike foreleg and began cleaning the gaps between its toes, extending its great claws as it did so. It watched Alphena with eyes as bright as spearpoints. Her hand hovered close to her swordhilt, but she didn't draw the weapon.

The gryphon lowered its paw. "Well?" it said, speaking in a haughty tenor voice. "Will you get on my back and ride, or shall I carry you to Poseidonis in my talons?"

It laughed, opening a hooked beak that could have snapped the head off a calf—or a man. Despite the shrill overtones, the creature's voice reminded Alphena of Lenatus and Pulto discussing their army service.

"You'll be more comfortable on my back, I think," it said. "But it's all one with me, mistress. I will serve you as you wish."

"I . . . ," Alphena said. "I'll ride you, then."

She stepped close to the gryphon; it had a warm, animal odor, strong but not unpleasant. It hunched down, lowering its withers and folding its feathered wings tightly against its torso.

"You'll need to sit just below my neck, I'm afraid," the creature said. "If I'm to fly, that is, and there's not much point in this excercise if I don't."

Alphena put both hands on the gryphon's neck. The fur was as stiff as hog bristles, though the feathers into which it blended had a silky texture.

This isn't going to be comfortable, she thought. She grinned wryly. *But there may be worse to come.*

She vaulted aboard. The scabbard slapped her left leg, but she got her seat easily enough.

Alphena straightened. The gryphon rose to its feet and stretched like a cat before looking back at her. "Hold tight, mistress," it said. "If you fall, it will be a long way."

It laughed again; not cruelly, but with a hard carelessness. "A very long way," it added.

"All right," Alphena said, digging her fingers into the fur. It was long enough to give her a grip, though not a very good one.

What am I going to do when we reach Poseidonis?

The gryphon sprang upward with the strength of all four legs. Its wings beat with a fierce suddenness, more like the release of a catapult than that of a bird flying.

The ground fell away into a gray blur. The islands of Atlantis hung in the sky, seemingly as far as they ever had been.

But first we have to reach the city.

BECAUSE THERE WERE SEVEN SLAVES to be freed at one time and Varus knew that other slaves would want to watch, he had suggested that his father hold the manumission ceremony in the courtyard instead of in his office. Saxa stood with his back to the central pool. His chief lictor was to his left holding one of the rods which, bound around the helve of his axe, were the symbol of his authority.

Varus and Tardus were off to the right side, witnesses rather than participants in the process. The recording secretary sat cross-legged in front of them.

The entire household, as well as Tardus' considerable entourage and very probably servants from nearby buildings, crowded around. They filled the courtyard, pressed against the second story railing, and—younger males in particular—sat on the roof looking in with their bare legs dangling.

"I, ah . . . ," said Tardus. He glanced toward Varus, then looked down again quickly when the younger man tried to meet his eyes. "I must apologize for the way I behaved when I visited the other day. I wasn't in control of my actions, of course, but even so I'm embarrassed at what I remember. The very little that I remember."

Varus lifted his chin in solemn agreement. He hadn't been sure how Tardus was going to react to the invasion of his house by a gang of slaves. The wrath of a senior senator would be no slight thing, even if the senator was regarded as a superstitious fool by most of his colleagues. It appeared that Tardus primarily wanted to distance himself from the business, which Varus—and Saxa—were more than willing to help him do.

"It must have been awful to be under the spell of foreign magicians that way," he said sympathetically. "I'm glad Father was able to devise a way of freeing you—"

Would Pandareus approve of me lying in that fashion? Still, an orator should phrase an argument in the fashion which his audience was best able to appreciate. That's all Varus was doing when he attributed the plan to another senator instead of to a youth from the frontier whose father was merely a knight.

"—from their domination."

"All present attend the tribunal of Gaius Alphenus Saxa, Consul of the Republic!" boomed the chief lictor. He had trained his voice to silence the crowd when court was being held in the Forum, so the relative constraint of this courtyard was no challenge whatever. "Let the first petitioner state his business!"

The first—the only, of course—petitioner was Agrippinus. The majordomo stepped through the line of lictors arrayed in front of the consul and said, "I come to the magistrate to proclaim the formal manumission of seven slaves who are the property of myself alone."

"I had understood that Saxa would be freeing his own slaves today," Tardus said in a puzzled tone.

"That's correct," Varus explained, "but Father first sold them to our majordomo for a copper each. That way he can act as magistrate in the manumission without questions being raised about the owner and magistrate being the same person."

Agrippinus took the first of the slaves by the hand and brought him in front of Saxa. He said, "I declare this man to be my slave Himilco."

The lictor touched Himilco—a North African; short, swarthy, and muscled like a statue of Hercules—on the head with his rod and said in his resonant voice, "I declare Himilco to be free from this day onward!"

"Surely no one would have objected?" Tardus said doubtfully.

"I assent," said Agrippinus, releasing Himilco's hand.

"My father is a stickler for the correct forms," Varus said. He started to smile, but that would have projected the wrong image. Tardus was if anything more focused on foolish detail than Saxa was . . . though apparently not the same details. "He deemed this to be the safest route."

"It is hereby noted that the former Himilco, now Gaius Alphenus Himilco, is a freeman," Saxa said. The secretary duly jotted the information down on a wax tablet.

Himilco stood with his mouth open. Instead of showing enthusiasm, he looked as though he had been thrown bound into the arena with half a dozen lions.

He'd probably be more comfortable with the lions. They would be more in keeping with his past experience than being stood before a pair of senators, one of whom was also consul.

Agrippinus leaned over to whisper in Himilco's ear. A smile of understanding spread across the new freedman's face. He threw himself onto hands and knees, lifted the consul's foot and placed it on his neck, and then shambled back to where he had been before Agrippinus brought him forward. He hadn't overbalanced Saxa in his enthusiasm, as Varus had rather feared he might.

"I would say . . . ," Varus murmured to Tardus. "That the willingness to grasp a sword and charge armed enemies does not require a high intellect."

Before he met Corylus, he would have said that it *couldn't* be paired with high intellect. Still, he suspected that his friend was the exception.

"You freed me, Gaius Varus," Tardus said. He made a small gesture with his left hand as the second slave was brought forward. "From a worse servitude than that. Me, a Senator of the Republic and a Commissioner for the Sacred Rites!"

Varus considered the unexpected confidence. He said, "I'm glad we were able to offer you a service, Lord Tardus. That is, to a man of your stature, and to the Republic through you."

That certainly didn't sound like the admission of a man who had invaded the house of a senator with a band of armed slaves. Pandareus would be proud to see the effects of his teaching.

When we find Pandareus.

Agrippinus was bringing the third slave forward now. After the ceremony was complete, Saxa would be providing each of the new freedmen with a gift of a thousand coppers, the amount the emperor had given each legionary upon his accession at the death of Augustus. Lenatus and Pulto would be given property worth four hundred thousand coppers: the requirement for becoming a Knight of Carce.

Corylus—when he returned—would be offered nothing, at Varus' insistence despite his father's protests. That saved his friend from embarrassment and saved Saxa from worse embarrassment when Corylus refused the gift.

There wasn't enough money to have induced Corylus to plan and execute the raid on Tardus' home. By the same token, Varus knew Corylus wouldn't accept money for doing what friendship and the needs of the Republic had made necessary. Saxa, to whom money meant nothing, couldn't understand the logic of a principled man to whom money was important—but not overwhelmingly important.

"The sages brought me the murrhine tube," Tardus said, lowering his eyelids as he looked back in memory. "They said that it was an artifact of great power. They burned herbs in it, drawing the smoke out through a reed tube at one end."

Varus lifted his chin. "That's what they were doing when we broke in on them and Pandareus," he said, frowning. "The one with the censer blew smoke onto Corylus—he was the first one of us through the doorway. There was a flash and I couldn't see anything—none of us could. When we could, Corylus was gone as well as the sages and Pandareus."

"One of them blew smoke at me too," said Tardus. He was turned toward the manumission ceremony—the fifth slave was being freed—but his mind was clearly in another place. "I couldn't move except by their choice after that—until you freed me."

He shook his head as though trying to cast out the memory. "They said the murrhine pipe was half the representation of an amphisbaena. It had great power."

"The snake with a head on each end of its body," Varus said, speaking to solidify the reference in his mind. "Yes, I understand now. And Father has the other half."

"They knew that Lord Saxa has it," Tardus said. "They took me to your house to gain it. I was a slipper and they were the foot that wore me, whether I would or no. I was less than a slave to them."

"Father and I sympathize with you, Lord Tardus," Varus said in a suitably solemn tone. It was a relief to learn that the senator was more concerned with forgiveness for his own behavior than redress for what Varus and his friends had done. "Were you present when the sages discussed their plans, perchance? Though—"

He frowned at his error.

"I suppose they would have been talking in their own language, even if you could hear them."

Tardus looked at him, frowning in concentration. "Yes, I suppose they were . . . ," he said, "but I could understand them perfectly well. I hadn't thought of that."

He shook his head. "I wasn't myself, you see," he said. "That is, the sages *were* me; but that means I was them too, I suppose. But—"

He shrugged. "But I can't tell you where they took Master Pandareus," he said. "From what you describe, they must have acted in the crisis. Certainly they didn't plan anything of the sort when I was with them."

"I understand," said Varus; and he did, though he'd hoped that Tardus would be able to help them. "Well, we'll have to find Pandareus—"

And Corylus, but no reason to emphasize that.

"—in some other fashion. Will these sages stay here in Carce, do you think? If they do, perhaps they'll reappear and we'll be able to find them."

"I suppose they will remain," Tardus said. "Their business is here, after all."

"Their business?" said Varus, irritated at himself for not having asked the most obvious question before Tardus reminded him of it. "What are they doing here, your lordship?"

"They don't think they can hold Uktena where he is for very much longer," Tardus said. As he spoke, his voice became thinner and his face began to look gray. "They plan to gain time by releasing him here in Carce, a long distance from the Western Isles, while they either create defenses or find a way to bind the monster again."

The manumission ceremony had just concluded. Hundreds of servants shouted, "Yo, hail Lord Saxa!" waving caps and pieces of cloth in the air.

The cheering smothered Tardus' voice, but his lips and the obvious logic left Varus in no doubt that Uktena terrified the old man.

It terrifies me as well.

CORYLUS COULDN'T MOVE and he couldn't see his own body. He wasn't sure that he had a body in this place.

"Where am I?" he said to the slim, straight woman. Her hair was a lustrous dark brunette, but there were green highlights in it.

She laughed with friendly amusement. "You're here, cousin," she said. "That's all one can ever say, *I* think. Though I know you humans have other ideas about it."

That was the answer I should have expected when I asked a dryad about geography, Corylus realized. Though he wasn't sure that "geography" was the right word.

The inhuman creature squatted on its haunches. Its narrow mouth opened enough to let its tongue loll out between hedges of small, sharp teeth. It rested its arms on its thin thighs; its hands stuck out before it.

"Mistress . . . ," Corylus said, looking at the woman but really concentrating on the creature beside her. Standing, it would be no taller than the sprite and it wasn't nearly as heavily built as Corylus himself. Its bite could be unpleasant but no more dangerous than that of one of the mongrel dogs which lived on Carce's streets, and its claws were as blunt as a dog's also.

Despite that, Corylus really hoped that the creature wouldn't decide he was an enemy. He recalled Caesar's description of Germans laughing the first time they saw the soldiers of Carce who were so much smaller than the barbarians themselves.

They didn't laugh after the first battle, though; those who were still alive. Corylus wasn't laughing at this creature.

"I am Publius Cispius Corylus," he said. "May I ask your name?"

"Of course you're Corylus, cousin," the woman said with another trill of laughter. "And I'm Coryla, silly. My tree was struck by a rain of burning glass from the moon. The rest of it perished in the fire, but the glass sealed the air away from one nut, so I still survive. As for the Ancient—"

She ran an affectionate hand through the fur over the creature's spine. It writhed toward her touch but continued to keep its unwinking eyes on Corylus.

"—I don't know what his name is; I don't know if he has a name. My tree grew over his grave, but he wasn't with me until the glass fell."

Corylus would have touched the tektite amulet if he could have moved his hand. Or if he'd had a hand to move, which might be closer to the real situation.

"Is the glass, ah, magical?" Corylus said. He was speaking and she was understanding him, but he couldn't feel his lips move.

"What?" the sprite said. She bent to rub the base of the creature's ear. It tilted its fox-like head toward the touch, but it never took its eyes off Corylus.

They had the same golden cast as its fur, but the pupils were slitted horizon-tally instead of vertically like a cat's. "I shouldn't think so, no."

She gave the creature a final pat over the ribs and straightened. "But *he* is, of course," she added. "He's a great magician. Did he bring you to him, do you suppose? I'm not always sure what he's planning, even though he's part of me, in a way."

"Him?" said Corylus in amazement. "*It?* But it's just an animal, isn't it?"

The sprite's laughter was as sweet and musical as a nightingale singing in the dusk. "Of course he's an animal, cousin," she said. "You're *all* animals, you and him and the squirrels in the branches of my tree. Didn't you know that?"

"I mean . . . ," said Corylus. "It doesn't think the way a man does. Or you do. It, he, isn't he your pet?"

The creature made a clicking sound at the back of its throat and stood up. It continued to stare at Corylus. Its hind legs folded the way a man's did, not a dog's.

"Pet?" said Coryla. He thought she would laugh again, but the look she gave him had nothing of humor in it. "Him? Are you mad, cousin?"

The creature reached toward Corylus; toward where his face should be, if he had a face. It had four slender fingers. One was opposed to the other three like the hind claw of an eagle, not a human thumb.

I am a soldier of Carce. I will not flinch.

Fingertips as gentle as a fly's wing touched Corylus' cheek.

I can feel it! he realized, and as he did, light bloomed around him. He was lying on his back on the cliff top where he had fought the Cyclops. He breathed with a gasp of surprise—and shouted with the sudden pain of it. *My ribs are broken!*

Coryla and the creature were looking down at him. She seemed sympa-thetic and perhaps a little concerned; the creature . . .

It wasn't safe to read the expression on a face as inhuman as that of the creature, but it certainly *seemed* to be laughing at him. *How did I ever imag-ine that it wasn't intelligent?*

"You can sit up, can't you?" the sprite said. "Because there are other gi-ants besides the one you killed. And worse things."

"I don't know," Corylus said. He touched his chest gently, trying not to move his body. He must be bruised as badly as he ever had been in his life, but there wasn't the stabbing, grating pain that would have meant that he had broken ribs. "You said I killed the Cyclops?"

Coryla offered him her hand. He took it carefully, expecting the lightly built sprite to stagger forward when he started to put real weight on her. Instead, she remained as fixed a support as a deeply rooted hazel tree.

After a flash of blazing agony, the pain in Corylus' chest subsided to a throbbing ache, as though he were sitting too close to a hot fire. Several of the catches of his breastplate had popped. He undid the remaining one, then dropped the dented armor to the ground. That done, he turned slowly. He was looking for the Cyclops and hoping to see its body.

"Well, you did and he did himself, I suppose," she said. "He stumbled after you stabbed him and broke his neck. But if you hadn't stabbed him, he probably wouldn't have fallen, don't you think? So I said you killed him."

Corylus walked cautiously to the edge of the crag and looked over. His chest hurt and his left leg was as stiff as a statue's, except for the hip joint. That felt like the blazing pit of Aetna.

Two ships lay on their sides just above the water; their decks were tilted at a thirty-degree angle. That much was the same as the mural he had seen in the instant before the smoke swept him here. Close-up he now saw that the vessels were winged craft like those of the vision, not ordinary fifty-oared galleys as he had assumed.

The mangled bodies of their crews were scattered on the shingle. On the ground near the Cyclops' cave was an iron-bound club the length of a ship's mast. The monster's strength would have made it devastating.

Among the dead were two figures whose bright armor hadn't saved them from crushing blows. One's corselet had been dished in; the other's helmet was flattened so completely that blood and brains oozed through the grille that covered the face.

Directly at the base of the crag was the Cyclops, sprawled on his face with his head cocked sharply to the right. Corylus frowned. Any of the Scouts could have jumped the twenty feet to the shingle and expected— reasonably hoped, at least—to have staggered off without serious injury, but the giant weighed more than an ox. Even the bones of its short, thick neck couldn't take the shock of that hard landing.

"I told you he was dead," the sprite said chidingly. "Don't you suppose we'd better leave? That you should, I mean. It's all the same to us, you know."

Corylus looked at her. The slope rising above the Cyclops' cave wasn't nearly as steep as the escarpment to the beach, but he wasn't sure he could climb it in his present condition.

He *was* sure that he couldn't get down to the beach, unless he did it the way the Cyclops had. And probably with the same result, since he couldn't land with flexed legs and roll as he'd learned to do with the Scouts.

"Mistress," he said, "I can't go anywhere until I've recovered some. If I ever do: my leg may be permanently injured. If you can save yourselves, you'd best go do it."

The furry creature stood a pace behind her, its torso leaning forward and its hips thrust back for balance. It clicked in its throat and stepped to Corylus' side. He couldn't jerk away—he stood on the edge of the crag—and if he tried to run, he suspected he'd faint with pain.

"What's he doing?" the sprite said. She cocked her head quizzically.

And by Hades, how would I know? Corylus thought, but he kept his face impassive.

The creature touched Corylus' left hip; moved its slender hand down to his knee; and then dropped into a near squat to touch his ankle as well. The fingers *pressed*, but instead of greater agony, they brought relief.

The creature straightened. Its tongue waggled from the side of its jaw again; perhaps it really was laughing. It reached out with both hands and caressed Corylus' chest through the sweat-soaked tunic. The pain in his ribs vanished like chaff in a windstorm. Its tongue still lolling, the creature backed to where it had been behind the sprite.

Corylus swallowed. "Thank you, master," he said as formally as if he were addressing a magistrate, not something frighteningly inhuman. To the sprite he added, "I believe I can walk normally now. Where do you suggest we go? Since you appear to be more familiar with this place than I am."

She shrugged. "Let's take one of the ships," she said. "I suppose it shouldn't matter to me, being as I am now—"

She gestured toward the amulet now hanging outside Corylus' tunic.

"—but those hills are bleak, not fit for anything but tamarisk and bergamot. And besides, you'll need to eat. There'll be food and water on the ships."

"I can't—" Corylus began, then stopped himself. *I don't need to push the ship down into the water; it flies. But—*

Correcting himself aloud, he said, "Mistress, I'm not a magician; I can't make the ship move. Though we can take the food and water, or some of it. Maybe I can make a cart."

In a bemused tone the sprite said, "You are *such* a silly, cousin."

She turned to the creature and chirruped like a hen on her eggs. It—he—didn't reply in a fashion Corylus could see, but the sprite beamed and stroked the golden fur of his throat. He writhed toward her, even more like a serpent than before.

"Which ship shall we take?" she asked Corylus.

"We'll take a look at them before we decide," he said. "Ah, can you make it down the slope by yourself?"

The sprite ran her fingers through his hair in the same affectionate fashion as she had just petted the creature. Without answering, she started down the escarpment facing forward, as though she were descending a staircase. Corylus felt his eyes narrow; then he smiled. Of *course* the soles of her feet would be able to cling to crevices too tiny for his eye to see.

The furry creature watched him. Corylus thought about asking if it too could get to the beach unaided, then simply turned around and started down himself. He'd been called silly quite a number of times since he met the sprite, and he was beginning to wonder if she wasn't correct.

His body no longer hurt the way it had immediately after the fight with the Cyclops, but he had taken enough of a pounding to leave anybody groggy. Maybe that was an excuse for being slow to understand what was happening.

The cliff was limestone, steep but corroded by salt and storms. There were plenty of hand- and footholds, though Corylus had to test each one before he put his full weight on it. He simply kept going down until his hobnailed sandal clashed on the beach.

He looked up. The creature was peering over the edge at him. When it saw that he had reached the ground, it leaped like a squirrel.

Corylus flattened against the escarpment reflexively. His first thought had been to try to catch the creature, but keeping out of the way was a better idea.

Its narrow feet sprayed shingle. It bounced up as part of the same motion, spun in the air, and landed again: lightly this time, and facing Corylus.

It's laughing. I'm sure it's laughing.

Whether the creature was or not, Coryla certainly laughed merrily. "You males," she said affectionately. "Always posturing to each other."

She turned and walked toward the nearer ship. She was still giggling.

Instead of following the sprite and her companion, Corylus walked to the man in armor with his skull crushed. He had been killed very recently, but the fierce sun was already beginning to rot the blood and other leaking fluids.

The fellow's sword was still in its scabbard. Corylus drew it. The blade was made of the same fiery metal as the armor. It was slim, slightly curved, and a little longer than the infantry sword he was used to. He'd practiced with the horsemen's longer weapons, though.

It wouldn't be his first choice, but it was the only thing available here. Maybe he would have a chance to replace it with steel before he found himself in a real fight. He squatted to unfasten the sword belt. Instead of a buckle it had an unfamiliar latch that opened when he turned it.

"You should take orichalc armor for yourself too," the sprite said as she wandered back from the ship she had been looking at.

"Orichalc?" Corylus said, pinging the breastplate with his fingernail. "This?"

The orichalc he knew about was a copper alloy which could be polished to look like gold. Whatever this metal was, it certainly wasn't that.

"Yes, orichalc," she said, rocking what was left of the corpse's head back and forth with a toe. She giggled again and added, "You'll have to take the helmet from the other Minos, I guess, won't you?"

"Yes," said Corylus. The body armor had the same kind of catches as the belt; he began to turn them. He wasn't squeamish, but he didn't care to strip bodies quite so thoroughly dead.

The furry creature had prowled the deck of the nearer ship, then disappeared through a hatch into what must have been a very small hold. When it reappeared, it dropped to the beach and walked to the other ship.

It walked in a hunched posture. Its arms were long enough that it could have put them down without stooping further, but instead it kept them close to its chest.

Like a praying mantis, Corylus thought. *Not a snake.*

He grinned, remembering the sprite's comment about posturing. She was a perceptive little thing.

Corylus belted on the sword, but he carried the armor in his left hand as he walked to the second corpse; the second Minos, the sprite had called him. "What do you mean by Minos, mistress?" he said. "Are they a tribe?"

"They claim to be a different tribe from the commoners," Coryla said without particular interest. She continued to stand beside the corpse whose armor he'd taken. "They're probably lying, though. You humans always lie to make yourselves look bigger than you are, don't you?"

"Some men do," Corylus said. Getting angry because a comment had some truth in it would be childish and, well, silly.

He set down the armor and squatted by the figure whose chest had been flattened. The helmet seemed undamaged, though. The screen covering the face blurred the corpse's features.

"Well, anyway, the Minoi rule Atlantis," Coryla said. "They're magicians. When they're born, they get a tattoo on their foreheads. Not that you'd have been able to tell with this one."

She toed the corpse again. Her sense of humor was a lot like that of a veteran soldier, a fact that Corylus found oddly comforting in this place.

A single catch released the faceplate. Corylus lifted it up on the hinge to remove the helmet. He stopped and looked over his shoulder at the sprite.

"Mistress," he said. "This was a woman."

"The armor adjusts," she said. "It will fit you, even if you're not a magician yourself."

I suppose that's all that really matters, Corylus thought. He lifted the helmet off, supporting the dead woman's shoulders with his free hand; then he lowered her with as much care as he could. He wondered about burying her, but there were at least twenty bodies, some of them mangled beyond certainty that they were human.

Treat them like the German dead after a battle, he decided. *Unless you're going to camp on the field, let the wolves and crows take care of the job.*

The creature leaped thirty feet from the deck of the second ship back to the upper railing of the vessel near to Corylus and the sprite. It squatted there, watching them. The shape of its face gave it a look of bright interest, but there was no real way a human could read the expressions of something so utterly inhuman.

"We can go, I suppose," Corylus said as he straightened. "That is, if you're ready."

He held helmet and corselet in his left hand. They weren't unmanageably heavy, and he preferred to keep one hand free.

Instead of answering, the sprite walked past him toward the ship. The creature watched her, moving only his head, and that just enough to follow her approach.

"Aren't you going to put the armor on?" she asked. She didn't look back toward him. "It won't protect you if you're not wearing it."

It didn't help the Minoi who were wearing it before, Corylus thought, but of course there might be dangers besides the chance of being clubbed by a giant whose strength was all out of proportion to its considerable size.

Aloud he said, "It looks uncomfortable, mistress, especially the helmet. Is the armor necessary now?"

"Am I a soothsayer?" Coryla said. "If you know the future, cousin, then do as your wisdom directs."

She caressed the polished deck planks, then stepped aboard by the low side. She stood easily, despite the slope.

Corylus stopped, set the armor down, and took off the belt so that he could put the corselet on. When he closed and latched it, the metal seemed to flow against his ribs.

He lengthened the belt that he'd taken up to fit his waist under only a tunic, then donned it also. Finally he set the helmet on his head. It too fit, just as the sprite had said it would.

The orichalc equipment was less constricting than the mail and legionary helmet with which he was familiar. He didn't latch the grille. That would take only a sweep of his hand to complete, if necessary.

He climbed aboard. The sprite watched him with a smile.

"The flames that the projector in the bow throws . . . ," she said, nodding toward the knotted apparatus that Corylus had taken for a stubby winch of some kind. "The armor will help you with them. And there are other things."

"Thank you, mistress," Corylus said. He bowed toward her.

The golden furred creature hopped to the deck and took three mincing strides to the stern. Its narrow tongue licked the air. The ship gave a shudder and rocked upright on its keel.

THE SILENCE OF THE CROWD as Serdain and Kalpos marched Hedia across the plaza was disquieting. Their retainers followed in line. They wore their daggers, but their nets and poles remained in the ships.

Ropes of light rippling like molten glass bound Hedia's waist to the nearer hand of each Minos. They didn't hinder her so long as she kept in step with her captors, but when she deliberately hesitated in midstep, the bonds jerked her forward with a jolt of pain. It felt as though she had been dropped into boiling water for an instant.

Well, she hadn't expected to be able to break free by force. Violence wasn't a tool she had ever found congenial.

The entrance was a slender triangle, echoing the design of the spire itself. It was twenty feet wide at the base, but it seemed narrow because its top was almost a hundred feet overhead. Hedia glanced up: the orichalc ball must be at least a thousand feet in the air.

She almost stumbled again—in genuine shock—when she and her captors stepped inside. The spire's interior was the largest enclosed space Hedia had ever seen. Indeed, it was larger than her dreams of what was possible.

It was all a single room, from the glassy floor to the peak so high that it made Hedia dizzy when she looked up at it. The bonds dashed pain over her again, but because that pulled her back to the present, it was an almost welcome relief.

Almost. The shimmering fetters cut like the whips of the Furies. *One more thing to pay back when opportunity presents itself. . . .*

Ramps like those of an amphitheater slanted around the interior in narrowing helixes. People stood against their railings for as far up as Hedia could see before the light through the crystal walls blurred everything into a bright haze. There were unthinkably many people present, perhaps as many as the crowd in the Circus Maximus for a full card of races.

They were all watching Hedia and the Minoi holding her. *I'm scarcely looking my best,* she thought as her captors led her to the center of the huge hall. Though since nobody else cared, she didn't suppose she ought to either.

Cool air rushed up through narrow slots in the crystal floor. It dried the sweat on Hedia's body and made her scrapes and scratches itch less. She would still give a year of her life for a bath; though—she smiled coldly—a bath wouldn't be at the top of the list if she were being offered wishes.

Of course, her life might not have a year remaining. Thought of the amphitheater brought to mind watching lions being loosed on prisoners who had been bound to posts and were as naked as she was now.

"Stand here," Serdain said. Hedia stopped. She couldn't see anything different about this patch of floor. It was translucent with a vaguely blue cast.

The Minoi each muttered something and stepped away. Hedia's waist was free, but the flowing hardness now gripped her ankles. She tried turning with care prompted by the vicious bite the bonds had given her when she fought them.

She was able to do that so long as she remained on the same patch of crystal. A tentative step forward caused the flowing light to bind her; she didn't try pushing beyond that point. She could stand such pain as she needed to, but it wasn't an experience she cared for.

Until she turned, Hedia hadn't realized that the crowd from the plaza had followed her into the hall. The scores of Minoi formed a circle around her. Their armor caught the light wicking through the crystal walls; the metal shone like cold fire in the cool blue ambiance.

They had taken off their helmets. Hedia could see that at least a dozen were women, but that left her with many possible ways to improve her situation. Retainers formed blocks behind individual Minoi as they had done on the plaza earlier.

"The Council of the Minoi is in session," said a voice. "Let all the world take notice and obey!"

Hedia couldn't tell who was speaking or even be sure of the direction from which the voice came. It was ordinary sound, not ideas forming in her mind, and the words hadn't been shouted.

From the way the whispers and shuffling stilled, everyone in the vast enclosure must have heard it. Perhaps it was magic, but it might have been simply an improvement on the excellent acoustics of the theaters with which Hedia was familiar.

"Our Servitors have succeeded in capturing and bringing to us the wizard who is the key of the threat to us," the voice continued. "All that remains to ensure our safety is to bring her to the notice of Typhon, then send her to the Underworld by the path that she has already traversed. Typhon will follow and be bound inextricably."

"The Servitors have made a mistake," said another voice, this time clearly a woman speaking. "Look at her! *She's* not a Minos."

Although Hedia couldn't identify this speaker either, she noticed this time in her survey that each Minos held an object and was gazing into it. The individual talismans differed: crystals of one sort or another were common, but some of the Minoi had what seemed to be common pebbles like the one Serdain had used to fly the ship that brought her here. Occasionally she saw a tiny orichalc machine or a sculpture.

"She doesn't have the mark, but that means nothing," said what might have been the first voice. "Her culture has its own forms; we mustn't be parochial in our views."

"But look at her aura!" said the female voice. "She cannot possibly be a Minos. She's as common as the serfs who spread night soil on the crops!"

If I learn who you are, dearie . . . , Hedia thought as she continued to smile. *I may one day serve you out in a fashion that will make you less eager to insult a lady of Carce.*

"She has visited the Underworld and returned," responded multiple voices in near unison. "No one but a great wizard could do that. None of us could do it: therefore we sent Servitors."

What if they decide I'm not a wizard? Hedia thought. *If they think they're going to put me to spreading manure on flower beds, they're going to get an unpleasant surprise.*

The alternative, being dangled before a monster like a strip of pork on a shark hook, wasn't ideal either, but Hedia had never assumed that monsters had snatched her from her bed for her own benefit. Being bait seemed to offer more possibilities.

Thought of being snatched from bed reminded Hedia of the Servitors. The glass men with the hunting party had remained aboard the ships, and she didn't see others here in the hall. Were the creatures really alive? Were they absent now simply because there was no need of their presence, or were they barred for the same reason women were not allowed to watch the Senate in session: out of fear?

That thought made Hedia smile wider and more harshly. Most men wouldn't have agreed with her assessment of the real reason women weren't allowed in the Senate chamber, but she had no doubt that she was correct. Men demeaned what they feared, and they were rightly afraid of women's power over them.

"And she is linked to Typhon," said another voice, male and elderly as best Hedia could judge. "She is best suited, perhaps uniquely suited, to draw the monster away from Atlantis and to that bourn from which it cannot return."

Why in heaven do they think I'm connected with that monster? But Hedia had to consciously smooth the frown from her forehead. *Am I connected with it? There's so much I don't understand.*

I don't understand any of this!

"We don't know that," said what was certainly the female voice which had objected to Hedia's aura—whatever an aura was. "The link is to the place but not to the person except by conjecture. I say the Servitors took the wrong person."

"The link from Typhon to her home is clear," said what must have been a majority of the Minoi present. "It is certain that this is the one whom the Servitors tracked back from the Underworld, where only a wizard could go and return. Logic indicates that one and the same person is responsible for both. We will offer her to Typhon and lead the monster to the Underworld."

"I am Hedia, daughter of Marcus Hedius Fronto, consul and descendent of consuls!" Hedia said. The vastness seemed to drink her voice; she didn't know if anyone, even Serdain and Kalpos a few feet away, could hear her. "I am a lady of Carce! Return me to my home or face the anger of the gods who have raised Carce to the throne of nations!"

Instead of a response, she heard a burst of unintelligible chittering, like that of a frog pond during an evening shower. After a moment—a few heart-beats, no more—a chorus said, "The Council of the Minoi decrees that this female shall be offered to Typhon, then brought to the Underworld where she and it shall be sequestered forever. It shall be done!"

"I am Hedia, wife of Consul Gaius Alphenus Saxa! Release me and take me home!"

"She should be clothed," said the female voice. Hedia didn't know whether the woman was an ally in some fashion or if she simply enjoyed disagreeing with her peers. "We must provide her with a garment."

There was a further brief interval of wordless chirping. A number of voices—many, but not the great consensus of Hedia's condemnation—said, "She shall have a garment."

Almost immediately the Council in unison said, "Then she will be taken to the cells and held till we have made the necessary preparations. It shall be as we decree."

A youth, a commoner in a bleached white kilt, stepped between a pair of armored Minoi and trotted toward Hedia with his head lowered. He held a bundle which he tossed at her feet, turned, and scurried back the way he had come. He never looked up.

Hedia considered for a moment, then bent and opened the bundle. It was a shift folded from a single piece of cloth, with armholes in the sides and a head opening cut at the top. It was off-white with a dingy blue cast, but it seemed clean; its straight lines could be made attractive with a sash and a few judicious gatherings.

She shrugged it over her head. Though the garment was obviously utilitarian, the fabric itself was as soft as cobweb.

Hedia stood straighter, wondering if the female voice would demand that the prisoner be given a bath. Instead, and without warning, the floor beneath her feet began to sink. Her stomach flipped twice; for a moment she was afraid that she would disgrace herself by vomiting in public.

She wasn't in public. The floor of the hall was high above her; she could see only a glint of brighter light when she turned her eyes upward. The shaft in which she fell was as smooth and featureless as ice.

Hedia's descent slowed; weight threatened to buckle her knees. She stopped in a rotunda, facing two glassy Servitors.

"Where are you taking me?" she said.

Instead of answering—could they answer?—they bent and shifted the bonds from her ankles to her waist again. That done, they marched her down a corridor with cells to either side. Through the door gratings Hedia saw shapes moving. She didn't think they were all human, or at least fully human.

"When will I be released?" she shouted.

The Servitors shoved her into an empty cell. The flowing fetters vanished.

The door of the cell clacked shut before Hedia could turn around.

ALPHENA COULDN'T SEE VERY MUCH from the gryphon's back. The sky was black and filled with stars, but they weren't the constellations of Carce. Indeed, they didn't seem to be grouped at all, just scattered as randomly as a field of daisies.

Straight ahead were a pair of larger, diffuse blobs which didn't appear to be coming closer though the gryphon's wings beat strongly. Alphena thought she saw detail in what at first had been featureless blurs, however.

By leaning forward carefully, clamping her knees, and gripping the longer feathers above the eagle head, Alphena was able to look past the wings and see that her mount had folded its legs beneath it like a cat. Which it was, she supposed, so far as its body and hind legs went.

The gryphon turned its head to fix her with his right eye. "If you fall," he said, "you will probably fall forever. Unless I should manage to turn and catch you in time, which has its own—"

He stretched out his right foreleg and extended the claws. They were thicker at the base than Alphena's thumbs, and the points were vanishingly sharp.

"—difficulties for you."

The gryphon laughed, a croaking sound from deep in its throat. If a man had behaved the way this creature was doing, Alphena would have struck him. That wasn't a practical response here.

She felt her expression softening into a grin. *I take myself too seriously. By now I should realize how little I matter to the cosmos.*

Aloud she said, "I appreciate your concern, Master Gryphon. Do you have a name?"

The gryphon chuckled again. "Who is there who could name me?" he said. "And I have not chosen to give a name to myself."

The creature's wings were relatively short and broad, like those of a raven. Though they beat powerfully, Alphena didn't feel the slap of air that she would have expected if a tame pigeon had taken off from her wrist. She seemed to be breathing normally, but she was beginning to wonder whether this was real or a dream.

"Is the light ahead of us Atlantis, master?" Alphena said. She knew she was speaking to occupy her mind. She had decided it was better to react to her nervousness than let her thoughts about the near future spiral down into paralysis.

"It will be Atlantis," said the gryphon, glancing back. "And Poseidonis. And then my task is completed, is it not so?"

Alphena felt her chest constrict with terror. *How will I get home?*

She let out her breath slowly. Because she hadn't immediately reacted aloud, she'd had time to realize that blurting, "You have to take me and Mother back to Carce!" would be as useless—and possibly as dangerous—as a similar shrill demand directed to the emperor.

"I will not venture to tell you your duty, Master Gryphon," Alphena said. "You will act as your honor requires you to act."

The great eagle head faced front again; the gryphon chuckled. "Such a clever little chick you are," he said. "Such a clever little wizard."

Alphena swallowed. That could have gone very badly wrong if she'd reacted as she would have done a few weeks ago, before she really started observing the way Hedia moved in a world where men had all the public forms of power.

She whispered, "Thank you, Mother."

The stars moved visibly though still without forming familiar combinations. The vague light directly ahead became a view of a glade in which women in flowing garments stood or walked, sometimes hand in hand. Alphena didn't recognize the place or the faces, though she scanned them intently, hoping to see Hedia.

A spring-fed pool sent a trickle out into the forest. Eyes watched the women from the leaf-dappled water, but nothing moved except the ripples.

The gryphon flew on; the scene blurred to a desert under moonlight. Trees as large as temple pillars threw shadows onto sand, rocks, and thorny brush. Their trunks and upraised limbs were covered with needles.

A slight, stooping figure walked across the landscape. It had a fox's head and was covered with lustrous fur. It reached out a startlingly long forearm and snatched a scorpion from a rock. It snapped off the tail with delicate jaws, then swallowed the remainder of the scorpion like a moray eel taking a shrimp.

"Master?" Alphena said. "What is that beast?"

"Do you pray, little wizard?" the gryphon asked. "If you do, then pray that you never get close enough to him to learn what he is."

The scene blurred to a village near the seashore. Fields hacked from the forest were turning green with spring crops.

Alphena's focus swooped from the rounded huts to a reed mat at the edge of the clearing, then beneath it into an underground chamber. The light that seeped through the mat-covered entrance shouldn't have been enough for vision, but Alphena saw a man squatting in the center of the room. He wore only a breechclout, and his iron-gray hair was bound in two braids. He held a reed pipe to his lips as if he were playing it, but there were no finger holes in the tube.

At the other end was fitted a murrhine cylinder. If it wasn't the artifact from Saxa's collection, it was the mirror image of it.

The man lowered the reed and looked at Alphena, still-faced. Smoke curled from the end of the reed and from the murrhine cylinder in which chopped herbs smoldered. There was no threat—no emotion whatever—in his expression, but for an instant Alphena had the feeling that she had stepped around a corner and found a tiger waiting.

He's the man I saw in the theater! When the others said they saw a monster!

The man smiled at her. His lips barely quirked, but the change was as profound as that from cloud to full moonlight.

Then he and his chamber were gone. The crystal city, by now a familiar image, formed in the globe of light.

"Little wizard," said the gryphon, "we have company, and I do not think they are friends."

Alphena had been concentrating on the window into other worlds toward which the gryphon was flying. If she was honest, as she tried to be at least with herself, she was doing that not only because it interested and affected her, but also because that allowed her to forget all the other things that were happening.

When the gryphon called her into the wider present, she saw that what had been the second blob of light now had the face of the moon; it was silvered over with light that seemed to come from inside. On the sphere, like a statue on a rounded plinth, stood the cold, angry woman who had appeared when Anna chanted over the basin.

The woman no longer held the leashes of her vultures. Alphena wondered for a moment where they had gone; then the woman faded away and two specks rose from the moon's cratered surface.

As they swelled toward her, Alphena saw that they were the three-headed vultures and that a figure in orichalc armor rode astride the middle neck of each bird. She didn't have to wonder anymore.

"Your magic won't help you against the Minoi, little wizard," the gryphon said. "Not while we are between worlds."

"I'm not a wizard!" Alphena said. She drew her sword. "Can we fight them?"

This time the gryphon's chuckle was deeper and there was a catch in it. He said, "Of course we can fight them. Of *course*."

The gryphon shifted. Alphena swayed with her mount, gripping the feathered neck again with her free hand.

The vultures and their riders were becoming rapidly larger. Judging from the size of the armored figures, the Minoi, the birds were at least as big as the gryphon.

The hanging image of Poseidonis rotated into one of raw jungle. Alphena couldn't tell if it was the forest beyond the crystal city or if the scene was as distant as that of the desert minutes before.

She supposed it didn't matter. Nothing mattered until they had settled their account with the vultures.

The birds were approaching from above and below. The higher one banked slightly, allowing Alphena to meet the stare of the rider. The Atlantean's mesh-fronted helmet blurred her view of his features, but she could see that he had a moustache.

The Minoi had proper saddles, and they held reins to their mounts' middle head in their gauntleted left hands. They had drawn their swords also; the orichalc blades curved slightly upward at the tips. Alphena wondered how that fiery metal would fare against the demon-slaying blade she had brought back from the land of dreams and spirits.

We'll know soon enough.

The vultures edged closer. "Watch yourself," the gryphon muttered. With the words he stooped on his lower opponent. His fore claws were extended, and his eagle beak opened. His challenge could have pierced stone.

The vulture twisted with unexpected agility, spreading its talons to meet the attack. Its rider held his seat; his legs were locked at the ankles beneath his mount's neck.

When the gryphon dived, the second vulture plunged down from the left. Alphena turned to meet it, slashing with her sword instead of trying to thrust. Her blade met the Atlantean's with a shock that numbed her arm and scattered ropes of blue fire through the starry firmament.

The Minos fell backward out of the saddle, but his mount collided with the gryphon. Alphena lost her sword. She grabbed at the gryphon's neck with her right hand, but her arm had no feeling and her fingers, as lifeless as a statue's, slid over the feathers.

The gryphon snapped, catching one of the vulture's necks with a beak big enough to shear a bull's haunch. The violent movement flung Alphena off.

The first vulture had circled, gaining altitude; now it slanted toward her. The Minos leaned over his mount's neck, his sword poised to strike as he drove past. Given the way a similar sword had resisted her own lost blade, he would probably cut her in half.

The gryphon screamed and dived again on the circling vulture. Locked together, the giants tumbled away in a confused melee that Alphena couldn't have sorted out even if she had leisure to try.

You will fall forever, the gryphon said. Well, this wasn't his fault, but Alphena didn't really blame herself either. Sometimes you lose. It was as simple as that.

She couldn't see either the gryphon or the vultures. The stars glittered and shifted as she fell. The window in darkness which had been their destination had faded again to a glow.

The same thing might have happened if I'd gotten there. How could I have fought an army of these Minoi?

The blur of light coalesced again. Alphena saw the seashore village and the man with braided hair. He held his smoking pipe in his left hand, but with his right he reached out and gripped her wrist.

Smiling minusculely, he drew Alphena toward him.

CHAPTER XIII

Alphena awakened and sneezed violently. Her eyes stung and the light was dim. She thought, *Was I dreaming?* Then, *Where am I?*

She was lying on a reed mat on the floor of the underground room where she had glimpsed the man with braided hair. He sat cross-legged, watching her over the bowl of his pipe. He drew a lungful of the smoke up the reed stem, then blew it out through his nostrils. Smiling faintly, he lowered the pipe.

He's a magician. He has to be a magician to bring me here!

"Who are you?" Alphena asked. She rolled her feet under her but didn't try to get up. She wore the tunic she had donned before joining Anna in the garden, and the scabbard still hung from her sword belt. The weapon itself was missing, just as it should have been if what she remembered about the fight with the Minoi was true.

The man leaned forward, stretching the index and middle fingers of his right hand out toward her. Her reaction was to flinch, but she forced herself to hold still. *If he was my enemy, he'd have left me to drift forever as the gryphon warned would happen. . . .*

Alphena couldn't guess how old the man was. Older than her father, certainly; but he gave her the feeling that she was sitting beside an ancient oak. His fingers were like lengths of tree root.

He touched her left ear, her right ear, and finally her lips. "I am Uktena," he said, smiling again. "I have seen you before, little one, but I do not know who you are."

She licked her lips. "I'm Alphena," she said. "Ah, daughter of Gaius Saxa. But I came here—that is, I was going to Poseidonis to save my mother from the Atlanteans. Do you know who the Atlanteans are?"

Stated baldly like that, Alphena realized how foolish her plan had been. It hadn't been a plan at all; but she'd had to do something!

"I know one Atlantean," Uktena said. His smile suddenly had something terrifying in it. "But I would venture that in any case no enemy of yours would be a friend of mine. Come, I will show you our village . . . and perhaps we also will see the Atlantean."

Uktena knocked the dottle from the pipe into his palm, then scattered it on the bare ground at the edge of his sunken chamber; some of the embers were still glowing. He slipped the reed stem under his waistband and rose smoothly without using his hands. Alphena knew the effort it required to do that when seated cross-legged, but she didn't have the impression that her host was showing off: he was just extremely fit for a man of *any* age.

"Master Uktena?" she said. "Are you a magician?"

He weighed her with a glance. "Say rather that I remember some things that the spirits have taught me," he said after a moment. "As they will teach any man, who asks them in the right way. My fellows call me a shaman, but—"

His smile was very slight, and there was again the hint of a tiger beyond the calm expression.

"—I would prefer you call me Uktena, little one."

A pine sapling leaned against the opening in the chamber's roof. The bark had been stripped and the thickset branches trimmed, but stubs projected alternately to right and left. Uktena climbed it, using the stubs as rungs for his big toes. At the top he tossed aside the mat covering the opening and looked back to Alphena.

"Do you need help?" he asked.

Alphena couldn't decide whether he was mocking her or being polite. "No, but the ladder won't hold us both," she said, thought it probably would have. She rose to her feet rather less gracefully than her host.

Uktena swung out of the opening. Alphena followed, moving briskly but thankful that she wore hobnailed military sandals whose thick soles gave her solid purchase. *Her* big toes weren't up to supporting her full weight on such short stubs.

The field nearest the chamber had been planted with some kind of bigleafed grass. Two women had been cultivating it with clamshell hoes, but their voices had stilled when Uktena came out of the ground.

They remained upright with respectful expressions for a brief instant when Alphena appeared also. The women cried out; one dropped to her knees, the other turned to run. What looked like a cloak of bark cloth over her shoulders turned out to be a sling holding a sleeping infant.

"Sanga, why do you run from my friend?" Uktena said. "Fear me if you like, but Alphena will not harm you."

Sanga took two strides more, but she slowed and turned to face them. The kneeling woman opened her eyes and said, "But master—she did not go into the kiva with you. Is she a demon, or did you form her from clay by your power?"

"Uktena caught me when I was falling from a far place," Alphena said, stepping forward. "I am in his debt for my life. I will not harm anyone whom he regards as a friend."

The words formed in her mind as she spoke, replacing those she already had on the tip of her tongue. She wouldn't lie; but there might be advantages for both her and her host if these peasants chose to believe she *was* a demon held in check only by Uktena's benevolence toward them.

He laughed, but he didn't amplify her statement. "Come, little one," he said. "I'm sure my colleagues will want to meet you."

Women and children were appearing from the fields and the semicircle of huts; a few men carrying bows came out of the woods. Three older men—the trio which had come to dinner with Sempronius Tardus the night Hedia disappeared—stood before the dwellings. They watched Uktena the way jackals eye a lion.

A dune separated the grain field from sight of the shore until Alphena and her host were near the village proper. She looked past the edge of the sand and almost shouted in surprise.

"Mas—" she said, then touched her lips to mime silencing herself. She resumed, "My friend Uktena? What is that?"

Rather than pointing, she nodded in the direction of what looked like a spire of black glass, well out from the shoreline. The mild surf curled around the base of it, outlining it in foam.

"That is the house of Procron, little one," Uktena said. "He came here from Atlantis flying in that tower. He is our enemy, and I think the enemy of all men in all times; an enemy even to his own people."

"You have meditated all day, Uktena," said the man with a stuffed bird pinned to the roll of his hair. "Have you found the wisdom to send our enemy from us?"

His tone was outwardly respectful, but Alphena could hear the under-current of anger in it. She eyed him narrowly.

"Who knows what the spirits intend, Wontosa?" Uktena said, stroking the murrhine bowl of his pipe with his fingertips. His voice was as gentle as his touch on the stone, but Alphena wouldn't have wanted the words directed at her. "But soon, I think, I will try my knowledge against that of Procron."

"He may be gaining strength while you wait, you know," said the sage with a gold ring in his ear. He wore a tunic of familiar pattern rather than a breechclout or an off-the-shoulder robe, and his features were broader than those of the other men Alphena could see.

"I *don't* know that, Hanno," Uktena said. "Do you know it? You're wel-come to try your wisdom against Procron. Or make trial with me, if you wish that."

Hanno—a North African name, which explained his face and dress, but what was he doing in this place?—backed a step. "You know I don't mean that, master! We have no hope except in you. It's just that—"

He fell silent. Glancing sideways toward the sea and the spire standing in it, he backed up another step.

Not before time, Alphena thought.

"Do you have something to add, Dasemunco?" Uktena said to the third sage, who had been eyeing Alphena with a guarded expression. His head was shaved except for a fringe above his forehead.

"I wondered who the woman is, master," he said, lowering his eyes as if in humility. "Have you created her to aid you in your battle with Procron?"

"It may be that the spirits have sent Alphena to help me, Dasemunco," Uktena said, smiling without affection at the sage. "Until we know their will better, I will continue to take pleasure in the company of a brave friend who does not fear me."

Turning to her, he said, "Come, Alphena. I will show you Cascotan, where I live and where my colleagues are visting since Procron's arrival."

He stepped forward as though the sages were not there; they hopped quickly out of the way. He and Alphena walked side by side between a pair of huts and stopped in the bowl of the semicircle. Villagers watched with the air of deer poised to flee at the first sign of a threat; none of them spoke. The sages had not followed.

"Why did you say I'm not afraid of you?" Alphena said, as quietly as she could and still be heard. "I know I haven't seen all you can do, but I've seen enough."

"Respect is not fear, little one," Uktena said with a chuckle. "And is not someone who rides a thunderbird worthy of respect as well?"

Alphena started to speak, then decided not to. She realized that Uktena might know more than she herself understood about the way she had come here. Certainly he didn't speak lightly; so she shouldn't lightly disagree with him.

The flat-ended huts didn't look very sturdy. The roof and walls of each were supported on poles that had been bent into arches with both ends fixed in the ground. The frames were covered with reed mats like the one Uktena used to cover his kiva.

Inside were wicker benches and a variety of baskets, but no pottery that Alphena could see. They were unoccupied, except for an old woman who stared toward the doorway with milky eyes.

Something moaned from the near distance. Alphena looked out. It didn't appear to come from the spire on the horizon. One of the watching women turned and began to cry into her hands.

"Come," Uktena said. "Mota must be in the lagoon. It is good that you should see her, little friend."

They walked beyond the village, paralleling the shoreline but a furlong inland. There were fields here too, planted with the same heavy grass. Vines grew at the base of each stalk.

The deep moan sounded again from ahead of them. "Who is Mota?" Alphena said. "Ah, what is Mota?"

"We will see her soon," Uktena said calmly. "She grubs clams in the shallows. She wanders some distance up and down the coast, but she always comes back here eventually. Her mother used to go out to meet her, but she no longer does."

"The woman who was crying back in the village?" Alphena said. *Did Mota go crazy? Did Procron drive her crazy?*

"Yes," Uktena said. "Lascosa. There is nothing she can do. There is nothing I can do either, for Mota. Perhaps I can save other girls, though, if the spirits wish me to save them."

They stopped on the edge of a steeply sloping bank. Sedges grew down it and continued out into the water, which was black from rotting leaves. Recently stirred mud streaked the surface. Alphena looked to right and left, expecting to see a naked girl with wild hair digging in the muck with her hands. There was no one.

Water gurgled as a woman's head broke the surface. She looked at Alphena and her host, then lifted further.

Alphena shouted and stumbled back. She would have fallen if Uktena had not already had his arm behind her in anticipation of just that occurrence.

Though the eyes and forehead were human, the broad jaws were those of a beast. They worked side to side with a sound like stones turning; mud, muddy water, and bits of broken shell dribbled out from the thick lips.

More of the body lifted to the surface. It was rounded, tapering to a tail that was flattened sideways instead of horizontally like that of a porpoise. The skin was covered with fine scales which gave it a jeweled appearance.

"That is Mota," Uktena said. "She was raking for clams with her mother when Procron arrived in his dwelling. His glass servants came from the spire and took her. In a week's time she was back, as you see her now."

The creature—the *girl*—opened her mouth. Her jaws were filled with massive grinding teeth. She gave another terrible moan, then submerged again.

"But why?" Alphena whispered.

"Because he could," said Uktena. His voice was as calm as a frozen pond. "There have been others. There will be more, until someone stops him."

Alphena started to say something optimistic—and empty. She looked at Uktena and caught the words unspoken. There was no place for silliness around this man.

"How can I help?" she asked. Trying to keep her tone from slipping into defensive anger she continued, "I *know* I'm a woman but I've trained, I can fight. I lost my—"

She didn't have a word for sword.

"I lost my long knife fighting the vultures, but if you have something here, a knife or an axe, I can help you fight."

Uktena looked at her. Instead of the objection—or worse, dismissive laughter—that Alphena was poised for, he said, "A battle with Procron will not be fought with knives and axes. It is always good to have a friend nearby in a hard place, though. I welcome your presence."

Alphena lifted her chin in understanding. She'd had to ask, though. She glanced toward the lagoon. Mota hadn't surfaced again, which was a mercy; but she was there.

"Uktena, who are the other men?" Alphena asked. "The sages?"

"Come, we will walk back now," he said. Turning, he continued, "They are the wise men of neighboring villages. Hanno was brought to our land by a spirit wind, which whispered secrets to him. He, Wontosa, and Dasemunco all think that I have great power because of the talisman that came here not long before Procron did."

He touched the murrhine bowl of his pipe.

"Are they right?" Alphena said, responding to the tone she heard in Uktena's voice.

"The talisman is a tool of great power," he said, smiling at her. "But it is half the tool it was before Procron split it and crushed the sage who had used it to fight him. Procron too has a talisman. He *is* the talisman himself. But tools do not win battles, little one."

"No," Alphena said. *If you fail, I hope Procron kills me at once.*

They had reached the Cascotan again. At least a dozen men were present. Most people faced her and her host, but those Alphena glimpsed from behind had three lines scarred into their left shoulders.

"My friend and I will eat now," Uktena said to the assembly. "Bring our food to my kiva."

Wontosa stood slightly in front of his two fellows. He said, "When will you fight Procron, master? Tomorrow night will be the full moon. That is when he takes captives."

Uktena looked at him. "When the spirits inform me," he said, "I will try my knowledge against that of Procron."

He smiled. "You have an axe, Wontosa," he said. "An axe of copper that came from far to the west, do you not?"

"You know I do, master," Wontosa said. He touched the stuffed bird woven into his hair, obviously nervous. The other two sages eased away from him. "The axe is my talisman, though not so powerful as your pipe. Not nearly so powerful."

"Give your axe to my friend Alphena," Uktena said, still smiling. "She may have need of it."

I've seen sword blades with more humor in them than the line of his lips.

"But—" Wontosa said, and stopped. Then he said, "Yes, master. I'll fetch it at once."

"Send it to the kiva with our dinner," Uktena said over his shoulder as he and Alphena strode through the village.

Quietly, to Alphena, he added, "It is possible that you will need the axe tomorrow morning, little one."

VARUS STOOD BESIDE THE SIBYL, looking over an escarpment toward the jungles of Atlantis. He didn't recall climbing the opposite slope to meet her this time.

He grinned. *Perhaps I'm dreaming.*

Below, flying ships made slow circles about a spire of black glass. "How many are there, Sibyl?" he asked. "There must be hundreds of them."

"One hundred and thirteen Minoi rule Atlantis," said the old woman. "All are here in their ships, and most are accompanied by other ships directed by Servitors who draw power from the talisman of the Minos they serve."

Unlike the other crystal mansions Varus had seen in his visions, there had been no ordinary human dwellings around the base of black spire. The nearby forest smoldered where flames from the ships' weapons had glanced. The spire, untouched, rose from bare rock like a toadstool.

"The Minoi have gathered to punish Procron, who is also a Minos and who defies them," the Sibyl said. "All are present, because even so they fear that they will not be strong enough to prevail. And there is Lann, who is no longer a Minos but still lives in a fashion."

"Why are they fighting?" Varus asked. As he spoke, three ships turned inward from the circle. A Servitor stood alone in the stern of each. Smoke rose from a dozen patches of forest, ignited when ships crashed there burning.

"Procron and Lann were neighbors and enemies," the Sibyl said. "The Minoi have always fought among themselves; they have no other recreation, save diddling their serfs and drugging themselves. But instead of burning out Lann's cantonments, Procron destroyed Lann's keep and practiced other arts on Lann himself. Procron sculpts human beings."

As she spoke, Varus saw as if at arm's length an unfamiliar animal hanging by all four limbs from a tree limb; the ground was at least two hundred feet below. Lichen streaked the beast's shaggy gray fur; if it had not been for the jaws' slow movement, Varus might have thought he was looking at a bizarre swelling of the tree bark.

The eyes and forehead were human, or a parody of human.

"That's enough," Varus said, his voice clipped. As the thought formed in his mind, the creature shrunk to a blur beneath the forest canopy over which ships maneuvered in battle.

"Lann's talisman was an amphisbaena which he had carved from murrhine," the Sibyl said. "It was hollow to concentrate the thoughts of the one who used it. No other Minos thought he could have stood against Lann and his talisman; but Procron broke the talisman and broke Lann, so in fear they attacked Procron together. And even united—"

A line of shimmering purple curved from Procron's fortress with the casual grace of a trout leaping. It arched above the three approaching vessels, reaching instead for a ship in the distant circle. In its stern a Minos hunched over a rod of balas-ruby.

The line halted just short of the ship in an explosion of sparks that spread to right and left, following the curve of the circling fleet. Not only the target but several vessels ahead of and behind it began to glow in a faint violet echo. A human seated along the railing of the central ship threw up his arms and jumped overboard. His body burned in the air like thistledown; ashes drifted onto the treetops.

The balas-ruby exploded into sand. The ship's stern vanished; molten blobs of orichalc armor flew in all directions.

The bow dived into the forest. The three ships which had been approaching the spire settled somewhat less violently, like driftwood flung onto a beach.

Lines of yellow light began to reach inward from the encircling ships; some strands were brighter than others. They twisted as they stretched toward Procron's fortress, weaving a net that grew brighter as it extended.

Purple fire from the spire snapped like a whiplash, ripping the meshes of light for a hundred feet to either side of the contact. Trees in its path toward the spire sizzled and flared, but Procron's stroke faded into orange afterimages. The net rewove itself brighter and denser than before.

Light spat from the spire again, this time as a thrust toward a ship on whose deck a Minos spun a top turned from moss agate. The air along its track into the netting roiled into a spitting rainbow.

Almost, but not quite, the fire reached its target. It finally spluttered out no more than an arm's length from the hull. The woman in orichalc armor looked up once, then went back to her stone spindle as it spun and spun back, and spun. The soil beneath was burning, and gobbets of molten bedrock bubbled along the track as from a volcano.

The net was near about the fortress, now; the ships of the Minoi closed in behind its protection, while the vessels captained by Servitors stayed behind, wobbling just above the treetops. The net's upper edge was higher than the top of the spire, and at the bottom it burned the rock clean.

Varus expected Procron to try at least once more to break through the closing meshes. The spire began to sizzle with fuzzy light, like fruit infected with purple fungus. Instead of spitting another bolt, the fortress rocked sideways, then ripped free of the mountaintop. It began to rise.

Many of the Minoi closed in when they saw what was happening: portions of the net's upper edge looped inward as the ships turned bow-on to the spire. At least a third of the great fleet hung back, however. Either the Minoi directing those ships were concerned for their skins; or, more charitably, the tightening circle didn't permit all the vessels to approach without fouling one another.

The spire lifted raggedly, like a wounded man trying to climb a palisade. Cords of yellow light, by now brighter than the sun, wrapped its base. Instead of slowing, the cone of black crystal steadied into a smooth climb. The cords of light stretched, and the nearest ships jerked nearer still. Their prows lifted skyward.

The black fortress was several hundred feet off the ground when it paused. Varus thought, *Has Procron finally exhausted his power?*

The spire began to slip westward, moving hesitantly. Two ships had been lifted to the crystal's height and were directly in its path. Varus expected splintering crashes. He had once seen a storm hurl a pleasure boat onto the cliffs of Capri. Instead he had a momentary impression of each ship intersecting with a mirror image of itself and vanishing.

The spire moved with gathering speed, leaving the net of light in tatters behind it. Several ships had crashed into the jungle, whipsawed by bonds of light which their directing Minoi had not loosed in time.

One vessel whirled in circles behind the spire to which it was attached by a vivid hawser of light. The Minos with the moss agate spindle had been directing it, but when the vessel overturned the first time, it flung her and her talisman out. A dozen human servants had been aboard with her; all of them dropped into the sea or the jungle despite desperate attempts to cling to the railings.

Four Servitors remained on deck, as firmly fixed as the mast. Varus could see them as glittering refractions of sunlight even after the ship and the spire which dragged it had vanished into the west.

The edges of the vision began to blur. The images became fog from which the color bleached, filling the valley in which Varus had watched the battle.

He turned to the Sibyl. Her lined face smiled. She said, "You have seen Procron, Lord Wizard. Can you stand against him?"

"Is he my enemy, Sibyl?" Varus said. He had no way to measure the strength of one wizard against another—or against a hundred others—but he had seen rock melt and lush forest blaze at the touch of the powers the opponents were using. *That* he could understand.

"He is the enemy of all men and all life," said the Sibyl. "Can you stand against him?"

Varus wet his lips with his tongue. *I am a citizen of Carce.* "Sibyl," he said, "I will face Procron for as long as I can. I will face him for as long as I live."

"Then return to the waking world for now," said the Sibyl. "The time is coming. *Strong necessity demands that these things—*"

"Your lordship?" said Manetho. "I, ah, didn't hear all of your command. You were saying that something needed to be accomplished?"

Varus sat up, disoriented for a moment. He had been lying on the couch in the library. On the floor lay the wax tablet from which he had been reading his notes on the manumission ceremony to the clerk transcribing them in ink to a scroll.

The clerk still stood beside the desk, though he looked logy and had almost certainly just been awakened. The windows were shuttered, but sunlight came through the louvers. The librarian, Alexandros, was also barely awake, but Manetho by the doorway looked brushed and alert. Varus wondered whether he and another deputy steward had been taking shifts so that one was sure to be ready when the young master woke up.

"Your lordship . . . ," Manetho said carefully. "The decision was made not to awaken you when you nodded off. If that was a mistake and you should have been helped to your bed, I will personally search out the servant responsible and have him sent to the fields. Ah—or perhaps to your noble father's silver mines in Spain?"

Varus grimaced at the thought. Manetho wasn't joking, though he surely didn't—Varus hoped he didn't—think the young master would demand that sort of punishment for a servant who had simply guessed wrong about which of two equally probable outcomes Varus would prefer when he woke up. Not so long ago Alphena might have reacted that way, though Varus had the impression that she too was becoming more measured in her behavior.

"Of course not," Varus said. He was suddenly angry when he realized that Manetho might be looking for an excuse to send a rival to brutal labor and an early death. "Don't *ever* suggest something like that to me."

It had been bad enough to imply that the young master might be savage and unreasonable rather than the philosopher he strove to be. It was much worse to use him as a weapon against a victim who was not only undeserving of such punishment but even innocent.

Varus got to his feet. He said, "Open the—"

Before he got the rest of the sentence out, three servants were throwing open the shutters. His whole entourage—the day and night shifts together—was here in the library or in the corridor outside.

He bent to pick up the tablet which had slipped from his fingers, wondering just how far he'd gotten in his dictation. He had thought he was too tense to get to sleep and that focusing on scholarship would calm him. The plan had apparently worked better than he had hoped.

"Permit me, your lordship!" said the girl who had snatched the tablet from the floor. She put it in his hand, pressing his fingers as she did so. She must have been sleeping at the foot of his couch.

Varus didn't remember her name, though he had seen her repeatedly in the past several days. He couldn't imagine why she had been assigned to him. If in fact she had been: in a household as large as Saxa's, it was quite possible for recently purchased servants to float for weeks or months without being given specific duties.

He straightened abruptly without trying to hide his look of irritation. Just as he didn't want to be a tool of vengeance between servants, he disliked the notion of some illiterate girl using his favor to elevate herself among her fellows. She didn't even speak good Greek!

"I believe I'll go to the baths now," Varus said to Manetho. "Or—are the baths in our gymnasium warm, by any chance?"

Saxa's little exercise ground was fully equipped, though it had rarely been used before Varus invited his friend Corylus to visit. The attached bath had a steam room and a cold pool only big enough to sit in rather than swim, but that would be sufficient to relax the stiffness of a night spent sleeping awkwardly.

Manetho smiled. "When I learned your lordship was here," he said, gesturing to the bookcases, "I ordered the furnace to be stoked. The water should be ready now."

You just redeemed yourself, Varus thought. And after all, it was possible that the deputy steward hadn't had any evil motive in talking about punishments.

Aloud he said, "Have a fresh tunic brought there for me," and started for the door. Manetho whisked out ahead of him.

Frowning, Varus added, "Manetho, do you know what happened to the slaves whom my father freed, ah, yesterday?"

"They were enrolled in a section of their own," Manetho said. "Master Lenatus was appointed as the decurion who will lead them."

"Ah," said Varus, lifting his chin in understanding. His face was blank as he started downstairs toward the gymnasium at the back.

It would not do for the emperor to hear a rumor that Gaius Saxa was raising a private army of former slaves. On the other hand, Saxa's new clients had to be dealt with in some fashion, and keeping them in Carce under Lenatus was probably as safe as any choice could be. Besides, they might come in useful again. . . .

Varus thought of a wizard with the power to lift crystal mountains and to scour swathes of forest to bubbling rock. The emperor wasn't the worst threat which Saxa and the world faced at the moment.

INSTEAD OF HANGING its sail from a single spar, the Atlantean ship had two booms joined separately to the mast. When they began to flap like wings, Corylus looked up to see how they were attached.

There was no joint: the booms grew out of the mast the way branches spread from a tree bole. Corylus laid his palm against the mast and felt the wood bunch and flex as though he were touching the flank of a running horse.

"Cousin?" he said. "Is this ship alive?"

The sprite turned from the bow, where she had been looking out to sea. "I suppose it's alive the same way a crystal is," she said. "Does that matter?"

"Perhaps not at the moment," Corylus said, a trifle sharply. The sprite's lack of curiosity disturbed him, but he had met no few human beings who also disregarded the world unless it had some immediate application to themselves. The soul of a tree which had been dust or ashes for untold thousands of years had a better reason to lack a sense of wonder.

They were far enough out over the sea that Corylus could barely see the land they had left. They had slanted upward until the keel was—he looked over the railing—about a hundred feet above the water, but they were no longer climbing. There was nothing ahead or to either side, as best he could tell.

The ancient wizard grinned at him. It didn't seem to need a talisman like those he had seen the Atlanteans in visions use when they propelled their ships.

The ship's wings beat with slow, powerful strokes like those of a vulture gaining altitude on a gray day. Corylus said, "How long can we fly before we have to land? Or—"

He knew he was being optimistic, but that didn't cost any more than anxiety would.

"—can we soar without flapping?"

The sprite looked puzzled. "How would we do that?" she said. "But we can fly as long as the sun shines. Why would you want to stop flying?"

There was no useful answer to that—because of her disinterest and his ignorance, they were talking at cross purposes—so Corylus said, "Will we get home—to my home, I mean—before sunset, Coryla?"

She shrugged. "You humans worry about time," she said as she returned to where Corylus stood at the railing just forward of the mast. "I don't know when we'll reach the waking world. I don't know if we ever will."

She slid her hand through the sleeve of his tunic and began fondling his chest. He took her wrist and firmly placed her arm at her side; she pouted and turned her back, but she didn't move away.

Corylus looked up. There were no clouds, but the sky itself had a pale cast that suggested haze. The sun remained bright, though not hot enough to make him wish for better shade than he had available.

"I should have thought things through before we left the beach," Corylus said. "Does, ah, your friend know how long we must fly to get back?"

The sprite turned and glowered for an instant. Then her mood broke and she said, "I don't think he cares any more about time than I do, cousin. You humans are hard to understand."

She walked toward the bow but threw a glance over her shoulder to show that she wasn't stalking away; he followed. "But there was nothing good about that island, not for me and certainly not for you. I'm glad you left. And—"

She raised her eyebrow.

"—what would you have done when another Cyclops came? Though I might have asked the Ancient to help. Even though you're not as friendly to me as you should be, cousin. Don't you think I'm pretty?"

"At another time I'd . . . ," Corylus said. "Well, I might find you very pretty. But not now, please, mistress."

The Cyclops had almost crushed him to death, and in this place he wasn't sure he was alive to begin with. *Is my body lying on the floor of Tardus' library, turning purple and cooling?*

He grinned at the thought. So long as he could imagine things being worse, the way things were didn't seem so bad. Any soldier could tell you that.

"Well, *I* think you're being silly," the sprite said with a pout, but she wasn't really angry this time. "What else is there to do?"

"I'm going to check the food and drink," Corylus said, removing a pin so that he could slide the wooden bolt that fastened the hatch cover. He had spoken to change the subject, but as soon as he formed the words he realized that he was very thirsty.

The shallow hold was empty except for a tank with a spigot and a net bag holding hard, fist-sized lumps that looked like plaster. He supposed they were rolls. The tank wasn't metal, wood, or pottery of any familiar sort. It had flowed like glass, but it didn't have the slick hardness of glass when Corylus tried it with his fingertip.

He turned the spigot and ran fluid into the mug of the same material chained to the tank. It was water and too tasteless to be really satisfying. He drained the cup regardless, then took one of the rolls back on deck.

"Do you need something to eat?" Corylus said to the sprite. "And there's a cask of water, too."

She brushed the thought away moodily. "I don't eat; I can't eat. And I no longer have a tree."

She caught his glance toward the creature in the stern and laughed. "No, not the Ancient either," she said. "What a thought, cousin!"

At least I've cheered her up, Corylus thought. He wondered what it would be like to be imprisoned for millennia—imprisoned forever, very likely—in a bead of glass with an inhuman sorcerer. Of course the sprite was inhuman also. . . .

He took a bite of the roll as he leaned over the railing, looking down. He started to chew, then stopped and spat out the mouthful. It tasted like stiff wax.

"Mistress?" he said. "What is this stuff? I thought it was food."

"It's the food that the serfs eat on shipboard," the sprite said without much interest. "The Minoi have fresh food, but that's probably all gone now. The ships were cast up many seasons ago, you know."

"I see," said Corylus. He leaned on the railing again, eyeing the roll again. His teeth had left distinct impressions, just as they would have done in wax. He might become hungry enough to eat the stuff; but though he *was* very hungry, he wasn't to that point yet.

Swells moved slowly across the face of the water, occasionally marked by flotsam. Spurts of foam suddenly flecked the surface well off to starboard.

Corylus focused on the flickers of movement: flying fish were lifting from the sea and arrowing above it for several hundred feet, slanting slightly to one side or the other of their line in the water. Following them closely were the much larger shadows of porpoises, curving up from the surface and back. Their motion reminded Corylus of a tent maker's needle as he sewed leather panels together.

He looked at the roll. "Mistress," he said, "we don't have fishing gear or any way to make it that I can see, but I think if we get right down on the surface ahead of those fish, some of them will fly aboard. I've seen it happen before, on regular ships."

He grinned. "Flying fish are bony," he said, "and I don't suppose there's any way to cook them, but even fish would be better food than these rolls."

"It doesn't sound very good to me," Coryla said, "but if that's what you want. . . ."

She called to the creature in the language they shared. He barked in obvious amusement.

Corylus didn't see him change what he was doing—he simply squatted in the stern, occasionally looking over one railing or the other—but the ship slid downward as smoothly as it had risen. They were bearing to the right as well, putting them into the path of the school of fish.

Feeling triumphant, Corylus tossed the roll he held over the side. He felt a catch as the ship's keel brushed through the top of the swells. Spray flew backward on the breeze. Droplets splashed the creature, who calmly licked his golden fur smooth again.

A fish slapped onto the deck, wriggled, and flung itself back through the railing as Corylus tried to grab it. Almost immediately, two more fish came aboard. He hadn't replaced the hatch cover—from laziness, not foresight—but that allowed him to scoop first one, then the other catch into the hold.

They were each the length of his forearm. Corylus was more pleased at having come up with a clever idea than he was at the prospect of eating them raw.

"Cousin?" the sprite said. "Have you looked into the water over the stern recently?"

Corylus grimaced to be interrupted: another fish had landed on the deck and there was one caught on top of the port sail as well.

She didn't sound concerned—but she never *sounded concerned.*

Corylus leaped past the Ancient, looking back while holding onto the inward-curving stern piece. There was only swelling water, a translucent green that darkened—

"Take us up!" he shouted. "Higher, by Hercules!"

The Ancient laughed like a chattering monkey. The sails slammed the air back and downward, thrusting the ship upward and making it heel onto its port side. Corylus grabbed the starboard railing with both hands and kept his grip though his feet skidded out behind him.

The sails flapped again. The ship wasn't gaining height—the port rail barely skimmed the tops of the swells—but they had turned at almost right angles to their previous course. The golden-furred creature continued to laugh.

It was going to let us die without saying a word!

But then, it was already dead. Presumably nothing would change for the Ancient and Coryla if the glass amulet was in the belly of a—

The sea exploded upward where the ship would have been if it had continued dawdling along catching flying fish. The head of the monster was ten or a dozen feet long in itself, and its gape was wider yet. The fangs were a foot long, back-slanting and pointed like spears.

The jaws clopped shut on spray and air. If the ship hadn't twisted to the side, they would have crushed the hull.

The monster curled to follow its prey's new course. Its head and body were a tawny bronze, with darker mottlings as though brown paint had been dripped over metal.

The eyes, prominent and well forward in the snout, glittered with what Corylus read as anger. He knew he was projecting his fear onto a beast whose small brain likely had room only for hunger. Hunger was quite enough of a threat.

The ship was rising at last, describing a slow curve which would bring it back on the course which Corylus had left to go fishing. He looked at the magician in the stern. His right hand trembled toward his sword hilt.

The anger flooded out of Corylus; he laughed also. He leaned over the railing to see the monster which had almost devoured them.

Coryla's friend had done what he told it to do. If Corylus stabbed in the dark and cut down the wrong person, would he be angry with his sword? In the future, he would be more careful, but—

He turned to the creature and bowed. "Thank you, Master Magician," he said. "By turning the ship instead of just rising as I ordered, you saved us from the danger I put us in by my ignorance."

The Ancient very deliberately touched the tips of his long fingers together, then put his hands on his thighs as before. Corylus didn't know what the gesture meant, but it was clearly an acknowledgment.

Corylus looked down at the giant fish which now was swimming near the surface. It had a fin the whole length of its back, but nothing else marred the serpentine smoothness of the several hundred feet of its body. The ship was drawing ahead, but it was clearly following.

"Our magic drew it from the bottom," said the sprite. "The eel isn't a natural creature, you know. Well, most of what I've seen in this place you brought me to isn't natural, as we know it in the waking world."

Corylus cleared his throat. They were a hundred feet above the water and leveling out. He thought of going higher, but—

He smiled grimly.

—experience had taught him to trust the magician's judgment over his own.

"Will the eel chase us far, mistress?" he said to the sprite. His hands ached from their grip on the railing; he began to spread and clench the fingers, working circulation back into them.

"Until it dies, I suppose," Coryla said, "or we leave its world."

She shrugged. "Or until it catches us and you die, of course."

"Of course," Corylus said. By squinting when he looked back along their course, he could see the eel as a long shadow rippling in the water.

The sun was past zenith. It would go below the horizon in five or six hours. For now, the ship flew on.

WATER TRICKLED DOWN A BACK CORNER of Hedia's cell. It wasn't because the walls sweated like those of the cells under the Circus during the winter:

this stream was guided by a channel. When it reached the floor, it ran down a channel cast into a tile with a beveled hole in the middle.

A greater flow echoed hollowly in the sewer beneath the cells. Though the floor was probably nearly transparent like the rest of the building, there wasn't enough light below for Hedia to see through it.

She walked to the grating on the corridor side. Two Servitors stood against the far wall, watching her. Each held an orichalc spear; a dagger of the same gleaming metal was thrust beneath a sash of coarse fabric.

"I need food!" she said, not shouting but in a commanding voice. The glass men didn't move any more than she expected them to.

She rattled the grill. It was steel, or at any rate some gray metal. The hinge pins were discolored, but there was no rust despite the damp conditions. The bars were too thick for her to cut through in less than a month even if she'd had a saw.

Which she certainly did not. There was nothing with her in the cell except the garment which the Council of Minoi had given her after their decision. She had taken it off and used the wetted cloth to rub herself clean as soon as she had taken stock of the situation. She didn't need clothing, and she would feel much better to be rid of the filth and dried blood in which she was covered.

"Your masters don't want me to starve to death!" Hedia said. "If you don't bring me food, that's what will happen. What will they do to you then?"

The Servitors were as still as statues. She wasn't sure that they could understand speech anyway—or even hear.

A steel grating of about the size of the cell's floor covered a section of the corridor roof. It stood out as ridged black against the faint blue glow of the crystal in the walls, floors, and the rest of the ceiling. Air rose through it with a low-pitched whistle, drawing cooler air along the corridor.

A human servant shuffled down the corridor, carrying a nearly empty sack made from rope netting. He was a stooped old man with his eyes fixed on the floor in front of him.

"Good sir!" Hedia called, pressing herself against the bars. "Come here! I will make it worth your while."

He ignored her as completely as the Servitors had done. Stopping, he rummaged in his bag and brought out a lump the size of two clenched fists. He offered it to a Servitor, who took it in his glass hand.

The human continued onward without ever having looked toward

Hedia. The Servitor crossed the corridor and thrust the doughlike lump through the bars. They were set closely, but Hedia could have reached between them.

She didn't bother, since she knew from experience that she couldn't have overpowered a glass man. Even if she had, it wouldn't get her out of this cell.

She grinned. It would be satisfying, though. Throttling *anything* would feel good right at the moment.

Hedia bit into the lump as she walked to the back of her cell. It reminded her of overcooked octopus: bland, resilient, and tough. She chewed mechanically, wondering what it had been originally.

The cooks of noble households in Carce prided themselves on disguising the ingredients of their dishes, fashioning "roast boar" from mackerel and "rack of lamb" from peacocks' tongues. She doubted whether even the most experienced of them could create something quite so namelessly nasty as this, however.

Because she didn't have a cup, she held her lips to the groove in the wall and sucked the trickle which followed it. It was good water, at least.

She resumed eating. The situation was unpleasant, but the fact that she didn't like the food wasn't close to the top of the list of things she didn't like. If the guards had been human, she might have complained; though without expecting anything to change. Railing at the Servitors was as pointless as screaming at her bronze mirror.

A clang like a cartload of armor overturning sounded in the corridor. Holding the lump of food in one hand and her garment in the other, Hedia walked in a dignified fashion to the grilled doorway. Walking was about the only dignified thing she could do under the circumstances, and she didn't imagine that her moving faster would change anything that was going on outside her cell.

The Servitors had leaped into action. They stood beneath the grate in the corridor ceiling, pointing their spears toward the dark bulk that had crashed down hard enough to dimple it. Had a block fallen from the top of the airshaft?

Fingers from above thrust into the grating. It rocked, then lifted slightly. Hedia touched her own bars. If the grating was the same metal, it had to weigh five or six times as much as she did.

A guard thrust upward, nicking the steel. His orichalc point missed the gripping fingers.

The square grate lifted a hand's breadth higher, then shot down into the corridor. One guard dodged in time, but it struck the other squarely and slammed him back against Hedia's cell. His spear flipped into the air like a spun coin, bounced from the corridor ceiling, and landed ringing on the floor. The grating toppled to lie on the point and half the shaft.

Lann hung within the air shaft, his broad palms pressed against opposite walls. He had lifted—and thrown—the grate with his feet. Weight alone held it on studs cast into the sides of the bottom course of crystal blocks.

The ape's tattooed human face scanned the situation below; then he leaped onto the standing guard, catching his spear-shaft in his toes. They hit the floor together with Lann on the bottom.

Hedia pushed the rolled-up garment between the bars with her right hand and caught the end with the other hand, lacing it back through the next opening to the left. The guard had fallen with his back against the cell. He started to get up.

Hedia looped the garment around his glass neck and crossed the portions on her side around one another. She didn't have time to knot the ends, but even so the fabric took the strain instead of her hands and arms. The Servitor half-rose, then recoiled into the bars with a clang almost as loud as that of the grating hitting the floor.

Lann used his hands and feet together to fling the other Servitor against the wall of the corridor. The glass head shattered to dust; the Servitor's torso and limbs crumbled into gravel-sized chunks a moment later.

The remaining guard jerked forward again. The steel bar flexed noticeably outward, but to Hedia's amazement the makeshift noose didn't break: the fabric had made her itch, but it was clearly stronger even than silk.

The Servitor turned and reached through the bars. Hedia jumped back, avoiding a grip that she knew could squeeze her bones to powder. The glass hands pulled the loop open, now that she was no longer able to keep the ends tight.

Lann grabbed the Servitor by the ankles. The glass man reached for Lann's wrists instead of holding onto the bars. Lann swung him sideways like a huge club. His head hit the opposite wall and powdered like that of his fellow guard.

Hedia stared at the ape-man, scarcely able to believe what she had just seen happen. *How strong are you?* she thought. But unless he could tear apart steel bars as thick as her two thumbs together, killing the guards wouldn't change her situation.

Lann gripped the spear of the guard he had just killed and jerked it from under the grate. He thrust the point into the door's lower hinge. Gripping the shaft in his hands and the bars with his toes, he pulled. The slender orichalc blade didn't bend, but the hinge pin snapped and the lower corner of the door twisted noticeably inward.

I might be able to slip through, Hedia thought; though she knew that slim as she was, she wasn't really *that* slim. But if Lann would break the upper hinge also—

The ape-man dropped the spear and gripped the corner of the door. With his feet braced on the crystal jamb, he used the bars' own length to lever them outward.

"There, I can squeeze through!" Hedia said. She got down on her hands and knees.

Lann continued to pull. *Can he understand Greek?*

The corner of the door squealed as it bent upward like a scrap of cloth caught in a breeze. The ape-man dropped to the floor again. He was breathing hard and the fur of his chest and shoulders was soaked with sweat.

Hedia started to crawl out. Lann pushed her back with the brusque gentleness a nurse uses toward an infant who insists on going somewhere she shouldn't. To Hedia's surprise, he crouched and squirmed into the cell, twisting partway through so that his massive shoulders would clear. She hadn't thought he would fit, but the ape-man had a better eye for the problem.

Although that didn't explain why he apparently wanted to imprison himself. Hedia could think of one possible reason, but she supposed she should discount that because her mind *always* tended to run in that direction. So, however, did the minds of many men who came in contact with her.

The ape-man ignored her and shuffled splay-legged to the drain. He thrust his right hand into it and planted his left hand flat on the floor. The muscles of his shoulders bunched again.

Hedia thought for a moment that Lann's hand was trapped; then she realized that the tile was lifting. The ape-man straightened till his long left arm was straight; the tile wasn't completely out of the hole in which it had nested, but she could see the underside shimmering close to the level of the floor.

Lann leaned backward, using the weight of his body to balance that of the massive tile: it was square, three feet on a side and eight inches thick. He gripped the upper edge with his left hand and tilted it further upward; his right hand was clenched into a fist, creating a lump too big to slip back through the drain hole.

He rotated the tile in the opening, then gave it a slight shove sideways and unclenched his fist. The tile, aligned with the diagonal, dropped through the square hole and smashed into the sewer beneath.

Lann turned, grinning, to Hedia. His right wrist was ringed with blood. He pointed down into the opening, grunted, and then climbed through. He held the rim for a moment, then dropped.

Hedia looked into the hole. She couldn't see the bottom, but she caught the motion of the ape-man waving. He grunted again, louder and this time imperiously. The sound echoed like a lion's cough.

Hedia darted to the front of her cell and stretched through the bars for the spear Lann had used for a lever. She pulled it in with her, then managed to reach the belt from which the second guard's dagger hung. The previous wearer was now a pile of sharp gravel which spilled away when she tugged the scabbard. She hung the belt over her shoulder like a bandolier instead of bothering with the complex buckle.

Lann called a third time, obviously angry. She doubted he could climb up again to fetch her, but she had learned not to discount the ape-man's strength and resourcefulness.

Hedia thrust the spear through the opening butt-first and waggled it until she felt a powerful hand snatch it away from her. She slid into the opening, bracing her arms on the sides as Lann had done. Relaxing them, she dropped.

She hoped Lann would catch her instead of letting her fall onto the edges of the drain tile. Even if that had happened it would be better than being dangled as bait for a monster.

Besides, trusting Lann had proved to be a good idea this far.

CHAPTER XIV

Lann caught Hedia not only easily but gently; his hands were like a pair of leather pillows shaped perfectly to the contours of her body. He lowered her till her feet touched water. She twitched back for an instant, but the ape-man was standing so she straightened her legs.

The bottom of the channel was no more than six inches below the surface. The trickle down the wall of Hedia's cell had been fresh, but this was salty enough to sting her many cuts and scratches. The Minoi must use a constant flow of seawater to flush the sewer.

The current was noticeable but not hazardous. Lann set off against it, hunching as before. He looked as though he were fighting a fierce wind.

Hedia fished up the spear—Lann had dropped it—and followed. She wished that the ape-man could talk, though his strength was certainly more valuable an asset than speech would have been.

She visualized a frail, scholarly monkey declaiming to the crowd in the Forum in a toga. The thought made her giggle and feel better.

As her eyes adapted, she could see that the walls of the sewer glowed faintly blue up to within a foot or two of the high ceiling. She scraped the spear butt along it, finding crystal beneath. She left a mark on the surface and lifted a blob of bluish slime which she flicked off.

Algae, she supposed, or perhaps moss like the sheets that grew on the ancient well in Saxa's back garden. About all the light showed her was Lann, sloshing on ahead, but he was a comforting sight.

Hedia couldn't see into the water, and there was no walkway to the side of the channel. She decided not to worry about what she couldn't change. Occasionally her foot squished instead of splashing, but that could happen in the streets of Carce. If she had been squeamish, she would have missed out on quite a lot of what life had to offer.

It was growing brighter. There was something ahead, a cross-hatched pattern glimpsed past the ape-man's bulk.

It was a grating across the sewer. Vegetation so dead and dry that Hedia couldn't tell what it had been originally clung to the bars. It was a solid curtain at the bottom, and stray wisps remaining almost to the top from when the channel had been flooded. Through gaps Hedia could see the end of the tunnel; open water gleamed in the moonlight.

Lann reached out with both hands and shook the grate. It was fixed so firmly to the crystal that Hedia couldn't hear the metal ring—though she told herself that she did.

The ape-man cried out in echoing rage. He took the bars in his outstretched feet and hands, trying to bend them toward the middle. He shrieked like a bull being gelded.

"Lann?" Hedia said. He ignored her.

She shouted, "Lann!" at the top of her lungs. He continued to shake the bars vainly.

Hedia knew better than to touch him. She had been around a number of very angry men, and had learned how bad an idea startling one could be. She had never known anyone as strong as Lann, however.

Hedia stepped to the wall and rattled the orichalc spear-butt across the grating, making a musical clamor that cut through even the ape-man's bellows. Her hands tingled on the verge of numbness from the vibration.

To Lann, the grate must have felt like the breath of nearby lightning. He shouted, "Waugh!" and leaped backward.

Hedia offered the spear to him. He stared at it for a moment in confusion; then his expression brightened into a smile that displayed fangs which could have cracked the joint of an ox.

Two bolts on either side locked the grate to the crystal wall. Lann thrust the spear between the grate and the left-hand wall.

Hedia stepped away as the ape-man worked. He knew his own strength, but she had the impression that he didn't fully appreciate the weakness of those around him.

The ape-man was clearly more than just a beast. He had entered her prison by coming down the air shaft, but even he hadn't tried to climb back that way while carrying Hedia. He had known the way the sewer was constructed—he had been one of the rulers, after all—and he had intelligently exploited that design to escape with her.

But though Lann had used a spear to break the cell door loose, he hadn't thought to bring it along in case he needed a lever again. His enemy Procron hadn't put a man's brain into an ape's body . . . but it did appear that he had put *part* of a man's brain into an ape.

The grating rang like anvils falling together. Hedia thought the spear must have snapped, but the orichalc shaft had held. The sound was the thick steel bolt breaking.

Hedia thought the obvious way to proceed was for Lann to use the lever to break the remaining bolt on that side. Instead he dropped the spear, gripped the edge of the grate with both hands, and set his feet on the wall.

The grating was taller than the cell, giving the ape-man more leverage on the upper bolt than he'd had on the door hinge. It flexed upward only a few inches when the bolt sheared with another ringing crash.

Water trapped behind the debris at the bottom of the screen gushed through. Grunting in thunderous triumph, Lann walked backward along the wall, dragging the grate with him.

At last he dropped to all fours in the water, snorting like a winded horse. He had bent back the grating so that it left a broad passage, but the ape-man was blocking it.

Hedia smiled wryly. She didn't intend to go on without him, even if she had been able to get by.

Lann rose to his usual crouch, glanced at Hedia, and shambled past the grating. She fished out the spear again and followed. His strength was incredible, but even so his exertions must have taken a toll; he seemed logy, though—

She was thinking of him as human. An ape couldn't be expected to be sprightly in human terms.

They sloshed from the inlet into a sea which got deeper very quickly. Lann hooted in concern and pulled Hedia with him to the muddy bank.

The water shone in moonlight. In the far distance she could see the opposite shore, not as a place but as a boundary to the shimmering smoothness. Occasional streaks indicated that things were swimming close to the surface, and the water slapped once.

They continued along the edge of the water. Behind them Poseidonis rose as a series of glittering angles beyond a band of jungle. Hedia didn't see

man, and we would be considering how to proceed after dessert, Hedia thought. But considering the alternatives, the present situation was just fine.

She leaned over the rim and looked down. All she could see was her own reflection, distorted by ripples from the pad's motion. Absently she trailed her fingertips in the water. It was cool if not cold, unlike the warmth of the Bay of Puteoli. She thought of the relaxing days she had spent in villas at Baiae, wondering if she would ever—

"Waugh!" Lann shouted. The leaf bucked as he flopped across it and caught Hedia's leg.

He jerked her away from the edge with the kind of violence he had displayed toward the Servitors. She let out a startled yelp, then broke into tears: a defensive reflex honed by the number of times powerful men had attacked her.

The pad lurched again. Hedia twisted around just as jaws clopped shut like the stroke of a battering ram. She didn't know what the creature was— fish or snake or something still worse—but it could have bitten Lann in half, let alone her.

It sank back and swirled off, brushing the pad with its tail. Hedia stopped crying. Now her fright was completely real.

Muttering to himself, the ape-man resumed stroking the boat forward. Onward, at any rate.

Hedia crouched, well back from the edge. She wanted to apologize, but she didn't know how to. At least she could avoid repeating her mistakes.

Though the sky wasn't visibly brighter, Hedia no longer saw the stars as clearly as she had when she emerged from the sewer inlet. She wondered what would happen if they remained on open water during daylight.

Under other circumstances she might have suggested to Lann that they climb into the water and kick their way along, using the leaf for flotation. The only value she could see in that now is that she would wind up feeding Atlantean sea life instead of becoming bait for an even larger monster as the Minoi planned for her.

Hedia looked forward again and to her surprise saw trees. *We're going to make it!* she thought, delighted that the shore hadn't been as far as she thought when last she strained her eyes to see ahead.

Lann rumbled a challenge from deep in his chest. The sound rose and fell as though its jaggedness caught his throat when it tumbled out. Hedia jerked around, wondering what she had done wrong this time; but the ape-man was looking beyond her.

She turned again. What she had thought were trees were walking off. The trunks leaned to the side and the roots—or dangling branches?—bent and lifted and set down again well forward of where they had been. She supposed they had to be walking on the bottom, but in the doubtful light it really looked as though they were skimming the surface of the water.

"I thought they were trees," she repeated, this time in a whisper. And perhaps they *were* trees. . . .

Lann resumed paddling. Hedia watched him; in part because she was afraid to look at anything else in this terrible place, but also because she was beginning to appreciate the economy of the ape-man's movements.

She had thought he was clumsy, but she now realized his seeming awkwardness was a result of the sheer mass of his muscles and the skeleton that anchored them. She had seen warships carrying out combat maneuvers. Their long, slender hulls resisted turning, but even so a trained crew could send its ram crushing through the center of a target or could slip between pillars with only a hand's breadth of clearance to either side for the oar tips.

The boat jerked violently again: something was scraping along its underside. Hedia wailed, but she jumped up with the spear in her hands. If she plunged it straight down between her feet, whatever was under the lily pad would—

Lann closed his hand over the spear shaft, preventing her from thrusting. He hooted in question. Hedia looked over her shoulder: they had grounded on the other side of the sea. The pad had been rubbing the sloped edge of the land.

"Oh," she said. "I'm very sorry."

Lann strode past her into the lowering jungle. Hedia, still carrying the spear, followed.

I'm almost back to where I started, she thought. Which meant she was was a great deal better off than she'd been a few hours earlier.

THE SUN REMAINED ABOVE THE HORIZON, but its ball had flattened and its light was deepening to red. Corylus pressed his hands together, wishing there was something he could do.

The sails continued to beat, but it seemed to Corylus that the strokes were slower and becoming flaccid. The ship was certainly descending, though the keel was still a hundred feet in the air. Almost a hundred feet.

Something thrust up from the sea about three miles ahead, or it looked like something did. Corylus grasped the sprite's shoulder and said, "There, isn't that an island, Coryla? Or anyway a rock. Is it big enough to land on?"

"Am I a sailor?" the sprite said. "Or a magician? I don't know what this ship can do."

Corylus turned toward the Ancient and bowed. The wizard didn't acknowledge his presence except by the focus of his golden eyes.

"Master," Corylus said. "Would you please take us toward that island—" He pointed.

"—so that I can take a look at it. We're going to need to land, soon."

Corylus looked beyond the magician, back over the course they had travelled since leaving the Cyclops' island. They had outdistanced the great eel, but he didn't doubt the sprite's warning that it would follow until it died or it caught them. A night spent rolling on the surface would be long enough for the latter—and he didn't see any reason why the monster should courteously manage to die before that happened.

Corylus had taken his hand from the sprite's shoulder when he turned. She nuzzled close to him again. He eased back, though he didn't break contact. He said, "Is there anything alive on the island? It looks pretty barren to me."

He couldn't decipher the look that Coryla gave him. "It's barren," she said. "But there is life, of sorts."

The island was a square-sided vertical pillar that rose out of the sea to the level of the ship's keel. The top was about twenty feet on a side and slightly domed rather than flat. Grass grew in patches and there were occasional bushes, but it was mostly bare rock.

Because of the island's shape, Corylus wondered if it might be artificial. As they drew closer, he could see that the striations which he'd taken for masonry were actually natural rock layers. Some were reddish, darkened further by the setting sun. Iron had bled from them and draped rusty banners down the paler rocks beneath.

He estimated how difficult it would be to climb the rock face. He could still do it, he was pretty sure; but he'd been in Carce for long enough that he'd like to have a few days to train on lesser slopes first. He grinned.

The Ancient made a sound that started low but climbed in pitch and volume. Corylus had his sword out by the time he had faced completely around, expecting to see the eel or something worse rising toward them from the sea.

He almost didn't recognize the Ancient. The golden fur was fluffed out, making him look more like an angry bear than the starving cat Corylus would previously have used as a comparison. His mouth was slightly open: irregular teeth gave his jaws the contours of saw blades. He extended one long arm toward the island.

Corylus followed the gesture. A man with wild hair and a dark tunic climbed to the center of the dome. Could he have been hiding in the vegetation? That would seem impossible to a civilian, but Corylus had twice seen a hulking blond German lunge from a bush that shouldn't have been able to hide a coney.

A dozen more men appeared; they must have come out of the rock or condensed from the air itself. They were gesturing and speaking among themselves. Corylus could hear the sounds, but he couldn't make out words if they even were words.

The ship wallowed from side to side and lost way. They were sinking as well, though slowly. That wasn't what most concerned Corylus. This savage outbreak on the part of the magician he depended on mattered more than mere details of the ship's course.

The Ancient extended both arms and shrieked, still louder than before. His hands bent toward one another as though he were holding an invisible globe. Blue-white flashes glittered between his palms; then a line of sparks curved raggedly from them toward the island.

Scores of men stood now on the rock, impossible numbers to exist on so small an island. Several dropped to all fours and began to howl. Their companions took up the sound.

As swiftly as images change when a mirror tilts, human forms became wolves and as swiftly changed back to human. The top of the island seethed like water coming to a boil, and the howls seemed to Corylus to echo from the roof of heaven.

"Sheer off!" he shouted. He stepped between the Ancient and the wolf-men who had driven him to frothing rage. "Take us away! We can't land here, no matter what the choice is!"

For a moment, Corylus thought that the magician was going to ignore him—or worse, strike with the power which allowed him to lift this ship and drive it hundreds of miles in a day. *The armor might protect me, but—*

The Ancient hunched back to the stern where he had been standing until the wolfmen called him forward. His fur began to settle, though hints lasted like the flush on the face of a man who had controlled his anger.

The sails beat more strongly; the ship rose sluggishly as it left the island behind. The wolfmen continued to howl behind them.

Only the upper half of the sun showed above the horizon. Corylus hugged himself.

How long? How long before the eel catches up with us?

VARUS REMEMBERED TALKING with his father, but now he climbed the craggy, fog-wrapped hillside. He never took the same route to the Sybil's eyrie, though the differences were trivial: here white gravel had spilled across the path, marble chips perhaps; there was an outcrop which in the mist looked like an unfamiliar human profile.

He reached the top of the ridge. The Sibyl sat like a senator on a folding ivory stool. Beside her was a wicker basket from which she took peas. She was shelling them into an earthenware pot on the other side and tossing the hulls down the opposite slope. She turned to watch Varus as he approached.

"Mistress, I greet you," he said. "I hope that you are well."

The Sibyl gave a broken chuckle. "I am the creature of your mind, Lord Magician," she said. "There is no well or ill for me."

Varus felt his lips wrinkle as though he were sucking a lemon. *She knows things that I do not know,* he thought, *and I'm not a magician.*

Then he thought, *But if I were a magician and afraid to admit it to myself, I might know things that I allowed myself to see only in these visions.*

The Sibyl smiled as Varus argued silently with himself. Embarrassed, he looked into the valley beyond. Instead of a landscape, he saw a globe hanging in blackness. Its surface was moving.

"This is the world, Lord Magician," the Sibyl said. "Not today, but one day."

"It's a sphere," he said, not asking a question but voicing the statement to file it in his mind. "Then Eratosthenes was right."

Varus didn't have a mind for mathematics, but Pandareus told his students that they should attend the lectures of Brotion of Alexandria who was visiting Carce. He and Corylus were the only members of our class who did so.

He grinned at the memory. Corylus seemed to understand what Brotion was saying. Varus himself was pleased just to have remembered Brotion describing Eratosthenes' calculations.

He looked at the globe. As before, the object of his attention became clear. For an instant he saw the tossing sea; then the surface of the world became a single throbbing creature: a myriad of heads, arms, and legs, but only one monstrous body. The whole world . . .

Varus jerked back with a shout, though there was no need to react physically. The globe and its pullulating surface first blurred, then vanished completely as fog filled the valley.

If I even have a body in this place.

"That is Typhon?" Varus said, trying to prevent his voice from trembling.

"That will be Typhon," the Sibyl said. "Not today, but one day."

Varus swallowed. "Sibyl," he said, "how do I stop him? How do I stop *that?*"

He nodded toward the vanished image. He didn't want to point, and he particularly didn't want to describe what he had seen in words.

"Typhon will rule the world," the Sibyl said. She took more pea pods in her right hand. "No one has the power to change that. Not even a magician as powerful as you, Lord Varus."

Varus made a sour expression again, but he didn't argue pointlessly. "Sibyl," he said, "what should I do? What *can* I do?"

"What did the sage Menre tell you, Lord Magician?" the old woman said. She resumed shelling the peas, dropping them one at a time into the jar on her left.

"That was a dream, Sibyl," he said, thinking back to his vision in the shrine of Serapis. "I dreamed that Menre gave me a book, but when I awoke with Pandareus, it was all as it had been when we entered the chapel. There was no book."

The Sibyl's jar was decorated with a single long band which wound from the base of the vessel to the rim. People of all ages and conditions walked up the slanting field. When Varus looked at the figures closely, he saw that they were moving, and he thought that some of them were looking out at him.

The Sibyl smiled. "Was there not?" she said. "What are you holding, Lord Magician?"

Varus held the winding rods of a large papyrus roll, open before him. He looked down and read aloud, *"I remember the names of my ancestors. I speak their names and they live again!"*

A causeway stretched before him, over the mists which hid the valley where Varus had watched the triumph of Typhon. The Sibyl crooned softly as she resumed shelling peas, paying Varus no attention.

He walked onto the causeway. He glanced over his shoulder once, toward the Sibyl. He wondered whether she was counting years or lives or some further thing . . . but it didn't matter to him.

Gaius Varus was going to meet with his ancestors; and perhaps he would one day return.

ALPHENA WOKE SUDDENLY from a fitful sleep. Throughout the night she had been dozing off and on. Whenever she wakened, Uktena remained sitting cross-legged in the center of the chamber, smoking his pipe and mumbling rhythmically under his breath. Now he had gotten to his feet.

"Is it time?" she asked. Her voice caught. The acrid smoke—dried willow bark mixed with some broad-leafed local herb—had flayed the back of her throat. She coughed to clear it.

Uktena thrust the stem of his pipe beneath the cord of his breechclout and stepped to the simple ladder. Either he didn't hear her, or he was ignoring her.

Alphena got up. She had sat, sleeping and waking, with the copper axe in her lap. She gripped the haft firmly as she waited to follow the shaman. She wasn't used to the way the axe balanced in her hand, but it was lighter than a sword and she ought to be able to handle it without strain.

Uktena lifted the mat away from the kiva's entrance. His movements were slow and exaggerated, as though he were performing a ritual dance.

Alphena scrambled to catch up as the shaman strode through Cascotan. Villagers watched silently; no one was working.

The sky seemed bright after the smoky kiva. Though Alphena couldn't see the sun from where she stood, dawn had turned the tip of Procron's fortress to black fire.

Uktena walked with deliberation toward the shore. He didn't look to either side.

The three sages waited midway between the village and the saltwater. As before, Wontosa stood a half step ahead of his companions. He said, "Greetings, master! Are you ready to drive the monster away from our shores?"

Uktena did not speak, but for the first time since he emerged from the kiva, he turned his head—toward Wontosa. The sage stiffened and his eyes lost focus momentarily.

Alphena followed Uktena. As she passed, Hanno called, "You, girl." He didn't shout, but he managed to put a threat in his tone. "Where are you going?"

"I'm going to stand with my friend," she said, pausing to look squarely at the sages. The axe head rose slightly as she spoke. "Come with us, why don't you? Aren't you all magicians?"

Hanno didn't respond. Wontosa and Dasemunco were looking out to sea, pretending that they weren't aware of Alphena's presence. She spat on the ground and hurried on to join Uktena.

The shaman had reached the shore and stopped; his bare feet were just above the tide line. He dropped the murrhine pipe on the beach behind him. The surf was sluggish, like the movements of the chest of a sleeping dog.

Lightning flashed in the far distance; no thunder accompanied it. Alphena looked up in surprise. The morning had been clear when she saw the sky from the mouth of the kiva, but a scud of clouds was racing in from the west.

The sun rose, throwing the shadow of the black spire toward Uktena. He lifted his right arm, the palm toward the east.

Alphena, to the shaman's left side and a pace behind him, glanced at *his* shadow. It was elongated but as sharply chiseled as the reliefs on a temple facade, then—

Something squirming and huge spread across the shoreline and beyond, covering the land. It was not a shape but a blackness too pure to have form.

The shadow was gone as suddenly as it had appeared. Uktena faced east.

The top of the black fortress split open. Procron, a figure in orichalc armor without the helmet, drifted out like a wisp of gossamer. In place of his human head flashed a diamond skull brighter than the fiery metal.

Uktena walked forward with the same awkward determination as before. His feet touched but did not sink into the slowly moving water. He raised his right arm, bent at the elbow; his left hung at his side. He was chanting, but Alphena could not make out the words.

She went out fifty feet from the shore, trying to follow. There the low waves caught the hem of her tunic and with that purchase threatened to pull her over. She lifted the garment, preparing to fling it away, but she stopped when she thought about what she was doing. Grimacing, she backed to where the water reached only to mid-shin.

Alphena had seen many gladiatorial battles. Splashing in water that would shortly be over her head, she would be completely useless in a fight against an enemy who walked on air.

Worse, if Uktena took notice of her, she would handicap him. She didn't mind risking her life, but she dared not risk the life of the friend she was supposedly helping.

Brilliant purple light flashed from Procron's skull, sizzling against a clear barrier an arm's length short of Uktena's chest. The bolt dribbled off like rain blown against a sheet of metal.

The sea beneath Uktena hissed. Alphena—near the shore now, a quarter mile behind him—felt her legs tingle and the hair rise on her arms and the back of her neck.

Uktena continued forward. Alphena thought she heard his voice in the thunder rumbling overhead.

Procron drifted closer, his arms folded across his chest. He slammed out another bolt, brighter than the sun at noon.

Uktena staggered, half-turning. Alphena fell backward in the water from the visual shock. She blinked furiously, trying to clear the orange afterimages flaring across her eyes.

Uktena resumed his advance. His form was shifting, swelling.

Alphena squeezed her eyes closed, pretending that what she saw was because afterimages were distorting her vision. She whispered, "Vesta, make him safe. Make him not be changed."

Huge, tentacled, and many-legged, the thing that had been Uktena approached the Atlantean. Both hung in the air. Procron loosed a series of dazzling, crackling bolts, flinging Uktena back. Tentacles shriveled and the swollen body seemed to deflate, though the purple haze which spread about the scene blurred the forms of both combatants.

The sea beneath them was bubbling. Dead fish and stranger creatures rocked on the surface, many of them boiled pink or red. Alphena's skin itched as though she had gotten a bad sunburn.

Uktena surged toward Procron again. A purple flash and thunderclap drove them apart short of contact.

Procron tumbled, his armor flashing brightly, but he regained control above the water. Wobbling, dipping like a skylark instead of rising smoothly, the Atlantean took an aerial post midway between the shore and his gleaming fortress.

Black and smoking, the creature Uktena had become dropped into the sea. Spray and steam spouted fifty feet in the air.

The wave from the impact sent Alphena tumbling. She got to her feet and began sloshing toward where the shaman had hit. She screamed and raised her axe to threaten anybody who came close to her.

Uktena bobbed into view. For a moment he lay sprawled facedown on the slow swell; then his head lifted and he shook himself.

Treading water, Uktena looked out toward his opponent. Procron showed no signs of returning to try conclusions again. Carefully, painfully, the shaman began to stroke for shore.

Alphena, waist deep when the sea was at rest, watched for a moment in hesitation. She bent and took off her sandals, throwing them to shore. Holding the axe helve with her knees, she pulled her tunic over her head. After rolling it into a loose rope and retrieving the axe, she walked in the shallows toward the line Uktena was taking.

Overhead, the clouds were breaking up again. Alphena thought it had rained briefly, but the swirling battle had whipped the sea to froth; the spatters she felt might have come from that.

Uktena had paused. A swell lifted him; when it dipped away again, he lay as motionless as a mass of seaweed.

Alphena sloshed forward. "My friend!" she called. "My friend Uktena!"

The black spire had closed again. Procron must have returned to his fortress; at any rate, Alphena couldn't see him anymore.

Uktena roused and splashed feebly. Alphena shouted, but it wasn't a word. She bobbed out as far as she dared and flung the end of her rolled tunic toward the shaman. For a moment she was afraid that he wouldn't take it; then one of his sinewy hands twisted itself into the fabric.

Alphena's feet didn't touch bottom when her nose was above water. She dipped, digging her toes into the sand as she pulled hard on the makeshift rope. With the slack that gave her, she fought a foot or two closer to shore and repeated the process. She could swim, but not well and not while holding the axe. She wasn't going to let go of the axe.

After a very long time, she could walk normally. Uktena tried to get to his feet. His eyes were blank. Alphena threw his right arm over her shoulders and gripped that wrist with her left hand. Staggering—she was exhausted, and the shaman was a solid weight, not large but all bone and muscle—she started for the kiva.

She saw the pipe. Bending carefully she retrieved it and held the reed stem alongside the axe helve.

Smoke hung over the village. The end poles of one of the huts stood at the edge of a blackened oval. In the center, the ground had been blasted into a waist-deep pit on whose edges grains of sand in the soil had been fused into glass. Several other fires lifted coils of smoke from the pines in the near distance.

The three sages squatted with their heads close together, whispering among themselves. They didn't call to Alphena, but their eyes followed her and the shaman. The villagers watched also, in silence.

"Bring us food and water!" Alphena shouted. "At once!"

She didn't know whether she would be able to get Uktena into his underground chamber. There was time enough to decide that when they reached the entrance.

"And bring my sandals and tunic!" she added. "I left them where we came out of the water."

They would have been that much more to carry. She still had the axe, though.

Alphena walked slowly toward the kiva under the weight of her friend. She tried to forget the image of the monster which had battled the Atlantean wizard.

A BIRD—OR FROG, or lizard, or Venus knew what—squealed imperiously from the canopy above them. Hedia didn't bother to look up. She was numb from stress and from stumbling through the jungle.

And from lack of sleep, now that she thought about it. She hadn't slept since the previous morning when she was on the run from the Servitors, and she hadn't slept well then.

Lann gave a sharp bark and halted. Hedia stopped also, but she lost her balance and almost toppled into the ape-man. She lifted the spear—with difficulty; the muscles of her arms didn't obey any better than her legs were doing—and tried to look in all directions to find the threat.

There was no threat. They were back in the ruined keep where Hedia had first escaped from the Servitors. It was Lann's keep, she had been told by one of the hunters on the ship. Now Lann was squatting, pulling apart the vegetation that had grown through the blocks of shattered crystal.

Hedia looked for a place to sit. An oval slab of roof had fallen without breaking further. Its longer axis was greater than she was tall. Vines had squirmed up from around its edges, but no shoot could penetrate crystal which was nearly a foot thick. She used the dagger to saw through a few stems, then pulled them out of the way and seated herself.

She had wanted to get off her feet even more than she wanted something to eat, but she was hungry enough to eat a snake raw. She looked around hopefully, then reminded herself that she might better watch what the ape-man was doing. Her chances of escaping the Minoi—not to mention her only realistic chances of getting something to eat—depended on him.

Lann raised a piece of charred wood. *A branch flung burning into the fortress when Procron shattered it?* Hedia thought. Then she noticed that the underside of the wood had been carved in the supple likeness of a woman's calf. It was part of a wooden statue; the fragment had been perfectly modeled.

The ape-man put the leg down beside him and dug again into the pile before him. The fortress had crumbled into chunks of varying size, ranging mostly from as big as Hedia's fist down to sparkling sand. No more wood appeared, though his spade-like hands came out blackened by charcoal. His palms were longer than a man's whole hand, with relatively short fingers.

Hedia wondered if Lann—when he was human—had carved the statue himself, and who he had used for a model. Absently, she rubbed her own right calf.

The ape-man rose to a half-crouch, not quite as erect as even his normal bent posture. He walked splay-footed a few paces further into the ruin. Bending, he began to tear out saplings with spindly trunks and a few broad leaves.

The bird called again. Lann leaped erect and screamed a challenge. Sweeping up a block as big as his own head, he hurled it toward the sound. The missile crashed against a tree trunk as loudly as a ballista releasing, but it must have missed. The bird gave a startled squawk and flew away. It sent back a diminishing series of complaints.

Hedia rolled her legs under her so that she could leap off the slab in any direction if she needed to, but she continued to smile. She was confident that none of the men she'd met in the past would have realized how tense she was, although Lann might smell it in her sweat.

She was watchful rather than afraid. This wasn't a new experience for her, though it was unusual in that the ape-man wasn't drunk.

Lann gave a final growl, then pulled up another sapling. Its roots bound a piece of garnet or ruby, a fragment of a triangle which would have been four inches on a side when it was whole. Lann buffed it clean with his thumbs and set it on a woody runner thick enough to have been the trunk of a small tree. He went back to work.

Hedia wondered how long ago the destruction had occurred. Her first thought would have been "decades," but the night she had spent in this soggy jungle had shown her how quickly plants sprouted here.

Cooing with excitement, the ape-man came up with two more crystal fragments. He rubbed them clean like the first piece, then licked the mating surfaces with a black tongue the size of a toilet sponge.

He fitted the parts together with care that Hedia wouldn't have thought his broad fingers were capable of. Holding the recreated triangle in his left hand, he touched it in the center with his right.

The crystal buzzed and turned a brilliant, saturated red which didn't illuminate the ape-man's hand or anything else. Music played and dancers, both male and female, whirled about the jungle with high steps and complicated arm movements.

Hedia would have said they were real human beings with identifiable features, but they danced unhindered through trees and piles of rubble. The music was bewitchingly unfamiliar, similar to that of an organ but much finer and more clear.

The pieced-together crystal gave a pop and shivered to sparkling powder. The dancers vanished, leaving only ruins and the jungle.

Lann gulped, then gave a series of gulps like nothing Hedia had heard from him before. She looked closely, afraid that the toy had injured her protector when it burst.

The ape-man squatted on his haunches, his head bowed and his fingertips touching the dug-up soil in front of him. He was crying.

Hedia got to her feet and went to Lann's side. She placed her hands on his shoulders and began rubbing them. His long, reddish hair was softer than she had imagined, more like a cat's fur than a horse's. The ape-man's skin was loose over the muscles, but those muscles were as firm as a bronze statue.

She squatted, still massaging him. She would rather have kneeled, but she didn't want to chance lumps of broken crystal in the dirt.

"There, now," she said. He wouldn't understand the words, but he could hear her tone. "We're alive, dear Lann. You saved me. You're so strong, darling. I've never met a man as strong as you. *No* one could be as strong as you."

The ape-man turned his head to look at her; his biceps rubbed her breasts. She smiled.

His broad, flat nostrils suddenly flared. He stood, taking Hedia by the shoulders.

His member protruded from its furry sheath. It was not, she was glad to see, nearly as much out of ordinary human scale as the remainder of Lann's physique was.

Lann turned Hedia around and started to bend her over. *Not on this ground, not even if you were no stronger and heavier than I'm used to.*

She wriggled free of his hands. He hooted in obvious surprise, but he followed when she touched his fingertips and led him to the slab where she had been sitting.

It took a series of gestures and pats for Hedia to convince the ape-man to sit on the edge. She was about to straddle him in a sitting position when a whim struck her. She touched Lann's shoulders again, then mimed shoving him backward. Still puzzled but willing, the ape-man lay flat.

About time, Hedia thought as she stood over him, *because I'm really ready!*

She lowered herself, carefully at first but then driving herself down with a scream of satisfaction.

The last time I did this . . . Hedia thought. She burst out laughing.

It would never have been like this with poor dear Saxa. Even if the Servitors hadn't appeared.

CHAPTER XV

Alphena laid the shaman down full length on the mat that he'd used to cover the entrance to the kiva. She sat beside him for a moment, waiting to catch her breath.

Nobody seemed to be coming from the village with food and her garment. She got to her feet. The axe was balanced in her hand, the shaft upright. She had gotten the feel of the weapon and was coming to like it.

Two women—Sanga and her companion from the field—immediately started from the huts carrying pots. Moments later a boy followed at a run with Alphena's tunic.

Alphena smiled in a fashion and sat down again. She supposed she looked foolish, muddy and nude, but these westerners weren't laughing. That showed they understood the situation. She might not be the magician that they thought she was, but with this axe she could certainly teach a few barbarians to respect a citizen of Carce.

The women approached with their heads bent so low that they were looking at their own bosoms rather than at the ground. "Mistress," Sanga muttered. She didn't have her infant with her.

They had brought a pot containing maize and flat beans cooked into a porridge, a separate container of meat stew, and a skin bottle. Both pots were of red clay. They weren't glazed but they had been blackened during firing and were marked on the outside with herringbone scratches.

The women started off as soon as they delivered the food. Alphena said, "Wait!" to stop them.

She tried the skin. It was water, but some kind of berries had been crushed into it to counteract the brackish taste; it would do.

"You," she said, pointing to the woman whose name she didn't know. "Bring us a basin of plain water. I want to wash off."

The boy handed the tunic, damp but folded, to Alphena. He seemed about six years old, and as naked as she was. Unlike the young women, he stared at her in fascination.

Uktena rolled onto his elbow. Sanga wailed softly. She didn't disobey Alphena's order to remain, but she sank to her knees and turned her head away. The other woman scampered away.

The shaman's muscles bunched as though he were about to sit up. Instead he relaxed and smiled. He said, "You brought me out of the sound, little one."

"I said I would stand with you, my friend," Alphena said. "We have food. Is there anything else you want from the village?"

"No," Uktena said. "Sanga, was anyone from Cascotan injured when we fought?"

"No, master," the woman mumbled. Her eyes were closed. "We ran into the woods when we saw what was happening."

Sanga looked up cautiously—she seemed more afraid of Alphena than of the shaman. Perhaps she was right in her concern, because Uktena wouldn't deliberately hurt his own people.

She said, "Bocascat's hut burned. And trees near where we were hiding burned. It was like lightning, but purple and much worse."

She lowered her head again and whispered, "Master, will it happen again?"

"Yes," said Uktena. "It will happen until the Atlantean dies or I die."

"Sanga, you can go," Alphena said, hearing the rasp in her voice. *Didn't they see what Uktena was risking for them?*

"You too, boy," she added to the child. She wondered if the word meant slave in this language as it did in her own.

Sanga turned thankfully. The boy might have lingered, but the woman twined her fingers in his hair and dragged him yelping after her.

Uktena scooped porridge with three fingers of his right hand. He swallowed and said, "Will you go with me tomorrow, little one?"

"Yes," Alphena said. She was bone tired. She had been at the end of her strength by the time she got the shaman to shore; if he had fallen a little farther out in the sound, she would have been unable to help.

But she would go. She would try.

Uktena gave her a smile that looked straight into her heart. She blinked.

"We will eat," he said, "and sleep. I will be able to manage the ladder. And in the morning, my friend Alphena, we shall see what we shall see."

"Yes," Alphena said.

And every morning. Until Procron dies, or Uktena dies.

Or I die.

HEDIA STRETCHED LUXURIANTLY while the ape-man resumed rummaging among the overgrown rubble. She ached, and she suspected she would ache still more by the next morning, but she wasn't complaining. No, quite the contrary. . . .

The bird or one like it sounded its clear gong-note from the canopy again. Lann ignored it as he lifted a block of crystal at least half the size of the one Hedia now lay on. Apparently she wasn't the only one who had found the recent break to have been a much-needed relief from stress.

Lann tilted backward at a thirty-degree angle and waddled to the edge of where the undamaged fortress had stood. He pitched the block outward. A simple beast wouldn't have bothered to discard it where it wouldn't get in the way of further excavation. His huge flat feet seemed to grip on any slope.

Someone so big should be clumsy. Hedia had known—briefly—a pair of acrobats, and they even in combination weren't nearly as flexible as Lann had proven. She grinned broadly and got to her feet.

The ape-man returned to the cavity he had opened in the foliage. He squatted, cooed with delight, and plunged his hands deep in the hole. Whatever they gripped resisted for a moment; then he lifted it to the surface.

Hedia went over to him and placed a hand on his shoulder, both to warn him of where she was standing and—as she knew in her heart—to proclaim her ownership. She looked at the object Lann was cleaning with his thumbs, then tongue.

Blurs of light swirled about them. They sometimes seemed to resemble paintings viewed sharply from one side or the other.

Making tiny burbling noises, the ape-man displayed a circular orichalc ring holding a lens six inches across, ground from a material so clear that only the few remaining streaks of dirt on its surface proved that the frame wasn't empty.

The posts to which the frame had been attached, though barely wires, were orichalc; Lann had wrenched them apart. That was the most remarkable feat of strength Hedia had seen him perform yet.

Lann held the apparatus by one of the broken posts. He glanced toward Hedia to make sure he had her attention, then touched the lens with a finger of his free hand. Though the finger looked like a watercock from a public distribution point in Carce, the motion was precise and delicate.

Images appeared, this time vivid and complete. Hedia wasn't so much seeing them as existing in their midst in place of the jungle where she had been a moment earlier.

They were close to the keep of a Minos, a tall spire whose crystal walls were as black as the smoke rolling from a funeral pyre. Around it spread the usual village of huts, but the figures living in them were not human—or at any rate, were not wholly human.

A woman pranced on hind legs like a zebra's, and a man with the head of a deer turned the wheel of a pump. Many residents had the arms, legs, or head of monkeys like the one which had chittered in the canopy when Hedia sailed past in the grip of the Servitors.

One pair, an obvious couple, aroused her interest as well as her disgust. Each was half human, half goat: the male's upper half was human; his mate was human below the waist.

Hedia didn't see any hybrids with great apes like Lann, but she now knew what she was looking at. This was the keep of Procron, before the other Minoi grouped to drive him from Atlantis.

Lann moved his index finger slightly. Hedia was almost sure that he didn't actually touch the lens, but its viewpoint shifted slowly toward the smoky crystal walls.

She wondered if anyone else—herself, for example—could control the device, but it didn't really matter. That wasn't the sort of business that a lady, that a *citizen* of Carce, bothered with. There were slaves to handle mechanical things.

She and Lann entered the spire. About them objects moved with the detached silence of vultures circling in the high sky.

Procron, helmetless but otherwise bright in orichalc armor, was the only human or part-human figure present. Three Servitors—no, four; one stood in an alcove midway up the inward-sloping walls—waited motionless.

Are we actually present, watching this? Hedia wondered. *Or is it a stage show, being acted by ghosts or demons?*

Procron turned so that he would be facing Hedia if she were present in his reality. He had dark, narrow features, black hair, and eyes as fierce as an eagle's. He cradled in both gauntleted hands the skull of something nearly human. Either it had been carved from diamond or diamond had replaced the original bone.

Purple light crackled, blurring the edges of the orichalc armor and the surfaces of objects close to Procron, including one of the Servitors. The Minos began to rise gradually; for a moment Hedia thought that he was simply growing taller.

The diamond skull seemed alive. Fire blazed in its cavities and highlighted its complex sutures.

It's real. No sculptor could carve pieces of crystal so perfectly.

The spire was over a hundred feet high. The purple light brightened around Procron as he rose. As he passed, the Servitor in the alcove spread its glass arms, then let them fall to its side like those of a marionette whose strings had been jerked, then cut.

When Procron reached the peak, his gleaming form paused for a moment. Nothing in the tall room moved; the wheels and spirals and other spinning objects—Hedia wasn't sure whether they were glass or merely forms of light—remained frozen.

The top of the spire split open, the two halves folding down like black wings. Procron stood in open air. The sky had been clear when Lann took their viewpoint through the crystal walls; now it was a roiling black mass, sending down sheets of rain which splashed on the hovering Minos and dripped into the fortress.

Procron lifted the diamond skull. Lightning struck him. To Hedia everything went white, then shimmering purple. Lightning struck again, a huge bolt which boiled water from the surface of the spire and ignited several huts in the cantonments built at its base. The walls were dimly transparent from inside, making the smoky yellow flames visible.

Procron lowered the skull toward his own head. The third lightning bolt seemed to focus the whole sky onto the Minos. Sizzling fireballs spat out like blobs ejected from the heart of Aetna.

Nothing moved; there was no sound in all the world.

Procron raised his empty hands to the sky. Purple fire from his spreading fingertips split the clouds, shoving them away with the violence of waves bursting through a wall of sand.

Where Procron's human head had been, now the diamond skull rested. The mouth opened, and the Minos laughed. His voice was the thunder which had not followed the third lightning bolt. His armored form began to sink toward the floor of the fortress as the peak folded closed above him.

Hedia was transfixed. She was only dimly aware that the ape-man beside her had pointed toward the lens—now invisible—again.

They were back in the jungle. Lann set the lens on a section of wall which hadn't been thrown down during Procron's attack. He stepped into the cavity from which he had lifted the device.

Hedia looked around, disappointed to return to this wilderness of destruction but thankful as well. Procron was frightening, even when viewed from a great distance through time and space. Even without the transformation she had just watched, she knew that Procron wasn't a man whom she could expect to twist to her will.

The ape-man was straining at another large fragment of the ruin. Hedia frowned and moved a little farther away. People concentrating on a difficult task tended to forget everything else, and she didn't want to find herself under a slab of crystal because Lann didn't remember she was present.

The distant *thump, thump* she heard was a flying ship; probably several of them. The Minoi had found them.

"Lann!" she said urgently. "I hear ships coming!"

The ape-man straightened slowly, pivoting a block too large for even him to carry. His lips were drawn back in a grimace which bared his teeth.

There was a deeper blackness in the leaf mold over which the crystal had lain: the entrance to a tunnel. Lann had been aware of the approaching vessels long before she was.

The ape-man gave a great cry and with a final push sent the overbalanced block toppling into the surrounding vegetation. It had been almost too much, even for him. He fell forward, sprawling across the edge of the pit he had just created.

Hedia hesitated for a moment. Lann drew in whooping gasps that sounded as though he were being strangled, but the beating sails of the Minoi were drawing closer.

She jumped down beside the ape-man and put her hand on his shoulder. "Lann?" she said. "I'm ready to go."

The ape-man straightened as much as he ever did. It was like standing beside a horse: powerful, exciting, but for the moment not even marginally human.

"Wook!" he said. He took the lens in his left hand and wormed his way through the mouth of the tunnel.

His hand reached back to summon her, but Hedia was already poising to follow. She wore the dagger on the bandolier and dragged the orichalc spear behind her.

She didn't know where they were going, but she knew what it would mean to be captured again. That wasn't going to happen if she could prevent it.

THE SAILS BEAT ONLY FITFULLY, like the breaths of an animal in its death throes. Corylus looked back on their course, his face as blank as he would have kept it if he were on the wrong side of the Rhine and the bushes around him were rustling. He didn't see the giant eel, but by now it couldn't be far behind.

"There's an island," the sprite called from the bow. "To the west, see?"

A finger of stone thrust up from the horizon, casting its long shadow toward them against the glowing red water. Only a thumbnail edge of the sun was still visible.

"Yes!" Corylus said with a rush of relief. He moved to her side, calling, "Master, steer to that island, if you please. Ah, will you, will we, be able to rise to the top?"

It was another nearly vertical pillar, at least as tall as the first one, and again there was no beach at the base. The ship's keel was some twenty feet above the wave tops; not nearly high enough to land on the island, and probably not safe from the eel if it caught up with them either.

The Ancient chuckled but said nothing. Corylus felt the ship turn slightly. It moved like a piece of driftwood which had been in the water so long that it could barely float.

Corylus had tied his helmet to the base of the mast, using a cord clipped from the netting which held the bread. He slipped it on, though he didn't close the face guard yet. He lifted his sword and let it fall back, just making sure that it was free in the scabbard.

"Are you afraid of what's on this island?" the sprite said. "Nothing lives here. Nothing for longer than you can imagine."

Corylus lifted his chin in understanding. "I'm glad to hear that," he said.

And he was. But they were going to land anyway, even if it meant battling wolfmen until he or all of them were dead. There was at least a chance with that, but an eel several hundred feet long was an adversary as hopeless as an avalanche was.

If we can land, that is.

The ship suddenly plunged at a steep angle. Corylus grabbed the railing, certain that the Ancient had lost control of the vessel. The sprite gave him a mocking smile, standing arms akimbo on the deck. The antics of the hull didn't affect her any more than a branch feared to be shaken off a swaying tree trunk.

They heeled as the ship curved upward. The sails slammed convulsively, once and again. The vessel lurched like a horse on its last strength. Corylus, looking over the bow, could see land beneath him but the stern with the Ancient was a hundred feet back: much lower and over the sea.

The keel ground on the lip of the tor. The bow tilted down and they scraped to final safety. Only the curved sternpost stuck out over air and the clashing waters.

The sun had dimmed to a bloody smear on the horizon. The ship toppled onto its starboard side. Corylus jumped to the ground, clumsy because he hadn't been expecting what had happened.

I expected to crash into the side of the pillar, drop into the sea, and drown. If the eel didn't get me first.

The moon was low but already so bright that it cast black shadows now that the sun had set. Corylus surveyed the top of the pillar where they rested. It was circular, about a hundred yards in diameter, and as flat as a drill field. In the middle was a tumble of rocks which must have been brought there: nothing else marred the sandstone surface.

The sprite stepped away from the tilted vessel with far more grace than Corylus had managed. Reassured that she was right about the island being untenanted, he walked to the cliff edge and looked down. The helmet felt awkward, so he took it off and held it in his left hand.

The sea around this spine of rock glowed. At first Corylus thought it was only froth from waves hitting the hard stone, but as he watched, he realized that the water was covered with luminescent seaweed. Eddies formed whorls which curled several hundred yards out from the base. He had a feeling that they formed a pattern, but it was beyond him what it might be.

The great eel rose from the shimmering foam, its jaws open. The monster was silent save for the roar of contact as the huge body slid up along the stone flank of the island. Corylus shouted and drew his sword.

The eel lifted halfway up the sheer rock face. It wriggled for a moment as the sinuous body lashed the water for purchase, then hurled itself another thirty feet upward.

That was all. Still twenty feet short of the top, the jaws clopped shut. The eel arched downward and struck the water sideways with a cataclysmic splash. It dived for a moment, then rose to curl sunwise around the rock with another flick of its tail.

Corylus stepped back from the edge, sheathing his sword. He looked critically at the ship and said, "If we could drag the stern in a little so that it wasn't visible from below, maybe the eel wouldn't be so agitated."

The great body hit the rock again and again slid back. Corylus wasn't watching, but the splash as the eel returned to the ocean didn't seem as loud. He presumed—he hoped—that it meant that the creature was tiring and hadn't risen as high on its second attempt.

The sprite shrugged. "I don't think anything you can do would make the eel less angry," she said. "Why? Do you suppose it can reach the top of this rock?"

Corylus laughed—at himself, really. "I hope it can't," he said. "And I'm pretty sure that we can't move the ship until daylight regardless, so it doesn't matter. Except that it's one more thing for me to fret about, which I'm good at doing."

The Ancient was prowling among the rocks, dropping occasionally to all fours. *Is he searching for bugs?* But that couldn't be, because neither he nor Coryla ate.

The Ancient squatted and turned his face toward the rising moon. He howled with bleak misery.

The sound chilled Corylus, though he wasn't disturbed by the splash and slapping waves as the eel tried again to mount the rock. He half-drew but released his sword as he ran to the rocks in the center of the island; the sprite was beside him.

The Ancient cried out again. He remained oblivious of his companions when they reached him. Corylus looked at the ground to see if there was a material cause for the misery—a scorpion, some sort of trap that gripped even the being of an ancient ghost.

The rocks had once had squared edges, though Corylus had to bend close to be sure of that after the long ages they had weathered. He couldn't tell what the structure had been. There weren't enough blocks to construct a dwelling, but a pillar or an altar could have been constructed from what was present. There might have been more originally.

He reached down to turn a block over to see whether its protected underside was ornamented. Coryla stopped him with a hand and pursed lips.

Oh, of course!

Corylus backed away cautiously, then bowed low to the Ancient before turning to the ship. He hadn't eaten—hadn't wanted to eat—while it looked as though they would have to land on the waves at sunset. The rolls weren't appealing, but he was very hungry; and anyway, he had to eat to live.

The Ancient wailed again. Corylus could only guess, but he would bet his life on that guess: the magician's golden-furred race had raised the structure from which the present ruins had crumbled.

He tried to imagine what it would be like to stand in the Forum after the surrounding buildings had fallen and goats browsed among the scattered blocks. He couldn't really feel that, but he could come close enough to shiver at the thought.

Before he clambered aboard the ship, he looked down into the sea again. The eel was some distance out in the weed, but it drew a serpentine curve toward the rock when Corylus reappeared. Its leap was halfhearted, though; scarcely more than lifting its wedge-shaped head from the sea.

A fragment of verse returned to him, from a manuscript Varus had found in the library of the Raecius family which had links to Gades and Spain more generally, going back before the Second Punic War. The document was very old and had been written on leather rather than parchment; it seemed to be a geographical description written in archaic Greek.

Here weed floats in the water and great beasts swim, bringing terror to mariners. . . .

Corylus mouthed the words as he remembered them. Then he climbed over the railing to get food.

VARUS HEARD THE MUSIC OF PIPES and sistrums, wishbone-shaped rattles whose bronze disks clinked together on the double arms. He might be imagining the Egyptian instruments because the book from which he had read the phrase was Egyptian also.

He thought he heard the wind sighing also; but down where he walked on a stone pavement, the air was dead still. The light was like that of the moon above a thin overcast, enough to see the path but not to make out distant shapes.

I wish the Sibyl were here to tell me what all this means.

Varus laughed. He said aloud, "I even more wish Corylus were here.

There probably won't be anybody to attack with a sword, but I'd feel better if I knew I had a friend who could do that if needed."

His words didn't echo, but they had a fullness which suggested he was in an enclosure rather than in the middle of a barren wilderness. That made him feel better, though as a philosopher he knew that the grave was an enclosure also.

He could just as easily wish for a cohort of the Praetorian Guard. Though from comments he remembered, Corylus would probably protest that the Batavian auxiliaries were better combat troops.

Varus walked on, his sandals busking against the flagstones. He grinned.

A group of men stood to the right of the path. They wore togas and were arguing. He paused, but the men didn't seem to notice him. Beyond them he could see the forms of buildings, softened as though by thick fog. The men talked on the steps of the Aemilian Hall, but the Julian Forum which Caesar had built more than seventy years ago wasn't beside it.

One of them turned from the group, hesitated, and stared at Varus. His features could have been the original of an ancestral death mask on the walls of Saxa's office, but it was hard to compare flesh with age-blackened wax.

The man shrugged and stepped away. He and his companions vanished into the grayness. Varus nodded and kept on walking.

He had learned that to keep on going was often the only choice. Well, the only choice besides lying down and waiting to die. Resignation to fate was a proper quality for a philosopher, but giving up most certainly was not. Not for a philosopher who was also a citizen of Carce, at any rate.

The road had become a rural path. Varus walked beside a single track which had been worn by animal hooves. Not even a country cart with solid wooden wheels could navigate this hillside.

A vista opened, this time to the left. A man struggled behind a crude plow being drawn by a single ox. The animal was small and shaggy, with a blotchy red-and-white hide and forward-curving horns. The farmer wore a simple woolen tunic and a broad leather hat with a low crown; he was barefoot. Between the field and the path was a wall piled from stones plowed out of the field in past years.

The man looked up as Varus passed, then dropped his plow handles and lifted the brim of his hat. "Varus?" he called in accented Latin. "Gaius Varus?"

His voice had become thin by the last syllable; the grayness was returning.

Varus waved, but the fog grew thicker yet and there was nothing more to wave to.

He trudged on. That was the only acceptable choice.

Varus no longer had even a path to follow, so he kept to the center of the terrain that opened before him. For a time he walked through woodland, even crossing a narrow brook, but very shortly he found himself skirting the edge of a dry lake. A yellow-gray dog, scraggly and thin, ran off with its tail between its legs. It glanced back over its shoulder.

There was a tree ahead. Someone sat at the base of it, apparently waiting. The trunk and branches curved, and the leaves dangled in long double rows from central stems. *Corylus would know what it was. . . .*

Varus continued straight. The ground was a thin layer of leaves and yellow clay over limestone, with frequent outcrops and spreading roots.

The seated figure was the corpse of a woman with a heavy jaw, prominent brow ridges, and black hair over all her exposed skin. The right half of her body was skeletal; it had been picked as clean as if it had been boiled. Ants might have been responsible; no beak nor jaws bigger than an insect's could have done so neat a job without disarranging the bones.

The woman's arms and torso had been tied—wrapped—to the tree with vines. Her legs, one of flesh and the other bare bones, splayed out in front of her. Between them were a few fist-sized rocks which had been broken to a crude point on one end.

"Greeting, child from the children of my womb," the dead woman said. She chuckled.

Her jaws worked normally though only half of them were clothed with flesh; Varus could see her black tongue moving; it had been sectioned lengthwise as neatly as a razor could have done. Her voice was low-pitched and rough, but not really exceptional.

Varus swallowed. "Greetings, mistress," he said. His mouth was dry. "Should I, that is, *may* I release you?"

She laughed again. "Release me from death?" she said. "Do my descendents have such power, then? I think not, though I see that you are a great wizard. You are my worthy progeny, child."

"Mistress," said Varus, "why have you brought me here? I will do whatever you wish, if I'm able to. But I don't understand."

"Take a piece of my jawbone, child," the corpse said. She couldn't move either arm because of the way she was bound with vines, but the tip of her half-tongue thrust to the side and licked the bare mandible. "Take the bone, for the time will come when you will need it."

Varus had been standing at arm's length. The dead woman wasn't threatening, but the situation was too uncanny for him to approach unbidden. He stepped forward and squatted, putting his face more or less on a level with hers; he didn't know what to do next.

"Crack it, child," she said in a testy voice. "Use the hand axe at your feet."

"But . . . ," Varus said.

"Do it, boy!" the woman said. "End this business for both of us. Crack my jaw and take the splinter!"

"Yes, mistress," Varus said; meekly, as he would have responded to Pandareus when he was being called down for an error in class.

There were several stones, all of a size to fit in the cup of his hand. He picked one that seemed to have started as a stream-washed pebble, dense and black. It had been egg-shaped, but the small end had been flaked to a point which was irregular but surprisingly sharp.

The dead woman opened her jaws wide. "Forgive me, mistress," Varus muttered as he moved to the side to get a better angle on the task. She chuckled.

He struck. The axe clocked loudly, but it didn't break the heavy bone.

"Harder, child!" the corpse said. "End this!"

Varus struck again with the full strength of his arm. The jaw cracked and a splinter flew away. Varus dropped the hand axe to catch the spinning bone. He held much of the right mandible including the teeth. It had split from front to back across the jaw hinge, forming a long spike beyond the massive final molar.

"Well done, my child!" the dead woman cried. "You are worthy of me indeed!"

She began to laugh again. The sound echoed as Varus felt himself spinning into gray fog.

"Mistress?" he cried, but he could no longer hear her. He lurched bolt upright.

He was on a couch in the library. The book he had been reading was on the floor; the lamps were lighted. His father was looking at him in concern while the servants kept to the background.

"Son?" Saxa said. "What's that in your hand? It looks like a bone."

Varus stared at the fragment of jaw, just as he remembered it from his dream. "Yes," he said, "it is. But—"

He smiled lopsidedly at his father.

"—I'm not sure why I need it, my lord." He took a deep breath and added, "Just that I do."

ALPHENA WALKED INTO HER DREAM, a perfectly flat pavement that flickered red/orange/yellow as though it were the heart of a fire. It seemed boundless, but in the far distance a group of people stood about a throne. Almost before she could wonder what they were doing, she was among them.

The people—women as well as men—with her at the base of the throne were dressed as imperial servants in vividly dyed tunics. Alphena didn't recognize any of them, but they nodded and bowed as though she were known and respected.

She felt awkward: her tunic was much the worse for wear, and even clean it had not been intended to be seen in august company. For that matter, her person was scarcely fit for the public either. Coiffeur had never been Alphena's concern, but she knew that the events since she mounted the gryphon in her father's garden had left her hair in a state that would have embarrassed a whore at the gate of the gladiator barracks after a hard night.

The throne was made of ivory and gold. Its frame and high back were carved with the greatest delicacy. Alphena raised her eyes to the man seated on it in imperial splendor.

"Uktena!" she said in surprise. "What are you doing here?"

Then, as she heard her initial words, she added, "Where is your pipe, your talisman?"

The man enthroned leaned toward her with a frown of wonderment. "I know you, do I not?" he said. "Or I knew you once, I believe. Who are you, little one?"

"I'm your friend Alphena!" she said. Being called "little one" without any recognition in the shaman's tone, hurt her to hear. "We fought—"

That isn't true.

"I was with you when you fought Procron," she said. "The Atlantean."

As Alphena spoke, a vision of Poseidonis formed to her left. She turned. This was a closer view than she had gotten when she approached on the gryphon's back. Something was rising from the harbor—

Alphena stifled a scream with both clenched fists. When she focused on the image of the city, the silent courtiers in the corner of her eye became brightly colored fishes swimming in a sea of fire.

Beyond them was a horrific monster, all tentacles and heads and huge beyond fathoming. It was the creature other people had in the Pompeian Theater.

It was the monster Alphena herself had seen Uktena turn into when Procron's magic lashed him. It was horrible, *horrible*. . . .

"Alphena?" the shaman repeated. Her name rolled softly from his tongue. "I have heard the name, or I think I have. Do you know how I came here, Alphena? I was in another place, but I cannot remember where that was."

"You were in Cascotan, my f-friend," Alphena said. She had closed her eyes. Even when she forced herself to open them, she couldn't bring herself to look up from the pavement to the enthroned figure. "You fought Procron. You fought for your people and for the world."

She looked up. Uktena's was the same stern, steady visage that she had first seen in the theater. He looked puzzled but not worried. She wondered if anything could really worry him.

"You fought for me, Uktena," she said. "You drove the Atlantean back." *And almost died*. . . .

"I don't remember," Uktena said sadly. "But you are welcome here, Alphena. Anyone who says she is a friend of mine is welcome. I do not think I ever had friends; or not at least for many ages. Instead I have power."

His words echoed about her. Vast though it seemed, this was an enclosure, a prison. But as the sound trembled to silence, the shaman's form began to quiver in turn. The human shape blurred and spread and became again the foul immensity of Typhon.

"I am your friend, Uktena," Alphena said. Her eyes stung with tears, but she *wouldn't* look away, wouldn't permit herself even to blink. "I am your friend!"

"Little one?" said a voice from outside her. "Are you having bad dreams?"

Alphena sat upright. She had been curled on the floor of the shaman's kiva; the promise of dawn brightened through the reeds of the mat over the entrance. Uktena was looking down at her, his pipe in his hands.

She got to her feet. "It was nothing that matters, Uktena," she said. She looked at the axe in her right hand, then hefted it. "Is it time to go?"

"Yes, child," Uktena said with a faint smile. "It is time."

He paused to light the herbs in his pipe bowl with a pinch of punk which he kept smoldering in a hollow gourd.

"And perhaps it is the last time," Uktena said.

CHAPTER XVI

I was talking with my friend Marcus Priscus last night, Varus," Saxa said.

Even half-dazed by the dream of his conversation with the corpse, Varus felt his lips lift in a tiny smile. His father was *so* proud to be able to claim Priscus as a friend.

A man as wealthy as Saxa could easily have scraped acquaintance with military, political, or social leaders. What he had wanted, however, was to join those whom he regarded as truly wise, the only group which could not be bought with money. The disasters threatening his family and the world had at least allowed Saxa to achieve his greatest ambition.

"He pointed out that Hedia's disappearance," Saxa said, "and that of Master Pandareus as well, of course, weren't the start of this business. It started with the vision of the monster that we saw in the theater."

He cleared his throat and added in a small voice, "I talked to Meoetes, you see. The climax of the mime wasn't his doing after all. It was a real vision that surprised him as much it did the rest of us. In fact—"

Saxa smiled ruefully.

"—it surprised him more than it did me, because I thought it was a trick that I was watching."

Varus looked at the splinter of bone. It fitted his hand like a leather-worker's awl. He thought, *I can't have been dreaming. But what does it mean?*

Aloud he said, "I don't know the answer any better than you, Father. There's nothing in the books I've read—and Lord Priscus would know better than I anyway. Though—"

As he spoke, an answer presented itself.

"—there is a person I could ask. I'm not sure she would tell me, though."

Or even that she exists outside my own imagination—since she claims she doesn't.

As suddenly as the thought, Varus felt himself dropping out of the present, onto a fog-ridden hillside. Instead of the familiar track which would lead him to the Sibyl's eyrie, this was bare black rock. The Sibyl waited for him at the foot of the slope.

"Sibyl?" he said. "Why are you here?"

"You have need of me, Lord Wizard," she said. Her smile was unreadable, another seam in the wrinkles that covered her aged face. "Where else should I be, since I am wholly a part of you?"

"Mistress, tell me what I should do," Varus said. He didn't care what meaning she gave to the question. He needed help in so many fashions that any answer would be welcome.

"Come with me and meet your enemy, your lordship," the Sibyl said, taking him by the hand. She started up the slope. Ancient though she seemed, her pace was both quick and steady.

She doesn't have a body, of course. And neither do I in this place. I don't think that I have a body in this place.

Varus didn't ask further questions: he would have his answer when the Sibyl chose to volunteer it or he had the wit to determine it for himself. *If she is really part of me, I'm a difficult person to get information out of.*

They reached the top of the hill. In front of them stretched a bleak moor. The sparse grass or sedge—he couldn't be sure—was gray with hoarfrost; the sky was gray as well. The sun, huge but orange, hung in mid sky; its light did nothing to temper the bitter wind.

A spire of black crystal stood on the moor half a mile away. From horizon to horizon, it was the only object which was taller than the occasional black bush which might have risen to Varus' knee.

"Is that Procron's keep, mistress?" he said. "Or is there another Minos in this place?"

"This is where Procron hides," the Sibyl said. She continued to walk forward; Varus kept pace. "This is your enemy, Lord Wizard."

His feet crunched on the sere vegetation. Something small—perhaps a rabbit, though it didn't move like one—scurried ahead of them; Varus thought he heard it squeal. The air was thin, and it didn't seem to fill his lungs.

"Why did—" Varus began. He caught himself, grinning with what he thought was a pardonable degree of self-satisfaction.

"Sibyl . . . ," he said, a philosopher and a lawyer now instead of a youth too frightened to use his education. "*Did* Procron abduct my mother? Because I *know* that the sages took Corylus and Master Pandareus. I was there when it happened."

The old woman glanced toward him. He thought she was smiling again, but he couldn't be sure.

"Procron did not take Hedia," she said, "but those who took her are for others. Your duty is to deal with Procron, for no one else can."

The Sibyl made a chuffing sound that Varus thought was a laugh. "And even you may be unable to stand against Procron, Lord Wizard; though your world will end if you fail."

Varus sniffed; for a moment he was solely a son of Carce. "My world will certainly end if I fail," he said in a haughty tone, "for I will have died in the attempt. Of course."

They had come within a furlong of the crystal fortress, the length of a footrace. The high-arched door at ground level remained sealed, but the top of the spire split open. The angled sides moved soundlessly, catching sunlight and scattering it across the bleak landscape in a shower of orange droplets.

A figure in fiery armor slid from the fortress, standing on the air. He did not wear a helmet. In place of his head was a skull carved from diamond.

"Who are you who dares come to me?" the figure said. "I am Procron, Lord of Atlantis! Submit or I will crush you as I crush all my enemies!"

"I saw you run from your fellow Minoi, magician!" Varus said. The words leaped to his tongue without his conscious volition. "And you must have run again, or I wouldn't find you here. Bow to Carce or take the consequences, barbarian!"

Procron raised a hand, but it was from his glittering skull that purple fire leapt at Varus and the Sibyl. The ground in a circle about them flashed into steam and bitter smoke.

Varus started back, but the bolt had halted at arm's length from him and splashed in all directions. The Sibyl stood, smiling faintly. The sparse vegetation could not sustain the fire.

Am I physically here *in this cold wasteland?*

Embarrassed to have recoiled from the purple fire, Varus strode forward. He didn't know why it hadn't incinerated him, and he certainly didn't know whether he'd be as lucky the next time. Besides which, the Atlantean wizard was a hundred feet in the air; unless Varus had developed an unexpected ability to fly, he couldn't get at his enemy even if Procron failed to blast him to ash in the next instant.

No matter. *I am a citizen of Carce. If I don't know what to do in a crisis, I will go forward.*

The flame-scoured moorland was hot beneath his feet. He was wearing silk slippers, suitable for a gentleman doing research in his family library. He grinned wryly. Blistered feet were the least of his worries.

Procron's diamond jaws opened as if to shout, but no sound came out. He spread his hands. Light the color of orichalc danced from his gauntlets. It formed walls in the air, tumbling and joining until they locked suddenly into a faceted sphere. It surrounded Varus and the Sibyl, slanting into the hard soil beneath their feet.

"Did you think you were safe because you could block my spells?" Procron said. "Stay here and starve! You cannot return to the world from which you came. I will watch you die and rot and crumble to dust—and even the dust will remain, for all eternity!"

Varus reached out with his left hand, touching the tip of his little finger to the amber gleam. The light was as solid as bronze. It had neither texture nor temperature, but he could no more step through it than he could the doors of the Temple of Jupiter Best and Greatest.

"Die, you puppy!" Procron said.

The Sibyl said, *"May the doors—"*

"—*of heaven be opened to me!*" Varus said, completing the phrase in a cracked, ancient voice which caused his father to jump back in alarm.

"My son?" Saxa said. "I don't understand."

Varus rubbed his forehead, then bent and picked up the book he had dropped: a copy of the *Aetna*, the Stoic response to Lucretius' *On the Nature of Things*. He had always been in sympathy with Lucretius' Epicurean disbelief in the gods, but recent events had made him think the Stoics might be right after all.

"I don't understand either, Father," Varus said. "And I'm afraid I don't know what has happened to Mother. But I know what I must do."

Unfortunately, I don't have the faintest notion of how to do it.

CORYLUS AWAKENED when he felt the ship begin to tremble. The sky had brightened, and the sails were quivering.

Corylus ached pretty much everyhere. He had slept on the ground beside the tilted keel, using a biscuit—or whatever they were—to cushion his head. They did better for that than they did as food, though he supposed they would sustain life.

He'd had a few bites of one to supplement the raw fish. He would probably eat more today, because he didn't trust the remaining fish to be safe without smoking or at least a drying rack. Though being doubled up with the runs didn't seem quite as terrible as it would have been if the alternative were something other than the chalky blandness of the ship's stores.

Coryla was watching him. "Good morning, cousin," he said politely. She pouted.

The Ancient had stopped shrieking some time in the middle of the night, but he still sat in the ruins. Under other circumstances, Corylus might have built the scattered stones into a shelter; the ship lay almost crossways to the prevailing wind, which was as bitter as that of the Hercynian Forest in November. It was better to feel chilled to the bone than to cannibalize the Ancient's shrine, however.

The same concern, perhaps even more strongly, had convinced Corylus not to use the sprite's warmth to shelter him. He needed the Ancient as an ally if they were ever to get off this needle of rock. Even without that, he was sure that the result of provoking the golden-furred wizard into a rage would be unsurvivable, and he'd seen more than one man knifed or battered to death because of a disagreement over a woman. The sprite's pique was a cheap price to pay for avoiding that risk.

Water slapped loudly, then rebounded from the base of the rock. The eel hadn't slept during the night either. Judging from the sound, none of his leaps had equalled his first attempt. Corylus hadn't looked over the edge again, however, for fear of spurring the creature to a sufficiently greater effort.

The Ancient squatted with his wrists resting on his knees. His fingertips dangled almost to the ground. He watched as Corylus approached.

Corylus bowed. "Master Magician?" he said. He doubted whether the Ancient could understand his words, but he thought it was better to speak directly rather than to use the sprite as an intermediary. "I would like to leave as soon as you determine that there is light enough to lift the ship."

He gestured toward the brightening east without turning his head. He bowed slightly. The Ancient simply stared.

I depend on his goodwill, Corylus thought. He turned his back and began walking toward the ship. *When both parties know that one cannot force the other to his will, then only a fool attempts to threaten.*

There was a scrape on the dirt behind him. Corylus started to look over his shoulder. The Ancient shot past him in a flat leap that carried him to the stern of the ship. He slammed into the deck and straightened, his claws biting the wood. He grinned at Corylus.

Corylus grinned too, then broke into laughter.

"Men!" the sprite said. Her voice held a mixture of amazement and disgust.

"Time to board, cousin," Corylus said as he lifted himself over the railing. "And very glad of it I am, too."

He continued to smile. The sprite was quite correct. He and the Ancient *were* both men—not just males—in all the important senses. That had risks if you weren't properly courteous in the other fellow's terms, but Corylus understood that: he'd grown up with the Batavian Scouts.

If you were in a hard place, you wanted your companions to be men also. Corylus was in a very hard place now.

The hull rocked upright. When the first bright edge of the sun showed above the horizon, the sails gave a mighty stroke and the ship lifted. Below and behind, the sea slapped to the desperate fury of the monster eel.

The moon, just short of full, hung in the western sky as though it were the beacon toward which the Ancient was steering. For an instant, Corylus thought he saw an angry woman standing astride the orb; then she was gone, but two specks lifted from the silver surface.

Corylus watched the specks, his eyes narrowing. He couldn't be sure, but they seemed to be swelling . . . which meant they were headed toward the ship.

"Cousin?" he said. "Do you see those dots? Are they coming toward us?"

The sprite joined him in the bow; she seemed to be over her irritation. She had a basically sunny personality, which made up for an obvious lack of intellect.

"The Minoi have guards on the Moon," she said. "Are the Minoi your enemies?"

Corylus had taken off the armor to sleep and hadn't bothered to don it in the morning. Now he removed the sword belt so that he could latch the breastplate in place properly.

"I didn't know anything about the Minoi before I was thrown onto the cliff with the Cyclops and the ships on the beach below," he said. "Maybe they think I've stolen their ship."

The sprite shrugged. "Perhaps," she said without interest. "Anyway, they'll certainly kill you if they can, now that they see you're wearing their armor. They're a haughty lot; worse than olive trees, even, for thinking that they're better than everyone else."

Corylus hung the cross belt over his shoulder again and latched the buckle of the waist belt; then he reached for the helmet. He would like to have a spear, or better still a sheaf of javelins. He had been pretty good at throwing a javelin, even by the standards of the Scouts.

The orichalc armor of the Minoi glinted identifiably even while they were too distant to have shapes. Corylus noticed that the ship was descending. He looked back at the Ancient.

The Ancient wrinkled his lips. Corylus hoped that was a grin and returned to watching the Minoi.

The golden-furred wizard knew what he was doing. At any rate, he knew better than Corylus knew to direct him. The giant eel should be far behind them by now; and if not, it still wasn't the most serious danger.

The Minoi were riding huge, three-headed vultures. They turned after they closed and for a time flew parallel to the ship, a furlong to either side. After a moment they drew ahead, demonstrating that their mounts were far swifter than the ship's throbbing sails.

"Cousin?" said Corylus, though he was a little afraid to put his hope into words. "Have they decided to ignore us now that they see who we are?"

Before the sprite could answer, the Minoi drew their swords. The vultures banked, turning inward. Their powerful wings beat as, side by side, they drove toward the ship.

Corylus drew his sword also, but he didn't expect it to be of any use. He wasn't a sailor, but he could see the danger easily: the Minoi didn't have to attack *him*. All they had to do was slash the sails and cause the ship to drop into the sea. The eel would finish their work, and even if it didn't, Corylus would eventually starve.

The Ancient gave a savage, rasping howl, the same sound he had made in response to the men/wolves of the first island they had approached. Corylus didn't look around. His concern was for his enemies; his allies—he hoped the Ancient was his ally—could take care of themselves for the time being.

The sea ahead lifted. For a moment, Corylus thought the eel or another like it had reached them after all; but this was water alone, rising in a spray of droplets.

It shuddered into an image of the Ancient, formed of the green sea and surrounded by a rainbow halo. It poised, hunching toward the Minoi. The vultures sheared off, but the simulacrum lunged forward, striding on the waves, and snatched one out of the air.

The image of water used its arms the way a praying mantis does, drawing its victim back to its pointed jaws. A huge black wing dropped away, its flight feathers quivering. The helmet flew in one direction and the rider's legs and torso in the other.

The simulacrum flung the vulture's body into the sea. The remaining bird was flying toward the rising sun. The thing of water pursued it for as far as Corylus could see.

The ship began to rise to its usual height. The sails had slowed their stroke, but they were picking up the rhythm again.

Corylus sheathed his sword. He turned and bowed as deeply as the breastplate allowed him to do.

"Thank you, master," he said to the Ancient. "I am honored to be in the company of such a warrior as yourself."

The ancient wizard's tongue lolled. He laughed. This time the sound was as terrible as his shrieks of a moment before.

ALPHENA SNEEZED AND AWAKENED. *I must have slept like the dead.*

Uktena had lighted his pipe. Holding it between the thumb and forefinger of his left hand, he started up the ladder. Alphena saw brilliant white sparkles wherever his skin touched the wood.

"Uktena?" she called. She began to lace on her sandals; she had taken them off to sleep. "Wait a moment."

The shaman did not pause, but he was moving with great deliberation. By the time he had flung the entrance mat aside and disappeared onto the surface, she was ready to follow.

Her hands and calves tingled when they touched the ladder. She swallowed, but it didn't matter. *It can't matter. He's my friend.*

Black clouds filled the sky, seething like water at a rolling boil. Alphena expected thunder, but she heard none. The air on the ground was still. Dead still.

Uktena stalked toward Cascotan. The villagers were not in sight, but the three sages waited in front of the huts as they had on the previous day.

Alphena trotted to catch up. The copper axe head sparkled as her arms pumped, and the hair on her right arm stood up as though lightning had struck nearby.

"Master," Wontosa said, standing slightly before the fellows to either side of him. "We have discussed the dangers, my colleagues and I. It is not safe that you approach the Atlantean from the land as you did yesterday. Use your powers to circle him from the sea and—"

Uktena put the pipe to his lips, drew on it, and lowered it again. He expelled an expanding jet of smoke toward the sages.

Wontosa shouted, "Hai!" and leaped back. His rolled hair burst into smoky red flames. Screaming, he tried to beat out the fire with his bare hands. His companions were running toward the forest.

Uktena gestured with his right hand. Wontosa sailed toward the marshes on the north side of the island. Moments later, Alphena heard a faint splash from that direction.

Uktena had not paused. Alphena reached his left side and fell into step. She tried not to look at the shaman, but what she saw in the corners of her eyes shifted in disquieting ways.

He is my friend. I am his friend.

They reached the shore. Procron's tower was a glittering spike against the textured black of the sky. A thunderbolt crashed, striking the sea and turning it momentarily as clear as smoky quartz.

Uktena dropped the pipe again. White fire wreathed him. He stepped forward, onto the surface of the water. Sparks popped and hummed about his feet. Alphena would have waded in also as she had done the previous day, but the sea threw her back with a loud crackle.

She fell onto the coarse sand. Her right leg was numb. She reached across to massage the calf with the opposite hand, but even seated she continued to hold the axe ready in her right.

Uktena, but no longer Uktena, advanced in a haze of sizzling light, changing and growing. The peak of the crystal fortress opened slowly. Procron drifted out with the stately majesty of an emperor being drawn in a triumphal chariot.

What Uktena had become gathered speed as it advanced. Its swelling mass concealed Procron from where Alphena stood.

Purple fire blazed, reflecting from the clouds and sea. The crack of thunder jolted the shore beneath Alphena and sent waves leaping across the sea in both directions.

Uktena staggered. His wrapping of light dimmed; Alphena saw clearly the tentacled, many-legged monster he had become. Hundreds of bestial heads lifted from the mass and bellowed in agony.

It—*he*—surged forward. Procron rose higher. A second purple bolt spat from his diamond skull. Uktena staggered, but the thunderclap jolted the Atlantean backward as well.

The white fire surrounding Uktena congealed, brightened, and swelled again. Like the sun settling off the island's shore, the shaman halted momentarily, then rushed forward. Great arms spread to right and left, threatening to envelop both the spike and the Atlantean himself.

Uktena's arms closed. Purple light flashed, through the white and from the clouds. The sea exploded from beneath the magicians, throwing out a wave as though a mountain had been dropped into the water.

Alphena had risen to her feet. She had a brief glimpse of the shelving bottom before the wave knocked her down and tumbled her up the slope. She did not let go of the axe.

The water that had washed over her was hot. It recoiled from the shore, carrying with it hundreds of fish—bellies up and parboiled white.

There was silence for a moment. Alphena's ears rang, but she had felt the previous thunder through her sandals. Now there was nothing.

Procron broke free, rising unsteadily. The glow that had surrounded Uktena faded.

Wobbling, shrinking like a pricked bladder, the shaman spiraled toward the land. The Atlantean hovered for a moment, then vanished within his fortress again.

Uktena dropped into the surf, twenty feet from the normal shoreline. Alphena waded out, sliding the helve of the axe under her sash to free both hands. Waves from the battle slapped and gripped her, but the water was no more than knee-high in its resting state. The air was thick with the stench of death and burned ooze, but the deluge which broke from the clouds began to clear it.

The shaman was flaccid, a dead weight. Alphena lifted his arm over her shoulders and started back. Crackles of white fire licked the sea around them.

They reached the shore. Alphena thought of laying the shaman down now that he was out of the water, but she was afraid that she might not be able to get up again for hours if she paused even briefly.

They staggered through a line of sea oats at the top of a ridge of sand. Where the heads brushed Uktena's body, they sparkled and were transformed to crystal, which as quickly crumbled to sand.

Alphena walked forward. Uktena's feet had been dragging. Now he lifted the right one for a hesitant step.

White light infused the ground. Three earthworms squirmed up, twisting into the air as though they had bones. Alphena grimaced but walked on. The worms sprouted wings and flew ahead of her and the shaman, making high, keening cries.

He is my friend. No matter what happens, he is my friend.

Uktena took his weight on his own legs, but his head sagged and his eyes were blank. Alphena guided him, though she was dizzy and her eyes blurred so badly that she could barely see.

"Food!" she croaked as they passed through the village, as clumsy as a dog with a broken back. "Bring us food or by Hecate, I'll kill you all!"

They reached the entrance of the kiva. As they sank to the ground, the boy who had brought Alphena's clothing the previous day now appeared again. This time he carried a pot of porridge.

"Eat, my friend," Alphena whispered. She dipped out porridge with her right hand and held it to the corner of the shaman's mouth. "Eat, warrior. We will need your strength tomorrow."

HEDIA WORMED DEEPER into the tunnel so that Lann could jump in behind her. She expected him to close the entrance to conceal them until the Minoi and their servants gave up the search. The ape-man jumped in all right, but instead of trying to pull the slab back over the opening, he gestured Hedia forward with hooting violence and a scooping motion of both hands.

She turned again and stumbled on. The six-foot spear was impossibly awkward in the twisting passage; she abandoned it regretfully.

The tunnel had been cut through the coarse limestone underlying the jungle. To Hedia's surprise, it wasn't completely dark beyond the dim light from the entrance. The water oozing through the porous rock had a faint green glow. Her eyes adapted to it the more easily because the forest itself had been so dim.

She reached a raggedly wider spot. Her feet crunched uncomfortably on what she thought was sharp gravel; then she saw the hand of a Servitor against one wall, and a little farther on was part of a glass skull. From the amount of glittering debris, at least a dozen of the not-men must have been destroyed here—by one another or by survivors.

There was a piece of apparatus also, but it had been melted into a mass that Hedia couldn't identify. It probably wouldn't have meant anything to her even if it were whole. The battle that shattered Lann's fortress had been conducted by Servitors advancing underground as well as by the ships which she had seen in the vision which the ape-man's lens had summoned for her.

Lann pushed past her, not harshly but with no more delicacy than to be expected from a beast. Hedia was happy to let him lead, though she was uneasily aware that the entrance in the ruin was open for those hunting her to find.

She smiled wryly. On balance, she supposed she preferred to have the ape-man between her and whatever might be waiting ahead of them. Regardless, she had no choice in the matter unless she decided to overpower her companion and force him to follow. She suspected that she would have more chance of breaking through the Minoi with her bare hands.

Not only Servitors had fought in these tunnels. Something rocked beneath Hedia's foot; when she looked down, she found she had stepped on most of a human pelvis. The right socket had been burned off.

Because Hedia was looking down, she almost ran into Lann when he stopped abruptly. She gave an unintended squeak and hopped back, placing a hand on his hip to steady herself and remind him where she was.

The passage ahead had been blocked when a section of the roof caved in; apparently during the fighting, because a single glass arm stretched out from beneath a tilted block the size of a litter. Strong as the ape-man was, Hedia didn't think he could budge *that*, especially because it seemed to be wedged against the unbroken portion of the ceiling.

Lann gave a low hoot of dismay. He had the lens in his left hand, but he tugged at the block tentatively with the other. It didn't move any more than Hedia had expected it to. He hooted again.

She touched the ape-man's left wrist. When he turned to look at her with a frown of surprise, she touched the lens and gestured him to give it to her. His frown deepened for a moment—either he didn't understand or he didn't want to give it up—but he finally gave her the device.

Hedia drew the dagger with her free hand and stabbed at the block. Even with no more than her strength, the sharp orichalc point chipped a noticeable divot from the stone. She turned the weapon in her hand and offered the hilt to Lann.

The ape-man snatched it. Using both hands, he attacked the block.

Hedia had stepped away, but she had to back still farther. Dust and chunks, some of them fist-sized, sprayed from the soft limestone. She had seen when Lann freed the lens that orichalc wasn't unbreakable, but gouging through what seemed to be hardened clay wasn't an excessive strain.

The block split crossways. Lann dropped the dagger and gripped the lower portion. Hedia ducked low, knowing the risk she was taking, and retrieved the dagger just in time.

The ape-man waddled backward, dragging the half-block with him. It scraped along the floor of the tunnel, then crashed flat in a cloud of choking dust. The top portion hesitated for a moment, then slid after the part which had been supporting it. Rubble was piled beyond, but at least for a distance there was room between it and the tunnel roof.

Lann clambered up the pile on all fours and started through the choked passage. Hedia hesitated a moment, but there wasn't any choice. She sheathed the dagger—which would have been buried under the slab of rock if she hadn't grabbed it in time—and followed.

The gap wasn't as tight for her as for the ape-man, but he was more agile and she was carrying the lens. The ape-man seemed to have forgotten for the moment that he'd given the device to her, but Hedia had seen how important he considered it.

She decided she would give up the dagger before she would drop the lens. It might not be directly useful, but any woman knew the importance of symbols. If you lack physical strength, you quickly find other tools to give yourself an advantage over those around you.

The floor beyond the blockage again glittered with shattered Servitors. Hedia pressed her lips together as she followed. She had hoped that by shuffling her feet, she could avoid the worst of the pain, but the tunnel floor was too irregular for that to help. The next time, she'd wear hobnailed army sandals of the sort Alphena affected.

She laughed. *The next time!*

The tunnel straightened and the walls became smoother. It was marginally wider as well, though Hedia still could not have walked alongside the ape-man. The problem wasn't only his broad shoulders but also the fact that he tended to weave side to side as he shambled.

She smiled affectionately. She stretched her right hand out toward Lann's hip, but she didn't let the fingertips touch his coarse hair. He needed to pay attention to what was in front of them, not to his companion's whim.

They came out into an underground chamber. It seemed to be roughly circular, though roots had penetrated from above and brought down part of the ceiling. Many—certainly more than a dozen—tunnels led off from the chamber.

Most were like the one Hedia had followed, but almost opposite her was a wider, taller opening with an arch rather than being crudely cut square. That one was noticeably brighter. Lann dropped to all fours in his haste to reach it.

Hedia followed, suddenly excited that there might be a way out of this place, this *world*. The only reason for her hope was that this was a change from what she had been through since the Servitors took her from Carce; and the change that she most desired was to be back in her home.

This short tunnel was lined with crystal, though Hedia could see the texture of the limestone beneath. They entered an enclosure the size of an amphitheater, also of crystal. Originally it had been open, but the forest had grown up on all sides to overhang it, turning sunlight into a green haze. It had seemed bright only by contrast with the dim glow of the tunnel.

They had reached the foundations of Procron's spire, left behind when the assembled Minoi drove their fellow and his fortress out of Atlantis. Hedia realized that the battle between Lann and his neighbor had involved a warren of tunnels, not just the one she had followed. Procron had created the underground gallery so as not to have to pierce his own quartz walls for each attack.

Though the floor was thick crystal, impermeable to roots, the enclosure's interior was covered with forest debris. Leaf mold was ankle deep everywhere, and even Lann chose to skirt a tangle of fallen branches which reached over the wall to the right.

Lann stopped. Hedia, fully alert now, stopped and moved to the side to see past the ape-man's broad body. She thought for a moment that she was looking at a pool ten feet in diameter in the middle of the enclosure, but what she had taken for water was instead a colorless blur. It hung in the air six inches above the level of the floor around it. She saw no sign of the rotting leaves, bark and branches which otherwise carpeted the enclosure.

The ape-man turned. He gestured urgently toward the crystal he had given her. Hedia held it out with both hands; he took it with the delicacy which had already surprised her.

Lann squatted with the device. Hedia turned, largely because the shimmering disk made her uncomfortable. It didn't have real color, but she got a feeling of blue when she looked at it.

Someone shouted. The sound was faint and distorted, but Hedia was sure it was human. She had learned it was impossible to tell where noises came from in this jungle, but she thought it was out of the tunnel.

They did *come after us!* Of course they had, but with the difficulty of her journey through the tunnel, she had forgotten to worry about pursuit.

Hedia looked at the ape-man, apparently peering through his crystal toward the disk before them. She licked her lips, wondering if she should warn him about—

She straightened in disgust at her presumption. She had seen how keen Lann's senses were. If there was something he needed to know about his surroundings, he knew it.

The *whop . . . whop . . . whop . . .* of beating sails sounded; distant but seemingly approaching. Certainly approaching.

Lann lurched upright with a warbling cry. The hazy disk was spinning into a maelstrom, spiraling down into infinite distance.

An Atlantean ship drove into the canopy of trees, cracking through branches and sending down a shower of leaves and fragments. Two humans carrying nets pushed through the arch from the tunnel complex. Behind them was a Servitor with an uncertain device

Lann took Hedia's wrist in his huge right hand. Gripping her firmly, he jumped into the whirl of light he had just opened.

CHAPTER XVII

Corylus frowned. Though the moon had set, the sky ahead had become noticeably brighter than it was behind them, where the sun was fully above the eastern horizon. Rather than a blue that would grow paler as the day wore on, it looked as though the ship was flying into the white heart of a furnace.

The sprite curled at his feet in the far bow. His toes projected between the straps of his army sandals; she was playing with them. It was disconcerting, but it didn't actually hurt anything—Corylus had initially kept a careful eye to see if the Ancient reacted; he hadn't—so he didn't object.

"Cousin?" he said. "There seems to be something odd about the sky."

The sprite continued her game, touching his nails in a pattern that he felt sure must be meaningful. He didn't have a clue *what* it meant, though.

"Is there?" she asked in a disinterested voice. She didn't look up. "It isn't going rain. I'd know if it were going to rain."

Corylus caught his response unmade. The sprite was being forthcoming within her limitations; which, regrettably, were of considerable extent.

He turned to look back at the Ancient. The sprite chirped an objection when he moved his feet out of her reach. That hadn't been Corylus' whole purpose in turning, but it had been part of his purpose. He suppressed his slight grin quickly.

The Ancient stood at his post, unmoving and unconcerned. He met Corylus' eyes and let his tongue loll.

Corylus grinned in response. He absently touched his breastplate above where the glass amulet rested against his chest.

The Ancient's nonchalance would have been more comforting if he hadn't been willing to let a giant eel swallow them. It was time for a real answer.

"Cousin." Corylus said sharply. "Stand up, if you will. Tell me what you see ahead of us."

The Atlantean ship had a chest-high shield over the far bow, like that of the small warships with which Corylus was familiar. In the squadrons of Carce, the shield would have been made of tightly woven wicker, as much to turn waves as for protection in battle—though it would stop a javelin or slow an arrow.

This one was of some material Corylus couldn't identify, a resilient black film. He suspected it had something to do with the fire-projectors.

The sprite rose with her usual liquid grace. Corylus realized that he'd been expecting the ill-temper—or flat refusal—that he might have gotten from a human female. His—distant—cousin wasn't everything he might have wished in a companion, but she had a remarkably pleasant personality.

She looked at the sky ahead; it was by now as pale as lime-water. Frowning, she said, "But that's what you wanted, isn't it? You wanted to go back to the waking world."

Corylus looked from her to the sky, then back to the Ancient. He had been taken off-balance by what he had just heard. "That's what's happening?" he said. "We're returning to Carce?"

She shrugged. "I don't know where Carce is," she said. "Your world, though. What used to be my world before the meteor, and then you taking me with you into your dream."

The sprite's lovely face grew as thoughtful as Corylus ever remembered seeing it. "I wonder what will happen?" she said. "You're real, and the Ancient and I are real as long as you hold the amulet. But I wouldn't have thought the ship—"

They drove into the brightness. Corylus felt everything dissolve.

"Greetings, little one," Uktena said. "I am glad that you are visiting me again."

He walked down the three steps of the throne's base to join Alphena on the fiery pavement. He was dressed in gold and purple as in her previous dream, but he greeted her as warmly as if he were her brother.

"F-friend," Alphena said. Her dream body didn't feel tired, but mentally she was weary to death. "Please, where are we? Where *is* this place?"

Fish flashing with all the colors of parrots' plumage circled them at a distance. They always kept one eye or the other on her and the shaman. At the edge of Alphena's awareness she thought she heard them murmuring in frightened voices.

Uktena took her left hand in his and looked down into her eyes. He was not tall, but she was short for a woman.

"I do not know where you are, Alphena," he said. "Your soul visits me, but I cannot see into the waking world where your body rests. As for where *I* am—"

Still holding her hand, he looked about them. The fish scattered from the sweep of his cool, gray eyes, like minnows in a pool with a pike.

"I am in a world of my own," the shaman said. "I do not know how I came here, and I do not remember who I was in the waking world. Except that I remember you, little one."

His tone was musing, appraising. Alphena heard no anger or bitterness in the words, but she had the sudden feeling that she faced a crouching lion rather than a fit man who, despite his black hair, was as old as her father.

"You were a great magician of the Western Isles," she said fiercely. "You still are! You're fighting an Atlantean wizard named Procron. Your name is Uktena and you're beating him, you *will* beat him!"

Uktena touched her hair, tracing a tangled curl with his fingertip. He said, "I do not remember Procron or the Western Isles; I do not remember Uktena, child. But I remember you, and you are my friend."

"I am!" Alphena said. She turned away because she was afraid she was about to cry. "You're going to break out of here and come back home and *crush* Procron. You will!"

She felt the shaman touch the curl again; then he must have lowered his hand. "I will never break the bounds of this place, little one," he said quietly. "This is my universe. I would have to go outside everything that exists for me to escape it; which I cannot do, no matter how great a magician you think me. No magician, no god even, can do that."

Perhaps there was sadness in his measured tones as he added, "It is good of you to visit me, Alphena."

She blinked, then rubbed her eyes fiercely with the backs of her hands before opening them again. They still stung, but she could see.

Alphena could see *people* beyond where the fish circled. Their figures were hazy, and they didn't sharpen when she focused on them the way everything else in this place did.

They aren't in this place!

"Uktena!" she said in excitement. She pointed toward the figures, still visible though they were fading into a greater distance. "Who are they? Could they help you?"

The shaman laughed. "Little one, little one," he said. "They perhaps could, for only one who remembers much of the arts which the spirits whispered to him could even be in the place between universes. But they will not help me."

Alphena clenched her fists and squeezed her eyelids almost closed. "They might," she said. "They may!"

"Alphena, look at me," the shaman said in a voice of command. She turned without thinking.

The monster of heads and arms and legs beyond number filled her awareness. There was nothing in this place that was not *it*. Typhon was all.

Instead of screaming, Alphena closed her eyes and began to cry. Hands took hers gently; arms drew her cheek against a human chest.

"Don't cry, little one," Uktena said softly. "There is no reason for sadness. What is, *is*. What other kind of universe could you or I be content in?"

Instead of rubbing her eyes, Alphena put her arms around the shaman. It was like hugging a muscular tree trunk.

"I'll free you!" she said. "Someway, some*how*, I will!"

But her voice faded and her arms dissolved. Very faintly she heard, "Farewell, little one. . . ."

Alphena awakened from her dream. It was dawn, and Uktena had risen to do battle.

HEDIA SAW NOTHING and heard nothing as she dropped into the blue light, not even the screams she tried to force through her throat. She felt Lann's hand, however, so she clung to it as a shipwrecked sailor does to a floating spar.

With a coldness in her heart beyond any previous fear, Hedia knew there were worse dangers in this place than mere drowning. How long could she be trapped in this place before oblivion replaced even madness?

Her feet touched—the ground? Something solid, at any rate. Her eyes flew open; she hadn't realized that she had closed them to shut out the terror of nothingness.

Lann was looking at her in concern, but he hooted cheerfully when she smiled. They stood on a plane that was the same almost-blue neutrality as the disk into which he had drawn her. She thought there were bulks in the far distance, but they had no more shape than clouds on a moonless night.

The ape-man grunted, then turned and started forward. Hedia felt an instant's terror when he let go of her hand, but she didn't vanish into gray limbo again. She caught her breath and strode after him.

I wish he'd warned me before he did that.

She grinned away her scowl. If he had given her any warning, she would have clung to him in fear and despair.

An arrow with red fletching and an orichalc point dangled from Lann's left hip, wobbling as he walked. It had pierced loose skin, apparently without touching muscle.

Hedia had been vaguely aware of a *zip! zip!* as the ship drove into the shielding canopy, but only now did she realize that bowmen aboard the vessel had been shooting at them.

Shooting at the ape-man, more likely. Though the Minoi might have been willing to cripple Hedia in the hope that they wouldn't nick an artery in the process.

The arrow was a quivering reminder of how nearly she had been recaptured. It was possible, of course, that before long she might think being in the hands of the Minoi would be preferable to having escaped to this place.

Hedia grinned again. That seemed unlikely. And so long as she was with Lann, there were compensations.

She had believed that they were walking along a level plane. That might be true, but the strain on her thighs suggested that she was climbing. There was nothing to judge their progress against; she had only her faith in the ape-man that they were actually going somewhere instead of just going on.

Movement jerked her attention to the right. What had been foggy distortion when she first reached this side of the disk now resolved to people, or—

Hedia started back. "Lann!" she said.

She tugged the ape-man's wrist till he turned to face her, then pointed with her whole arm. "What is that? I thought I saw—"

She would either have finished the sentence with "—my daughter Alphena," or with, "—the terrible monster I saw in the theater." In the event she said neither, because Lann snatched her arm down with a haste that was just short of violence. Hooting, he swung her around him so that his body was between her and the shifting images. It was the closest thing to anger that he had yet displayed toward her.

He's afraid of that, whatever it is, Hedia realized. Or anyway, the ape-man was afraid of what might happen if she called attention to them by pointing. That might be a real concern or just the sort of superstition that made a peasant unwilling to claim that his crop was shaping toward a good harvest.

She wouldn't make that mistake again.

Lann released her and started forward again. Hedia followed submissively, keeping her arms by her side. When she had reached out to point, her hand had met a resistance which it couldn't feel. There had been nothing visible between her and the *beings* that she glimpsed, but she was sure that the place her arm went was not really toward what she saw.

After a dozen paces, Hedia became sure that the ape-man wouldn't turn around to check on her. She glanced to her right.

Alphena was no longer present. Where there had been a monster indescribable in its vastness and complexity, now stood a man in a loincloth who wore his hair in two braids. He wasn't young, but he was *very* well set up. Large fish of varied colors circled him at a distance.

A reflexive smile started to lift the corners of Hedia's mouth. The man's eyes flicked toward her. She could see him as clearly as if they were facing one another at dinner.

She stiffened; her face, unbidden, set itself into regal lines. *I am Hedia, wife of Gaius Saxa and a noble of Carce. . . .*

For this man was a noble also. She didn't know where he came from, but she accepted at a glance that he was her equal in every fashion; and, being male, was possibly a little more equal in some fashions.

That was all right with her. Hedia's smile was slight but real. *In its place.*

When she focused on the man, Hedia had the impression of courtiers standing nearby in obsequious silence. Her eyes followed the motion.

She saw fish, the same colorful fish as before. When she didn't focus on the nobleman, she saw around them, filling existence, Typhon: a writhing, swollen horror which hungered to grow for all eternity.

Hedia faced away, grimacing. All this business had started with the vision of Typhon destroying what she now knew was the city of Poseidonis. If that had really happened instead of it being a mirage in the bowl of the theater, she would have been spared these recent days of unpleasantness.

Though she would have missed Lann also, which would have been a shame. Not tragic, but a shame nonetheless.

Lann turned. Hedia gave him an impish smile, her reflex when she feared she had been caught in some wrongdoing, but the ape-man wasn't concerned with whether she had continued to look at the figures to their right. Instead he stared past her, back—she could only assume this, as she saw empty gray on all sides—the way they had come.

The ape-man hooted in concern. He started to go on, then stopped without warning and squatted over his disk.

One of her first husband's friends had an ape trained to play the dice game Bandits. Lann looked so much like that animal peering over the game board that Hedia half-expected to see him react as the ape had—by suddenly flying into a rage and hurling the board, the counters, and all in every direction.

That had been unexpected and exciting; and dangerous, but danger added spice to life. She giggled, as she had giggled when she watched the screaming ape knot a bronze lamp stand as easily as a man might have done a blade of grass.

New images appeared around Hedia and the ape-man, replacing their gray surroundings with a blankness indistinguishable to her—save for the pair of Atlantean ships which flew out of a spiraling blur. Their sails beat, driving them forward here just as they had on the other side of the portal.

The Minoi pursuing Hedia in the jungle had not given up when Lann took her through the portal. They would never give up.

Armored figures stood in the sterns of the vessels. The human servants holding wooden bows and spears were huddled against the railings. Their eyes were closed and many seemed to be mumbling prayers. Several even curled their knees against their chests and wrapped their arms around them.

The Servitors—four on one vessel, two on the other—were upright and alert; their weapons were orichalc. Hedia couldn't imagine that even Lann's strength would prevail against those odds.

The ape-man dropped his lens; its images dissolved like sand ramparts in the tide. Facing the Minoi in the unseen distance, he rose into a bandy-legged posture of threat, his head cocked forward and his great fangs bared. He roared loudly, even with no walls to echo from. He roared again, then drummed his broad chest with fists like mauls.

There was no response. That would come soon enough, Hedia knew, in the form of fiery swords or arrows.

The ape-man dropped to all fours. Hedia thought he planned to run in his chosen direction until the ships caught them; and perhaps that was all that had been in his bestial mind until his knuckle touched the crystal disk.

Lann paused, as motionless as a statue covered with shaggy fur. Then, with the deliberation of a torturer raising the poker he had heated, he turned with the disk toward the unseen barrier between them and Typhon.

Hedia wrung her hands. She shifted her eyes from the crouching ape-man, back to the way they had come. She couldn't see the Minoi, but expectation of their arrival frightened her less than what the ape-man was doing.

She couldn't bring herself to look at what was happening beyond the barrier. Even so she was aware at the corners of her eyes that something twisted and flowed. It moved like a serpent or a thousand serpents, and she knew what it was even without looking; what it was, and how huge it was.

The ape-man grunted with angry satisfaction. He was using both hands to force the edge of the disk against *nothing*. The crystal suddenly lurched forward against his pressure.

He drew back quickly and got to his feet. The lens swung in his left hand; it appeared unharmed.

"Lann, what have you done?" Hedia said. Tiny cracks were running across the surface of the unseen, like tendrils of mold through bread.

The ape-man grunted and gestured her on. When she hesitated, he caught her shoulder with his free hand and dragged her. She stumbled for a dozen steps before she properly got her feet under her so that she could keep up. Lann released her only when he was sure that she would follow at his own best speed.

Hedia glanced over her shoulder as she trotted beside the ape-man. The cracks were expanding swiftly.

And the immensity beyond writhed closer.

VARUS STOOD IN A CORNER of the Forum, looking up at the Citadel and the Temple of Jupiter Best and Greatest. It was past the close of business, but the pavement was still crowded.

The son of Gaius Saxa wasn't being jostled, of course. A contingent of servants faced outward around him, shoulder to shoulder. That kept him clear to the length of his arm.

No one, including Candidus who was in charge of the escort, had asked Varus why he wanted to stand by himself in the Forum. He wasn't sure that any of the servants had even wondered.

Everyone in Saxa's household knew that the master's son was a literary sort who pondered things that no ordinary person could even imagine. A reputation for being unfathomably strange seemed to buy one a degree of tolerance for acts that would have aroused comment if committed by someone normal.

Varus smiled wistfully. He wasn't sure himself why he had chosen the Forum for what he had come to do. This wasn't where Carce had first been settled: traditionally, that had been the Palatine Hill, behind him. The Citadel would have provided a better view of present-day Carce, and it had been the religious and military core when the city first came to prominence.

But the Forum had been and to a degree remained the civil heart of Carce, and a city *was* its citizens. The first great act of the citizens of Carce had been to drain the Forum through the Cloaca Maxima, transforming a marshy pasture into a plain in which they could assemble and decide their laws. Rather than to look down on the Forum from the Citadel, Varus had chosen to stand where his forefathers had gathered in times of peace.

His vision had shown him Typhon engulfing the Forum. But Typhon, the Sibyl had told him, was not the business of Gaius Varus. . . .

Varus unrolled the book of Egyptian magic in his mind. He found the verse and read in a loud voice, "I open the doors of heaven!"

A jagged gash tore soundlessly through the sky, splitting it down to the pavement beside Varus—where the Sibyl was now standing. There were no stars in the gap between halves of cloud-swept blue.

"Sibyl?" he said in surprise. "I thought . . . that is, you've never come to me this way before. In Carce. I thought I'd be climbing the hill to see you as usual."

The Sibyl sniffed. "All this is mummery, Lord Varus," she said, gesturing toward the crack in the sky. "I am a shadow of your will, no more. How shall a shadow direct the wizard who casts her?"

She gave him one of her unreadable smiles and patted his arm. Looking about the Forum, she said, "In my day, Evander pastured his cows in this valley. Everything changes, Lord Varus. Everything changes, and eventually everything ends."

If you're not real, then how can you talk about Evander? Varus thought.

He grinned in sudden realization. The statement had brightened his mood by posing him the kind of question he understood: a literary question. Now he could smile as he considered the matter that had brought him—brought them—here.

"Sibyl," he said, "what is Procron doing that I should stop? If he simply lives in that barren world, what harm can he do to Carce?"

"That place, that barren world . . . ," the Sibyl said. She turned away from him to view the huge hall which Aemilius Paullus had built from the spoils of conquered Greece. "Is this world, this Earth, Lord Varus. In the distant future when there are no men save Procron himself in exile, but still the Earth. He hates his fellow Minoi, because they drove him out of Atlantis."

She paused to look up at the Citadel. Seemingly off the subject, she said, "You thought Evander was a myth, did you not, Varus?"

Varus felt his smile spread wider. "I thought *you* were a myth, Sibyl," he said. "I have made other mistakes besides that."

"If it is a mistake," the Sibyl said musingly. "If it really is."

In a businesslike, relatively firm, voice, she went on, "Procron cannot return from his place of exile, but his powers gain him agents in other times. He works to loose Typhon from the place he was bound. Typhon will destroy Atlantis and the Minoi; but he will destroy all things, save Typhon himself."

Varus took a deep breath. Members of a family—two families, he realized—were sacrificing at the altar in front of the ancient Temple of Saturn. The heads of house were probably consecrating a marriage contract. They were planning for the future; a future which would not exist, for them or for anyone, unless Gaius Varus prevented an Atlantean sorcerer from freeing the greatest of the Earthborn Giants.

The Sibyl looked at him and smiled again, this time without the gentle humor she had shown before. "You cannot prevent Procron from loosing Typhon," she said, responding to Varus' unvoiced thoughts, "because Typhon is already loose. What you must do is to slay Procron before he does further harm. And you see—"

Her lined face was suddenly grim, as fearsome as a bolt of lightning.

"—Procron is no more. His body is dead, and the skull that rules him is in a dimension that nothing human can reach; not even the Sibyl, who once was human and is now the shadow of a great wizard."

A small fire smoked on the altar. The families watched in satisfied silence as the priest, his arms lifted, prayed to Saturn . . . the king of the gods

"—and I don't imagine a port hostler will give me mules and a cart on credit, even if I take off this armor."

Which I'd better do. Swanning about armed and wearing armor that shines like a bonfire is pretty well guaranteed to bring the attention of the Watch Detachment here in Ostia, not to mention the Praetorian Guard if I somehow reached Carce.

Corylus took off the helmet and started turning the latches of the breastplate. "I guess," he said to the sprite, "that I'll hike into Carce, go to—"

His apartment or Saxa's house? The latter, because it was closer to the Ostian Gate where he'd enter the city. The servants knew him as a friend of the family; someone would find him a clean tunic and give him a meal.

His stomach growled at the thought. He wasn't starving, but food—a loaf of real bread in place of the bland *putty* in the ship's hold—was suddenly his first priority. That too would have to wait till he reached Carce, unless he tried snatching a loaf from a stallkeeper here.

Unless—

"Can we fly here, cousin?" he asked. "I mean, now that we're back in the—"

What term had she used?

"—the waking world?"

"Of course," the sprite said. "At least if he—"

She nodded toward the grinning Ancient.

"—is more powerful than the western magicians. I think he is, but there *are* three of them."

She looked at the open cart which was clattering down the quay toward them behind a pair of mules. One of the magicians who had accompanied Tardus to the theater was driving; the other two were in back with a bundle which squirmed beneath the mat that concealed it.

Pandareus, trussed but conscious.

The cart pulled up alongside the ship. The driver was the North African. He slid from his seat, drawing a curved knife. A second magician got out of the back of the wagon, holding an axe with a stone head. The ship floated with its deck almost level with the pavement.

They're seeing a ragged stranger whom they probably take for a sneak thief, Corylus realized. He bent.

The westerners glanced at one another to coordinate their attack. They jumped aboard simultaneously, to either side of him.

As before, Corylus had laid the weapons belt on the deck in order to take off the breastplate. He drew the orichalc sword in the same sweeping curve that sent its tip toward the African. He shouted and managed to twist in the air, reinforcing Corylus' belief that he had been a sailor.

The last hand's-breadth of the blade carved through the fellow's ribs and lung. Blood droplets sailed from the sword tip and the victim's mouth spewed a red mist.

The other westerner was older and less agile, but he chopped with the stone axe while Corylus was off balance. Corylus grabbed the railing with his free hand and jerked himself clear.

A large chip of wood flew from where the axe struck the deck. The fellow might not be a real warrior, but he was clearly strong and willing.

Corylus thrust. The orichalc sword didn't have enough of a curve to make it clumsy. The point entered above the westerner's breastbone and came out through his spine in the middle of his back. The blade was sharp and as stiff as a granite obelisk.

Corylus leaped to the quay to finish the business. Too late he saw that the third westerner, the one with a stuffed bird in his hair, was sucking on the stem of his murrhine pipe.

A puff of smoke wreathed Corylus. His muscles froze and he toppled backward onto the ship.

The magician sang a short phrase, smoke jetting from his mouth and nostrils with the syllables. Two Servitors reached down to grasp Corylus' upper arms.

"Stop them," the sprite said.

The Ancient wailed. The sound started high and rose, a jagged edge of sound. The western magician shouted with surprise and leaped toward the ship.

There was a *crack!* like nearby lightning. A Servitor vanished in a shower of glittering dust.

There was a treble *crack!* All the glass figures were sand and dust finer than sand. The shrilling cry ended. Corylus still couldn't move.

The Ancient jumped to the railing. The westerner had teetered to a halt when the Servitors vanished. He blew smoke toward the Ancient and began chanting.

The Ancient reached out, gripping the magician's head with both long arms. He twisted sharply.

There was a muted pop as the victim's spine parted. The Ancient laughed and hopped onto the deck again.

Corylus got up. He didn't need the help of the long, golden-furred arm that the Ancient offered him, but he took it anyway.

Pandareus, gagged but sitting upright, watched from the back of the cart.

CHAPTER XVIII

Alphena hadn't thought she could sleep, but of course she had. This time she must have slept through the herbal smoke when Uktena lit his pipe, but she awakened at last because her skin prickled and the hair stood up on her arms and legs.

She opened her eyes to a haze of crackling light. It shrouded a form that was not the shaman's. Then Uktena expelled a final puff of smoke and thrust the pipe stem under his sash.

Without seeming to notice her, he started up the ladder. Ghosts of his body hung in his wake when he moved. They grew paler and finally dissipated.

Alphena hadn't taken off her sandals when she lay down, but she had loosened the laces so that her feet wouldn't swell uncomfortably during the night. She tightened them now without waste motion and got up to follow. The copper axe was in her hand.

She couldn't have described how she felt. She climbed, ignoring the jabs and flashes of numbness where her skin touched the wood which Uktena had touched.

I don't feel any way. A thing happened and I am doing a thing in response. The rain falls and the seed sprouts; but the seed feels nothing.

Clouds piled high in the western sky, red with the light of dawn. Lightning flashed within them, bringing out momentary shades white to dark gray; Alphena heard no thunder.

She caught up with Uktena. The ground around him popped and sizzled, and he dragged a train of glittering insubstantiality.

The three sages and some of the villagers watched from the edge of the forest beyond the planted fields. Wontosa's hair had been repaired with a weave shorn from someone else; the stuffed bird was different, also. He flinched when Alphena looked at him.

Does he think that I have powers? she wondered. Although—

She wriggled the axe in her right hand. It wasn't a magical talisman for her, but it did give her power over such as Wontosa.

The crystal fortress had already split open. Procron lifted from it, bathed in purple light that hurt Alphena's eyes. She shaded them with her hand, wishing she had her broad-brimmed hat. She had lost it from the gryphon's back while battling the Minoi. If she'd been thinking, she could have replaced it as she had the sword which she lost at the same time.

The sword was important. The hat was not.

She tried to walk close beside Uktena, but the power spreading from him drove her back like a fierce wind armed with sand grains. Grimacing, squinting, Alphena lowered her eyes and turned her shoulder to the discomfort. Even so, she had to stay twenty feet away from him.

Uktena probably didn't notice. He hadn't paid any attention to her since she awakened.

They reached the shoreline; Uktena dropped the pipe as before. A gentle wave rolled up the sand. When it touched the shaman's bare feet, the water disintegrated in hissing sparkles—not steam, though the gleaming motes stung when they touched Alphena's calf.

Spreading, swelling, the shaman moved outward. He was no longer Uktena, and she wasn't sure that he was her friend or even mankind's friend.

He's our defender, though. He's putting himself between us and our enemy.

Purple light ripped from the Minos, lashing the shaman and the sea. Water boiled away in a thunderclap, but the huge bulk continued to advance. The protecting white fire partially concealed the creature within, but Alphena could see enough of its writhing immensity to feel sick.

Clouds filled the eastern sky, coalescing out of clear air as suddenly as vinegar curdles milk. Black and lowering, they rushed toward the shore to meet the cloudbank that hung above the land. The storm broke in full earnest: rain and howling winds bent the tops of pine trees and sent a hut flying out to sea like a huge bird.

The thing that had been the shaman engulfed Procron despite the unrelenting sheets of purple flame spitting from the diamond skull. The monster had grown to the size of the island from which it came.

The white glow had dimmed so that Alphena could see clearly what

Uktena had become. Some of the heads were of beasts she had never seen before, and some could only be demons.

Tentacles spread toward the Atlantean. Hissing purple light burned them away, but they regrew and redoubled like the Hydra's heads.

Alphena fell to her knees. Windblown rain slashed her, washing away her tears. Like the thousand arms of what had been her friend, more tears sprang from her eyes.

Inexorably, the monster's bulk forced Procron back. The painful purple light didn't slack, but its punishment no longer slowed the advance of what had been the shaman. Where the flame now touched the creature, flesh bubbled and swelled and changed still more horribly, but it continued to crawl on.

Alphena unlaced her heavy sandals. They would help to wading depth, but she couldn't swim in them. She would be ready. . . .

Procron burst upward from the encirclement. He began to accelerate like a dropping stone. A hundred tentacles rose and snatched him down. They stripped him of his armor the way a cook shells a crayfish, flinging away the gleaming bits. Even under a storm-covered sky, the fragments shone like the tears of the sun.

The fight is over.

Procron suddenly blazed with shimmering violet energy. The gripping tentacles shrivelled and dropped away.

The Atlantean hung shimmering in the air for a moment. As fresh arms reached for him, he flung himself back into his spire.

The monster surged forward like the tide driven in by a storm. The doors at the top of the fortress slapped closed like the shell of a clam reacting to danger. What had been the shaman covered the spire and mounded above it.

How much larger can it grow? How much larger can my friend Uktena grow?

All the world grew transparent to her eyes. Alphena saw Procron in his crystal spire and saw the fortress in the monster's swollen body like a pearl in the oyster's mantle.

The crystal *shifted*. It could not break free in space, but it stretched into another dimension; fading, losing color and form, becoming a sparkling ghost of itself.

The creature made a convulsive movement like a whale swallowing. Even the ghost vanished. Procron and his fortress were cut off forever from Alphena's world.

The monster, swelling still greater, trembled. The storm paused, the clouds frozen in place and the winds still.

Alphena rose to her feet. She shouted, "Uktena! Come back to me, my friend! Come back!"

The monster slumped toward her like a wall of sand collapsing. She stood with her arms crossed. Heads and tentacles drew into the vast body and the body shrank.

"My friend!" Alphena shouted.

Uktena took a step toward her and collapsed into the surf. She thrust the axe helve through her sash and waded out to get him.

The sea spit light and occasionally stung her flesh like sparks from a bonfire. Uktena's compact body wobbled on the swell. He was facedown.

Alphena hurled herself against the water, but her tunic dragged her back. She should have taken it off with the boots before she left the shore.

The tide was going out. It was taking Uktena with it.

Alphena untied her sash and snatched the tunic over her head to drop on the waves. The axe was gone also. That didn't matter. Nothing mattered except that she reach Uktena before he drowned. She swam toward him, wishing she had spent more time in the swimming bath even if that meant less at sword practice.

She didn't know how long it was before she reached the shaman. He turned his face to breathe, but she wasn't sure that he noticed her presence. She rolled him onto his back. Kicking and stroking with one arm, she began to return to the shore. The storm was passing, though the wind still whipped froth from the wave tops.

Alphena felt momentarily weightless; the water about her glowed white. Everything returned to normal, except that six flounders rose to the surface and began a round dance on the tips of their tails.

The fish dived back toward the bottom, their white bellies gleaming. Alphena continued to stroke shoreward. Maybe she had imagined the fish, and anyway it didn't matter.

She didn't realize how close they had come till her knees scraped sand and bits of shell from the bottom. She gasped in shock and managed to swallow water.

She squatted because she wasn't able to stand. She laid Uktena's head in her lap to keep it above water. He was breathing, but he didn't seem to be aware.

Awareness would come. He was breathing. That was all that mattered.

Alphena didn't know how long she squatted there with her eyes closed, getting her breath under control and easing the white ache of her right arm and shoulder. The surf only came to her ankles at its flux and retreated well out into the sound.

She heard voices. After a further moment, she raised her eyes. The three sages were coming toward her, chanting in unison. Forty-odd people, probably the whole village of Cascotan, waited at the high water mark.

"Help us," Alphena said. "He's all right, he's just tired. Help us back to the kiva."

Still chanting what must be a prayer, the sages lifted Uktena from her. Hanno and Dasemunco took the shaman's arms. Wontosa, carrying the pipe, walked ahead of them. They paid no attention to Alphena.

She got up and wavered. She should have put her hands down to help herself, but she hadn't wanted to appear weak. *I could scarcely appear weaker than I really am.* She followed the four men higher up the shore.

Wontosa said, "Here. The sand is dry, so he won't be able to take power from the water."

He began to fill the murrhine pipe with herbs from the embroidered deerskin pouch. Uktena had left it behind in the kiva.

"What are you doing?" Alphena shouted. She stumbled forward. Arms caught her from behind—the women Sanga and Lascosa; the latter the mother of the thing Procron had created in the marshes.

"He's too dangerous," Sanga said. "Don't you see? He has to be sent away or we'll never be safe!"

Uktena sprawled on his back on the sand. The sages squatted around him and continued to chant. Wontosa puffed on the pipe he had taken from the greater magician.

"He saved you!" Alphena said. Her vision blurred with anger and tears. "He saved you all!"

"He's a monster!" Lascosa said in a venomous tone. "He didn't save my Mota. He would destroy us all!"

The chant reached a crescendo. Wontosa blew a great jet of smoke over the torso and head of his exhausted rival. Uktena's form blurred.

"No!" Alphena shouted as she tore loose. She flung herself over her friend's body.

The world shifted like a mirror tilting. She was alone, falling again through the emptiness from which Uktena had rescued her.

But now he cannot rescue even himself.

LANN RAN HEAVILY. He was faster when he dropped down and used his knuckles as forehooves, but even then Hedia had no difficulty keeping up. He didn't seem comfortable on all fours, however. He regularly lurched upright and tried to run on two legs like a man.

He wasn't a man, poor dear, except in his mind. And not really all of his mind, though enough to satisfy Hedia. She focused on the virtues of the men whom she liked, and Lann had most of the virtues which Saxa lacked. Between them, they made a truly wonderful man.

Hedia smiled. She'd found over the years that if she tried, she could like most men.

The ape-man paused, rose on his hind legs, and sniffed the air. He frowned in doubt. Turning, he looked back the way they had come. He didn't seem to see any more there than Hedia did—blank grayness—but he noticed the lens she carried.

"Hoo!" he cried, as delighted as if he were meeting an old friend. He snatched the device from her without ceremony.

Hedia felt her lips purse, though she didn't object. It was his, after all, though he might have been more polite.

Except that Lann *couldn't* be more polite. He was a beast, an animal, with major virtues. And, like Saxa, he was devoted to her.

The ape-man held the frame in one hand and touched the lens with his index finger. When he did so, he and Hedia stood on a pavement of dull metal in place of something firm but unseen in the universal grayness. She tested it with her toes.

This is what we've been walking on all the time. This isn't a mirage of the past, this is real.

Other paths branched from this one. Each was of a different material: brick laid in various patterns; concrete; a hard material as black as muck from a swamp; and uncountably many others. Some tracks were dirt, sun-baked or rutted or even grassy.

One of the paths was leaf mold on which Hedia could see her own footprints pressed delicately onto the broad, splayed marks of the ape-man who had led her. An Atlantean airship flew above that side-branch and vanished through the portal at the end; the second ship followed only moments later.

The hunters who had chased Hedia and the ape-man on foot were also running back the way they had come, but it was too late for them. Typhon crawled on its many legs from the prison which Lann had breached.

The monster seemed deceptively slow because it was so large, but its tentacles swept fleeing humans into its slavering maws. Typhon had as many heads as it had legs. They were equipped with beaks and fangs and muscular gullets to squeeze and crush and swallow. Some of the victims turned to fight, but that was like watching mice bare their teeth at a forest fire.

None of the hunters reached the jungle path. Instead of stopping when it engulfed the last of them, Typhon swelled through the portal with scarcely a pause.

For an instant Hedia thought she saw not a monster but a man in a loincloth who wore his iron-gray hair in braids. Then Typhon again filled the path from its ruptured prison to the portal, flowing onward without seeming to diminish.

The ape-man hooted joyfully and resumed his journey. He held the lens in his left hand, walking on either his legs or his legs and the knuckles of his right hand. He continued to chortle.

Hedia swallowed. The Atlanteans weren't her friends, Venus knew, but . . . all of them, the Minoi and their servants and their little dogs and the very worms in the dirt of their gardens? Because she didn't imagine Typhon would halt while there was still something to destroy.

She mentally shrugged as she accompanied the ape-man. The pavement was wide enough that she could stay within half a step of him while keeping far enough to the side that they wouldn't collide if he stopped abruptly.

She wouldn't have chosen that end for the Atlanteans . . . but she *hadn't* chosen it. Besides, it was done now. In this world—in all worlds—women get used to making the best of situations which they can't change.

Hedia grinned. Men really weren't much better off, but they were less likely to accept reality. That was another case of the woman having the advantage, if she had wit enough to use it.

They had passed numerous branchings, but Lann continued to follow the central metal path. Now at last he bore to the right, onto flagstones of volcanic tuff which appeared to have been set in concrete. Though a byway, it was wide enough that Hedia didn't feel uncomfortable as long as she kept to the middle of it. She wasn't sure it was possible to fall off the path, but the thought of drifting forever in this limbo frightened her more than the risk of death.

The ape-man paused again and concentrated on his lens. Hedia bumped him because her thoughts were elsewhere. That was no harm done: it was rather like walking into a tree with furry bark.

For a moment Lann and Hedia were in a vision of a bleak waste on which Procron's fortress stood under an orange sun. The ape-man made an adjustment by changing the angle of his right index finger. Their viewpoint shifted to the air above Poseidonis as Typhon advanced on the city like a tidal wave.

In the distance was the ring island outside the one on which Poseidonis stood. The monster had torn a gap the size of itself in the land as it emerged on the site of Procron's keep.

Typhon was larger than that now. It would continue to grow for as long as there was space for it, spreading like the sea.

Nothing can stop it. Hedia swallowed again.

Ships were rising from the harbor as they had done in the vision of the theater, but in this reality they were not attacking the monster. Instead, heavily laden with liveried retainers, they wobbled toward a shimmering disk hanging above the pinnacle of the great tower. The portal rested on the orichalc finial, which blazed now brighter than the sun.

The Minoi and their households were abandoning Atlantis rather than struggle against an inexorable doom. Typhon would triumph, but not over them.

Perhaps some of the women have carried along their little dogs, Hedia thought. The worms and the common people could take care of themselves. Though as an aristocrat herself, who was she to object?

Lann grunted in disgust and resumed his swaying course up the stone pavement. Hedia looked down at the blocks with a sudden question—and a recognition.

Where are the Minoi going in their flying ships? And—

The ball on top of the Atlantean temple is the same as the one we saw on the sundial in the Field of Mars.

"I'M VERY GLAD TO SEE YOU, Master Corylus," Pandareus said as Corylus finished undoing his bonds. He pursed his lips and added, "How did you know the westerners were carrying me to their ship, if I may ask?"

Corylus had untied the knots instead of cutting them because he was trembling in reaction to the fight. It had involved every fiber of his being—but only for a few heartbeats. It was over now, but his blood was still flooded with the emotions which had carried him through.

"I didn't know," he said. His mouth was dry as sunbaked sand and he felt a wash of dizziness as he finished freeing his teacher's wrists. He stepped back. "I don't think it was luck, though. My companion—"

He nodded to the Ancient, who was grooming his fur with his tongue.

"—is a great magician, and I've found him a better friend than I had any reason to expect would be the case."

"I see," said Pandareus in a neutral voice. He turned his head; Corylus followed his eyes toward the sprite.

"Ah!" Corylus said. He'd gotten so used to Coryla that he'd completely forgotten about certain matters that should have been obvious. "Cousin, while we're here in, ah, the waking world, would you put some clothes on, please. Ah, I think this fellow's tunic—"

He toed the corpse with the stuffed bird in its hair. The two he'd killed were covered with blood . . . as was his own right forearm, now that he noticed it.

"—will do."

"He can see us too?" Coryla said, giving Pandareus a thoughtful look as she walked over to the dead man. "Is it because we've been in the dreamworld, do you think? Or are you that great a magician?"

"I'm not a magician," Corylus said. He said to his teacher, "She's a cousin of mine, master. A very distant cousin."

There were quite a number of people watching them now—a score or more openly, and doubtless many times that number peering from cover or through slatted shutters from the buildings facing the harbor. The mule cart had drawn attention, which the sudden bloody violence would have multiplied.

Nobody had tried to interfere: a gang which killed three men in broad daylight wasn't anything for civilians to trifle with. A section of the Watch was bound to be arriving shortly, though.

"Master, where were they taking you?" Corylus asked. "That is, if you know."

He had already decided that they had to use the ship to escape Ostia, though there weren't any good places to fly *to*. They would have to land in daylight unless he wanted to wait six hours for nightfall. Even then someone would probably notice them in the air unless they landed in a barren location or came down at sea and rowed in, as presumably the glass men had done when the sages arrived.

Corylus couldn't handle both sweeps by himself. Pandareus wasn't strong enough to help, and asking the Ancient to do that sort of physical labor would be . . . a matter for cautious negotiation.

"I think they were taking me home," Pandareus said. "To their home in the Western Isles, that is. They were joining my mind to theirs to force me to use my powers of magic—"

His smile was wry.

"—to control the monster Uktena, so my consciousness listened to their discussions. They had decided to leave because the fleet of their enemies, the Minoi, was going to attack Carce at any moment."

The Watch had arrived at the end of the quay. Though—if he was reading the standards correctly, they were accompanied by a number of Marines as well. Part of the detachment at Misenum must be stationed in Ostia.

"The Atlanteans *here?*" Corylus said. "I thought Atlantis was destroyed thousands of years ago. That is, if it were even real to begin with."

"So did I," Pandareus said with a rueful smile. "If I understood the westerners' discussion correctly, *Atlantis* was destroyed but its rulers are coming here to escape. The sages couldn't stand against them, so they were taking me home to continue trying to find a way to control Uktena."

He looked down the quay toward the armed men advancing, then looked back at Corylus. He said. "I suspect that the Minoi will only put off their danger by fleeing to Carce. If their weapons are as terrible as the westerners seem to believe, however, Carce's present population won't survive to be threatened by the monster."

Pandareus coughed into his hand and added, "Uktena appears to be the westerners' name for Typhon."

Corylus sighed. Taking longer to think wouldn't give him a better result. There *were* no good results.

"Come, master," he said, offering Pandareus a hand more to get him moving than because he needed help getting up. "We'd best get aboard the ship."

The Watch and Marines were advancing at a deliberate pace, but they would arrive soon even if they didn't decide to make a final rush. Corylus had a frontier soldier's contempt for the Watch—and even more for the

Marines, who filled their ranks with freed slaves. Even so there were forty of them, and some of the Marines were carrying long pikes.

Pandareus moved with commendable speed, hesitating only when he reached the edge of the quay. Before Corylus could speak, the Ancient took the teacher in his long arms and hopped with him across the three feet of open water to the ship's deck before setting him down.

Pandareus remained tense for an instant, then broke into a broad smile. "Publius Corylus," he said. "You have in one fashion and another added more to my education than I can possibly have done to yours. Where are we going now?"

"To Carce," Corylus said, tossing the anchor aboard and trotting to the stern to loose the hawser there. "A moment ago I wondered what people would say if we flew over the city, but it sounds as though there'll be a good deal more to worry about than our presence."

The oncoming troops raised a shout, but it didn't look like any of them wanted to double-time into the kind of trouble which had brought them out in such numbers. They would be here in a moment regardless.

Corylus tossed the hawser aboard and leaped to the deck himself. He could have cut the rope easily, but he didn't want to give the Watch a chance to gloat.

The ship wobbled, then started to rise without Corylus needing to give an order. Well, it would have been a request. The Ancient was at his post in the stern, laughing in his fashion.

Corylus saluted him, then strode to the bow where the sprite waited. The sails beat strongly above them. The company on the quay had scattered, all but three Marines who butted their pikes on the stone and tried to follow the rising ship with the points of their weapons.

"Cousin," Corylus said, patting the tangle of dull black tubes which must be the flame-spitting weapon which he had seen in visions. "Can you teach me how to use this? Because if you can't, I'm going to have to fight shiploads of Atlanteans with just a sword."

He patted the hilt and grinned. "And I don't fancy my chances," he said.

VARUS STOOD IN THE BACK GARDEN of his father's house. He was alone.

A few days ago he had believed that none of the servants would have been willing to join him here even if he ordered them to do so under threat of torture. Today, Lenatus and three of the just-freed slaves in the new squad of servants had offered to stay with him. Lenatus said that the whole squad would attend if Lord Varus ordered them to.

Varus had found his voice growing thick as he assured the men that it would be better for him to be alone. He knew they were all afraid of magic, and he was sure that they had a good idea of how dangerous this was going to be . . . though probably not a real understanding of the *ways* it was going to be dangerous. It didn't make any sense that they should volunteer.

Nobody had ordered Gaius Varus to take on this duty either, but he was a philosopher: he knew that the flesh was of no importance. He didn't imagine that the squad of bruisers was nearly so blasé about questions of being and nonbeing . . . but they were willing to stand with him

Varus swallowed. He was beginning to understand what it meant to be a man. And perhaps that was because he was becoming a man himself.

He took a deep breath. He didn't have a weapon, just a splinter of bone. He had his mind and the knowledge in it. Those, not steel points or edges that would be more danger to him than to an enemy, were the tools with which he would fight Procron.

Varus wore a toga and leather-soled walking shoes. Remembering the terrain in which Procron's fortress stood, he had been tempted to get a pair of cleated army sandals. He wouldn't find them comfortable, though. He instead put on a pair of the shoes he would wear if he were going out on the streets of Carce.

"*May the doors of heaven . . . ,*" Varus said, reading aloud from the book which unrolled in his mind. "*Be opened to me!*"

It was the same phrase he had used to escape when Procron attempted to hold him. He was coming to realize that the words he used were not important. Hundreds or even thousands of Egyptians must have read the same phrase in past years. The words had power when *he* read them, because he read them with a particular intent.

The garden darkened. Varus stepped forward into a dark valley. The Sibyl waited for him at the base of a track up the hillside..

"Greetings, Lord Varus," she said. Crinkling her face still further in a smile, she added, "Intent is important, of course; but it would mean nothing if you were not a wizard."

She's replying to what I thought.

"Why would I not know what goes on in your mind, Varus?" she said. "Since I am a part of your mind."

Varus nodded politely. "Good morning, Sibyl," he said, ignoring her question. "I am glad you have joined me. I've come here again, because if I'm to stop Procron, I know of no better way to do it than by facing him."

Pandareus would appreciate the delicacy of his phrasing. Varus didn't believe that facing the Atlantean would enable him to defeat him—but he knew of no better way. Sitting in the library and pondering endlessly would lead nowhere. Choosing to face his enemy at least meant that by dying Varus would avoid having to watch the results of his failure.

"Come then," the Sibyl said. She started up the track, as she had done before.

She said, "Procron loosed Typhon on Atlantis in revenge for his exile, but he opened *all* paths when he did so. Typhon has chosen to attack Procon's enclave on this aged world, putting Procron on his mettle to prevent the monster from entering."

She cackled with amusement. "It is a struggle like no other in the history of the Earth," she said. "But there is no one to watch it except you and me, Lord Varus; and I do not exist outside your mind."

They reached the top of the low ridge. The sky was black with clouds congealing from the thin air. Procron's keep rose from the chill moorland in the near distance. The air was clear directly above the tower's peak, but a writhing mass of flesh tried to force entry against a net of violet lightning.

There was a continual thunderous hiss; the plain shuddered. Typhon's heads and limbs lashed at the lightning. They blackened, vanished, and were replaced as quickly by others swelling from the gross body.

"What—" Varus said. He stopped, smiled grimly, and began hiking toward the beleaguered fortress.

I already know what to do: enter Procron's fortress and stop him. Or die.

"Sibyl?" he said. "How long will this—" He waved. "—last if we don't take a hand?"

"For eternity, Lord Wizard," said the old woman, walking at his side. The air grew warmer as they approached the center of the struggle. The hoarfrost had melted, and the low vegetation was wilting. "Procron has pulled this world out of time, save for the one portal which his mind holds open to gain vengeance on the world that expelled him. Not even Typhon has the power to force that gate. Typhon will never cease trying, but—"

She shrugged.

"—if Typhon is blocked for very long here, it will enter Carce through another portal."

"But *I* will be able to leave?" Varus asked. He licked his lips. "As I did before when Procron tried to hold us?"

"If you slay Procron, whose power holds the portal open, his power vanishes," the Sibyl said. "Then only Typhon and Typhon's power remain, and Typhon destroys all things."

Varus was breathing fast as they approached the high arched doorway of the crystal fortress. *The air is thin. I breathe quickly only because my lungs don't fill as they ought to.*

"I see," Varus said. *I am a citizen of Carce. I will carry out my duty.*

He faced the spire and read out in a strong, steady voice, *"May the doors of heaven be opened to me!"*

IF I HAD MY AXE, Alphena thought, *I'd take care of all three of those sages! Even without the axe, I'd—*

Through the red haze of her anger, she glimpsed herself as she was: not only unarmed but stark naked. The hobnailed boots she had imagined grinding into Wontosa's face lay on the shore. Her waterlogged tunic had probably sunk to the bottom of the sound, where the copper axe certainly was. And ever since the vulture-riding Minoi had attacked her, her hat and her sword drifted in the eternal gray between worlds.

Where she was now.

"How could they?" she shouted. No one but herself would hear, but the words were empty anyway. "He saved them all, he saved *us!*"

Alphena felt mild pleasure as she realized that she was angry but not afraid. Fear might come later; she supposed she would be here until she starved. For now, though, she was furious with the sages and the whole village of Cascotan for what they had done to Uktena.

To cast *her* into this drifting prison—well, she was a stranger and she had never pretended to like any of them. What they did to her was fair, though of course she would know how to repay them if she ever got the chance.

But Uktena was their champion. He had saved Cascotan and probably the whole Western Isles from what had been done to Mota . . . and instead, Mota's mother blamed Uktena for not saving her daughter.

It's not fair!

The Earth, or Alphena supposed it was the Earth, was the pale ball which she had seen reflected in the basin when Anna chanted her spell. That seemed infinitely long ago; everything that had happened since she mounted the gryphon's back was another lifetime.

Alphena smiled again: a lifetime which had lasted longer than the life which had followed was going to. She had heard Lenatus talking about the army with Corylus and Pulto; so long as she kept quiet, the old soldiers had treated her as though she wasn't there. At the time she hadn't fully understood the stories of sudden death which they told, generally with laughter.

Now she understood. Alphena, daughter of Senator Gaius Alphenus Saxa, would never listen to stories in the exercise yard again.

She looked at the Earth, wishing that she could see it in detail as she had when the gryphon carried her toward Atlantis. Perhaps the omnipresent gray wouldn't disturb her brother or Pandareus; they seemed to live in their minds more than she did.

More than I ever wanted to, Alphena thought; and smiled, but she wasn't very cheerful at the moment.

Because she had nothing else to do save drift in emptiness, she considered again what had happened to Uktena. Resignation had replaced the anger, allowing her to look dispassionately at the situation.

No, what the villagers had done *wasn't* fair, and the sages who led them had certainly acted out of envy as well as fear; but Alphena no longer pretended that they had no reason to be afraid. Uktena was her friend and he had saved them all from a cruel monster; but the thing Uktena had become to win the battle was a monster as well. Nothing and no one would have been safe if that monster had remained in the world he had saved.

She now understood where it was that she had visited her friend—and why he was there. The sages had robbed Uktena of his memories and placed him in a vast prison beneath the sea, cut off from the cosmos in which humans lived. By doing so they had preserved not only themselves but all men.

"I would kill you all . . . ," Alphena whispered to her memory of the villagers. She could understand how they thought, even Mota's mother, blaming the hero because he hadn't saved her daughter and thus excusing her own willingness to betray him.

But Uktena was her friend. The fact that she understood the villagers' reasons didn't mean that she was willing to accept what they had done.

Alphena laughed. Not that they knew or would care if they did know.

But it made her feel better to have determined the truth to her own satisfaction.

She was rotating slowly as she drifted. She could see the lesser blur, now; the Moon, if the larger blur was the Earth as she assumed.

I'd take my chances with a magician riding a vulture, now, she thought, quirking a smile. She considered waving, but she didn't really believe that would rouse the attention of the Atlantean outpost. Besides, she would feel silly doing it.

Alphena thought she saw something. She squeezed her eyelids closed. She was afraid to hope, but she really thought she had seen something. When she opened her eyes again—

"It is!" she shouted. "It's wings! I see wings beating!"

She *didn't* see the glint of orichalc armor. If this was one of the vultures, would it attack without its rider?

She was seeing the gryphon. The gryphon was coming back for her!

Alphena waved and shouted, "Gryphon, it's me!"

The gryphon had obviously already seen her, so flailing about didn't help; she just spun a little faster. She didn't care. She had to do something!

The great beast banked around her in a lazy circle. His brindled fur had a sleek sheen, but there was a long scratch on his right flank that could have been caused by either a sword or a vulture's claw. The tuft of feathers over his right eye had been clipped off also.

"If you will stop pretending to be a rope dancer, girl," the gryphon said, "I will approach you from the front and you can catch me at the root of my right wing. If you're strong enough—"

He had swung out far enough that his deep voice was fading. He paused and with a quick, strong wing-beat angled back toward her again.

"If you are strong enough, as I say," he resumed, "you can pull yourself onto my back as before. Saving me the necessity of catching you myself."

Chuckling, he flared his foreclaws again. Like his beak, they were those of a giant eagle.

"I'm strong enough," Alphena said. "I'm ready."

The gryphon swept toward her. He looked huge, and however well-intentioned he was, the hooked beak really was capable of biting her head off.

He flared his wings like a hawk landing, bringing his great body to a near halt in space. Alphena, tense in expectation of the lion smashing into her, caught the gryphon's neck and the base of his right wing. He flapped, and she used the renewed momentum to swing herself back into a safe seat on his back again.

Alphena felt relief so profound that it made her dizzy. Laughing hysterically, she threw her torso down on the gryphon's neck and wrapped both arms around him.

"I am glad you find humor in your situation," the gryphon said with a touch of pique.

"I don't, please, I don't," Alphena said through her giggles. "I was afraid I was going to faint and make you do this all over again. You would have, wouldn't you? You wouldn't leave me here?"

The gryphon snorted. "I hope I know my duty better than that," he said. Then, in a tone that seemed to be apologetic, he added, "I'm sorry about the earlier trouble. I saw that pair off, right enough, but by the time I did, the wizard from the Western Isles had gathered you in. I didn't try to take you away, because, ah . . . I wasn't sure that I could. In fact—"

He paused long enough that Alphena thought he had decided not to finish the thought. Then he said, "In fact I was sure that I *couldn't* remove you. But it seemed to be working out all right."

"Yes," said Alphena. "It was all right."

My friend. She felt dizzy again. She hugged the gryphon's warm neck and felt the play of muscles under the stiff fur.

"Lady Hedia isn't in Poseidonis anymore," the gryphon said. "I could take you there, but Typhon has destroyed the city and—"

"Wait!" said Alphena. "My mother isn't in Poseidonis? Where is she, then?"

"I believe she has returned to Carce by now . . . ," he said in a clearly guarded tone. "Though it isn't so simple as that, I'm afraid. I'm not avoiding your question, Alphena; I just don't know."

"Well, if you think Mother is in Carce, then take me there!" Alphena said. She heard her tone and added, "I'm sorry, gryphon. I'm tired and, and upset. And I spoke without thinking. I would appreciate it if you would take me back to Carce or wherever Lady Hedia is. Ah, if you can?"

"Lady Alphena," the gryphon said. "It is not my place to advise you. I have agreed to serve you where I can, and I can certainly return you to the woman you refer to as your mother, if you wish. She is or shortly will be in the Field of Mars in Carce. But—"

"Go ahead, if you please," Alphena said more sharply than she had intended. She noticed that though the gryphon's wings were beating in a steady rhythm, neither Earth nor any other world was coming into focus the way it had when they flew up from her father's garden.

"There is a place where, if I understand your thinking, you would wish to be if you were aware of facts which it is not my prerogative to tell you," he said. "But if you direct me, I will take you to the Lady Hedia."

"You're as bad as my brother and his teacher, playing at words instead of saying what you mean!" Alphena said; but as she spoke, she knew she was wrong. The gryphon had said what he meant very clearly.

"I apologize again, master," she said, hoping he understood the sincerity with which she was speaking. "I'm tired, as I said, which isn't really an excuse. And I'm afraid my brother was the bright child of the family. I'm bright enough to take your advice, though. If you're still willing, please take me to the place you think I should be."

The gryphon gave his throaty chuckle. "With pleasure, little warrior," he said.

He banked toward one of the lesser blurs to which Alphena hadn't paid attention previously. She saw purple lightning crash.

I wish I had my sword, she thought. *Or the copper axe.*

But she felt excitement, not fear.

CHAPTER XIX

The sprite looked in disgust from the flame projector to Corylus. "That?" she said. "It makes *fires*. Why would I know anything about that?"

She shuddered theatrically. "It's ugly," she said. "You shouldn't use it."

Corylus felt a wash of frustrated anger, then despair. He gripped the starboard railing hard, wondering if his gauntleted hands would leave dimples in the wood.

He had no power over the sprite, no threat to offer that could force her to do what he wanted. More to the point, the worst torture imaginable wouldn't give her knowledge that she didn't possess. He didn't imagine that she was lying when she said she didn't know anything about the apparatus. Why would a tree nymph know how to operate a flame projector?

The ship circled as it rose, banking slightly to the right so that Corylus could look straight down if he wanted to. Wholesale establishments and market gardens lined the road into Carce, interspersed with the occasional tavern for travellers.

People looked up and pointed. A sailor was lazing on his back as mules hauled his wine barge against the current. He stared at Corylus, then shouted, "Baali!" He leaped to his feet and dived overboard.

The Tiber was a textured brown flood, trailing occasional lines of bubbles. Corylus had never seen the river from high enough up to appreciate its whole presence before. It wasn't the Rhine, let alone the Danube, but it had a personality which compelled respect.

He visualized the river god rising from the stream with flowing brown locks and challenging him. *Perhaps Father Tiber would know how to use this flame projector*, Corylus thought. He felt better for the whimsy.

The Ancient spoke in a querulous, demanding voice, ending on an up note. Corylus turned, clinking the flare of his helmet against his armored shoulder.

The sprite said, "I don't want—"

The Ancient spoke again, briefly but with a snap in his tone. He was glaring at her.

The sprite made a moue. "The place that makes it work is there in the back," she said to Corylus. She gestured with her elbow toward a six-pointed star with curving tips imprinted in the back of the apparatus. "You turn it sunwise."

The Ancient was grinning at him. "Thank you, master," Corylus said. He turned his attention to the flame weapon.

The ship had risen higher than it had in the past. The ground was at least a thousand feet below, and Carce spread like a mosaic of tile roofs in the northern distance.

There was an unfamiliar shimmering disk in the sky beyond the Citadel; it seemed to rest on the granite pylon which Augustus had brought from Egypt for the gnomon of his sundial. As he watched, a bump in the center of the disk grew into the bow of a ship; a moment later, the whole vessel flew free into the air above Carce.

Corylus touched the star on his weapon with the fingers of his left hand, then turned it. He felt a clicking through the gauntlets.

The device had been as rigidly fixed to the structure of the ship as the mast itself; now it quivered into life, moving with greasy obedience when Corylus touched the left handgrip. A triangle of light four inches to a side appeared over the forward-pointing spout, framing a section of sky.

"When you push down with your thumbs," the sprite said grudgingly, "fire comes out the front."

She looked at the deck and shook her head. In a barely audible voice she said, "I don't know how you can think of doing that, cousin. Using fire!"

Corylus closed the mesh visor of his helmet. The thin orichalc wires cast a soft blur over his vision, but they didn't blind him as he feared they might.

He thought about what the sprite had said. For a moment, he visualized a world in which men recoiled in horror from the thought of burning other men alive; a world in which the Batavian Scouts didn't dry the ears of Sarmatian raiders whom they had tracked down east of the Danube.

That world was almost real to him, but not quite. Now he sighted along the spout of the weapon as their ship slid down through the sky of Carce. A second Atlantean vessel was pressing through the disk of rainbow light.

The wings of Corylus' own ship stroked hard, lifting the bow slightly. He tugged on the handgrips to keep the first of the two Atlanteans in the lighted triangle. The weapon was perfectly balanced, but it was heavy enough that adjusting the aim took some effort.

He kept the snout swinging, judging the Atlantean's course and their own. It was a matter of figuring out where the target would *be* and aiming there. *Like launching a javelin at a Sarmatian riding across our front. . . .*

The decks of the Atlantean vessel were crowded with people. Most of them wore brightly colored off-the-shoulder tunics, but there were also archers and spearmen in simpler garb and a handful of exquisites—women and children—who glittered like spiderwebs frosted with dew.

Many Atlanteans stared at Corylus, but they didn't seem concerned. They must think he had come through the portal ahead of their ship, that was all.

A Servitor stood beside the armored Minos in the stern; another held the grips of the fire projector in the bow. The glass men were looking down at the plaza between the sundial and the Altar of Peace where citizens of Carce were gathering to see the wonders despite the threatening clouds. The Servitor in the bow slanted his weapon to sweep the crowd.

In another world, the Minoi would meet the Senate in peace and their people would settle in this world, another nation among the hundreds already within the boundaries of a peaceful empire.

In another world. The Atlantean ship was within fifty feet, proceeding parallel to Corylus' craft but not as swiftly.

The Ancient howled a word. Corylus didn't wait for the sprite to translate—if she intended to—before he squeezed with his thumbs. Nothing moved beneath them, but there was a loud roar, a blast of heat on his cheeks despite the mesh visor, and a throbbing vibration through the hull.

A spray of flame washed across the sails of the Atlantean ship; they vanished into puffs of ash drifting on the breeze. The vessel rolled over on its side, spilling its passengers and crew before plunging after them. The Minos dropped like a blazing meteor.

Corylus lifted his thumbs. The Ancient was keening something as he brought their ship around to engage the second Atlantean. The Servitor at the weapon of that one was no longer concerned with the civilians below, though the projector's inertia slowed him.

A third ship was squeezing through the disk. Behind it were scores of others, more than Corylus could begin to count in a brief glimpse.

He adjusted his flame projector. He thought he heard the sprite sobbing, but that was a concern for another world, a world that didn't exist today.

HEDIA SAW A BRIGHTER PATCH in the blur ahead of them. There had been an omnipresent buzzing, like that of many distant insects; now it began to congeal into voices. To her surprise, Lann first slowed, then stopped and stood erect.

Hedia made a quick choice and stepped around him, striding briskly. She couldn't hear words, but the rhythms of the speech ahead were those of Latin.

The ape-man gave a plaintive chirp. She glanced over her shoulder and saw that he was shambling along behind.

The air changed and the brightness gained texture. When Hedia looked straight ahead she saw only the flagstones, but there were other movements in the corners of her eyes: a pair of sheep, long-legged and shaggy, stared at her with their jaws working in a circular motion. Again, a young man made a half-turn to loose a discus. His muscles were so chiseled and perfect that Hedia almost missed a step.

The vision faded. The athlete was gone with the sheep.

Without conscious transition she stepped from the path onto the pavement within the marble screen of the Altar of Peace. Around her marched in low relief the sacrificial procession with which Emperor Augustus had inaugurated the altar.

A huge storm boiled in the sky around the horizon, but shimmering light held clear the air directly overhead. The light blazed from the orichalc sphere on top of the pointer of the sundial which Augustus had erected at the same time that he built the Altar of Peace.

A portal almost a hundred feet in diameter balanced above the monolith. From it, as Hedia watched, struggled a flying ship.

The Minoi were here. They had caught her.

Hedia walked out through the west doorway of the marble screen. Directly ahead, the Egyptian obelisk rose above the heads of the spectators.

She was stark naked, with nothing to hide her cuts, bruises, and general grubbiness. At least she had gotten used to going barefoot, so the hard pavement didn't bother her now.

A ripping sound, not loud but savage, drew Hedia's attention to the sky. Two Atlantean ships flew past one another in opposite directions. A cone of flame, bright orange on the edges but a lambent white at the core, spewed from the bow of the more distant ship. It bathed the sails of the nearer vessel, setting them to blaze like gossamer.

The victim turned belly up like a dead fish, then dived toward the river. The pair of Servitors clung to the bow. The Minos was flung out with his screaming retainers. His orichalc armor caught light from a thousand angles. He smashed into the facade of the Temple of Saturn and slipped down broken.

The ship that had attacked rose into the air, its sails beating strongly. Hedia looked at it sharply. An armored Minos controlled the flame weapon in the bow instead of guiding the ship as had been the case every previous time she had seen the Atlanteans flying. *What on Earth is that animal in the stern?*

Lann came out of the enclosure behind Hedia, putting his knuckles to the pavement and swinging down the steps like a man on double crutches. He nuzzled her hand and made a deep moaning sound.

People nearby had begun to notice them, though the only one who seemed really frightened was a little girl who grabbed her mother's tunic and babbled in a high-pitched Eastern language. A naked woman and a huge ape must seem minor in comparison with flying ships battling in the sky.

"Make way for the noble Consul, Gaius Alphenus Saxa!" shouted a deep voice coming from behind.

Hedia spun around. She hadn't been thinking about her husband, but *of course* he would come here. Saxa wasn't what anyone would call a man of action, but he was dutiful to a fault. As consul—for another few days before his brief appointment ended—he would immediately have rushed to the site of the great wonder taking place on the Field of Mars. Household servants followed him, but his lictors led the entourage, adding official status to their husky presence.

The storm that filled the horizon rippled with nearly constant lightning, but the thunder was muted by the distance. Clouds seemed to strain at the bubble of clear air the way surf rolls against a cliff; but again like the cliff, the bubble cast them back.

Even the powerful voice of Saxa's chief lictor seemed thin against the background of crowd, storm, and the battle in the sky, but his men had opened their ceremonial bundles. Saxa's servants were carrying the loose rods and axes, but each lictor had kept out a rod which he used freely to open a path through the crowd for the consul.

The man who walked as the point of the advance, swinging his rod with both hands, saw Lann. He shouted, "Watch it there! Axes! Axes!"

"My lord husband!" Hedia said, stepping toward the procession and waving her right arm in the air. She wasn't sure that Saxa could see her through the press of his escort, and she was nearly certain that none of the lictors would recognize her in her current state. "Saxa, my heart!"

"That's her ladyship!" cried Callistus, forcing his way out through the lictors. Though soft, he was a tall man and more alert than Hedia would ordinarily have given him credit for. "Your ladyship—"

He paused to stare at her. Without a further word, he whipped off his ornate toga and settled it over her shoulders.

Lann growled and surged toward the steward. Callistus shrieked and fell back. Some of the lictors had retrieved their axes; they sprang forward. There was nothing symbolic about the axe blades now.

Hedia threw her arms around the ape-man's head and covered him. "He's a friend!" she shouted over her shoulder. Then—because in fairness to the lictors, they had every reason to be concerned for the consul's safety—she said, "Lann! No! These are my friends! Sit down and be good!"

"Dear heart?" Saxa said, forcing his way with some effort through his entourage. "What's happening here? You know, don't you? Tell me what I should do."

By Hercules, husband, how could I possibly know! Hedia flared; but that was exhaustion and frustration reacting, and the emotion—it wasn't thought, not really—didn't reach her lips.

The lictors had drawn back, allowing Callistus to get to his feet again. The ape-man unwrapped his head from folds of the toga, looking puzzled. His anger at the steward had passed, and he didn't seem to regard the men with axes as a danger. His only concern had been what he perceived as a threat to Hedia.

Stroking Lann's shoulder, she glanced up at the sky. The ship whose Minos was in the bow had climbed and was circling the other vessel. That second ship tried to keep its bow and the weapon there toward its pursuer, but it wallowed uncomfortably. There were at least a hundred people standing on its deck, a crowd that would have sunk a vessel of its size on the water and was threatening to do the same for this flying one.

Hedia *did* know why the Atlanteans were appearing over Carce. That was so obvious that she was embarrassed to remember her flash of unspoken anger at being asked the question.

She had watched the ape-man loose Typhon on Atlantis. The Minoi who could flee before the monster were of course doing so.

And she knew what Saxa must do. Unfortunately she didn't think that would be enough to save Carce, though.

"Husband!" she said. Her voice was crisp and her back straight. Nothing in Hedia's manner suggested that there was anything unusual in her presence or costume. "The ships full of people are Atlanteans trying to leave their island before it sinks. They'll destroy Carce to make a place for themselves—you saw in the theater what their weapons do, the way they spew fire."

The sky ripped as one ship sent a cone of flame across the other, lighting the sails and touching the passengers packed on the forward deck. People shrieked and threw themselves over the railing, their clothing afire.

Their clothing burned, and also their flesh: the smell of meat cooking was unmistakable. The emperor had lighted the Circus for a beast hunt one night with the households of four plotters, dipped in tar and hung from poles before being ignited. The screams had sounded the same that time.

Perhaps because the passengers in the bow jumped away from the jet of fire, the ship reared like a horse, then plunged into the ground stern first. It landed on a line of clothiers' booths toward the river. The hull shattered, killing those still aboard as well as spectators.

"But why are they fighting?" Saxa asked. He rubbed his lips with his left hand as if trying to muffle the admission of his ignorance.

"I don't know and it doesn't matter," Hedia said. "You have to summon troops with artillery."

Did the garrison of Carce have ballistas and catapults? The Watch certainly didn't, but the Praetorians might have some. *Some.*

"We have to be ready to fight the Minoi when they stop fighting one another."

Another ship was pressing through the portal. For a moment the scene reminded Hedia of a bubble on the surface of swamp, swollen about the stem of a reed. The defending vessel was climbing again.

"My dear!" Saxa said in obvious surprise. "I have no authority to do that. The Watch comes under the authority of the emperor's prefect, and as for the Praetorians—my heart, you *know* they wouldn't take orders from a senator. *Any* senator, but I'm afraid they would find me less impressive than most of my colleagues."

"But we have to fight them!" Hedia said, weak-kneed with horror that her husband had just corrected her on a question of political practicality. *Of course* the Praetorian Guard wouldn't take the orders of a senator. The Praetorians existed largely to keep the senators themselves in check. "Husband, look at the flames they shoot! If a hundred ships start lighting fires across the city, we'll all burn. Everything will burn!"

The people nearest Hedia were listening to the argument with frightened incomprehension. The words didn't mean anything to them, but anger and fear were obvious in Hedia's voice. Even a slave freshly dragged from the interior of Spain could understand what that meant.

Lann looked, perhaps for the first time, at the portal which seemingly balanced on the point of the granite obelisk. He hooted softly, then bared his teeth and boomed a challenge Hedia had heard before: in the forest immediately after her escape from the Servitors, when the ape-man confronted the lizard which was about to leap on her; and toward the Minoi pursuing them in the passage back to Carce, before he loosed Typhon.

Lann put his head down and bulled his way on all fours into the screaming crowd. The spectators were too closely packed for him to shove them out of the way: rather, he crushed them down or hurled them into the air like spray from the prow of a ship.

The warships in the sky continued to maneuver. Two more had struggled through the portal and a third was on its way. Carce's sole defender slanted toward them, but it couldn't forever stop a fleet as big as the one Hedia had seen in the skies above Poseidonis.

And when it lost the unequal struggle, Carce had no other defense.

VARUS STOOD AT what he thought was a safe distance from the spire's double doors. He expected them to swing outward and possibly to swing very fast, because he couldn't assume that they would be bounded by the constraints of the material world.

Instead of opening, the black crystal valves dissolved into a thin haze. Through it he could see figures moving.

Varus grinned wryly. He had been correct in realizing that the doors might not open like those of the emperor's town house. He had been wrong in his unstated assumption that they would open in the material plane. Pandareus would be disappointed at the blinkered viewpoint his student had demonstrated.

I wonder if I'll ever see Pandareus again?

A sheet of lightning covered the sky for long moments, pulsing among the clouds. Beneath the shadowed gloom that followed, Varus walked toward Procron's fortress. The Sibyl was at his side, her expression unreadable.

She looked toward him and said, "There are many futures, Lord Wizard. In some of them you meet Pandareus again. Do you wish to know which of the Fates' threads you walk?"

"It doesn't matter," Varus said. Until he spoke, he hadn't realized how completely true the statement was. "This is my duty, so I'll carry it out to the best of my abilities."

It was easier to get on with life when one disregarded questions of personal survival. Zeno of Citium and those who had developed his Stoicism would be pleased that a young scholar had achieved such understanding.

The Sibyl made a sound like a pour-spout gurgling. It was probably meant for a chuckle. Anyway, it allowed Varus to smile at himself as he walked beneath the pointed crystal arch and felt gray fog enter his bones.

Varus paused. He had expected—*without consciously framing the question; Pandareus will be disappointed*—the fog to be a membrane, a permeable replacement for the solid doors. Instead it was a dim cave which branched in more directions than he could count on his fingers.

The Sibyl pointed her right arm forward and said, "*Grant me a path—*"

"*—over which I may pass in peace . . . ,*" continued Varus in the same high-pitched voice. He was reading the scroll open in his mind. "*For I am just and true!*"

Despite the situation, he felt his lips rise in a smile. *Every philosopher should be just and true. I at least strive for those ideals.*

A tube of rosy light snaked through the fog, wide enough for two to walk in. It went farther—much farther—than should have been possible within the crystal spire, which Varus had judged to be no more than a hundred feet in diameter at the base.

Still, he couldn't be in doubt as to his path; he strode in and walked as briskly as he would have done in Carce, passing from his father's house to the Forum or perhaps to a temple whose library he wanted to consult.

In Carce Varus would have had a guard of servants, to keep his surroundings at bay; here the light did the same. Occasionally something came close enough to the glowing boundary to give him a good look at it. He passed three slender forms in flowing tunics who stood arm in arm, watching him with wide eyes. They were as supple as the Graces themselves; he couldn't guess at their gender or even—

"Sibyl?" Varus said. "Are they human?"

"What is human?" the old woman said. "Many scholars including Aristotle have debated that. None of them came to a decision that you were willing to accept, Lord Varus."

Then in a less whimsical tone she said, "Their ancestors were human. Whether or not they remain human is a question for philosophers, not for a soothsayer."

I can be a very frustrating person to talk with, Varus thought again. *If I'm really talking with myself.*

He smiled again. He was amused at the insight—and he was amused that he had found a purely philosophical question to take his mind off the problem of what lay in his own immediate future. Both problems were insoluble, but considering the definition of "humanity," weren't emotionally trying.

For a moment, Varus saw vast machines beyond the faint rosy membrane, deeper shadows bulking in the purple-gray dusk. They moved repetitively, the movement visible though the forms were only blurs. He could not tell how distant what he saw was, or even if he was truly seeing anything.

As suddenly, he stared upward in horror: Ocean given physical form. A thousand ravening maws slavered toward him, tens of thousands of limbs kicked and clawed and coiled—and then storm-tossed water surged down, a sea greater than the world itself. Froth flicked from the whitecaps. Monster or ocean met eye-searing purple lightning and vanished into haze, through which the reborn terror drove to vanish in turn. The roar was deafening.

"Perhaps, Gaius Varus, you should consider preserving your fine mind by leaving this place," the Sibyl said. "You are still able to, you know."

Varus glanced at her in irritation. "To go where?" he asked. "Back to Carce, where Typhon will be driven if I don't stop Procron here?"

She gave him another enigmatic smile. "You don't mind my suggesting that you are a coward," she said in a musing tone, "but flawed logic offends you. Does that make you a brave man, Lord Wizard, or a fool?"

"Nothing historians have taught me about battles," Varus said, "makes me think that one man cannot be both. Publius Corylus has many stories of the army which have caused me to wonder if it's possible to be a brave man and *not* a fool."

" '*It is a sweet and proper thing for a man to die for his fatherland,*' " the Sibyl quoted. "Was Horace a fool, Gaius Varus?"

"No," said Varus. "Because he threw down his shield and ran instead of dying."

He paused, rolling the thought around in his head. Very precisely he went on, "Horace was not a fool; but he was worse than a coward to urge others to act and therefore die in what he thought was a foolish manner."

Varus cleared his throat and continued, projecting as though he had an audience beyond monsters and a figment of his imagination, "I honor Horace as a poet, perhaps the greatest of our poets. But I would prefer to die at the side of my friend Corylus than to live with the soul of Horace."

The Sibyl chuckled. Unexpectedly, she reached out and squeezed his hand. "The men of Carce have not changed since my girlhood," she said.

Which is a puzzling thing to hear from a figment of my imagination.

They were walking down a tube through darkness again. Varus hadn't missed a stride beneath the threat of Typhon—or of the sea, if there was any difference—but he felt more comfortable in this neutral setting. Well, he felt less *un*comfortable.

He glimpsed movement to the side and turned, wondering if he would see another of the androgynous maybe-humans. Instead he frightened into scurrying panic a handful of the rabbitlike animals which he had seen scampering outside on the moor. They disappeared into the shadows of the low, black vegetation.

"Their ancestors were human also," said the old woman. She was watching Varus, perhaps to see how he took the revelation. "The world grows old, and her children age with her."

"I see," said Varus. The only emotion he felt was wonder. He was beginning to understand the passage of long ages, which had been only a concept to him in the past.

The Sibyl gestured toward flickering brightness ahead of them. "There is your goal, Lord Wizard: Procron the Atlantean. Are you his master, do you think?"

Varus sniffed. "It doesn't matter what I think," he said.

The light was a doorway barred by sizzling lightning; the smell of burned air made Varus sneeze. He wiped his nose with the back of his hand and said, "*Grant me a path over which I may pass in peace!*"

And stepped through, into Procron's sanctum. The Sibyl had vanished as though she never was.

Procron stood upright in the middle of a vast room. He was nude: an aged man whose chest had sunk and whose limbs were withered. Violet light flickered in the depths of the diamond skull which had replaced his head.

The firmament of heaven formed the room's walls; a needle of light from each star pierced the magician's body. Varus' presence blocked a few of the beams, but they shifted and reformed as he walked forward.

"Why do you come here, infant?" a voice boomed. Procron wasn't speaking, or at least his body wasn't; the words came from the air.

Four Servitors walked toward Varus at a deliberate pace. He didn't know whether they had just appeared or if he had failed to notice them when they stood motionless in the light of stars as blinding as a dust storm. The glass men were bare-handed, but they scarcely needed weapons to deal with a young scholar.

Varus continued forward. The scroll written in Egyptian holy symbols was unrolling in his mind.

"Look above you, infant!" the voice said. "Look! Is this what you want to bring upon yourself?"

Varus looked up, though he knew what he would see. Typhon and Ocean, the presence flicking from one to the other more quickly than his mind could process . . . or perhaps they were the same, infinitely huge, ravening against the barrier of hissing light; a pressing, roaring, mindless fury oblivious of pain.

Varus walked on. The Servitors stepped close, their arms lifting to seize him.

"*May the gods be at peace with me . . . ,*" Varus said. "*That I may crush my enemies!*"

He started to raise his hand to point at the Servitors in turn. At his words alone they shattered into dust so fine that it seemed to sink through the solid floor.

Varus smiled grimly. Sometimes being a scholar was better than being a swordsman.

He had walked to within a few paces of the Atlantean wizard.

"What do you think to accomplish?" the voice thundered. "Even if you are willing to feed yourself to Typhon, still you cannot affect me. My soul is one with my talisman in a universe nothing can reach; the wizard Uktena slew my body thirty million years ago. What escaped to this time is dead and immune to further harm!"

"May the gods be at peace with me," Varus said, *"that I may crush my enemies!"*

A ripple quivered through the chamber, like heat waves stirring the stars on a summer night; the dust that had been the Servitors danced in fitful eddies. There was no greater result.

Procron's laughter echoed like mountains crashing. "You cannot harm me," the voice said, "because I am dead!"

As my ancestor, who gave me her jaw, is dead.

Varus held the splinter in his left hand. He didn't bother taking it in his right, his master hand, because he was certain that physical strength and dexterity had nothing to do with this.

He thrust the jawbone toward Procron's chest. It slid through the wizard's ribs like a spear driving into loose sand. There was a sound as if the world itself was screaming.

Above, the net of lightning that held back Typhon vanished; the monster began to pour down through the sky. The myriad lights around the vast room went dark.

Procron's body crumbled like rotten wood, but the diamond skull blurred. It was vanishing by becoming more diffuse, the way fog lifts as the sun climbs higher.

The scream grew fainter also, but it continued for a very long time.

Varus turned and walked back toward the entrance. There he would wait for horror to engulf him. *I am a citizen of Carce.*

"WHERE ARE WE GOING?" Alphena asked. "Ah—that is, if you please, Lord Gryphon."

The gryphon's muscles rippled over his bones with the rhythm of a dance. His fur lifted and settled like the surface of a pond when something very large swims beneath it. Even as keyed up as Alphena was, she found the movement entrancing.

"To your world, little one," the gryphon said, cocking his eagle head just enough that he could look at her with his right eye. "To your world, though not to your time."

He gave a throaty chuckle and added, "We are going to your brother; or to where your brother died, if we are not in time."

Alphena tried to prevent her muscles from tensing. She couldn't, of course; and even if she had, the gryphon would probably have smelled her sudden fear.

"Thank you, lord," she said, proud that at least her voice didn't quaver. "I'll hope that we arrive in time."

Images began to pick themselves out the hazy light ahead. As before, their destination became clear but did not swell as her mount's wings beat.

At first Alphena thought the gryphon had made a mistake: the bleak world before them was nearly featureless. It was the Moon glimpsed in the moments before the Atlantean guardians lifted from it on their vultures, not the blue seas and green continents of the Earth.

The fortress of Procron the Atlantean stood on a plain covered with plants whose leaves were the color of charcoal. Alphena tensed again; then she smiled.

Uktena saw you off once, she thought. *Since apparently my friend didn't finish you, I'll see what I can do to what's left.*

She thought again about the axe, lost off the shore of the Western Isles. She flexed her fingers in the gryphon's fur. Perhaps she could find a rock when they landed on that stark plain. If not, well, she would do what she could with her hands and teeth.

"Such a brave little warrior," the gryphon said affectionately. "It is not Procron with whom you have to deal; your brother has settled that."

The world before Alphena changed. A mesh of glittering fire surrounded it, the violet fury which Procron had used to lash his enemies. As suddenly, the shield of lightning vanished and—unseen till that moment—a torrent of fangs and claws poured down to cover the stark plain on which the Atlantean's fortress stood.

The crystal spire itself remained untouched for the moment. As Alphena watched, her brother stepped through the gateway and stood facing his monstrous doom.

"I can try to snatch him up," said the gryphon. He sounded reflective, not frightened. "I will not be able to rise before Typhon catches us, however;

and I'm not sure that your brother will survive the haste with which I will be forced to act."

He added, "I am not sure why Typhon hesitates. Typhon *is* destruction; it has no purpose but to destroy."

"No," said Alphena, her lips dry. "He isn't destruction. Set me down beside my brother. If—"

She sat up stiffly. She had been about to say, "If you dare."

"If you please, Lord Gryphon," she said. *Since he knows my thoughts, he knows that my apology is sincere.* "I regret the danger that I cause you to face."

The gryphon's laughter was cruel and triumphant. "What warrior expects to die in his nest, little one?" he said in a voice so rumblingly deep that the words were scarcely distinct. "Did I not know who you were when I chose to accompany you?"

His broad wings fanned and his forequarters reared, halting him in mid-flight. Alphena hugged herself to the feathered neck. With no transition that she could see, the gryphon's hind legs touched the narrow strip between Varus in the gateway of the crystal spire and Typhon's looming presence. The wings beat once more; then the cat torso settled and Alphena slid to the cold ground.

"Sister?" Varus said. The gryphon, stretching his great body in studied unconcern, was between them now. "Alphena, what are you doing here?"

She ignored him. "Uktena?" she said. Before her, surrounding her and now dwarfing Procron's fortress, rose a solid wall: it was snarling flesh where she focused but in the corners of her eyes the foaming, high-piled ocean. "My friend Uktena!"

The wall trembled toward her: a cliff crumbling, a wave breaking. Alphena stood, looking up: scratched, naked; her eyes on the verge of tears, but she wouldn't cry, she *wouldn't*.

The shaman Uktena brushed a lock of her hair out of her eyes with his left hand. "I did not expect to find you in this place, little one," he said.

"You're back," Alphena whispered, the words choking her throat. She gripped the shaman's hand and held it to her cheek with both of hers. "I was afraid I'd never see you again."

She couldn't see him now, because of the tears. She squeezed harder. Uktena's hand was as firm as a hickory root.

"I will never come back, child," he said quietly, stroking her hair with his free hand. "What I was in my home is gone forever, just as the wizard Procron is gone."

"Uktena," she said. "Please. Please, my friend. Let my brother go and the gryphon too. He's a brave warrior, you'd like him."

She drew a deep breath. She didn't open her eyes because she was afraid of what she would see.

"Let them go," Alphena said, "and I will stay. My life for my brother's. That's fair, isn't it?"

Uktena laughed the way thunder boomed when he fought Procron in the sea. "Fair?" he said. "What is fair? Everyone dies and everything dies, and I destroy all things. I am the destroyer!"

"You are my friend," Alphena said against the shaman's hard chest. "You are my friend, no matter what anybody says. I don't care!"

"Little one, little one," Uktena said. "You stood by me in good times and bad. Indeed—"

He chuckled again, but this time there was humor in the sound.

"—a person less fearless than yourself might have said that there were only bad times. Go, take your brother and the mount who glares at me like a frog preparing to fight a stork. You will all die, for all things die. But not today, and not at my hand."

"Uktena, you deserved better," Alphena said. Her voice was so low that she heard the words mostly in her mind.

"I have the world to myself, Alphena," he said. "Who is there greater than I?"

He laughed, but the humor was missing.

"Sister?" said Varus at her side. "You might be more comfortable wearing this."

He offered Alphena his tunic. He must have taken it off, then put his toga on again with the coarse wool directly against his bare flesh as though he were a sturdy plowman of ancient Carce.

Which he was, Alphena realized, in the fashions that mattered. She had learned what a man was in these last few weeks; and her bookish brother, to her astonishment, was a man in all the best senses.

"Anyway," he said, smiling as though he were unaware of the horror poised over him, "I would be more comfortable if my maiden sister weren't prancing around as naked as a plucked squab."

"Your brother," said the gryphon, "cannot hear your conversation with the person whom you call your friend. *I* heard, however. May I suggest that this would be a good time for me to deliver you to your stepmother in Carce?"

"Yes," said Alphena, her voice muffled as she pulled the tunic over her head. She turned. Varus was staring at the shaman. She said, "Brother, what do you see?"

"I can't describe it," Varus said, wetting his lips with his tongue. It was a moment before he met her eyes and forced a weak smile. "But part of the time I'm seeing Ocean, if that's what you mean. I don't know why the wave doesn't fall on me. On us."

"Get on the gryphon's back," Alphena said, swallowing. "I'll get up behind you. He has kindly agreed to take us to Mother, who is back in Carce."

Varus looked doubtfully at the gryphon, who said in a tone of drawling boredom, "Or if the boy would prefer to stay, *I* won't object to leaving him."

"I don't know how—" Varus said tartly. He was probably going to say something about not knowing how to mount so large an animal.

He jumped up before Alphena could offer to help, throwing himself across the gryphon's back like a pair of saddlebags. He must have realized that this wasn't a time for debate or the decorous behavior of the Forum, though he really wasn't much of an athlete. Alphena grabbed his right ankle to keep him from sliding completely over their mount and landing headfirst on the other side.

Varus spread his legs on opposite sides of the gryphon's back. Uktena watched with a slight smile; his arms were crossed.

Alphena forced her lips together and hopped onto the gryphon, folding her legs under her. The other choice would have been to seat herself behind the wings, where she wouldn't have anything to hold onto unless she grabbed handsful of flight feathers. She gripped her brother's waist with both hands, hoping he had enough sense to cling to their mount's neck.

"Lord Gryphon," she said, "we are ready."

The gryphon turned his head to stare at Uktena, then dipped it in what must have been a sign of honor. He rose onto his hind legs and sprang upward, slamming his great wings down with the same motion.

Varus rocked violently, but he managed to hang on. Alphena suspected that the gryphon was deliberately keeping his back more level than he had bothered to do when she alone rode him. She wasn't used to riding, but she *was* an athlete and had a sense of balance.

They rose swiftly, curving away. Alphena looked back over her shoulder.

The world behind them tossed and turned in the grips of colossal vio-lence. Procron's spire shattered under what must have been an enormous impact from all sides at once. Reduced to powder, the crystal walls spurted upward like the flume of a spouting whale.

Uktena, a giant standing astride the world, looked up at Alphena from the midst of the destruction. He raised his hand in salute; then the scene became a spherical mirror and faded into the distance.

Good-bye, my friend.

CORYLUS WAITED. His thumbs were consciously raised above the triggers as his ship slid toward the stern of the vessel which had just come through the portal. The target slanted downward, trying to reach the ground under con-trol instead of plunging from the sky as a flaming wreck.

The Servitors in the bow had rotated their weapon as much as they could, but that was only sixty degrees off axis, and the ship itself couldn't turn quickly enough to face the renegade vessel which had already destroyed the two preceding Atlanteans. Escape was the best choice, but it wouldn't be possible.

The Minos controlling the ship looked back at their pursuer. Corylus triggered his weapon, touching the top of his target's mast but not igniting the beating sails. Most of the jet sprayed across the passengers crowding the bow. The humans burst into screaming flame, but fire ran off the Servitors without affecting them.

Corylus let their speed carry him closer, then squeezed the triggers again. The muzzle spat a fiery gobletful. It splashed the right-hand wing of the sail which blazed like dry grass. Still forty feet in the air, the Atlantean vessel rotated to starboard and spilled its human freight before nosing down into field.

Corylus turned. "The flame stopped!" he shouted to the Ancient. He didn't know whether the fox-faced magician could understand Latin—or any other human language—but he was pretty sure that he could figure out what was going on even without words. "We don't have any more fire!"

The sprite sat disconsolately on the deck between Corylus and the mast. She didn't look up when he shouted. Violence didn't disturb her, but the use of fire had obviously affected her the way wanton destruction of books would have done Pandareus, who stood at the railing near her.

The scholar wore a look of bright interest at present. Corylus knew that Pandareus wasn't a cruel man, but witnessing unique events was of more importance to him than the fact that the events involved hundreds of strangers burning alive or being smashed to jelly.

The Ancient looked at Corylus from the stern. He raised his right hand, crooked the fingers into claws, and with a terrible scream ripped them down.

Corylus grinned through his mesh visor. He and the Ancient didn't share a language, but they could communicate well enough. He drew his sword.

The ship was climbing again to get higher than the portal. A pair of Atlantean vessels were squeezing through together. The Minoi understood the danger now, but their ships were too overloaded for nimble maneuvers.

"Master Corylus?" Pandareus said. "Is there a way I can be of service?"

Corylus took a deep breath. His nose and throat were dry because of backwash from the fire projector. Even with his armor, he had found it unpleasant to use. No wonder the glass men crewed the weapons on Atlantean ships.

"Thank you, master, no," Corylus said. "We'll come alongside their ships now and I'll kill the Minoi who control them. You wouldn't—well, you don't have armor."

Pandareus laughed. "A matter of no present significance, as we both know," he said.

Corylus coughed into his hand. He had seen how many ships were lined up on the other side of the portal. Speaking as much to himself as to the scholar, he said, "There's a lot of them, but they're very sluggish. They should have landed the civilians when they realized they were going to have to fight."

"Do you think any of the passengers would have been willing to disembark, my student?" Pandareus said, arching an eyebrow in question. "Since they know what surely awaits all who are left behind in Atlantis."

"Ah," said Corylus. "Sorry, master. I wasn't thinking."

"You were thinking as a soldier, Master Corylus," Pandareus said. "As you should be, in the present circumstances."

The pair of ships wallowing through the portal would have been an ideal target if the flame projector were still working. The Atlanteans had to crawl even more slowly through the portal than usual so that the ships didn't smash one another even before they met the enemy.

Without the flame projector, though, it meant that Corylus had two enemies to deal with when they finally did arrive. The Minoi were using bad tactics, but they'd gotten lucky.

Corylus smiled grimly. That wasn't the first time such a thing had happened in battle. A pity that it was working against the defenders of Carce now, but it wasn't the first time for that either.

The Ancient had lifted them well above the portal and to the starboard side of their enemies. Their flame projectors would be lethal; Corylus could only defeat the Atlanteans if he approached them individually from the stern, and even then there were still more coming through.

Spectators on the Field of Mars were shouting with enthusiasm. Even the greatest fool born could see how dangerous it was to stand on ground where warships, each weighing as much as several elephants, were likely to fall, but the field was if anything more crowded than it had been when Corylus first arrived over Carce.

On the other hand, the spectators were likely to survive longer than he was. He balanced the sword in his hand as the Atlantean ships turned sunwise together toward their enemy.

The Ancient slanted down like an eagle stooping on an osprey, using their advantage of speed and maneuverability to curve toward the enemy's sterns. The Minoi weren't used to real combat. If they had turned against one another instead of in parallel, one or the other would be prow-on to the attack.

There was a new commotion in the crowd. What at first Corylus thought was a bear pushed its way out of the crush and loped through the relatively fewer spectators close to the obelisk. The portal gleamed and sizzled above him.

The creature ran with an odd rocking motion, swinging its forelegs together, then its hind legs. Only when it leaped to the obelisk and began climbing did Corylus realize it must be an ape. The pink granite was carved with Egyptian picture-writing, but he didn't think *he* would be able to climb it with such handholds. The bears he had frequently hunted on the frontiers couldn't climb as well as he did.

The ape was a question for another time, and probably for another person—a living person—to ask. Corylus gripped the railing with his left hand, then remembered that Pandareus might not understand what was about to happen.

Turning his head slightly—he didn't dare look away when they were run-ning up on the enemy's stern so quickly—Corylus shouted, "Brace yourself, master! There'll be a shock!"

Bare-chested bowmen on the Atlantean vessel were shooting at them. An arrow hit Corylus' helmet squarely and clanged off; another buried its head in the railing beside his left gauntlet. The archers were less accurate than he expected, perhaps because they were so crowded on the ship's deck that they couldn't draw their bows to full nock.

The Minos in the stern dropped his crystal talisman to dangle on the golden chain about his neck; his vessel lost way. Drawing his sword, he turned to face Corylus. The ships would glance against one another, port bow to starboard quarter. At any moment—

The sails of Corylus' ship, of the Ancient's ship, stroked back and down with unexpected force. Their bow lifted over the Atlantean's rail and coursed through the screaming passengers. It struck the mast—which held—and the boom supporting the starboard sail, which snapped off short.

Corylus rocked back, then slammed forward. His breastplate took the im-pact, but even spread across his whole torso the shock was bruisingly severe.

Driven by one sail alone, the Atlantean ship rotated on its axis, then broke loose and fell away. It was upside down when it hit the ground. The crash sent man-sized splinters spinning high in the air.

The remaining Atlantean vessel had turned and was approaching from the port side at the speed of a fast walk. Corylus ran toward that railing, forgetting in the stress of the moment his fear of a ship's wobbling deck. The Ancient swung them down and to the right, using the collision with their most recent victim to aid the maneuver.

The Atlantean wizard tried to follow, but his ship wobbled badly and nearly overturned from the excessive weight on its deck. Several of the pas-sengers fell over the side to starboard, and the rush of the panicked survivors to the port railing almost precipitated a reverse disaster.

The Minos shouted something which Corylus couldn't make out because of the excited cheering from the crowd below. The Servitor in the bow sprayed fire more or less toward the defenders. The jet burned out far short of its target, as the glass man must have known it would.

Corylus was breathing hard, although he hadn't been called on to really do anything. He was sweating furiously under the breastplate, and he half considered taking off the helmet for a moment to let his head cool.

He wouldn't do that: he didn't understand the situation well enough to predict the dangers accurately. Which was what the sprite had told him beside the body of the Cyclops on the beach.

He turned to her. Lifting the visor, he said, "We're done with the fire, cousin."

Pausing half a moment to choose his phrasing, he added, "I'm truly sorry for the situation."

The sprite rose by curling her legs under her in a movement more like that of a serpent than a human being. To Corylus' surprise, she gave him a cheerful smile and said, "Well, it all ends, doesn't it? I've been in that bead—"

She ran her fingertips over the orichalc breastplate where it covered the amulet.

"—for so long that it will be a relief. We hazels aren't like those ugly gnarled desert pines, you know."

She raised her hand and caressed Corylus' face instead. It felt like a butterfly walking on his cheek.

"I feel sorry for the ship, though," she said, looking up at the mast. "The magicians took the souls away from all the pieces when they made it, but the ship was starting to talk to me. It's broken now, and that lot—"

She glared at the Atlantean vessel turning toward them.

"—won't fix it. Well, they'll probably burn us all, won't they?"

"Yes, I suppose that's likely enough," Corylus said. He had shut down emotionally. The logical part of his mind had addressed the question which the sprite had asked and agreed with her analysis.

For the first time Corylus realized that they weren't climbing as quickly since the most recent attack as they had before. In fact they were scarcely climbing at all, and the sails beat with an irregular rhythm.

"The mast is breaking, I think," Pandareus said, looking upward. He spoke with the interest he showed in everything new. "I was holding onto it when we hit the other ship, and it shook very hard."

He touched his cheek with a rueful smile. It was swollen, and there was a pressure cut over the bone. The bruise would close his eye by tomorrow.

Corylus looked up. The collision didn't appear to have damaged their hull, but the mast had whipped violently at the impact. It must have struck Pandareus a short, massive blow where his face was pressed against it.

The yards grew from the central pole like branches from a tree. When they flexed with the weight of the sails added, the starboard one had started to split away at the crotch just as a fir bough might break in a heavy snow. It labored now, and as it did so the crack spread further down the mast. At any moment the yard and sail would tear away completely. The ship would overturn and drop like the one it had rammed.

Unless, as the sprite had suggested, they burned instead. Corylus let his visor drop and trotted back to the bow.

They weren't going to be able to circle around their opponent this time. They were only slightly higher than the Atlantean ship, and it was moving faster than they could. Two more ships were coming through the portal. It was unlikely that they would be required to deal with the only defender of Carce.

The Ancient swung toward the prow of their opponent: there was no choice. The Servitor lifted the spout of his fire projector, and several archers began shooting. One arrow thunked hard into the hull and another zipped not far overhead.

"Watch out, master!" Corylus said. His orichalc armor had shrugged off an arrow, but the teacher wore only a tunic. Not that it would make much difference. An arrow might even be merciful.

When Corylus turned his head slightly to shout the warning, he noticed movement on the obelisk. The ape had reached the top and was wrenching at the metal ball that Novius Facundus, the astronomer who erected the sundial, had placed there to diffuse light around the top of the granite shaft. The portal throbbed and pulsed just above the creature's head.

But that wasn't a present concern.

The Ancient lifted their bow an instant before the Servitor spurted fire toward them. Coupled with their existing slight advantage in height, the jet washed across the timbers of the forward bow and the lower hull instead of bathing Corylus and the deck beyond him. He wasn't sure that flames would affect Coryla and the Ancient so long as the amulet remained intact, but he knew from watching the victims of his own weapon what would happen to Pandareus and—despite the armor—himself.

The ships crashed together, not a glancing blow like the previous ramming attempt but a bow-to-bow collision between vessels which were each proceeding at faster than a walking pace. Timbers broke, scattering burning fragments. The flame projector and the Servitor crewing it had been crushed by the impact, but the hull of Corylus' ship was already alight.

The ships were locked together, rotating widdershins around their common axis. Their anchor flukes had become tangled; the sterns were swinging together. Both pairs of sails continued to beat, but the ships were sinking swiftly.

The crash had thrown many of the Atlanteans overboard, but the Minos in the stern gave a roar of fury and stumped forward. He used armored elbows and even his sword on his own retainers in his haste. Blood streaked his bright armor.

Corylus paused. The Minos was as big as a German warrior, and he held his sword with the ease of familiarity. Corylus had practiced with a sword also, but his real skill had been in throwing javelins.

He had never used a sword without a shield on his left arm. He wasn't afraid of the Minos or of any other barbarian, but if he were advising a friend how to bet on the match—

A thought struck him. He unlatched his chin strap, then pulled off his helmet. With the chin strap in his left fist, he presented the helmet like a buckler. Given his training, being without a helmet wasn't nearly as great a handicap as being without a shield would have been.

"Ears for Nerthus!" he shouted. He leaped across to the other ship's deck to meet the rush of its commander.

The Minos was poised for another stride, thinking that his enemy would wait for his charge, but without hesitation he slashed overhand at the base of Corylus' neck. Corylus met the edge with his makeshift buckler. The shock numbed his left hand to the wrist and dented the orichalc, but the helmet's curve deflected the blade to the side.

Corylus thrust. His blade was slightly curved and longer than the cut-and-thrust sword he was used to, but principles were the same. The point slipped in beneath the Minos' chin. When the point pierced the back of his skull, the tip lifted off his helmet with a clang.

The ships hit the ground together, throwing Corylus up in an unexpected backflip. He lost both sword and helmet, but his knees had been flexed for the thrust and the hull timbers breaking had absorbed the worst of the shock.

Corylus hit the deck again on all fours, then bounded to his feet. *I couldn't have done that once in a thousand tries if I'd been training,* he thought.

The whole world seemed to be shouting. Some of the Atlanteans may have been alive, but they were no danger to Carce now.

The two ships coming through the portal and the scores behind them, though—they would be enough.

Corylus looked up. As he did so, the ape wrenched the metal ball from its socket on top of the obelisk. The portal wavered, and an Atlantean screamed in terror.

The ape gripped the obelisk with both legs and smashed the ball down on the wedge-shaped granite point with the strength of his arms and upper body. The metal deformed with a hollow boom.

The portal shrank. The storm rushed from all sides as the bubble of clear heaven reduced. Lightning and thunder overwhelmed the sound of the crowd.

The ape swung again, ripping the ball open. The portal vanished like mist in the sun. The bows of the ships on the way into this world tumbled downward, their hulls sheared more neatly than a saw could have done.

The ape stood on the peak of the obelisk, shrieking a challenge to the sky. The thunderbolt that struck him was blinding in its intensity.

The ape froze where it was for a moment, its fur blazing. Then it tumbled, and rain from the breaking storm hissed on the flames.

Hedia watched Lann fall as stiffly as a burning statue. The lightning must have frozen his muscles. She had seen antelope shot through the head in the arena stiffen that way. *There is no chance he can be alive.*

Then, *He saved me.*

She felt nothing for a moment. She was floating in a prickly white fog.

Her vision cleared. "You, Lenatus!" she said; her voice clear, her enunciation perfect. "You and your men clear my way to the sundial!"

She'd thought the trainer might hesitate. Instead he instantly bellowed, "Come on, squad! Batons only until I tell you different!"

Leading the newly freed servants, Lenatus pushed through the line of lictors who had taken the place of honor in front of the consul. From the way they moved, each man wore a sword under his tunic despite the fact that it would be certain crucifixion to be caught with military arms within the sacred boundaries of Carce.

Hedia followed, holding the borrowed toga over her shoulders with both hands. It was a stupid garment, clumsy and ugly and *stupid*. She'd like to burn *alive* the man who decreed it for formal wear!

She knew she was being irrational. She didn't care. She had *never* cared what other people thought of her behavior.

Lenatus and his bullies formed a wedge that shoved through the crowd. Lann might have been a trifle quicker about it, but he hadn't been clearing a path for a noble lady. Instead of just knocking down spectators who hadn't gotten out of the way, the men in front of Hedia were hurling them to one side or another so that she wouldn't trip over their groaning bodies.

Rain had begun to hammer down by the time they reached the obelisk.

One of the men—a bulky Galatian well over six feet tall, named Minimus by a former owner with a sense of humor—shouted at something on the pavement. He jumped back, drawing his sword.

He's alive!

"Put that away or you'll be crow bait!" Lenatus bellowed. "It's dead, don't you see?"

"Let me through," said Hedia. Her voice was clear, her enunciation perfect. She floated in a white stinging cloud.

"Your ladyship?" Lenatus said in concern. His hand was under his tunic also.

"He's dead, you say, so there's no problem, is there?" Hedia said. She brushed past and squatted beside Lann. Beside Lann's body.

Despite the rain, the ape-man's fur was still smoldering. The smell was terrible. She brushed his cheek with her fingertips and felt crisp tendrils break off beneath them.

He was as stiff as bronze, though the body was still warm. Brains were leaking from his crushed skull, but he must have died from the thunderbolt. The fall had flattened his head in line with his heavy brow ridges. The poor dear had never had the high forehead of a philosopher, of course.

He couldn't have felt a thing. No pain, nothing. Triumph and then oblivion. Quite a good way to go, and certainly he was now in a better afterlife than that which awaited the noble Hedia. . . .

"Dear heart?" a voice said.

Hedia looked over her shoulder. Lenatus had formed his squad in a circle around her and the body of the ape-man. They had allowed Saxa through, but the lictors were on the other side.

She got to her feet, swaying with exhaustion—mental and physical both. She didn't know how long she had been kneeling on the marble pavement, but the borrowed toga was soaked.

"My husband, I'm glad you've joined me," Hedia said calmly. "I'll ask you to put a guard over Lann here. Master Lenatus and his men will do."

She flexed her knees to pat the big body for a last time, then thought the better of it and simply gestured.

She said, "Please have him cremated as soon as the rain permits. A formal funeral will not be necessary, but I request that you have his ashes interred in the family tomb."

"Him?" Saxa said in obvious puzzlement. "The monkey, you mean?"

Hedia's mind went buzzing white again. After a moment she said, "If you choose to name your savior a monkey, yes."

Then, like a whiplash, "See to it!"

"Yes, my dear," Saxa said quietly. "At once. Ah—I'll go back to the Altar and, ah, leave you and your pet . . ."

He turned.

Hedia caught him by the shoulder and embraced him clumsily. "No, my dear master," she said. "We will go to the Portico of Agrippa, you and I, where you will take charge of the crisis until someone else arrives—the urban prefect or one of the Praetorian commanders, I suppose. And I see our daughter coming toward us. She appears to need help also."

She pointed to Lenatus, then toward the ape-man's body. The old soldier nodded in understanding. Soldiers got a lot of experience with hasty cremations; he would take care of it.

Good-bye, my friend Lann.

VARUS SAT ON THE STEPS of the public facility north of the sundial, letting the rain beat on him and trying not to think. The Emperor Augustus had built a larger pyre with marble appointments a little farther out on the Flaminian Way, close to where he erected his huge family mausoleum, so this one got little business in recent years.

Today the whole district stank of charred human flesh. Varus didn't know whether there were interrupted funerals on the platforms of volcanic tuff behind him, the fires quenched by the downpour, or if corpses scattered when Atlantean ships burned and crashed were responsible for the odor.

Eventually he would rise and join his father, who had set up a headquarters in the Portico of Agrippa across the road. Since the urban prefect hadn't arrived, Saxa had taken charge of rescue and the firefighting—which, thanks to the rain, wasn't the danger which a shower of burning timbers could have posed.

Eventually he would get up; but not now.

"Good afternoon, Lord Varus," Pandareus said from close beside him. "A very good one, in as much as we are both alive and Carce is not a flaming ruin."

Varus jumped to his feet. "Master!" he said.

Then, more calmly and with a smile for himself, "I'm sorry, I was completely lost in myself. 'In thought', I would say, but I think what I was really doing was trying not to think."

Before Pandareus could reply, Varus really *looked* at him. "Alive, yes," he said, "but what happened to you, master? Are you really all right?"

The left side of his teacher's face was badly swollen. The greasy look was probably unguent smeared on the cut over the cheekbone, but it looked *terrible*. Both his wrists were splinted, though his fingers seemed to move normally.

"Quite well, really," Pandareus said. The swelling distorted his smile, but it was clearly meant to be cheerful. "Though our ship fell to the ground, I managed to hold on to the railing. Unfortunately—"

He lifted his forearms to call attention to the splints.

"—I appear to have injured myself that way as well, though not as badly as would have happened if I had been thrown out. Pulto assures me that in a month I will be able to swing a sword just as ably as I ever could."

Varus went blank, then giggled in what he realized was release. Only then did Pandareus let his battered face warm in a smile.

"Corylus is all right, then?" Varus asked, raising his head. A pair of mounted couriers raced up the road from the barracks of the City Watch and headed south down the Flaminian Way. Only Hercules knew what they were doing.

Varus grinned wryly, glad to realize that he was regaining an interest in life. The rain seemed to be slacking, though his toga was so sodden already that walking in it would be like wearing a waterfall. Wool could absorb enormous quantities of water.

"Master Corylus is well," Pandareus said, "which is quite remarkable— even granting that I knew from our first meeting that he was an athlete as well as a scholar. He took his companions into the enclosure around the Altar of Peace, and his man Pulto is standing in the entrance to see to it that they're not disturbed. Pulto seemed pleased to see me and bandage my wrists, though."

"I'm glad of that," Varus said. He wondered who his friend's "companions" were and why they needed privacy. He could ask Corylus about that later, if he felt he had to know and if the information hadn't been volunteered. He shrugged in preparation to getting up, but the sloshing weight of his toga made him hesitate a little longer.

"Lady Hedia is in quite her usual form also," Pandareus said, "although she seems to have had received some rough handling in the recent past. She has taken your sister in hand and they're repairing their wardrobe and toi- lette in the shops of the portico."

"I'm sure Mother is in better shape than whoever tried to get in her way," Varus said, smiling faintly. Until Father got involved with magic, he hadn't appreciated how terrifying an enemy Hedia would be.

"I thought . . . ," Pandareus said with a hint of reserve. "That I saw you and your sister arrive here on the back of a gryphon?"

"Yes," said Varus. "That's what it seemed to me also. It may have been a metaphor, though."

He lurched to his feet. The toga clung to his legs, threatening to bind him. Well, if that was the worst problem he had—and it was—then he was a very fortunate man, and Carce was fortunate also.

"Master?" he said. "Typhon isn't a danger anymore, because of my sister. Alphena saved us all."

Pandareus lifted his chin in acknowledgement. "I gathered from what Lady Alphena said to your mother that the danger was past. I'm glad to have that confirmed, though. Your sister, ah, seemed distraught."

I really don't know what has been happening to my sister since she disap- peared from our garden, Varus thought. *And I think it will be better if I never try to learn.*

Aloud he said, "Come, my honored teacher. I will greet my father, the consul; and then we too should look into a change of garments."

ALPHENA LAY ON THE TABLE under the hands of the masseur. He was a tall eunuch, a friend and perhaps relative of Abinnaeus, whose shop Hedia had taken over with her usual brusque authority. The clothier would be paid, of course, and probably greatly overpaid, but Alphena doubted he'd been thinking of money when he leaped to obey the cascade of orders.

Alphena had stopped crying. The rough toweling had warmed and dried her, and she'd found herself drifting into a blurred reverie punctuated by flashes of vivid memory.

She and Hedia lay with their heads in opposite directions on parallel tables—display tables, originally, but sturdy enough for this use—and each had turned her face to the right. When Alphena opened her eyes, her mother was looking at her.

"Are you feeling better, dear?" Hedia asked, her voice pulsing with the quick rhythm of the assistant masseur who chopped at her back with the edges of his hands. He was a Libyan with dark skin and tightly wound hair as coarse as wire.

Hedia had insisted that the master work on her daughter, so of course that was what happened. Alphena could watch the assistant, though, and she had been impressed by the economy, strength, and precision with which he moved. *He'd make a good swordsman. . . .*

"I don't feel anything," Alphena said as the masseur worked the muscles of her right buttock with fingers as hard as wood. "I don't think I'll ever feel anything ever again!"

Her voice sounded petulant, even to herself, and she knew as she spoke that the words were a lie. She wouldn't have been able to judge the Libyan's skill if she hadn't resumed taking an interest in the world around her.

"That isn't true," she said flatly before her mother could say anything. "I don't want to feel anything, but I do."

To her furious amazement, she started crying again. "I feel awful! *Awful!* What they did was wrong!"

Hedia sat up abruptly. "You may all leave," she said, gesturing toward the outer door.

"At once, your ladyship," said Abinnaeus, who with his two assistants had been standing before the hanging which covered the storage room and stairs to the upper level. "Since your own attendants haven't arrived yet, would you like me to leave one of my boys? He speaks only Aramaic, though I suspect he's picked up some Common Greek. Not Latin, though, as he's only been in Carce for the past week."

"I think my daughter and I can pour our own wine in a crisis, Abinnaeus," Hedia said calmly. "Though if my maid Syra arrives, you may pass her through."

Smiling at Alphena, she said, "I sent a messenger to the house to bring my servants when I arrived, but I don't expect them to reach us for some while yet. I'll get some wine, dear."

Alphena sat up slowly. The masseur, his assistant, and the four attendants accompanying them went out first. They had started to pack up their paraphernalia, but after a quick discussion with Abinnaeus they had simply left it behind. The clothier's assistants chivied them to move faster.

Abinnaeus himself followed at the end of the procession. Before he banged the outer door behind him, he dropped a neatly folded packet on the table beside Alphena.

She picked it up: it was a napkin. She wiped her face and eyes, then blew her nose on it and set it down again.

Alphena had known that people obeyed her stepmother's orders, but nobody had given the shopkeeper an order about the napkin. Hedia surrounded herself with people who thought for themselves, which was a very different thing.

Alphena was suddenly glad to have become one of the people around Lady Hedia.

Hedia handed Alphena the two cups she had filled at the sideboard and sat down beside her. They sipped together.

The wine was straight from the jar. Alphena had already learned that what she drank with her mother was likely to be the pure vintage.

That was all right this time. Alphena took a deep draft. It was probably better this time, though she didn't expect to get drunk.

Hedia took another sip and looked at Alphena over the rim of her cup. "Who treated you unfairly, daughter?" she said. Her tone was mild but her face was not. "I may not be able to put it right, but there's a chance that I can demonstrate to those who wronged you that they have made a serious mistake."

"It's not me," Alphena said. She snatched up the napkin but she managed not to resume blubbering. "It was Uktena. I know what you think but he's not a monster, not really, he's a man, a brave man, and he, and he—"

She broke off because she found herself crying after all. She felt Hedia take the cup from her hand though she'd probably sloshed out half its contents already. A moment later, Hedia's arm went around her shoulders.

After a time, Alphena snuffled. She blew her nose hard into the napkin, then wiped her eyes with the back of her hand.

"Uktena is your name for Typhon, dear heart?" Hedia asked. Her voice was calm, hinting of no emotion except kindly concern.

"No!" Alphena said. Then, very quietly, she said, "Yes, I guess so. But it isn't fair. He only got that way because he had to fight Procron. His own people sent him away, put him in *prison* because they were afraid of him. He saved them!"

"Drink some more of this, dear," Hedia said, offering the cup again.

Either she had somehow refilled it or it was the one she had poured for herself. Alphena took a gulp, then second and third gulps.

"Did they have reason to be afraid of Uktena?" Hedia said. She lowered her arm but she continued to sit very close.

"Yes," Alphena whispered. "But it doesn't matter. He got that way by saving them! They can't cast him away like that, it isn't right!"

Hedia turned her face toward a wall where bolts of silk were stacked, but her eyes were far away. In a voice which throbbed with an emotion which Alphena couldn't identify, she said, "I suppose it must be right, dear, because that's what happens to soldiers all the time. We give them land to settle on the frontiers, because that way they don't come back to Carce. They're far too dangerous, you see."

Alphena looked at her. "He's a warrior," she said. "He fought for them."

"Yes, dear," Hedia said, meeting her eyes again. She smiled; a sort of smile. "The tribunes don't spend long out there, a year to be qualified for office and then come back to find jobs in the government. But sometimes a year is too long. They go away boys like your brother, and when they come back they're not really human."

She hugged Alphena again, harder; taking comfort this time, not trying to give it. "And there's nothing anyone can do, dear one, not after it's happened," Hedia said. "Except that sometimes we women can bring a little solace. Remember that, when you're older. Remember your friend Uktena."

Alphena swallowed. She put her cup down to free herself to embrace her mother.

CORYLUS FUMBLED WITH HIS BODY armor as he climbed the steps to the west entrance of the Altar of Peace. The orichalc cuirass was heavy, awkward, and it shone even during the rainstorm, calling unwanted attention to him. He would have taken it off before now, except that he couldn't get the catches to work.

On other days, the naked sprite beside him would have attracted even more attention, but the scattered fires and confusion had left many people running about the Field of Mars in states of undress. Coryla was more attractive than most, but the crowd was too excited about the flaming battle in the sky to pay attention to women, even pretty women.

As for the golden-furred Ancient on the sprite's other side—Carce was used to exotic animals. Mostly they died on the sand, shot by archers who stayed on the other side of the fence from their victims, but not a few came as pets for the great and good.

Pulto halted at the top. "Here, master," he said, reaching for the catches.

Corylus heard the *click, click, click* and felt the breastplate sag from his right side. "I got it on with no trouble," he muttered. "I've had it on and off lots of times since, since . . ."

His voice trailed off. He couldn't remember when all this had started. Days ago, but was a day in that dreamworld the same as one here in Carce?

"You take care of your business," Pulto said, lifting away the breastplate. "Then we'll get you to the baths and a long soak in the steam room. I ought to know what you need, as often as I've been standing where you are."

Blood still streaked the orichalc despite the storm which was only now slackening. The Minos had bled like a whale spouting when Corylus jerked his sword free; gore had covered his right arm as well.

"Right, take care of my duties," Corylus said. He looked into the altar enclosure, feeling his mind sharpen a little; tactical awareness became reflexive on the frontier, especially if you regularly visited the far side of the river.

"Don't worry about the east entrance," Pulto said. "I had some of Saxa's boys block the doorway with the deck of one of them crashed ships. They'll make sure nobody tries to move it while you're inside. Ah—I told 'em you'd see them right for the work, you know?"

"Yes, of course," said Corylus. He had to finish this quickly; otherwise he'd fall asleep. "I don't think we'll be long."

The problem wasn't so much the stress of battle: he would normally still be keyed up by the humors which fighting had released into his system.

His present exhaustion came from the blur of time Corylus had spent in the dreamworld. The release of *that* tension, that existence in a place not meant for living men, had wrung him out more than he could have guessed before the strain released.

"Take as long as you need, master," Pulto said. "Nobody's going to bother you this way neither."

Pulto stepped to the center of the entrance and turned his back to the altar; his legs were spread slightly, and his hand was on a barely hidden sword hilt. *No, nobody's going to bother us.*

Pulto had stayed with Lenatus in Saxa's house after the attempt to catch the western magicians. That was the proper response for a noncommissioned officer in a crisis: if there wasn't an obvious solution, report to headquarters where people are paid to think beyond straight ranks and a sharp sword.

At the alarm, he had joined the consul's entourage—figuring that reports of ships throwing lightning bolts in the clouds were likely to be cut from the same cloth as Corylus disappearing into thin air. He'd been right.

It had stopped raining, but water stood in shallow pools in the marble pavement and on the charred top of the central altar. The Ancient scraped a finger across the ash, then sniffed what he had caught under his nail. He grinned at Corylus.

The sprite touched the glass amulet, visible now that Corylus had taken off the breastplate. "What now, cousin?" she asked.

Corylus licked his lips. "You both have helped me," he said. "You've saved me, many times. What is it that you want from me?"

The sprite laughed. "Freedom, of course," she said. "Freedom to die."

She looked at the Ancient. He gave a terse growl. He didn't move from where he stood by the altar, but the fur along his spine had rippled.

"Both of us want freedom," the sprite said. "But you would be a fool to free us, cousin. You need us."

Corylus took off the amulet and weighed the glass in his hand. He looked from the sprite to the Ancient. Neither of them moved.

"If I didn't treat my friends honorably," Corylus said, "I would soon have no friends."

He put the leather thong over his left index finger and held it out to Coryla.

She looked at the bead; her tongue touched her lips. Very softly she said, "The times are in crisis, cousin. The Spirits of the Earth are rising, against you and all who live on the surface."

"My honor is good!" Corylus said. "I am a citizen of Carce!"

The sprite hesitated. The Ancient took the thong from Corylus and settled the amulet between the teeth at the back of his jaw.

The sprite laughed merrily. She stepped forward and kissed Corylus hard, then put her arm around the Ancient; he bit down.

Then Corylus was alone within the enclosure, except for the pinch of powdered glass drifting to the pavement.